I0579302

RAINING MEN

Chaser, Book Two

Rick R. Reed

A NineStar Press Publication

Published by NineStar Press
P.O. Box 91792,
Albuquerque, New Mexico, 87199 USA.
www.ninestarpress.com

Raining Men

Copyright © 2020 by Rick R. Reed
Cover Art by Natasha Snow Copyright © 2020

This is a work of fiction. Names, characters, places, and incidents are either the product of the author's imagination or are used fictitiously. Any resemblance to actual persons living or dead, business establishments, events, or locales is entirely coincidental.

All rights reserved. No part of this publication may be reproduced in any material form, whether by printing, photocopying, scanning or otherwise without the written permission of the publisher. To request permission and all other inquiries, contact NineStar Press at the physical or web addresses above or at Contact@ninestarpress.com.

Printed in the USA
Second Edition
March, 2020

Print ISBN: 978-1-951880-65-1

Also available in eBook, ISBN: 978-1-951880-64-4

Warning: This book contains sexually explicit content, which may only be suitable for mature readers.

The character you loved to hate in *Chaser* becomes the character you will simply love in *Raining Men.*

It's been raining men for most of Bobby Nelson's adult life. Normally, he wouldn't have it any other way, but lately something's missing. Now, he wants the deluge to slow to a single special drop. But is it even possible for Bobby to find "the one" after endless years of hooking up?

When Bobby's father passes away, Bobby finally examines his rocky relationship with the man and how it might have contributed to his inability to find the love he yearns for. Guided by a sexy therapist, a Sex Addicts Anonymous group, a well-endowed Chihuahua named Johnny Wadd, and Bobby's own cache of memories, Bobby takes a spiritual, sexual, and emotional journey to discover that life's most satisfactory love connections lie in quality, not quantity. And when he's ready to love not only himself but someone else, sex and love fit, at last, into one perfect package.

Dedication

For My Husband

Love is a rare and beautiful thing

Most people spend their time trying to find someone to sleep with instead of finding someone worth waking up to.
—B.G. Thomas, *All Alone in a Sea of Romance*

So we'll go no more a roving
So late into the night,
Though the heart be still as loving,
And the moon be still as bright.

For the sword outwears its sheath,
And the soul wears out the breast,
And the heart must pause to breathe,
And Love itself have rest.

Though the night was made for loving,
And the day returns too soon,
Yet we'll go no more a roving
By the light of the moon.

—Lord Byron
"So we'll go no more a roving"

Part One

Prologue

BOBBY'S DREAM

Thunder rumbles. Rain hisses. Flashes of lightning—brilliant and blue white—rip across the sky.

I know I'm dreaming, yet something about this whole scenario seems as real as the nose on my face, the hair on my head, the dick swinging between my legs.

In addition to the natural sounds of the storm, there's another noise, and it makes me smile. Music. Rising. Percussion. Disco beats. And the powerful wail of Martha Wash and the Weather Girls singing "It's Raining Men."

I'm standing under some kind of awning—red, canvas—watching the rain pour down not in drops, but sheets. Blinding. The flashes of lightning are like a disco strobe light, revealing in flashes of blue and silver, a darkened cityscape. Night. But a netherworld cityscape, blue gray, unreal.

It's the music that makes me want to move out from under the awning. The music that has me smiling, my hips, head, and arms in synchronized rhythm with the beat.

Glorious!

Even the rain, a cold shock to my naked body, isn't enough to keep me from driving myself out into the downpour to dance to the song, which has long been a favorite of mine.

What a delicious notion—raining men! Men falling from the skies! More men than one can shake a stick at (or something that rhymes with stick, heh-heh).

I look up into the midnight-blue clouds, my mouth and eyes open to the water pouring down, and I see it: the first of the men.

I stare in wonder as he drops from the sky. A blond Adonis, smooth and muscled, allover tanned with a dick thick, long, and perfectly hard, pointing back up at the sky. He lands somewhere outside my vision, and I dance, spinning toward where I saw him fall, hoping to find him where he has landed so I can say hello, reach out and touch him.

But before I can make any progress, another man falls from the sky. This one is hirsute, bearded, husky but hard-muscled, putting me in mind of the actor Jeffrey Dean Morgan. He smiles. Before I can even smile back, other men tumble from the skies, and I want to laugh, cry out in jubilation at my good fortune.

It truly is raining men!

Hallelujah!

They start raining faster now—blonds, redheads, brunets, black, white, Asian, Latino (yum), lanky, beefy, short, tall—all the most gorgeous men I have ever seen. All naked.

All for me!

I raise my arms and shout, "Come to Papa!"

And they do.

The first body hits me hard, feeling more like a ton of concrete instead of the delicious marriage of sinew, skin, and bone that I have come to know and love as the male form. I collapse to the ground, wind knocked out of me, and look up at the man who has rained down on me. He seems to have no awareness that I am beneath him, and I scurry to get out from underneath the crushing weight threatening to suffocate me, pressing my bones into the wet concrete beneath my back.

I manage to get out just as another man drops from the sky, a hot African American, bald, and looking just like Taye Diggs. I scramble free of his path, but he lands on my leg anyway as I crawl through the rain-slicked street.

I hear my leg break with a sickening crack. It takes only seconds for the pain to radiate throughout my entire body.

I roll over, gasping, wincing, groaning, and look up to see an entire sea of naked men falling from the sky in ever-increasing velocity—all headed straight for me.

The music reaches a crescendo in time with my shrieks.

*

Bobby Nelson woke.

The sheets beneath him were twisted and damp with sweat. He gasped, trying to regulate his heartbeat, which was jackhammering so hard he expected to look down and see it lifting the skin off his chest. A cartoon heart.

The room was silent.

Where did the music go? Martha? Weather Girls?

Where was the rain? The thunder?

He breathed in deeply and exhaled slowly.

Calm.

Just a dream. A nightmare.

Where are all the men?

Finally, he grinned, turning over in his bed.

Why, there's one! Lying right next to me, looking at me with a concerned face, a handsome face. Even in a darkened bedroom, Bobby could still tell if they're hot or not. It was his specialty.

This one, with a mop of curly blond hair and pecs like Michael Phelps, was a ten.

His voice was husky, sleep-choked. "Dude. You were having a nightmare. You okay?"

He placed what was meant to be, Bobby was sure, a comforting hand on Bobby's chest. Bobby cringed a little, moving away.

This has never happened before.

I have no idea who he is.

Before Bobby could stop the words from tumbling out of his mouth, they came. "Who the fuck are you?"

Chapter One

Bobby sat on a leather chair in therapist Camille D'Amico's office, took in his surroundings, and mused on why the therapist had arranged the office as she had.

He made certain assumptions. Camille had placed the seating to be comfortable, yet not confrontational. Bobby supposed she wanted her office to have the effect, the ambiance, of a living room—a safe, calm place where she and her charges could relax like two old friends, just gabbing, getting to the heart of their problems. The office was dimly lit—blinds drawn and a Pottery Barn ceramic lamp the only illumination, sixty watt—and for Bobby, it had what he imagined to be the desired effect: calming. From the small charging/speaker unit on Camille's desk, the violin of Joshua Bell played softly, a warm background accompaniment.

Camille adjusted her halo of frizzy brown hair, running her fingers through it, and pushed her glasses up on the bridge of her nose. She didn't say anything, and Bobby supposed she was waiting for him to begin.

Bobby fidgeted with a button on his sport coat, not sure where to start. Camille eyed him up and down, and Bobby knew what she saw: a tall, lean man with above-average—well, *way above* if he were being honest—looks. And it wasn't just his vanity that informed him. He had been told more times than he could count that he was gorgeous, hot, that he had the kind of virile beauty seldom seen outside of men's fashion magazines. His clothes were expensive, tasteful—a soft navy blazer with a white, button-down, Egyptian cotton shirt crisp beneath it. His jeans were indigo blue, the kind that went for hundreds of dollars a pair. His red suede sneakers bore the subtle Prada logo beneath the laces. Bobby had thrown the look together to display a kind of casual elegance, and from the way the therapist was eyeing him, it succeeded in spades.

Even Bobby's face spoke of good health and clean living. Skin so fine it almost appeared without pores. His auburn hair, close cropped, had just a touch of product to give it sheen, even here in this dimly lit warren. From him wafted the aroma of Hermès, sprayed in a cloud that Bobby had walked into, to ensure he got just the right amount on him.

In short, he knew he appeared to be a man who had everything—health, looks, money.

He imagined the therapist must be thinking: *So what the hell is he doing here?* And then, sadly, he guessed her next thought might be: *And why is it impossible for him to erase that mask of sadness that seems to cling to his face, marring those perfect features?*

I'll wait for him to tell me.

Bobby knew how therapists operated, even if he had never been to one. He had read enough about them and seen enough of them in movies and TV shows to know their *modus operandi.* She would know, Bobby surmised, that silence was often the most powerful tool in a head doctor's arsenal. Silence prodded, pushing for respite, for release. It was human nature, these days especially, to want to fill that quiet void with talk.

But Bobby, too, waited. A full two or three minutes had passed since Camille had made her initial small talk greetings. Yet Bobby still played with the pewter button on his blazer, seldom lifting his arresting gray eyes to meet her gaze.

Camille tapped the toe of her shoe on the bamboo flooring, and Bobby wondered if she was beginning to get impatient. She stopped tapping suddenly when Bobby moved his gaze from looking around the room to her foot. He finally spoke.

"Caden sent me."

Camille nodded. The simple nod and the sudden light in Camille's eyes told Bobby she remembered his old friend. He imagined what the pair must have once discussed, here, in this very room. She had probably helped Caden through love problems that most young men experience and issues with his mother's battle with cancer. Camille smiled, and Bobby thought it was because she knew Caden was now in a good place, in love with a wonderful man.

Bobby wondered if she had heard Caden was moving in with his boyfriend, Kevin. Bobby wanted to tell her that Caden's mother was winning her battle with that hateful disease and that she was now recuperating at home, struggling through chemo treatments with grace and humor.

But he only knew these latter two things because he had heard them from a mutual friend one night at Roscoe's along the Halsted strip known in Chicago as Boystown. He had not heard them from Caden.

He had not heard a word from Caden.

"Caden DeSarro?"

"That's the one."

"He's a good friend to have."

"*Was.* Was a good friend." Bobby realized Caden must have stopped coming to see her before Bobby had betrayed him, and the shame caused a rush of heat to rise to his face.

"Oh?"

"He and I kind of reached a parting of the ways, I guess you might say. I..." Bobby sighed and his voice trailed off. He stared down at the floor.

Camille said nothing.

"I kind of screwed up our friendship. I was an ass."

Camille cocked her head, a subtle indication for him to continue.

"You want to know what I did, huh?"

"I want to know what you want to tell me, Bobby."

"I tried to steal his boyfriend."

Camille nodded.

"In my defense, I didn't think Caden wanted him anymore."

He guessed that the therapist's first reaction to such news would be to recoil. Why not? Here before her was a man who had done a very bad thing, a reprehensible thing, and it seemed like he was sitting here wanting to blame the victim. He didn't think Caden wanted him anymore? *Seriously*? What kind of defense was that? Even if that *was* the case, and it was, someone still didn't go after a person their best friend had fallen in love with, no matter how sweet and sexy the man was.

But Camille, if she had any judgments, kept them to herself. Her face revealed nothing but a sincere desire to know more.

Bobby shook his head and let a bitter laugh escape his full lips. "That's bullshit. True, they were having problems. Caden was away—dealing with his mom's cancer—and while he was gone, his boyfriend, Kevin, went from pudge to stud in six weeks." Bobby laughed. "Most guys would be delighted with the change. I know I would. But Caden's an odd duck. He likes 'em big and beefy."

Camille nodded. Bobby wondered if she already knew this from her sessions with Caden.

"So I moved in. Made a play for the guy. I mean, Kevin was smokin' hot. Blond, bearded, a real man's man, you know? You'd never guess he was gay." He looked up at the therapist with eyes that pled for understanding.

"I just wanted someone to love me."

There it was. The raw truth. Bobby was surprised at himself—that he had allowed the heart of the matter to come out this early.

Camille agreed with him. "We all want that, Bobby."

"Yeah, we do." He fell silent once more and cut his gaze to the little digital clock on the end table next to her chair. He was surprised to see they'd already used twenty-five of their fifty minutes.

Bobby went on. "But I don't seem to know how to go about getting it. I ruined a friendship trying to grab something that I knew damn good and well didn't belong to me. And now, not only do I not have the guy I was after, I've lost the best friend I ever had."

Bobby guessed, if he was human, the therapist might now see a glimmer of a tear or two in his eyes at that point. He would go on to make an admission she would recognize as honest, yet very painful.

But that was what Bobby imagined other people might feel. The truth was—and Bobby was aware enough to recognize this—he was a man who was so out of touch with real emotions that he wouldn't recognize them if they came up and bit him on the ass.

But there was hope, wasn't there? Hadn't he just acknowledged, after all, his own culpability and bad behavior? Wouldn't she see that as a start?

Camille took a deep breath and threw out the question therapists must be honor bound to ask at least once, if not many times, during a course of treatment. "And how does that make you feel?"

"Like dirt. Like the piece of shit I know I am."

Harsh! But the sad thing was—it was true.

Camille shifted her weight in her chair, crossing and uncrossing her legs. Had he made her uncomfortable? Was he being too frank? Was she having trouble imagining how such a fine-looking specimen could feel his life was in such a shambles? He saw her write something quickly in her notepad. He wondered if she had jotted down one word: *narcissist?*

I certainly would fit the label, he thought sadly, although at this point in his life, he didn't have a clue how to change it. "Do you think I'm a narcissist?"

"Bobby, I think I should be the one asking the questions here, if you're going to benefit from your time with me. Why do you ask? Do you think you are?"

"Tell me again what the word means—your clinical definition."

Camille looked undecided, not saying anything for several moments. Finally, she said, "Well, the clinical definition of narcissist goes something like this. It's a person with an inflated sense of self, a deep need for admiration. They believe themselves superior to others, with little regard for other people's feelings." She paused and then added,

"People who fit this trait are often people who have very fragile self-esteem, often hidden behind a mask of confidence. Because of that, it's hard for these people to form wholesome, healthy relationships." She stared at him, and Bobby felt forced to meet her gaze. "Do you think that sounds like you, Bobby?"

"That's why I'm here," Bobby said, looking away from her.

"Go on."

"To figure out *why* I'm a *narcissistic* piece of shit. Why I just want to grab, grab, grab at whatever I want, heedless of who I hurt. What's wrong with me? I must be missing something. In here." He puts a hand over his heart.

Camille laid a hand, for a moment, on Bobby's own. "I think it's good we're here to talk about that, Bobby. It's good that you recognize you needed to talk to someone. Only when that happens can healing begin."

He grinned, but the smile did not meet his eyes. "That, and the fact that I'm an irresponsible, unrepentant, insatiable...slut."

Camille looked up at him. She looked more amused than shocked, and that surprised Bobby. She adjusted her pencil skirt, rearranged her halo of frizzy hair (for the umpteenth time—she really must find a way to stop that nervous habit), and asked, "Why do you feel the need to call yourself a slut? Most people wouldn't take kindly to someone calling them that. So I wonder why you'd apply such a label to yourself."

Again, Bobby said nothing for a long time. Finally, he glanced up from the loose thread he seemed to be contemplating at the hem of his jeans and gave her a warm smile, wide and welcoming. "Last week, I hooked up with seventeen guys."

What he had said must have made her nervous, even giddy in a hysterical sort of way. Camille tugged on her earlobe and scribbled onto her pad, seemingly unable to meet his eyes.

Bobby thought he would jar her back to the present. "You're not saying anything."

"What do you think I should say?"

"I don't know. Maybe something like: Shame on you? Have you been checked for STDs?" He grinned, but again, knew the smile would not reach his eyes, which he was certain reflected only sadness and resignation. "Where'd you find the time?"

Camille cut her gaze to the clock, and Bobby saw that their time, for real, was up. "Listen, Bobby, I think we have a lot to talk about." She smiled. "Can you come in again next week? Same time?"

He nodded, back to silent mode.

"Good. Just set it up with Clarice, out at the front desk."

Bobby turned at the door. "It'll probably be eighteen before night falls." He winked. "Just how I am. Incorrigible slut."

Before she could respond, he had closed the door behind him.

Chapter Two

Outside Camille's Wabash Street office, the early spring air was pure and clean—well, at least as pure and clean as the air in the Chicago Loop could be said to be. Bobby emerged from the old building's revolving door, shaken, as though he had been through some course of treatment that involved electroshock. The L train, rumbling on its tracks overhead, startled him. He didn't quite know why his first session with the therapist left him feeling so mixed up, his breath coming in quick, staccato puffs, his heart racing.

"I just wanted someone to love me."

What he had admitted to the therapist came back to him, like some snatch of music on a distant stereo, taunting, raw, hurtful, and true all at once. Why had he admitted such a pathetic need to this woman, who was really nothing more than a stranger? If there weren't pedestrians and traffic all around, he might have shouted the question to the sky, seeing if maybe there was a God up there who would supply an answer.

So what? Who doesn't want someone to love them? Jesus, what a pitiable creep you are. You should march back in and cancel that second visit. That woman has a way of worming way too much out of you.

The bright spring day, unseasonably warm, was a lie. A shining, promising testimony to his failures in life. Sure, he was successful as a marketing executive (except he wasn't sure how long that success would last if he continued to slip out on weekdays for fucking psychotherapy), but really, he had no one. No friends. His family was half the country away, living in Seattle. And he certainly had no boyfriend.

He wished there was just one person he could call, someone to whom he could release the thoughts and feelings that had been brought up so unexpectedly in the short session. But he couldn't think of a single person who would be interested, even though his iPhone directory was full of numbers.

Being released from that shrink's office was like having a plastic bag snatched off his head, though. Bobby felt like he could breathe again.

I don't know if I want to confront my demons.

Who was it who said if we get rid of our demons, we might also get rid of our angels? I'm with that guy.

Right now, it was just good to breathe. Bobby looked around and noticed that the office buildings in the south loop had emptied, just so everyone could get out and enjoy the sunshine after the claustrophobic winter with its gray skies, arctic winds, snow, and sleet.

Bobby stepped out of the building's shadows so the sun poured down on him. He wished he could just blot out the last hour, lose himself in the warmth from the rays. He forced himself to take deep, lung-stretching breaths and let the air out slowly. *Calm down.*

Wow. I don't want to think about being in Camille's office. I don't know if I can go back. She's like a mirror, only her mirror made me see something ugly. Who the hell needs that? How is that therapeutic?

Bobby strode down Wabash Avenue toward the stairs that would take him up to the L, which rumbled overhead. On the platform, he considered the last time he saw Caden. Bobby had thought the guy would be his best friend for life, the only person he could speak of, outside of his immediate family, who seemed to like Bobby for himself and not for sex. Of course, when he and Caden had first met, Bobby had tried to get him into bed. He tried to do that with just about every "fucking gorgeous" gay man he met, but he was never Caden's type. That had turned out to be a good thing. Caden showed him, for the first time maybe, how two men could be friends without having a sexual component thrown into the mix.

But now Caden was gone. For good. Bobby stared down the L train tracks, empty as his heart, and thought how he had pushed Caden away with his selfishness and lies. Bobby kicked a flyer that had blown in front of him off the wooden platform and onto the tracks. *It was my own damn fault.* He knew that now, but how to fix it?

He knew he had only gone to see Camille because of Caden.

Bobby flashed back to last week when he had opened his mailbox to find a handwritten envelope inside. He had almost gasped. How often did people get handwritten envelopes these days? He had turned the envelope over and looked closely to make sure the handwriting was *bona fide* and not the work of a talented machine. It was real.

The return address on Fargo immediately rang a bell.

It was where Caden's boyfriend lived. Oh, how Bobby remembered that address! Sneaking out of the back door one cold, frigid winter night to avoid seeing Caden, who had just arrived unexpectedly. Bobby had been playing games, trying to create tension and drama, discord where none had existed. All so he could claim Kevin as his own.

Since that night last winter, when all his lies were exposed, like bugs being confronted by bright light, Bobby had been really alone. No matter how many guys he hooked up with at the baths, the bars, or online, he could never seem to fill the hole his deceit had opened up back then.

Why would Kevin be writing to me?
He wasn't.

Caden was.

Inside the envelope was a piece of paper wrapped around a business card—Camille D'Amico's. The piece of paper holding the card bore a hastily scribbled note:

> *You need help. Go see her. Then maybe we can talk.*
>
> *C.*

Bobby remembered looking around the lobby of his building, feeling guilty for reasons he couldn't quite put a finger on, and stuffing the note and card into his pocket.

He'd wondered, heading up to his apartment in the elevator, if he should call Caden to let him know he had received the card. He would thank him for reaching out, trying not to gush, but so relieved that Caden had, after all the weeks of silent reproach. Because he knew it would please Caden, he would promise to make an appointment with the therapist. He would do anything to make amends.

The doors had opened for his floor, and Bobby affirmed to himself that of course he would go see her. But calling Caden? A little voice inside Bobby's head had told him that wouldn't be such a bright idea. It would be precisely what his old friend wouldn't want. Bobby had been calling him, first every day after it all blew up in their faces and then weekly and then every other week.

Caden would never call back. Would never pick up. Bobby had toyed with the idea of calling from a different phone, one where Caden wouldn't have the number stored in his iPhone's memory, but gave up on that. More duplicity—just what had gotten him into trouble in the first place. Somehow Bobby didn't think Caden would take kindly to being tricked, yet again, even in a small way.

But as he'd pushed the key into his front door lock that day, Bobby had remembered how he had clung, with almost feverish hope, to five of the eleven words Caden had written—*then maybe we can talk.*

Now the train that would take Bobby north to Belmont and his apartment in the sky pulled into the station, crackling and rumbling. He boarded, wondering if one visit with Camille would be enough to get Caden and him talking again.

Nah.

Bobby pressed his forehead wearily against the glass, to stare out through a grimy window at the sun-dappled day, wondering what he should do first when he got home.

Log onto Adam4Adam or just post an ad on Craigslist?

In the end, he opted for Craigslist. For one, it was easier than wading through all the online profiles, playing the back and forth of instant messaging, narrowing things down, weeding out the fakes from the real guys. That had been his experience on Adam4Adam. *Online cruising used to be easy*, Bobby thought. Now it just appeared to be an elaborate game.

Craigslist, with its neat little time-stamped ads, cut to the chase quicker. Some guys even had clever ways of beating the system that forbade including phone numbers by writing the numbers out, interspersing them with actual words, anything to slip by whatever computer sentries the folks at Craigslist had set up. Bobby wondered why they bothered with this prohibition anyway, when all it took was a quick email to get a guy's phone number. Everyone was so impatient these days.

No matter.

Bobby was tired too, exhausted from the soul-baring he had just done with Camille. He wanted to forget that whole episode. *And nothing brings oblivion quicker than sex.* Sex had a way of blocking everything out, pushing all one's cares out of the picture, intensifying the physical while, at the same time, downplaying the emotional.

Craigslist men-for-men is a world unto itself. It's like a party with horny men that grows every time I refresh my browser. Usually, I post my own ad with a couple of hot chest shots that showcase my hairless, ripped pecs and one of my taut ass, but today all I feel like doing is cruising the postings, hoping I will find someone who looks, if not tempting, then at the very least, acceptable.

My God. It's only three in the afternoon on a weekday, and there are dozens and dozens of guys online and looking. Certainly, I can find one to come over and make me happy again, make me feel whole again. Feel my hole again. Fill my hole again.

Bobby snorted out a laugh. He got up from his desk and slipped into a pair of boxers and a loose-fitting T-shirt. *Gotta be comfortable for the hunt.* He also needed sustenance, so he wandered out to the kitchen to splash some vodka into a glass and top it off with a little cranberry juice.

He sat back down, comfortable, fortified, to begin clicking through the ads. He immediately eliminated the guys who were looking to host. *I'm too pooped to travel, even if it's just around the corner—hell, even if it's on another floor of this Lake Shore Drive high-rise I call home. I want someone to come to me.*

Then he eliminated the guys who were parTying. *Yes, the capital T is not an error. That T stands for Tina, and Tina is short for crystal meth. I don't need some nasty-ass tweaker coming over here with his dirty pipe, dirty spike, dirty straws, or whatever the hell he uses to get that toxic shit into his system. Besides, those guys almost always have trouble getting it up, and I don't want some hungry, high desperate-to-bottom playmate with spring-loaded legs today. Not today. Today I want a big dick inside me to take me away, like the old ad for Calgon bath powder used to promise.*

Surprisingly, or maybe not so much, cutting out the partiers and those who were looking to host immediately narrowed the field considerably.

Then he weeded out those who had posted more than an hour and a half ago. *If they're still on, something's wrong. But it's more likely they've given up, hooked up, or simply moved on and forgotten to take down their ads.*

He rose to pour himself another splash of vodka, this time skipping the cranberry juice.

At last, Bobby's fingers hesitated over one ad that looked promising. The guy in this ad said he was a student at Loyola University, downtown campus, so the proximity to Bobby was good. His stats: six one, 180, red/blue, swimmer's build. (*If the weight is accurate, I don't have to worry that "swimmer's build" means Shelley Winters—God rest her soul—in the original* Poseidon Adventure.) He claimed to have an eight-inch dick (but then, most of the guys on Craigslist seemed to have eight-inch cocks), low hangers, and loved to fuck. He claimed he was twenty-four.

But the two pics he had attached to his ad were what really set Bobby's heart to racing. One showed the guy's dick, which did indeed look sizable—long and thin and hanging down between two freckled, muscled thighs like a snake. It had a very pretty, very purple head, kind of like a plum. Unlike most guys on here, though, he had also attached a face pic, and there was something so sweet about his red hair, freckles, and wide, perfect-toothed smile that it just set Bobby's blood pumping quickly southward. *He looks like a bad boy, a gay Huck Finn come to life.*

Bobby readjusted his dick in his boxers and clicked on the hyperlink to respond. He typed:

Hey, man. Saw your ad and am looking to take cock down my expert throat and up my tight ass, as rough and as many times as you want to give it. Play safe, but lean more toward wild than mild. You look like my kind of hot-ass man. On LSD (the drive, not the drug) and am looking for company NOW. Hit me up if you're interested.

Bobby attached a full-body shot from last summer of him on his bed, loving the way the light defined his muscles and how the sun had crafted a perfect field of white around his hard dick. His face looked hungry. He attached another one that showed the other side. *My creamy white ass, framed by the deep tan of my thighs and lower back, should really entice this dude if he's truly a top like his ad claims.*

Bobby hit Send and went back to perusing the ads. He saw a couple more who piqued his interest—a black guy who claimed to have an eleven-inch dick and a daddy with a ripped bod and a face like the actor Sam Elliot—but he would allow Loyola big-man-on-campus a few minutes to respond.

But only a few—he'd found that if they didn't write back right away, they weren't interested. If they got back hours later, they were flakes. *Hey, I have learned the rules through hard-won experience.*

If it's gonna happen, I've learned, it happens quick.

And Loyola guy wrote back right quick. An email popped up in Bobby's Gmail from Chitown Top Stud. Perfect. He opened it to read:

You sound like my kind of guy. Looking to get my dick drained (four-day load built up) and can come multiple times. You up for some hard-core pounding? Depending on where you are, I can hop in a cab and be to you within the hour. I'm downtown right now, near the Water Tower. So?

Bobby typed back what was essentially a great big neon *hell yes* and threw caution to the wind, giving him his cell and his address. *Why waste time? The sooner he gets that fine dick over here, the sooner we can get down to business.*

His fish-on-the-hook seemed to be of a like mind because almost simultaneously with sending Bobby's email, his phone started to ring.

"Hey," Bobby answered, automatically deepening his voice.

"What's up? You messaged me from Craigslist. I'm the redhead."

"And I'm the bottom. You up for comin' over?"

"Yup."

"Then let's do it. Ask for Nelson in 2013 when you get here."

"See you soon, man. And—be clean."

"Always. How long?"

"Take me fifteen minutes, maybe less. I'll hop in a cab."

"See you soon."

It's time to hit the shower. God, don't let him be a flake.

A half hour later, Bobby's phone rang. He hurried to answer it, noting that the caller display indicated the call was coming from the front desk. *Thank God. There are so many flakes in this online hookup world, I'm glad this guy at least had the decency to show up, which is more than I can say for many of my so-called paramours.*

Bobby pressed the button that would connect him with the caller. As he did, he checked out his image in the large, gilt-framed mirror opposite the bed. He smiled. He looked good, skin glowing from the hot shower, ripped, everything in the right place. He had put on a pair of black Papi trunk briefs that outlined his package nicely. He turned to look at the back view and loved the rise of his cheeks. *Bubble butt... You could set a tray on this ass...*

"Mr. Nelson? There's a man here to see you. Says his name is Andy?"

I guess it's Andy. We never did exchange names. I wish we had one of those systems a lot of the high-rises have, where you can see what your visitor looks like on your TV, via a closed-circuit system. But I saw Andy's pics, and if he's even close to how sweet he looks in them, I know I'm in for a treat. "Send him on up, Jim."

"Sure thing." Bobby hung up and lowered the sheets on the bed. He adjusted the blinds open just a hair so the late-afternoon sunlight fell in filtered slats across the sheets. He queued up an old vintage porn—Joe Gage's *LA Tool and Die*—on his iMac and was distracted for a moment by the opening shot of a guy on his knees, giving head to a whole roomful of guys. *Hot.* He made sure to lower the moans, sighs, and groans—and the accompanying cheesy soundtrack—to just above audible. Popping his iPhone into the speaker unit on the bedside table, he clicked on his Pandora "trance" station.

He opened the nightstand drawer:

Lube, check.

Poppers, check.

Condoms, check.

It looks like we are all set to go.

Good thing, too, because right now someone was knocking lightly on his front door. The gentle tap, three times, set Bobby's heart to racing and an ineffable sense of exhilaration coursing through him, banishing to oblivion the worries he had brought up in that frizzy-haired therapist's office earlier that day. He hurried to silence the knocking, which was now sounding a second time, and hoped that soon someone would be pounding hard on *his* back door.

As Bobby reached for the doorknob, he held within his mind's eye the visual image of that big pink dick and that naughty-boy face as he peered into the peephole. *Shoot. He's standing away from the door. All I can see is a bit of shoulder—a white T-shirt that tells me nothing.*

Bobby shrugged and opened the door. The smile he had pasted on his face like makeup dwindled away to nothing.

He is nothing like what I expected. No, the pics, I'm thinking, weren't fake, but they were taken maybe ten years ago. Or more. Yes, the red hair is there, but it's rapidly thinning and has strands of brittle gray mixed in with the red. He's wearing a pair of rimless glasses that do nothing to hide his pale blue eyes, rimmed in red. His nose reveals a drinker—a bit on the bulbous side and marred by broken veins. The usual accompaniments to an aging man are all present in his face—lined forehead, crow's feet, and jowls that are starting to sag just a bit.

He's about thirty pounds overweight and looks like he hasn't seen the inside of a gym in decades. I wonder if the dick pic was even him.

Nonetheless, Bobby considered himself forever the optimist and hoped that at least the cock portrait was for real. *At least dicks don't age—much—or shrink, right?*

Bobby replanted the smile on his face and opened the door wide, ushering Andy inside. He muted the voices in his head that were yelling at him, a chorus of scolders. They wondered why he was taking this any further. *The guy is obviously not even in the same league. And I know what the voices are telling me is true—that, once upon a time, I would have just patted the guy's shoulder, looked into his eyes, and said, politely but firmly,* "Sorry you made the trip, but I think I'm gonna pass."

But now, Bobby just wanted sex, never mind that those same voices were telling him sex was just another word for oblivion. Bobby told himself: *he's a man with a presumably hard dick. I don't want to go back to square one online.*

You just want to get it over with. And how in the hell is that the right attitude for sex?

Bobby gestured toward the bedroom. "Wanna come back to my room? I've got some porn playing. Good stuff. You like Joe Gage?"

But the guy didn't reveal his feelings one way or another about the director Bobby considered the master of precondom porn, the best of the best. What he did do was follow along, like a puppy, as Bobby led the way back to the bedroom. Bobby noted that his breathing was heavy. *The guy is either a smoker— yuck—or he's already getting excited and is panting a little. Let's hope, for both our sakes, it's the latter.*

But the charred tobacco smell wafting off the guy told Bobby it was more likely the former.

In the bedroom, Bobby shut the blinds fully, deciding the atmosphere was no longer necessary. Bobby, just like everyone else in this warren of Near North Side high-rises had binoculars—which were used, as everyone else used them—for spying, *Rear Window* style, on neighbors. Bobby didn't want any prying eyes seeing, even through partially closed blinds, what he had "gotten lucky" with today.

He had a reputation to uphold.

Didn't he?

He stood by the side of the bed, watching dispassionately as Andy undressed, clumsy. His knees creaked as he bent down to unlace his sneakers. Bobby would have chuckled, if it weren't so sad when the guy's foot got caught up in the bottom of his jeans and he almost toppled over.

Slowly, with a sense of resignation Bobby hoped didn't show, he brought out the lube and set it on the nightstand, throwing a handful of condoms, like confetti, on the bed. He sighed and shut off the new age music, turning up the volume on the porn to fill the room with synthesizer music and the sound of butch men grunting, groaning, and whispering filth.

Bobby guessed he could just close his eyes and listen.

Bobby took one more glance at Andy as he pulled down his boxers. He was relieved to see that at least the dick shot didn't lie. Andy's dick was as big as advertised, and it appeared to be rock hard, almost so tumescent the thing looked about ready to explode. *I wonder if he popped a Viagra before coming over.*

Bobby slipped out of his briefs and knelt on the bed, facing away from his lover-of-the-moment, so he could watch the action on the screen while the guy stood beside the bed and fucked him. Although it was obvious, Bobby pointed it out anyway: "Condoms on the bed." No way was it worth catching something from this fucker.

Bobby squinched his eyes shut and held his breath as he felt the guy press close, his heavy breath on his back. Bobby lowered his head to his arms, crossed before him on the bed. He felt exposed, vulnerable. He reached down and tugged at himself and discovered he was not even a little bit hard.

A voice bit into his consciousness, one that sounded very much like his therapist's, and she asked, "So why are you doing this?"

Bobby had no answer, other than sending out one thought telepathically to the guy, who was now pushing himself inside Bobby, making Bobby wince. *Just get it over with quickly...*

It didn't hurt.

He pumped a few times, no more than three or four, and cried out, "Fuck!" gasping and groaning as though he was having the world's best orgasm. Instinctively, Bobby clamped his ass muscles down on the throbbing cock as it emptied—Bobby hoped— inside the condom.

Bobby peered back through his legs to witness the specter of fat thighs moving away. The condom, now full, hung from Andy's rapidly deflating cock. Bobby couldn't help it; he snickered. The whole scene wasn't funny, though.

It was sad.

He watched as the guy pulled the rubber from his half-erect dick and flung it to Bobby's bamboo floor.

Hot.

Bobby and Andy did not say another word to each other as Andy dressed. There was a palpable sense of embarrassment in the room. Reclining on the bed, Bobby eyed the man, sending out a telepathic message for him to hurry up—hurry up and leave.

The guy turned to him, a questioning look on his face.

Bobby said, "Just straight down the hall. The door out is on your right."

The guy smiled. "Thanks."

"Sure. It was great."

Bobby listened to the man's footfalls as he headed down the hallway toward the front door. When he heard the door close, he got back online.

Chapter Three

Bobby awakened to the synthesized jingle of Eddie Murphy's old disco chestnut, "Party All the Time," sounding from his phone. He opened his eyes to a room still steeped in darkness and glanced first at the pillow next to himself, ensuring he was, indeed, alone and then to the alarm clock on his nightstand table. A bottle of Eros lube blocked the digital readout. He slapped it aside as the inappropriately cheerful tune continued its manic melody.

It was four fifteen. He had to be up in two hours to pull himself together for work, despite the dregs of a hangover and a throbbing asshole from dick or dicks unknown at this foggy-memory moment.

Who could be calling now? Middle of the night calls such as these were always bad news, weren't they? It was this last thought that sent a bolt of adrenaline through Bobby, waking him fully and banishing his hangover, other aches and pains, and guilt to the background.

Duh. The ringtone, programmed into his iPhone, belonged to only one person—his mother, Michelle, in Seattle. Bobby had given her "Party All the Time" as a ringtone one drunken night as a joke, because he could think of no one less likely to party all the time than his staid mother.

Bobby sat up in bed, the sheets dropping from his sweaty frame, trying to ignore a stabbing, ice-pick-style pain behind his right eye, and groped for the phone on his nightstand. What time was it in Seattle, anyway? Bobby quickly calculated. It would be a little after 2:00 a.m.

He felt a nauseating clench in his gut. This couldn't be good.

Glancing down at the smiling face of his mother on the phone—blunt-cut blonde hair, a turned up nose, the dark brown eyes, looking decades younger than her current age of sixty-three—made him feel even sicker.

"Mom?" he whispered to the darkness, suddenly afraid of pressing the button on the screen that would connect them.

More to quiet the inane rhythm of the tune than for anything else, Bobby pressed Accept only a moment before he knew the call would have been sent to voice mail.

If Michelle was calling in the middle of the night, the last thing she would probably want to hear was her son's voice, informing her that he was not available right now.

"Mom?" Bobby said again, this time into the phone.

"Thank God you answered! I wasn't sure you wouldn't be asleep, and then you wouldn't pick up, and I just don't know what I would have done if you hadn't picked up. But you're there, and we're talking, and that's a good thing. Actually, the thing I prayed for. Oh, son, it's sweet to hear your voice."

Bobby cut her off before she could babble any further. This wasn't like his mother, who was usually found in the phrase dictionary next to "calm, cool, and collected." "Mom? Mom, you're babbling. Is everything okay?"

There was silence on the other end of the line, then a very embarrassing, wet-sounding snort. Bobby listened to his mother draw in a great, quivering breath. "No, sir," his mother finally said. "Everything is *not* okay, not okay at all."

Before she started off on a crying jag or babbling again, Bobby brought her to the point. At the same time, he felt a chill course through him, as if he knew already the words his mother would eventually utter. "What's going on, Mom?"

"It's your father."

"What about him?"

"He's dead."

The words hung in the air, oddly casual, as though she had said he's in the bathroom or he's playing canasta or he's a Republican.

"Dead? What do you mean? Dad's only sixty-two." Bobby knew his follow-up response made little sense, but it was true—this was not a call he expected to get at this stage of life. "Did I hear you right?" *Yeah. That must be it. She said he's red, meaning he somehow got a sunburn, or he's fed, meaning he downed the leftovers from that night's dinner.*

"Oh, Robert! Of course you heard me right." The anger in her tone seemed to usurp her despair. "What else would I have said? For heaven's sake. Your father got up a couple of hours ago to use the bathroom. The next thing I know I heard a bang, like something heavy going over. I got up to check on him—" And suddenly she stopped talking; the despair returned full force. When she was able to speak, her voice was like a little girl's, high-pitched and choked by sobs. "I called out, 'Bob? Everything okay in there?' and then I tried to push on the bathroom door to open it." She sobbed. "I tried to push on the door. I tried to push on the door."

"Mom?"

"I tried to push on the door, and it wouldn't open. It wouldn't open because—oh God!—he was lying there on the floor, blocking it. By the time I could move it enough to poke my head inside, I saw him lying there, white as a sheet, eyes just staring up, but not at me. You know? He had a heart attack is what they're saying. A massive heart attack."

This had to be a dream. This couldn't be happening. Bobby didn't know what to feel. Should he cry? Should he lie back and smile because finally his father, his perfectionist father for whom nothing was ever good enough, was finally gone? Should he...what?

He experienced nothing but a strange numbness that left him set apart, as if this whole scenario were happening to someone else. Aside from feeling devoid of thought or emotion, he felt weird physically, like his head had expanded to two or three times its normal size. His arms tingled. Wouldn't it be ironic if *he* had a heart attack now? Part of him almost wanted to press the End button on the phone, just fall back on his pillows and go back to sleep.

But he couldn't do that!

What about his mother? "Mom? Mom, I'm going to hang up now so I can check into getting the soonest flight I can to come home. Where are you now?"

"I'm at the hospital." As if to confirm her statement, Bobby heard a page in the background.

"Okay. Okay, I'll give you a call when I have my flight information. I'll rent a car and either meet you at home or down at the hospital, whatever the timing is."

"Thank you, Robert. I need you here." His mother's voice was weak.

"I know, Mom. I'll get there as soon as I can. Talk soon." He was about to push End when he hurriedly added, "I love you."

But his mother had already hung up.

*

Bobby peered out the window of the plane to look at the snow-blanketed peaks of the Cascade Mountains and saw, in the distance, the ethereal majesty of Mount Rainier. The brilliant sunlight poured down relentlessly, illuminating the cold, harsh landscape shimmering with crystalline snow. It was beautiful, Bobby thought, but it was a hard, cold, and unforgiving beauty.

He returned his gaze to the issue of *Entertainment Weekly* he had brought along for the trip, trying for the third time to read a profile of Channing Tatum. His concentration never allowed him to do more than gaze at the pictures.

He was almost home.

Soon the plane would be descending, and views of vast expanses of slate-blue water, hills covered in firs, and Seattle's skyline would come into view, and then it would only be an hour or so until he saw his mom again.

Home.

The word echoed, strange, in his mind. What did it mean?

Home, where they knew Bobby was forty, as opposed to the early thirties he told all his conquests back in Chicago.

Home, where he had grown up surrounded by mountains, tree-covered hills, and water just about everywhere one looked—including up.

Home, where his mother now lived, a new widow.

Home, where his right-wing, Christian fundamentalist sister, Dawn, lived with her husband and three kids in the northern suburb of Snohomish.

Home, where he was *not* the confident, successful, handsome, well-built man he was now, but a scared little boy who was made fun of nearly every school day for being a sissy and who hid out in his room, reading books far too adult for a child. (*Rosemary's Baby* in third grade, really?)

Home, where he had grown up living in a fantasy world bolstered by TV soap operas and sitcoms.

Home, where he was his mother's favorite man and chief confidante.

There were a lot of definitions, and none of them were good.

Bobby wanted to march right up to the cockpit and tell the pilot to just turn this plane around and head back to O'Hare. Mr. Robert Nelson, Jr. (also known as Bobby) was not going to Seattle today. No way. No how. No, sir!

The beautiful patch of the Pacific Northwest where he'd been raised simply held too many painful memories, and with what was waiting for him, he knew he would only be making more.

He slumped back in his business-class seat before leaning forward so he could peer down the aisle at the blond flight attendant with whom he had flirted earlier, to catch his eye. When the guy—with his spiky hair, blue eyes, and perfect body barely contained by his uniform—saw Bobby looking, he grinned and hurried up the aisle toward him.

Good Lord, are those shoulder pads? Are your shoulders really that broad? And that basket! Is there a sock stuffed in there?

Maybe he has a layover in Seattle? Bobby wondered and then chided himself. *Your father is dead.*

"Can I get you something?" The blue eyes peered down, locking with Bobby's gray ones, and Bobby couldn't help but think the question was a loaded one. Bobby held up his glass, along with holding up his own inclinations to flirt, to see if the guy would be amenable to hooking up once the plane had landed, and asked, "Could you get me another vodka cranberry?"

"Anything you want." He hurried away, and Bobby craned his neck to watch the rise and fall of the firm bubble ass as it made its way back to the galley.

What the hell is wrong with you?

*

By the time he had claimed his bags and rented a car (an unassuming Toyota Camry in burgundy), Bobby was exhausted. He made his way north on I-5 toward the city. No matter how much he traveled, or how far, he never ceased to be amazed at how draining simply sitting for several hours in a confined space could be. Add that to the trauma of losing a parent, and he supposed it made a great deal of sense that he was tired, that his eyelids burned, aching with their need for slumber. Or maybe what he really wanted was oblivion.

As Seattle's skyline came into view with its iconic Space Needle, Bobby wondered what kind of scene awaited him at home. Instead of the warm feeling of homecoming he thought he should be having, Bobby experienced only anxiety as he spotted the familiar landmarks, the Sound, the shipyards, the city, now grown even larger with new skyscrapers he'd never seen and the addition of Safeco Field. Bobby gripped the steering wheel tighter to compensate for the sweat seeping now from his palms. Again he was seized with an urgency to take the next exit, turn around, head back to the airport, and hop the next plane bound for Chicago.

But he couldn't do that. He had a funeral to attend and a grieving mother to comfort.

Home.

There was that word again. Bobby felt a pang in his heart because he wasn't really sure if he could define the word, especially not now, not this afternoon, as he headed toward a condo his parents had bought after Bobby had moved away from the "Emerald City" to set himself up in the "Windy City" some ten years ago.

Had it been that long? Bobby shook his head, knowing it had. There was always one reason or another not to make it back here. Work. More work. A long-planned vacation. A short-lived boyfriend who wanted to spend Christmas in Palm Springs. Another short-lived boyfriend… Another…

And, really, this "home" to which he was headed was a place he had never even set foot in. Bobby had grown up in the airy hilltop neighborhood known as Queen Anne, in a red-brick house overlooking not only downtown and the Needle but Puget Sound as well. When his parents had sold the five-bedroom Georgian-style home back in 2006, just before the real estate bubble had burst, they had made nearly two million dollars on the sale.

Bobby wondered briefly who now lived in *his* old house.

Now his parents lived in a penthouse condo on Dexter Avenue, just south of the Fremont Bridge and north of downtown. It was smaller, only a couple of thousand square feet, but no less luxurious than their Queen Anne home on Highland Avenue. Their condo had stunning views of Lake Union, Gas Works Park, and across the placid blue waters of the big urban lake, the neighborhoods of Eastlake and Capitol Hill. Leaning out from their balcony on clear days, one could view the eastern edge of downtown and Mount Rainier. On those same days, across the water, the jagged blue-gray silhouettes of the Cascades rose up.

Bobby knew all of this because his mother often sent him pictures. At first, they were actual photos, printed. Then, as his mother caught on to using her first laptop and twenty-first-century means of communication like email and social networking, he would get glimpses of their gorgeous condo views on his mother's Facebook page. The message, implied or not, of all of these panoramic views always remained the same: come home; come see your family.

But Bobby was always too busy. Never mind that, during the last decade, work or pleasure had taken him literally all over the world.

And now death had forced his hand, and here he was, taking the Mercer Avenue exit that would bring him to his mother within only minutes.

The traffic was bad, and for this Bobby was grateful. It delayed the inevitable, and that was fine with him. As he sat in the tangled mess of Mercer Avenue traffic, he looked at the sky and tried to admire its colors as the sun set—tangerine, gray, lavender. Night would fall soon.

At least it wasn't raining. The day had been a sunny one, obviously, and rare for March in this town.

He inched along and, too soon for his taste, was on Dexter Avenue, heading north to his parents' condo. Correction—make that his mother's condo. He took in all the new apartment buildings that had gone up along this stretch since he had lived in Seattle. He noted the dedicated bike lanes and within a mile counted at least a dozen bikers, probably on their way home from work.

Yes, he was in Seattle.

Finally, he spied the building he had seen so many photographs of. It was four stories, very modern, with clean lines, and its exterior had been painted a tasteful shade of beige. The building even had a name, Aerie, because it perched on a bluff above a greenbelt that was itself above busy Westlake Avenue, and then the harbor and the lake. Bobby remembered his mom telling him the *Sleepless in Seattle* houseboat was just beneath them, although trees blocked their views of it.

He found a parking spot only steps from the Aerie's plate-glass front door and pulled in. This kind of parking—his friend Caden had called it "Doris Day parking" because it was always right in front of where you wanted to be, as it forever was in the wholesome blonde's movies—Bobby seldom found in Chicago, where it wasn't uncommon to circle a neighborhood for a half hour or more, only to park three or four blocks from your destination.

Again, Bobby realized he would have appreciated the delay. Instead, he turned off the car, sat there for a moment just trying to get his breathing under control. He pulled the sweat-soaked shirt from his back, despite the fact the temperature outside hovered around fifty.

"You gotta do this, and no amount of sitting here is going to make it any easier," Bobby said in his best "chin up, shoulders back" manner of speaking. He took a deep breath, put his hand on the door handle, and swung his legs out onto the pavement—just narrowly missing a biker who barreled down the hill at top speed. "Watch it, dumbass!" the biker called over his shoulder.

Bobby sat for a moment, door still offensively open to oncoming bikers, waiting for his heart rate to slow. He flung his head back to the headrest and closed his eyes, but only for a second. Then he looked behind him and got out. He grabbed his Tumi bag from the trunk and started up the walk.

In the gloom of dusk, he spotted a man striding down the street toward him. A cold chill passed through Bobby, colder than the air surrounding him. The man's bearing was almost military—shoulders back, spine ramrod straight, swinging his arms forcefully in time with his very purposeful and rapid walk—and Bobby sucked in a gasp.

It was his father. "Stand up straight, son! A man who slouches is a lazy son of a bitch, and that's no one from this family!" Bobby could hear the man saying.

"Dad?" Bobby whispered, and for a moment, it all was clear: his mother had set up this elaborate—and macabre—ruse to finally get him to come home. He felt himself cowering a little as the man drew near.

But of course it was not his father. This guy's hair, Bobby now saw, was snow white, and he wore tortoiseshell glasses. His father had still managed contacts and kept the gray carefully dyed out of his own head of thick auburn hair. And this man wore a Seattle Mariners T-shirt and jeans, attire his staid father wouldn't have been caught dead in.

Caught dead in? Bobby snickered, ratcheting the laugher almost up to a hysterical giggle as he chided himself for his choice of words.

Stop it! Pull yourself together!

At last he stood at the front door, thinking it was odd that he would have to, for the first time ever, buzz his mother for admittance to the family abode. He located the Nelson name in the directory and punched in the code.

Just as he noticed the camera above him, Bobby heard the discreet click of the front door lock releasing. He pulled the door open and whispered, "Here goes nothing."

He moved quickly through the lobby, heading straight back to his mother's front door. Should he knock? He shook his head; knocking would just be too weird. He tried the doorknob and it turned easily.

Once he was inside, he didn't have much time to admire the condo's clean lines, elegant marble and dark wood décor, or the stunning views from the floor-to-ceiling windows that all faced east, showcasing the shimmering water, the Eastlake neighborhood lit up by the setting sun, and the Cascade Mountains behind it, looking gray, their tops shrouded in ribbons of silvery cloud.

He could only glimpse these things quickly, because his mother commanded his immediate attention. Bobby's first thought was unkind, and he quickly stomped on it with shame. But it couldn't be denied—it looked as though his mother had arranged herself on the living room couch as a portrait of despair.

Michelle Nelson had nothing out of place. Her fitted black slacks, white silk blouse, and Hermès scarf in tasteful shades of avocado, yellow, and cream all spoke of genteel elegance. Her legs were crossed, and Bobby noticed that her shoes, high-heeled pumps, bore red soles, a high-end designer signature. Bobby could not remember the designer's name, only that the cost of the shoes would probably feed a family of four for a month. Michelle's hair hung straight, blonde, and perfect to her shoulders. Now, as she stared down at her interlaced fingers, that hair hid her face. She didn't look a day over forty.

She could be his sister.

But the perfect, almost serene composure was marred by his mother's face when she looked up. This was one area she couldn't keep together. Her eyes were moist, red-rimmed, with smudges of black mascara. Her lipstick had worn off, and she looked much closer to her real age. The lines of grief, not concealed by foundation and blush, were etched deeply into her face and emphasized by the obvious crying she had recently done.

She didn't say anything, but simply raised her watery blue eyes to him as he closed the door and walked toward her.

He felt bad for thinking she had somehow staged this moment to create some sort of tableau of her grief. It was obvious from her quivering lower lip and the tears that sprung forth from her eyes upon seeing him that the sadness, the ache, were very real and very fresh.

Bobby dropped his bag and hurried to sit by his mother so that their shoulders touched. The two of them said nothing for several minutes. Bobby simply pressed in close, wondering if he should take her in his arms.

The Nelsons were not a big hugging family.

Finally, it was Michelle who spoke first. She extended her hand, closed fist, toward him. "I know he would have wanted you to have this." The simple admission caused her to hiccup out a small sob, and she wiped at her eyes.

Bobby allowed her to drop what she held into his palm. He looked down to see the ring his father always wore, a square-cut ruby set in yellow gold— his birthstone. His father had had the ring since he was a young man. His parents had given it to him as a gift when he'd completed his undergraduate studies at the University of Washington.

Bobby fingered it, recalling it on his father's hand, remembering it coming toward him as his father reached out to cuff him on the ear, and felt sick. That ring was a piece of his father, and Bobby felt an almost irresistible urge to simply fling it across the room. He would have done so if he hadn't realized how much that act would hurt his mother.

Michelle said quietly, "Aren't you going to put it on?"

Bobby peered down at the ring as though it were a foreign thing, like he needed an instruction manual to understand how to slide it onto his ring finger. Finally, because he could think of no way to gracefully decline his mother's urging, he slid the ring on.

It would go only as far as his knuckle. The ring was too small, and this surprised Bobby: that he would have bigger hands than his hypermasculine father. By no stretch of his imagination would Bobby ever dream that his father's hands were small, even delicate, yet the ring told that very tale.

"It doesn't fit."

"You'll have to get it sized."

Bobby nodded and slid the ring into his pocket. For now, at least, the matter of his wearing it was settled.

"Do you want to unpack? I put fresh towels on the bed in the guest room and clean sheets on the bed. Are you hungry? How long can you stay?"

"Mom. Mom—never mind that. Are you okay?"

His mother stared for a long time at the dying light outside the floor-to-ceiling windows, taking in small breaths through her mouth. Bobby could tell she was trying not to cry. He patted her shoulder.

"No. Not okay. I don't know what I'm going to do." She looked at him then, her eyes pleading, desperate. "He took care of everything—the bills, the car, the house—how will I do all of that myself? I don't know where to start." She grabbed Bobby's hand and held it tightly. Bobby looked down at the small hand, the bird bones, afraid to return her grip for fear of crushing them.

Of course his mother would be grieving the loss of order, of practicality, of being taken care of, as she had been her entire married life. Although she had gotten a degree in elementary education, she had never used it, never worked outside the home. Her occupations had been volunteering for charitable organizations and taking care of Bobby and his sister.

Of course she would not be grieving for his father—*not the man.* How could she? He was hard, self-centered, a son of a bitch, if Bobby didn't want to put too fine a point on it.

His mother could never have really loved this man, who had essentially given her lots of material things but rarely showed her any real affection. Conversation between husband and wife in the Nelson household was more about instructing, complaining, and chastising than it ever was about sharing or kindness.

Bobby suddenly flashed on a summer day back when he was a little boy. His mother had gone to have her hair and makeup done for a party she and his father were attending that night. She came home— only a half hour late—beaming with pride at how gorgeous she looked, flushed with excitement for the party.

But one didn't arrive late—ever—on Robert Nelson's watch. He took one look at her, frowned, and said, "Too bad you went to so much trouble when it will only be the four walls who will appreciate it." He had walked away. Later, he had gone to the black tie event on his own.

Bobby had comforted Michelle that night, telling her how beautiful she was and mixing her expert Stoli martinis until she fell asleep on the family room couch.

Good times...

It was almost on the tip of Bobby's tongue to say something along the lines of *You'll pick up that stuff easy. Everything you need to know and do is all online now. I'll show you*, when Michelle interrupted the flow of his words by saying something that shocked him, that actually caused his world to be jarred two inches to the left, as if an earthquake had struck.

"I loved him so much. I don't know what I'm going to do without him."

Bobby didn't know what to say. Those few words changed his entire perception of his parents, of their marriage. *She loved him?*

How could she?

Bobby had never felt more alone than he did at this very moment.

He got up from the couch and lifted his bag from the floor. "I think I'll go unpack now after all. Okay if I take a shower? It's been a long day."

His mother looked up at him, eyes bright, questioning. But all she said was "Sure. Go ahead.

The guest room has its own bath. I put new shampoo, soap, and conditioner in there for you. While you're doing that, I'll heat up some Thai for you. You like Pad Thai?"

"Sure, Mom. That sounds great."

Bobby hurried from the room. For the first time since he had heard the news about his father, he felt like crying.

Almost.

Chapter Four

Bobby never ate the Thai food his mother had promised to heat up. After he had hung his suit, dress shirt, and tie in the guest room closet and placed his other clothes in dresser drawers, he lay down on the four-poster bed. He planned to rest for only a moment, but found himself blocking out thought by staring out the window at the lights coming on across the water.

The next thing he knew, he heard voices in the other room. He sat up and listened. The voice of his sister, high, bordering on squeaky, was going on...and on. Bobby smiled sadly. You may never be able to come home, or so the saying went, but certain things never changed. His sister's running mouth still seemed in good shape, even though Bobby couldn't quite discern the individual words she was saying. It sounded to him like a monologue.

Bobby got up, looked in the mirror, ran his fingers through his close-cropped auburn hair, smiled at himself (he couldn't help it—it was an old and true habit), and crossed the room to open the door. He debated for half a second about just hiding out in his bedroom for the rest of the night. "I have a headache!" he could say, but he knew his sister would only bang on his door until he came out.

When he wandered from the hallway into the living room, Bobby saw pretty much what he had imagined. He had a moment where he simply stood there, unnoticed, so he could observe his family dynamics in action.

His sister, Dawn, stood in the middle of the room, talking, her hands gesticulating, as his mother sat on the couch, eyes glazed and staring ahead, looking like the poster child for complete and utter exhaustion. Dawn's husband, Drew (yes, Dawn and Drew—they had three kids who were thankfully absent, named Davio, Drenda, and Dalton), occupied an overstuffed chair by the windows, his wing-tip-shoed feet up on the ottoman before him. From the tight mien of his mouth and the way he held his eyes open wide, Bobby could tell he was trying desperately to stay awake. Drew, who Bobby remembered as a hunk, had not aged well. The thick black hair Bobby recalled was all but gone, replaced by a buzzed cap of salt and pepper that did little to conceal that most of the hair atop his head was rapidly taking a powder. Bobby had once lusted for (secretly, of course) the man's beefy and muscular wrestler's build, which had now, predictably, gone to fat. An enormous belly tested the endurance of the buttons on his dress shirt. His tie was loosened, yet it did not seem to offer any relief to his florid complexion.

Dawn, however, had not gained an ounce. She remained the wiry bundle of hyperactive energy Bobby recalled. His sister was tall, only an inch or two shorter than Bobby's six feet, and her flame-red hair was a dye job, a way of telling the world her natural mouse brown was not to be tolerated. Dawn had been dyeing her hair since she was about fifteen, and if anything showed she was getting older, it was her hair. Stylishly cropped short, with bangs, it nevertheless showed the effects of the chemicals that kept it at its Lucille Ball best—dry and flyaway.

"So, after the funeral, I was thinking we should see if we could rent Ponti's for the reception. It's just down the road from here, so if anyone wanted to come by, it would be easy for them. And they have great food there! The fish is amazing. Isn't it, Drew?" She didn't wait for her husband to respond. "The lingcod I had last time was a revelation, I tell you. They probably have a room we can rent, and the views of the water there are so pretty, with the boats going by."

Bobby cleared his throat and stepped from the shadows of the hallway to let them all know he was there. "It's not a reception."

Dawn stopped and dropped her manicured hands to turn and stare, openmouthed, at her brother. She wore chinos and a button-down powder-blue blouse and low-heeled pumps. Bobby wondered if she even owned a pair of jeans.

A smile crept across her features, as painted on as the foundation, blush, mascara, and lip gloss. "Well, hello to you too, stranger." She crossed the room to kiss his cheek and give him a brief hug. Over her shoulder, Bobby saw Drew struggle to get up out of the chair. "What's not a reception?"

"What one has after a funeral. I don't think you'd call it a reception. Mom?"

"What?" Michelle inquired from the couch. It was obvious she had not heard a word his sister had said.

"Whatever," Dawn whispered, sounding vaguely Valley Girl.

"I was just saying that we should let Dawn handle the arrangements for the funeral. She has some wonderful ideas, and she's such a good planner." He eyed his sister, who was looking at him with undisguised disbelief. "I know everyone will have a good time, if she's in charge."

"A good time?" Michelle looked confused.

"Dawn here is the Martha Stewart of funerals and their, what do you call them, receptions?"

Dawn shook her head and went to stand near her husband.

Bobby cut across the room and extended his hand to Drew. "Hey, Drew. How goes it?"

"Same old, same old." Drew's grip was nearly bone-crushing, and Bobby did his best to break away as soon as possible.

For probably the first time in at least an hour, silence hung in the room like an extra presence. Bobby thought that entire books could be filled with what was not being said. The emotions he picked up on—discomfort, sadness, and anxiety, all mixed together in a roiling brew with a dash of buried rage thrown in—were familiar to him.

Maybe *this* is what home felt like!

His mother broke the spell. She stood and did what mothers tend to do the world over to try to bring families together—she suggested food. "Is anybody else hungry? I'm starving. Let me pull out some menus, and we can see what looks good to order in. How does everyone like that idea?"

"I think that's an amazing notion," Drew said, smiling, looking genuinely pleased. "I'm hungry."

Did he actually rub his belly? Bobby rolled his eyes.

His sister said, "I suppose I could manage something."

And Bobby looked at twiglike arms poking out of her three-quarter-length sleeves and wondered if she would later visit the bathroom to get rid of anything she had consumed.

Stop. This is your family. You love them. Right?

Bobby followed his mother out to the kitchen. "You still have the menu drawer, Mom?"

Michelle snorted. "I'd be lost without it."

And Bobby knew they would bond, as any good dysfunctional family would, not over grief at the loss of their patriarch, but over what it would be: Chinese, Thai, or pizza?

*

The Stallion was in a less-than-fashionable area of the Capitol Hill neighborhood, which could range from old-world elegance on Federal Ave. and the areas surrounding its lovely Volunteer Park, to hipster chic along Broadway with its cool cafés and gay bars. The decades-old bathhouse was tucked away on Summit in a couple of blocks that could only be described as trashy. Here, crumpled papers, crushed cans, tiny Baggies, and even used condoms littered the streets. The buildings were beat-up, run-down, and old, their edifices concealing whatever their drab brick exteriors and dirty windows hid.

It was only fitting that the Stallion, one of Seattle's oldest and filthiest (in every sense of the word) bathhouses was located here, where its patrons sneaked through its discreet, signless black door with eyes either lowered or with a quick glance around to ensure no one witnessed their entrance.

The Stallion was not a fancy bathhouse. It was a ratty, red-lit sex club with a couple of common areas, one set up with a sling and a St. Andrews cross, and the other a nearly empty room with a concrete floor that smart men made sure their bare feet never came into contact with. A couple of mattresses, vinyl-covered, lay on the same floor, and God only knew what kind of stories they would tell if they could talk or what kind of bacteria they harbored. Otherwise, the Stallion was simply a warren of tiny, cubicle-like rooms. Unlike more high-end sex clubs, the rooms in the Stallion contained only a single thin-sheeted twin bed, a horizontal mirror on the wall opposite, and a small particleboard cube that served as a nightstand. There were no TV monitors playing porn, no lockboxes, and certainly no complimentary packets of lube or condoms.

Bobby chose to come here for three reasons. One, because it was completely unlike his family's home. It was seedy and decadent, dirty—the exact opposite of the Widow Nelson's airy and luxurious condo in lower Queen Anne. And Bobby sorely needed dirty and decadent after an evening spent with his mom, sister, and brother-in-law, where the talk had skirted his father's recent passing almost desperately with endless talk of his sister's three children, what was happening at his mother's church (St. Mark's Episcopal on Capitol Hill), and how the Democratic Party in this country could do no right. Bobby craved the silence, the smell of bleach, the wary eyes of strangers sizing him up and imagining what they would do with him. He wanted dim lights and gritty floors, underscored by a cheesy techno music soundtrack with a heavy bass beat. He wanted to hear whispered exhortations, moans, and even yells coming from behind closed doors. He wanted the impropriety of passing a room full of men, caught in a tableau of wanting-to-be-watched sucking and fucking, with at least one of the men beckoning with a gaze or a hand for Bobby to join in.

The second reason Bobby chose to come to the Stallion after his sister and Drew had left and his mother had retired to her bathroom, where her plan was to soak in a hot bath and then, with any luck, go to sleep, was that he was jonesing for sex. Bobby seldom went more than a day without some form of carnal congress, and even though it had only been a couple of days since he had last been fucked, with the travel and the trauma, it seemed longer.

The third was that the Stallion, unlike the other bathhouses on the hill, had lifetime memberships. They even touted it on their website and the recorded message on their phone, both of which Bobby had checked before heading out. Even though his last visit had been a decade ago, he would not need to purchase a membership, only the key to a room and a towel.

There was also a fourth reason—barely acknowledged by Bobby as he locked his rental (twice with the remote, for good measure) and started the short, half-block walk toward the bathhouse—what he knew his new therapist Camille would label "avoidance." The fact barely peeked out of his subconscious, but Bobby couldn't quite deny that this trip was a way to avoid thinking about his father's death and what it meant to him.

So now, room key and ratty towel in his right hand, Bobby kept his mind blank, focused only on the prospect of sex as he made his way to room number thirty-seven, taking it slow since the light was dim and the rooms were set up like a maze. He knew he'd be the belle of the ball here, not because he was vain (although Bobby certainly possessed that quality in spades), but because the Stallion simply had a reputation for attracting older men, men with pot bellies, men with hair on their backs, and, unfortunately, meth heads with brown, rotting teeth and skeletal frames who came here because the sex was easy, there were plenty of others of their kind, and the drug was freely dealt here.

Bobby didn't know this last part from his own experience at the Stallion, because meth wasn't quite the rage it was now when he last visited, but bathhouses almost everywhere had become Tina central in the twenty-first century.

And Bobby had no intentions of partaking. His drug of choice was sex, and he wanted plenty of it. Orgasms equal oblivion.

Bobby hoped to find someone at least close to his physical equal here, some young Seattleite slumming, looking for rough trade or, like Bobby, to be the big, pretty fish in the little, scummy pond.

He pressed the key into the red-painted door to room thirty-seven, entered, and closed the door behind him. On his way to his room, he had passed a balding daddy who ignored him (imagine!) and a lanky dude with a ponytail, who eyed him appreciatively while working his dick beneath the towel he had wrapped around his waist.

Down, boy. Give me a chance to catch my breath, at least get my pants off.

In the room, Bobby adjusted the rheostat bright enough so he could see, but not bright enough to closely inspect the floor, walls, and sheet upon which he would be lying. *Some things are better left in the dark.*

He set the leather backpack he had brought with him down on the bed and opened it to set up its contents on the bedside table: a bottle of Eros lube, several foil-wrapped Magnum condoms (Bobby was an optimistic girl), a bottle of hand sanitizer, and several hand towels swiped from his bathroom at home. (Michelle would have been horrified.) He didn't remove the bottle of RID, with which Bobby routinely showered after a night like this, as a preventive measure, of course.

He removed the jeans and long-sleeved T-shirt he had worn, rolled them up, and tucked them into the backpack, then slid the backpack under the bed where no one could rifle through it without his notice. He left the black jockstrap he had worn under the clothes.

Finally, he turned the rheostat to lower the room's light to just a shade brighter than dim, opened his door wide, then lay on the bed, ass up. He knew the rounded globes of his ass cheeks were akin to an invitation, one he hoped would be accepted again and again—with gratitude.

It wasn't long before Bobby heard the quiet pad of bare feet on carpeting, stopping at his open door. He raised his head, peering through the gloom to see an older black man staring in at him. Unlike most of the other bathhouse patrons, this guy was not wearing a towel around his waist, but a pair of faded Levis that gripped his body in very flattering ways. Bobby could make out a sizable basket, the denim worn lighter just there, as if to emphasize the treasure it hid. That Bobby could make out the size and shape of the basket at this distance and in this lighting boded well for his future with this man, who was, Bobby conceded, his equal in the looks department. Bobby estimated the guy's age to be early forties. He radiated sensuality, with his shaved head, close-cropped gray goatee, and the smooth, hard, and defined muscles of his torso, his bulging pecs jutting out above his gut's six-pack like a shelf.

Bobby got himself up on one elbow and grinned at the man. "What's a nice guy like you doing in a place like this?"

The man laughed, taking a cautious step into the room, his chocolate-brown eyes meeting Bobby's, asking for permission to come in. Bobby liked his laugh—warm, deep, throaty. He motioned for the man to come farther into the little cubicle.

Bobby sat up as the man closed the door behind him.

His voice matched his bass laugh. "I could ask you the same question. All that's out there right now are tweakers and guys who mistook this place for belonging to senior citizens." He moved closer to Bobby, and Bobby had to wonder if his eyes were deceiving him, if his mind was conjuring up some wishful-thinking fantasy.

He had hoped to meet a handsome man, but he had definitely lowered his expectations when he had paid for his room and collected his towel from the front desk attendant. His hopes hadn't extended this far. This man was a dusky god.

Bobby fell to his knees to worship, sucking in his breath as the man slowly, provocatively, and teasingly unbuttoned his fly, pausing after each button. Finally, the caged beast was released, and Bobby couldn't suppress the grin that spread across his face. He imagined he must look like a kid who had just gotten the key to the candy store.

Before lowering his head to graze on the tumescent column of flesh, Bobby had to ask, so he would know for the mental records he kept of his conquests. He gripped it with one hand, tried to get his fingers to close around the thickness of it—and failed. "Not to be crass, but have you measured this thing?"

The man chuckled.

"I gotta know."

"Ten by six. Now suck it, boy."

And Bobby opened wide and took the dick into his throat, slowly, inch by inch, using his lips, tongue, and the muscles at the back of his throat to work it down to the root, squeezing and releasing. When he had it all inside, Bobby paused, breathing through his nose, willing away his gag reflex. The guy's pubes were coarse against Bobby's nose and smelled of sweat and a pleasing funk that Bobby could only describe as man smell.

Bobby worked his magic on the cock, and the man conspired with him, rhythmically thrusting his hips, pulling his big dick nearly all the way out then ramming it back in to tickle Bobby's tonsils. *Heaven.* When he tired of sucking, of swirling his tongue around the pole, he would grip the thing with one hand, working it up and down, slick with sweat, as he worked on the dude's swinging balls, taking them one by one into his mouth, gently sucking, savoring, and then making his way back to lick at the area behind them, to flirt with flicking his tongue between his lover's taut ass cheeks.

His new friend moaned, and it wasn't long before he hissed. "Man, you keep that up and you're gonna get a mouthful of come."

Bobby stared up at him, the dick looking even more enormous from his vantage point down on the gritty floor. "Okay with me."

"Not okay with me." He reached down to briefly finger Bobby's hole, stopping long enough to wet his finger with spit and insert it in past the knuckle. Bobby gasped, hungry suddenly for so much more. He fell to his hands and knees, ass in the air, and let the guy insert two, then three fingers.

Finally, the guy pulled him up, tugging beneath Bobby's armpits. "Come on," he whispered, "Let's get you up on the bed."

And Bobby offered no resistance. He stood, legs against the back of the thin mattress, and asked, breathlessly, "How do you want me?"

"On your back."

Bobby complied, raising his legs up in welcome. His latest relationship positioned himself on the bed, cock pressed against Bobby's cheeks, and threw Bobby's legs above his shoulders.

He leaned into him, reaching out with one hand to grab a condom and the lube, forcing Bobby to meet his gaze with the intensity of his stare. Softly, he said, "I'm gonna start out slow, but then it's gonna get rough. You think you can take it?"

"Try me."

And he did. And could.

Later, Bobby walked stiffly back to his car as tendrils of dawn lit the sky with shades of orange, pink, and violet. The streets were deserted, quiet, only marred occasionally by the whoosh of a passing car. Bobby looked over to see the Space Needle, standing sentinel over the quiet city.

Bobby was sore. In his night at the Stallion, he had never found an equal to his ebony god, whose name he later learned was TJ. TJ worked as a law clerk downtown.

Bobby could not be faulted for not trying to find an equal to TJ. There was the beefy redhead, who fucked him in a bathroom stall and came within a minute. There was the couple, number one tall and blond, overeager, and number two, his partner, a cute boy/man with an overbite and a downward curving cock, who took turns with him for more than an hour, ensuring that both of Bobby's holes were filled at all times. There was the young boy, who barely looked the minimum age for entry (twenty-one), all lean muscle, shaved head, and nervously darting blue eyes, who couldn't handle more than receiving a hand job.

And, finally, there was a quick blowjob in the darkness of the big room, with someone Bobby had seen only in shadow. He delivered a huge load to the back of Bobby's throat, and it tasted odd, almost chemical, and Bobby nearly gagged at the horror of it. As the guy beat a hasty retreat without a word, Bobby spit his jizz on the floor, hoping he hadn't held it inside of himself for long enough to cause any damage that might rear its ugly head later.

Now clean, showered, and smelling of RID and cheap body wash, Bobby took a small measure of pride in knowing that, at least until the last guy, he and latex had remained on good terms and he had played relatively safe.

He got in the car, started it up, and pulled out onto Summit.

Heading home.

But where was home? What was home?

*

Using the keys Michelle had given him, Bobby attempted to slip into the condo cat-burglar style, quiet, so he wouldn't wake her.

But Michelle was already awake, sitting up on the couch in her nightgown, a quilted lavender affair, staring out the windows as the sun backlit the deep purple silhouettes of the Cascades across the water.

"Robert? Is that you?"

For one moment, Bobby froze, wondering if his mother, in these wee, small hours of the morning, had mistaken his arrival for that of his father. But Michelle called him by his Christian name more often than Bobby, so more likely she knew he had caused the creak in the front door as it opened.

"Yeah, Mom. It's me." Bobby dropped his keys on the secretary desk by the front door and came into the living room.

Michelle looked up at him with red-rimmed, tired eyes. She looked every bit her age. There was something deflated and defeated about her. Bobby sat on the couch next to her and gathered her up in his arms for a brief hug. He rubbed her shoulders, squeezing and stroking. She laid her head in the crook between his neck and shoulder and sighed.

"You smell good."

Bobby wanted to laugh. *So Mom is a connoisseur of the marriage of RID and bathhouse shower gel. God bless her.*

"Should I ask where you've been?"

"No, Mom, you shouldn't, but everything is okay."

"Good." Michelle sat back, moving away from her son but letting her head rest on his arm, which he had stretched out over the couch's back.

Michelle said nothing for a long while, and she and Bobby simply sat together in the early silence, watching as the morning light filtered into the room. The day grew cloudy, and soon, dark gray clouds hung over the water, which mirrored their pewter color.

"I couldn't sleep. I was just sitting here, thinking about your father."

Bobby stiffened, wondering if his mother could have come up with any good memories of the man. At the moment, he was certainly not able to.

"Did I ever tell you about the first time I met your father?"

Bobby shook his head, then whispered, "No," because his mother was staring straight ahead. He didn't really know if he wanted to hear this. He also found it peculiar that here he was, age forty, and he didn't know this piece of his family history.

"He had been in one of my classes at the University of Washington. It was one of those big survey classes—zoology, maybe. You know, where you sit in an auditorium with hundreds of other kids?"

"Yeah." Bobby expected to hear how his father made some grand play for his mother, bringing flowers to the class, writing her name on the chalkboard with a heart around it, something that would draw attention to him as much as it would to her.

But that was not the story. "Your father, believe it or not, was very shy. Painfully so." Michelle laughed, and Bobby could hear in her chuckle the warmth of memory, nostalgia. It was hard for him to imagine his demanding, often loud, often extroverted father as a shy boy.

"I found out later he had caught sight of me the very first day of class, and he would wait until I came in, hiding in a corner, so he could see where I sat. That way, he could pick a seat where he could observe me." Michelle giggled, and Bobby heard the girl who still lived inside his mother. It touched his heart.

"He did that all through the whole term. He told me he dreamed about me, fantasized about me, but could never get up the nerve to come over and introduce himself. He said he would plan on it, every day, but he just couldn't." Bobby's mother glanced over at him. "I was quite the sweet young thing, you see. He was intimidated by my beauty." She laughed, but Michelle was as vain as Bobby, and he didn't believe her self-deprecating laugh for a minute. Plus, he had seen the photos of his mother from that time, and she really was stunning. She had a sweet, kind of Reese Witherspoon thing going on. How she had ended up with a hard-ass like his dad had always been beyond Bobby.

Until now?

"Finally, end of term arrived and finals loomed. I was gathering up my notes and my books when this boy came up to me, gaze cast to the floor, just a whisper of a smile on his face, and threw a folded-up piece of notebook paper down on my textbook. Before I could even speak, he had hurried away. I watched him go, wishing he had stayed because, damn, he was cute. That whiskey-colored hair, a good build, a face to swoon over. A dreamboat." She took Bobby's chin in her hand to turn his face toward hers. "He looked just like you."

Bobby had seen the photos, and countless times he had been told he was the spitting image of his father, but he had always resisted the comparison, thinking that was simply what people said to sons.

Bobby had nothing in common with the man who had fathered him. Did he?

"Anyway, I opened the note, and I still remember pretty much what it said. He told me he had been watching me all term and that I was so beautiful that he just didn't have the nerve or the guts to approach me because he was so sure I was out of his league. But, he said, if he didn't at least let me know that my beauty had left him speechless, had brightened a miserable term at school, he would not only be doing a disservice to me, but to himself as well. He asked me if I would meet him the next afternoon in front of his dorm—he would take me to lunch. He said he'd be waiting outside and that he didn't really expect me to show up, but if I did, even if it never went any further than lunch, I would make him the happiest man on campus." His mother halted the memory abruptly then, and Bobby looked over to see the tears standing still and glistening in her eyes. One shot down her cheek. She wiped it away and continued in a barely audible voice, "No, make that the happiest man in the world."

She looked over at Bobby, and he let her have this quiet moment, this memory, which he could see burning brightly behind her tired eyes—the youth, young love, first love—of course his parents had had it.

Michelle took a deep breath and blew it out, quivering.

"So, did you meet him?"

The question, dumb as it was, made his mother laugh. "Well, of course I did. You're here, aren't you?"

"So what happened?"

"I walked over to his dorm. I was so excited. I don't mean to sound conceited, but back then, people did find me attractive. Maybe too much. I never got asked out! Maybe I did intimidate the boys...but I was just a shy girl who wanted to find her prince.

"So I walked over to the dorm, everything inside and out just shaking with nerves, and I saw him."

Michelle took a moment to stare at her son, drinking him in, and Bobby realized—all at once—that she was not seeing him, but the image of his father in his face. Tears stood poised to drop in her eyes, but there was a huge smile on her face.

"Oh, I will never forget that moment! He didn't see me at first, but he was just sitting there on the concrete steps of his dorm, his head down, reading. The book was Walt Whitman's *Leaves of Grass*. I remember it like it was yesterday."

Bobby was dumbfounded. His father? Reading poetry? What alternate universe had he just stepped into? "Dad read poetry? Come on!"

"No, no, it's true. And you're ruining the moment." Michelle went on. "His head was bent over the book, and the sun shone down on him, making that auburn hair almost red. He had on a plaid shirt and pair of chinos—I knew he had dressed for me. He looked so innocent, so fresh scrubbed, so boy into man, if you know what I mean, that I..." His mother's voice trailed off as she struggled to rein in her emotions, to get ahold of herself. When she could speak again, just barely, she said in a whisper, "That I just fell in love with him. Right then, staring at him. That image of him sitting there in the sunlight, reading, is like a snapshot burned into my brain. I will never forget it." She smiled at her son. "That very moment was when my fate was sealed and my heart was forever ruined for anyone else."

They were quiet for a while. Bobby asked, "What happened next?"

"We went to lunch. We courted. He wooed me. We had sex, lots of sex." His mother giggled.

"TMI, Mom, TMI."

"What's your favorite memory of your father?"

The question caught Bobby off guard. Favorite memory? He couldn't think of one. His father was a perfectionist, a self-centered man whose bookish, quiet, and delicate little boy could never measure up, no matter how hard he tried. Bobby had gone out for football, run the mile relay on the track team, things he thought would impress his sports-obsessed father, show him that Bobby, too, could be a manly boy like his father's friends' sons.

But his father never came to a game or a meet. He was always too busy. Bobby had gotten straight As. He even took the most beautiful girl in his class to the prom senior year. He remembered his mother calling his father down at one of his favorite watering holes, pleading with him to come home and see how gorgeous the couple looked in their gown and tux. His father had told her to take a picture.

Plenty of bad memories emerged. But good ones?

Bobby simply started talking. He didn't know where it would go or what he would say exactly, but he simply did not have the heart to break the spell his mother had woven. To tell her anything bad about his father at this moment would have been an act of cruelty.

"I remember Dad and I were driving, and he had the radio on. We heard this commercial for kayaking trips"—he looked at the window, at the view of the water—"on Lake Union. And Dad said, 'That would be fun for us, don't you think? We haven't had any quality father and son time in a long while. You want to take one of those kayaking trips, son?'"

Bobby felt as though he was sticking his neck out here. The words did not even sound like his father's. But Michelle never called him on it. She listened, head cocked, a small smile on her lips.

"So of course I said yes. Dad got it all set up, and I remember getting up that morning. He had come into my room, telling me to rise and shine. Well, I looked out the window and knew I'd be about the only thing rising and shining in Seattle that day. The sky was heavy with dark clouds.

"But we went anyway. And it started to rain once we were out on the lake. But we just laughed and kept paddling. We went all the way from the dock off of Westlake toward downtown, back across the lake to the Fremont cut. I was freezing, wet, and happy.

"We never spent much time together alone, and I remember how special I felt that day—having my dad all to myself. We cursed the rain. We laughed about it." Bobby could see it all in his mind's eye, and his real eyes—the ones on his face—pricked with tears. It was as though this had all really happened.

If only, if only…

"After we did the whole lake, hours kayaking and my arms felt like they were about to fall off, Dad took me to Ray's boathouse for lunch." Bobby paused, as though he was remembering. "That was the first time I had oysters on the half shell. I didn't want to eat them, thought they'd be gross, but Dad told me I didn't know what I was missing. And he was right. Those damn oysters were about the best thing I'd ever tasted.

"When we got home, he marched me into the shower, and when I came out, he actually tucked me into bed."

"Your father?" It was Michelle's turn to be surprised.

"Yes! Can you believe it?" Bobby then finished watching the little movie in his mind. "He paused at the door to turn off the overhead light." Bobby's voice choked on what he said next. "In the dark, he said—" Bobby needed to wait a moment, to allow himself to speak. "He said, 'I love you, son.'"

Bobby began to sob. He didn't know if it was because his father had never actually said these words to him or because he missed the man, even if he was a bastard.

He was still his father.

He couldn't stop crying. His mother pulled him close, wrapping her arms around him.

She whispered in his ear. "Thank you, son. Thank you for that."

Bobby didn't know if his mother was admitting she knew the story he had just told was all a lie or if she was just grateful for his sharing a memory that cast his father in a favorable light.

But it didn't really matter. He knew he had made his mother happy...and that was the whole point.

They sat together for a while, just quiet, as the room filled with dull light. Finally Bobby stood. "I should get some sleep. Viewing hours are tonight."

"Go on. I put flannel sheets on the bed."

"Thanks, Mom."

As he was heading to his room, Bobby pulled his phone out of his pocket and glanced down at the screen. It told him he had a missed call.

He checked the recent call screen, and what he saw made his heart still for a second.

The call was from his best friend, Caden. The one whom he had betrayed. The one who, at one point, said he never wanted to see or hear from Bobby again.

Caden had called him.

Bobby looked at the time and estimated it had come at about the time he was taking a large black dick up his ass.

He went into his room, sat on the bed, and stared at the screen.

Chapter Five

Caden had left no message. Bobby sat on his bed, the blinds drawn, staring at the screen of his iPhone, wondering if he should call him back. *He didn't leave a voice mail. If he'd wanted you to call him back, he would have said so.* Bobby shook his head. Bobby had felt the strain of not having Caden in his life, since Caden had been his only true friend. He missed him like he would miss a limb. His longing for his friend was more intense than any sexual desire he'd ever had. Once again, he cursed himself for being so stupid.

He couldn't blame Caden for deserting him. Bobby had, after all, tried to steal his boyfriend. The one Caden now lived with, in loving bliss.

But all Bobby had wanted was the same for himself. He just didn't know how to go about it.

But he had called. Finally, after months of silence, *he had called.* It was something Bobby never allowed himself to dream would happen.

Bobby glanced over at the clock. It was now after seven, so that would mean it was after nine in Chicago. *Don't do it. Let Caden come to you.*

Bobby couldn't help himself. He had always had poor impulse control. *Ha! As if that was news!* He smiled, but there was only bitterness in it. That impulse control was what made him the world-class tramp he was today.

He pressed Caden's name on his recent calls screen. Bobby rationalized calling him by the thought that if Caden really didn't want to talk to him, he would see Bobby's name on the caller ID and he could simply let it go to voice mail.

That's what he told himself as he listened to the phone ring, halfway across the country, in the city of big shoulders.

"Hey."

Bobby closed his eyes, and his lips lifted almost unconsciously into a smile. It had been so long since he had heard Caden's voice that the simple one word utterance lifted his spirits, was like a balm on his tortured and traumatized psyche.

"It's me," Bobby said.

"I know."

"You called?"

"Yeah." Caden blew out a breath. "I didn't leave a message because I wanted to talk to you personally, so I just thought I'd ring you back later. But here you are."

"Here I am." Was this it? The beginning of their reconciliation? Hope rose in Bobby's soul like a bird taking flight.

"Listen, Bobby, I called because I heard about your father."

"Yeah. He passed away. Heart attack."

"And I just wanted to say how sorry I was to hear that. I know you and he weren't close and that you had issues with him, but in the end, he was your dad, and I wanted to tell you that I know that must be rough. Kevin and me both send our condolences."

Bobby wanted to weep. "That's so nice of you. Thanks."

"That's all. I just wanted you to know you're in my thoughts."

Bobby clutched at a straw. "Maybe we can all get together when I get back to town? We have so much to talk about."

There was a long silence on the other end, and Bobby's spirits, soaring for a moment, crashed.

Caden finally broke the quiet with "We'll see."

"Just to talk. We need to clear the air."

More silence, and at last Caden said, "Listen, I gotta run. I'm at work."

"Thanks again for calling, Caden. It means a lot to me."

"Sure. 'Bye."

Bobby wanted to say 'bye too—and tell Caden to give his boyfriend, Kevin, his best—but Caden had already hung up.

Bobby slumped back on the bed, feeling like a starving man who had been given not a meal, but a crumb. The ache in his heart had only intensified with hearing his old best friend's voice on the phone.

Would Caden ever be able to forgive him for what he'd done?

*

It seemed like only minutes had passed when Bobby awakened to the soft knock on his door.

"Sweetheart?" his mother called. "You better be getting up. We're going to leave for the funeral home in about an hour to check everything out. Your sister and the kids are here." She tapped again. "Bobby? You hear me?"

Bobby sat up and rubbed his eyes, feeling disoriented. The room was dark. "Yeah, Mom. I'll grab a shower and dress and be out in a few."

"You want me to fix you something to eat?"

"Don't worry about it. I'm not hungry."

"But you have to eat."

Once a mom, always a mom... "Sure, anything will be fine. Maybe some scrambled eggs?"

He listened as his mother padded away.

Later that morning, he would see his father again. It had been ten years. Bobby forced himself to get out of bed, muscles aching from having had his legs in the air for extended periods, and ambled to the en suite bathroom for the shower he hoped would loosen up those same muscles. He felt like an old man.

And what would he feel when he saw *his* old man again?

*

Michelle urged him on. "Go on, take a look at your dad. Pay your respects."

The casket stood in the middle of the main viewing room of the Swain Brothers Funeral Home in the Green Lake neighborhood. The room was overly appointed, with heavy damask draperies and sheers at the windows, plush beige carpeting, and muted walls of cream, along which had been arranged pewter sconces with frosted glass shades. The place looked like some grandma's idea of wealth.

His father's casket was no less ostentatious. Crafted from sleek cherry wood with brass handles, it gleamed, mirrorlike, under the parlor's tasteful recessed lighting. He could see a bit of his father's head from where he stood, but little else.

"You need to go say goodbye." Michelle laid a hand on his arm. It was just him, his mother, and his sister, Dawn, and her family there right now. The other visitors weren't due to show up for another hour, when official viewing hours began.

Viewing. It sounded so tasteless. So macabre. Why did anyone need to "view" a dead body?

Maybe, as his mother had just told him, to say goodbye.

Bobby could see no way he would get out of looking down at his dad, maybe even, God forbid, touching him one final time. So, even though every impulse was urging him to flee, to simply turn tail and run from the funeral home, get in his rental and head right back to Capitol Hill, where he could drown his sorrows and fears in alcohol and a stranger's passionate embrace, he moved cautiously forward.

There he was. The man who had fathered him. Bobby stared down at an almost serene face, a face that wore a bit of blush and some foundation. Bobby let out a snort of laughter, bordering on hysteria, when he thought that his father would have never been caught dead in makeup. He glanced nervously behind him and saw his mother standing there, watching him. He hoped she interpreted his laughter as a sob, as grief.

He returned his gaze to his dad in repose.

It was strange, and now Bobby did want to cry, because if he felt anything at all, it was relief. The man was gone. No longer would he be able to cause Bobby's face to redden at the dinner table as he once had when a little Bobby asked him to please pass the salad. His father had smiled, holding the teak salad bowl aloft, and Bobby had smiled back. Then his father had said, "I don't know what it is, but something about you reminds me of a girl."

Bobby could still feel the sudden rush of shame and how he had wanted to push back his chair and run from the kitchen.

No longer would his father be able to laugh off Bobby's starring role as Tony in his high school's production of *West Side Story* and refuse to be in the audience because, as he had put it, "Musical theater is for fairies. You a fairy, son?" He had pretended to be kidding, but they both knew he wasn't. In spite of this, Bobby still caught himself hopefully parting the curtains before they opened, then dejectedly scanning the audience each night of the performance for his father's face.

No longer would they have strained holiday conversations.

No longer would he treat his mother like a servant.

No longer would he live to find fault, to ridicule, to ensure that nothing, nothing Bobby did would ever be good enough for his standards.

Bobby bent over the man and planted a kiss on his cold cheek. He whispered, "You can't hurt me anymore."

He turned and walked back to his mother and sister. Michelle grabbed his arm. "See? Didn't that make you feel better? To say goodbye and tell him just how much you loved him?"

"Sure it did, Mom." He glanced over at Dawn, who was also smiling at him as if he had just accomplished some great feat, which, he supposed, he had. Bobby lied to them both. "Doesn't he look great? Just like he's sleeping."

And he drew his mother and then his sister, into a hug.

But he didn't cry.

*

Later, there was a lunch at Ray's Boathouse in Ballard. The windows of the restaurant looked out on Puget Sound, which today was a churning mass of gray and silver, as if the restless waters were reaching up to touch the dark, low-hanging clouds. Drizzle pelted the windows of the restaurant, blurring the seascape outside.

Bobby stood near one of those windows, a vodka and cranberry (his third) in hand, simply watching the restless ebb and flow of the water. A lot of people had showed up at the funeral home, and then here, to pay their respects to his dear departed daddy. Many more than Bobby would have thought.

Behind him, the chattering of the wake guests sounded like a party in full swing. There was a lot of laughter, clinking glasses, animated talk. Bobby had expected something more, well, funereal.

As he stared outside, setting himself apart from the guests, he remembered the church service and all the kind words the priest had said, painting a picture of a man who was a stranger to Bobby. The priest had praised Bobby's father's generosity, his kindness, his good works, his devotion to Christ and most of all, to his family.

Bobby couldn't help but wonder if the priest had gotten his funerals mixed up and was talking about another man.

As he was pondering this, seated next to his sniffling mother, his stone-faced sister, her bored-looking husband, and their restless children, something odd happened, something unexpected, something that took Bobby totally by surprise.

He bowed his head and began to weep. He didn't shed a couple of tears, which until the moment the crying jag had begun would have been the most he would have expected from himself, but launched from silence to sobbing just like that. His shoulders heaved, his nose ran, the tears flowed freely. He could barely breathe.

His mother patted his shoulder comfortingly, her own tears ramping up to join his. He could barely get himself under control, and he wondered why. He had, more than once, wished his father dead, thought how much better his and his family's life would be without the self-centered, perfectionist bastard around.

What did Bobby have to cry about?

And then it hit him: he wasn't crying for what was, but for what might have been. For the promise that was never realized, for a connection that would never be made, no matter how hungrily Bobby longed for it.

Now, the possibility of the love of the one man that the little boy in Bobby thought could redeem him was removed, snatched from the realm of possibility forever.

He had covered his face with his hand and cried until his mother had nudged him, urging him to get up. The pallbearers were carrying the casket, now closed, out of the church.

"Stand up. Pull yourself together, honey," Michelle had whispered. "Your father's passing."

Now, Bobby shook his head, took another sip of his cocktail, and emptied the glass. He sucked an ice cube into his mouth, then felt its cold burn as it slid down his throat.

He was startled by a voice close behind him. "Beautiful view, isn't it? I think I like it better like this, all dark and stormy, than sunshine and blue skies. More dramatic."

Bobby turned. Standing behind him was a very handsome man, whom he estimated to be about his own age. He was taller than Bobby, with raven-black hair and eyes so dark it was impossible to distinguish pupil from iris. The dark hair was brushed back away from his face, and when he smiled, he revealed perfect white teeth. There was a sharp cleft in his chin that Bobby had a very irrational and very wrong urge to explore with his tongue. Bobby couldn't help himself as he looked the guy up and down, admiring the way his trim form filled out what looked like a very expensive charcoal-gray suit.

There was something familiar about the man, and the wheels in Bobby's mind began to turn, trying to recall where he had seen him before.

Wherever it was, Bobby couldn't help but be enchanted by the guy, who was simply stunning to look at. Inappropriate as it was, Bobby found it hard to tear his eyes away.

Bobby smiled. "I like it too. The grays, the waves... You can almost hear the rush of the wind outside, the patter of the rain on the ground."

"You're a poet."

"Who, me?" Bobby laughed. "Just a marketing manager. Nothing poetic about that."

"Well, that's some very poetic imagery."

Bobby cast his gaze downward, feeling somehow embarrassed by the man's words. *Poetry was the province of "fairies." Isn't that what Dad would have said?*

"You don't remember me, do you?"

For a split second, Bobby wondered if he could fake it. But he was simply too exhausted by the events of the day and the emotional toll they had taken to even try. He shook his head. "I'm sorry, I don't. Remind me?"

"Wade." The man smiled and locked eyes with Bobby, causing him, for just a second, to forget everyone else in the room. "Wade Carlisle. We went to high school together."

Bobby drew a blank. Once he had graduated from Cascade High School, he had never looked back. There were no class reunions for him. He thought such gatherings were the province of the desperate, of those whose glory days were far in the past.

Wade? Bobby rifled through mental images of linoleum-tiled corridors lined with lockers, of classrooms with combination seats and desks, of a shiny, waxed gymnasium floor, of a red-velvet-curtained auditorium, and he came up with nothing. Bobby couldn't understand. Surely he would remember a hottie like this, who would have stood out from the crowd, who would have certainly caught Bobby's eye and perhaps taken part in the secret masturbatory fantasies he indulged in late at night in his boyhood bedroom. But no memory registered.

Bobby shook his head. "I'm sorry, Wade. I don't remember."

Wade didn't look disappointed. He laughed. "You probably don't remember me because I looked quite different back in the day. Had a little more meat on my bones. Well, a lot more meat. Wade Carlisle? Fatty Fatty Two-by-Four?"

And it clicked. Bobby swallowed hard. And he remembered Wade, although it was hard to believe this drop-dead-gorgeous morsel of masculinity standing before him was he. Wade had been the fattest kid in his class, the very big butt of a million jokes, the kid who sat alone at lunch, looking out at everyone else with dark, brooding eyes.

Bobby had never been one to tease him. Not because he was so kind back then, but because the fat kid simply didn't register on his radar. He vaguely remembered sitting next to him in an American literature class, and then it came back to him—his clearest memory of Wade.

"You read that poem in class once? Everyone was floored."

Wade smiled. "You remember that?"

Bobby nodded. He did. There was such passion in the fat boy's voice as he read; it had touched Bobby's heart. He couldn't recall what the poem was, but remembered the effect it had on him. "Sure I do." Bobby cocked his head. "Something about being an outsider?"

Wade moved closer, and Bobby picked up on a citrus scent mixed with a little musk that went straight to his groin.

Wade said, "That poem is one of my favorites. So simple, but it says so much. It spoke to me then, and it still does, even though I've changed on the outside."

"What was it?"

"Emily Dickinson. 'I'm Nobody.' Wanna hear it?" He grinned and glanced behind him in an attempt, Bobby assumed, to make sure no one was looking. Wade began to recite the poem.

I'm nobody! Who are you?
Are you nobody, too?
Then there's a pair of us—don't tell!
They'd banish us, you know.
How dreary to be somebody!
How public, like a frog
To tell your name the livelong day
To an admiring bog!

Bobby said, "That's awesome that you remember it after all this time."

"Some things stick with you."

Bobby remembered the day in class clearly now. Their assignment had been to read aloud a poem that had meant something to them. It had been an autumn day, and their classroom windows revealed leaves in fiery shades of orange, red, and yellow. A few people had snickered as Wade stood to read from their Survey of American Literature textbook, his hand trembling, his voice barely above a whisper.

By the time he had finished, though, no one was snickering. He sat back down to silence, and a full minute passed before their teacher had called on someone else.

"It must have taken a lot of courage to stand up and read that."

Wade shrugged. "I had nothing to lose. When you're the least popular, most teased kid in class, where's the risk in identifying yourself with a poem called 'I'm Nobody'? The worst that could happen was that they would laugh at me."

"But we didn't."

"No. And that's why I'll always remember that day."

Bobby looked around him, at the assembled throng of people here to pay their respects to his father, and was struck again by how much this felt like a party. Perhaps they were just as happy as he that the guy was gone. He turned back to Wade. "So how did you do it?"

"What?"

"This." Bobby gestured at Wade's broad-shouldered, flat-stomached frame with his hands.

"When my doctor wanted to put me on high blood pressure medicine and told me I was heading rapidly down the road toward diabetes—and this was at the ripe old age of twenty-two—I knew I had to do something. I tried a bunch of fad diets and just yo-yoed, you know? Lose a few, gain a lot more back. Then I just said 'Fuck it' and decided to change my life—for good. It wasn't easy at first, but I thought I'd see if I could just stick to eating whole foods, nothing processed, nothing out of a box or a can or frozen. Man, it costs a lot more to eat like that! But I did it. I ate a lot, honestly, but kept to fresh fruits and vegetables, lean meats, nuts, beans and learned how to use lots of spices and onions and garlic. For a while I missed the chips and doughnuts, but after a while, they just seemed gross to me. Now, I can't imagine eating that shit.

"And I began to work out—weights and bicycling—every day. I've since added kayaking and power walking to my repertoire, and what was once hard is now a pleasure. I get antsy if I can't do something physical."

I'd like to do something physical with you. Bobby immediately banished the thought from his mind, shaming himself with the reminder he was at his father's funeral. *Can't you get your mind off sex even for an occasion like this? What are you, some kind of man whore who can't control himself?*

Bobby decided not to answer those questions. Instead, he smiled at Wade. "Well, you look amazing. I have to be honest, I would have never recognized you."

"Thanks." Wade laughed. "Not to sound vain or anything, but I was always fat. I didn't know that an okay-looking guy was hiding inside, not until I lost all the weight. It was a bonus."

"Okay-looking? Jesus, guy, you're way beyond okay. You're fuckin' hot." And immediately Bobby could feel a scorching surge of heat rise to his face, knowing that crimson was spreading up from his collar to envelop him. He was so used to being around gay men that he didn't stop to think the man standing before him could be straight. The odds were for it! He tried to backpedal. "I mean, you're a good-looking man, very handsome."

Wade grinned at him, a playful light dancing in his chocolate eyes. "You seem embarrassed." He scratched the back of his neck. "This should be the part where I embarrass you even more by pulling out my phone and showing you a picture of my gorgeous redhead wife and our two tots, smiling on the front lawn of our Bellevue McMansion."

"I'm sorry, man. I'm gay. No problems with it. Well, maybe a few, but..." Bobby's voice trailed off, and he looked everywhere but at Wade. Finally, he forced himself to look back. "I need to remind myself that we homos are in the minority. I do find you attractive, but I also know most straight guys don't want to hear that from another dude."

Wade winked at him. "Who said I was straight?"

"You're gay?"

Wade chuckled. "As a goose. As a handbasket adorned with ribbons and bows. As the love child of Rip Taylor and Liberace. My blood is rainbow-colored. My middle initial is a Lambda. I eat quiche. And yes, Bobby, I suck dick." He said the last three words in a whisper.

Bobby leaned his head in toward Wade's, and they had a private moment, laughing together.

When they pulled away, Bobby realized his mother was staring at him from across the room. He knew she wanted him by her side, and as much as he didn't like to end this conversation, he realized his mother needed him more. She had surprised him with the depth of feelings she had for his father, feelings he just had assumed didn't exist.

"I need to get back to my mom. She's sending me eye signals that she wants me by her."

"I understand."

"I just wondered, though, what brought you here? I mean, you and I weren't really close." Bobby was flustered and felt like sticking his foot in his mouth again. "I didn't mean that the way it sounded. I'm really grateful you came."

"It's okay. I understand. I just saw the obituary in the paper and remembered you—remembered you fondly—from high school, and I don't have classes today, so I thought I could come by and pay my respects. I was at the funeral, but I don't think you saw me."

No. And if I had, I would have certainly remembered.

Wade went on. "When I laid eyes on you at the funeral, I wanted a chance to talk to you, so I followed the crowd out here. I hope that's okay."

"It's better than okay. I'm really glad you decided to make the effort. I wasn't expecting to meet a hot guy at my dad's funeral."

Wade, for just a moment, looked uncomfortable, making Bobby wish he'd learn to keep his mouth shut, or at least slow down and consider what was coming out of it.

"You were one of the nice ones," Wade said. "You never teased me or bullied me. You could have. You were one of the popular guys."

"I was?" And then Bobby mentally kicked himself once more. Of course he was, and false modesty wasn't becoming. He knew that. It just seemed, though, he had been so closeted when he was in high school, so fearful that someone would discover his deep, dark secret that he spent all of his time trying to be some faux ladies' man—and the girls did love it. But the real Bobby, the one he faced alone in his bedroom mirror, recognized the truth and realized everyone would hate him if they knew what he was.

Especially his dad.

So he wore a mask through those years and had a vague, almost subconscious realization during all that time that, although many people seemed to like him, no one really did. Not *him*. They liked an image he projected, not the real Bobby. The real person, he hid from and hoped and prayed no one else would ever spy what lurked beneath his "popular" exterior.

God, that was a long time ago.

"You should probably go see your mom." Wade reached into his jacket pocket and pulled out his wallet, from which he extracted a business card. He held it out to Bobby. "I don't know how long you're here for, but if you have time for coffee, I'd love to talk some more."

Bobby glanced down at the card and saw that Wade was an assistant professor of English at Olympic Community College. He looked back up at Wade.

"Still lovin' the poetry." Wade winked. "I overheard you were in Chicago now but hope you'll have a chance to call before you go back. My cell is on my card. I'm easy like that with my students."

"Oh, I'll call." Bobby reached out and clutched Wade's hand, squeezing it in a gesture that could not quite be described as a handshake, but more like a small caress.

Their gazes met and locked. The connection was finally broken by his sister, Dawn, who came up to him and hissed in his ear, "Mom really needs you."

Reluctantly, Bobby walked away from Wade, casting regretful looks back at him. Wade smiled and turned toward the windows once more, where outside the wind continued to toss the waves and force the clouds quickly across the sky.

*

Bobby waited until the day before he was scheduled to go back home to Chicago to call Wade. He didn't want to wait that long or cut it that close, but family obligations, which included comforting a mother who seemed to believe that her life had died along with her husband, superseded Bobby's desire to get to know this unexpected blast from the past.

As he listened to the ringing, he prayed Wade would be available. It would be good to have a break from mourning, to talk to someone who wasn't so intimately connected to his family. If he was horrible for thinking that way, so be it.

No one answered the phone for four rings, and Bobby had just begun to think he had blown it and would probably never see Wade again when he picked up.

"Wade Carlisle."

"Thank God I didn't miss you," Bobby gushed. "I'm leaving tomorrow, and I was really hoping we could get together for coffee, a drink, or even dinner before I have to head out."

"Who is this?"

Bobby wanted to do the classic smack to the forehead. "I'm sorry. Let me start over. This is Bobby Nelson. How are you?"

Wade chuckled. "Actually, my powers of deduction are so great that I *did* know who was calling. I just wanted to give you shit."

"Well, thank you for that." Bobby paced the guest room, looking out at the Eastlake neighborhood across Lake Union and how the houseboats, regular boats, and buildings and trees rising up the bluff from the water reminded him of an Alaskan fishing village. "Anyway, as I was trying to say before I made an ass of myself, I was wondering if you'd have some time to get together today or this evening. I enjoyed talking with you at Ray's and was hoping we could connect again before I go home."

"Actually, my evening is wide open. Would your family mind if I stole you away for dinner? We could meet on the Hill at the Honey Hole."

Bobby rolled his eyes. "Seriously? The Honey Hole?"

Wade laughed. "I know. I know. Not exactly the most appealing moniker for a couple of homos, but the sandwiches are the best, and the place has a laid-back, kinda funky vibe that I like. We can talk."

"Okay, then. It's a date. Should I just meet you there?"

"Hey, no worries. I can pick you up."

"Okay; thanks." Bobby gave Wade his mom's address. "See you at what? Seven?"

"It's a plan."

*

They ended up not staying at the Honey Hole after they had their sandwiches and beer. The place was jam-packed with students, some of whom knew Wade. Things were just a bit too noisy and not private enough for them to actually talk.

So the pair of them ended up back in Wade's car—the Seattle staple, a Subaru—taking it up to the neighborhood's Volunteer Park. They parked on a drive that ran in front of the Asian Art Museum. Opposite the museum, the iconic Space Needle rose up, almost glowing, in the distance.

The park was quiet this midweek night in March, and Bobby ended up talking to Wade for almost two hours. He shared how dissatisfied he had been with his father growing up, how he longed for a more meaningful connection with the man.

"Sometimes," Bobby said, "I wonder if that's what made me gay."

"What?" Wade asked, a disbelieving tone in his voice.

"You know, missing out on the love of my dad. Maybe it made me want to go seeking it elsewhere. Maybe all my promiscuity is rooted in that affection denied."

Wade shook his head, and his dark eyes met Bobby's across the car's seat. "Bobby, I don't think it works like that. I mean, maybe some 1960's therapist might think that way, but we live in the age of Lady Gaga."

"Huh?"

Wade grinned. "Baby, you were born this way. I think it's pretty true."

Bobby stared out at the night. If all his fucking and sucking couldn't be tied to the affection he was starving for from his dad, what could all the endless hookups be tied to? Was he just naturally a libertine, a bottomless bottom who could never be completely filled? It was easier to think there was some rationale behind his promiscuity so he could understand himself, maybe even excuse himself. If, as Wade (and Lady Gaga) claimed, he was truly born this way, what did that say? That he had no scruples, no standards?

That he could do sex, but not love?

"Look," Wade said, "I'm no shrink, but I think it makes sense that your unfulfilling relationship with your father might connect to your behavior today, but not for the reason you think."

"I'm not sure I follow."

Wade put up a placating hand. "I may be just blowing smoke here, because as I said, my education revolved around stories and poems and not how the mind works, but it makes sense to me that a little gay boy might fixate on his father's love even more than a straight one. The fact that you didn't get the love you deserved, that you needed, maybe even made you fixate on it all the more.

"And maybe that's why you act out. Maybe that's why you let yourself be used so indiscriminately."

The words stung, and Bobby felt a sudden tightness in his chest. He wanted to bolt from the car. "What do you know about it?" he said softly.

A long silence followed. At last, Wade said, "I saw you."

"You saw me? Saw me where?"

"The other night. At the Stallion. You didn't notice me, but then you were pretty occupied."

Bobby felt a wave of nausea overtake him. He opened the car door, hurried outside, where the cool night air felt marginally calming against the heat that had risen up to burn his face. Droplets of sweat were forming at his hairline. He remembered the crowd gathering around to watch him blow that one guy. How another crowd had lined up, practically, outside his room to watch him get noisily fucked on the narrow bed.

Suddenly, he didn't want to see Wade ever again. He began walking rapidly away from the car, heading downhill, toward a copse of trees. He hoped to disappear into their shadows. He tasted the acid of bile at the back of his throat.

Wade caught up to him, gently touching his arm. Bobby yanked it away.

"I'm sorry. Are you okay?"

Bobby turned and stared at Wade. Even in the darkness, he could see the concern and sympathy radiating from Wade's handsome face. Wade hadn't said what he did to cause Bobby shame. Bobby knew that, but it didn't lessen his remorse and embarrassment.

Staring at the stalwart pine trees before him, Bobby didn't look at Wade as he asked, "So what were *you* doing there?" He couldn't contain the bitterness in his voice. "I mean, you were trolling for dick too. Right?" Bobby spat out the question.

Wade took a second to respond. "Actually, I was there as a volunteer with Lifelong AIDS Alliance. One night a week, I go with some of the other guys to hand out condoms, lube, and safe-sex literature at the different bathhouses. I've been doing it for years. Most guys don't want to make eye contact, but a few take what I'm handing out, and even fewer actually listen to what I have to say, but if I can prevent just one guy from getting infected with something that might be incurable, I can feel my time isn't wasted."

"So you watched me? What kind of sick shit is that? Did you get off on it?" Even though Bobby knew he was out of bounds, knew that voyeurism was not Wade's purpose in going to the baths, he couldn't stop the words, like bullets, from shooting out of his mouth, bitter. He felt violated, ashamed, defensive, and backed into a corner, all at once.

He remembered suddenly when he'd lived in Seattle and how this very park had been nicknamed Volunqueer Park because of all the lewd acts that took place in bushes, copses of trees, and even the old observation tower. He wondered if anything was going on right now and if he could join in, dropping wordlessly, facelessly to his knees, taking cock after cock into his mouth, obliterating the shame and embarrassment Wade had caused him to feel.

Bobby stared helplessly into the darkness, searching for figures moving in the trees.

There was no one, save for Wade, who had laid a hand on his arm. "Bobby. I do apologize. Really. I never meant to even bring this up to you, but the conversation sort of just led me there. I couldn't have handled things worse. What you do is your business. I saw you the other night and recognized you from high school." Wade stopped suddenly, as if it were hard for him to speak. He moved his hand away and put both hands on Bobby's shoulders, seeking out his eyes with his own.

Wade spoke softly. "It's none of my business, but I have to say it. What I saw made me sad. Because I think you're better than that."

"Oh, what do you know?" Bobby spat. "I was having a good time. I enjoy sex, okay?"

"That's just it, sweetheart. I didn't see you having a good time. Not on your face. I didn't see any joy."

Bobby shrugged so Wade's grip on his shoulders would fall away. He stared down, hard, at the ground, digging the toe of his shoe into the grass. "So, what did you see?" He knew he was pretending not to care, but he did. Oh yes, he did.

Wade seemed to think about it for a moment. "I saw—and you're not going to like this, but we've come this far—desperation."

Bobby sighed.

"I saw determination, a kind of grim determination. Like you were making yourself go through the motions, like you were doing something you had to do, not something you really wanted to do. Your body was making all the right moves, but your face looked like someone working away at a job he hated." Wade drew in a breath. "If I had seen you looking happy, looking like this was what you really wanted, I swear to God, Bobby, I never would have said a word to you."

Bobby didn't know what to say, probably because every word Wade had spoken was the truth. He could accept them on some deep, subconscious level. But Bobby didn't know if he was ready to admit that to anyone, especially himself. It was as though Wade had thrown up a mirror, and that mirror revealed things to Bobby he simply did not want to see.

He felt like crying, but he wasn't about to let that much weakness show. So he, as he always did, shoved his emotions deep down inside himself and blew out a big sigh. He gestured with his head to a row of benches behind them. "I appreciate your saying what you did. I know it must have been hard to get up the courage to talk to me like that, but can we start over? Can we just go over there and sit down on one of those benches and talk about, oh, the weather, or movies, or music? With all I've been through this week, I don't really want the spotlight on me. And I don't really want to psychoanalyze myself. I have someone I pay for that," Bobby said, thinking of Camille D'Amico, back in Chicago.

Wade walked over to one of the benches and sat down. Bobby sat beside him. Wade said, "I apologize. I should never have thrown that stuff at you, not with your father just passing away and all. It was insensitive."

Bobby simply nodded, staring straight ahead as the hill sloped down before him, revealing the glow of the Space Needle rising up into the night. He did *not* want to tell Wade it was okay. Because it wasn't. Whether it needed to be said or not—well, that was something Bobby had a feeling he would be mulling over through the course of a long, sleepless night.

Once they sat down, though, silence hung in the air between them. The night had taken a cold turn, with a wind out of the north that brought a light drizzle. Bobby leaned into Wade so their shoulders touched, and he could feel the other man's warmth.

"Can you just hold me?" Bobby finally said softly, his voice plaintive.

In response, Wade slid his arm around Bobby's shoulders. They sat like that for a long while, the mist and chill seeping into their pores, invading their clothes, until at last the two of them shivered.

"We should get back to the car, maybe get you home," Wade said.

In the car, Wade started the ignition, turned the heater on, the fan to high, but did not pull out of the parking space. In the darkness of the car, he asked, "We okay?"

"Oh yeah. I'm really glad you made the effort to reconnect with me. It was an unexpected bonus."

"Me too. I wasn't sure I'd even talk to you when I came to the funeral, but I couldn't help myself." Wade paused and then said, "I always admired you from afar back in high school. I couldn't help it. You were the best-looking boy in class."

"And now I pale, standing next to you."

"Not at all, not at all. You're still gorgeous. Probably even better looking than you were back then."

Bobby took the compliment as an invitation. He leaned over and kissed Wade. The kiss was tender at first, and Wade didn't pull away, as Bobby feared he might when he first inclined his head toward him. Bobby put a hand on the back of his neck, drawing him closer. Tentatively, he snaked his tongue inside Wade's mouth, forgetting everything as his erection caused his pants to tighten.

Forgetting everything...

He used his tongue to part Wade's lips, then his teeth, exploring the man's open mouth, which tasted of the beer he had drunk, an echo that was both tart and sweet.

Wade let out a little moan, lifting his tongue to meet Bobby's.

And then Bobby reached down between Wade's legs, unable to help himself, to see if the kiss was having the same effect on Wade as it was on him. It was. He squeezed the column of flesh he could feel pressing against the denim. He moved his hand up to tug at Wade's zipper.

And just like that, it was over.

Wade pulled away suddenly. Even in the dark, Bobby cringed because he could see Wade's eyes flash with outrage. "What are you doing?" he asked.

Bobby grinned, but suddenly his stomach felt like there was a rat inside, gnawing with razor sharp teeth, trying to get out. "I was just taking things to the next logical step."

"That's not the next logical step for me." Wade stared out the window, shifting his weight restlessly in his seat. He pulled his zipper back up.

"You were excited," Bobby said softly.

"Yeah, so? You're a hot guy. Nature took its course, but that doesn't give you license to just grab my dick. The kiss was nice. Why did you have to go and ruin it?"

"What are you, some kind of prude?"

"No." Wade shifted the car into gear and began driving, hands taut on the steering wheel, eyes sharply focused on the road.

He wouldn't look at Bobby, certainly wouldn't talk to him. They headed in silence, west down John Avenue to where it turned into Olive Way and finally Denny Way, which would intersect with Dexter Avenue. Bobby knew he was taking him home.

Because it had grown later in the evening, the traffic was sparse and the ride home took fewer than ten minutes. But the journey seemed longer, with an almost palpable sense of tension in the car, as if there was a third presence riding with them.

Wade pulled up quickly in front of Bobby's mother's condo building. Bobby didn't dare venture a word. He opened the car door to exit, and Wade grabbed his arm.

"Wait. Don't go. I don't want to leave things like this."

Bobby reclosed the door, slumping into his seat. "Look, I apologize if I stepped out of line. Most guys I know wouldn't have minded me grabbing their junk. Sometimes that happens before we even exchange names." Bobby laughed, but there was no mirth in it. "I misinterpreted or misjudged or something."

"I'm not most guys, Bobby."

"I know."

"This might sound silly in this day and age, when everybody's hooking up online, making easy connections, changing lovers as frequently as they change their designer drawers." He snickered. "But me? I'm a romantic." He drew in a big breath. "You know what?"

"What?"

"Once upon a time, I was just like you. See, back when I lost all the weight, then had the surgery to get rid of all the excess skin left over, I was left with this hot guy I didn't even recognize in the mirror."

"That must have been exciting."

"I don't know if it was. Because I still had that fat, insecure guy living inside me. *That* guy never got any admiring glances. *That* guy never got cruised. And, sadly, *that* guy believed he didn't deserve those things.

"So when guys began to notice me, began to hit on me, it was unreal. And I went a little crazy. Every guy—and there were many, too many to count—became a validation for me. That I was hot. That I was desirable. That I was not that fat guy no one wanted. The sex became like a drug for me. If I wasn't hooking up, the old insecurities crept right back in. The fat guy showed up in the mirror again."

Bobby heard what sounded like himself in Wade's words, and it shook him. He longed to bolt from the car, hide away in his room, and contemplate what Wade had said. "What did you do? How did you get to be this romantic?" Bobby really wanted to know.

"I did a lot of hard thinking. When I got diagnosed as HIV positive, that was a wake-up call, and I started seeing a shrink. What I just told you? About validating myself in sex? In the arms of dozens of different strangers? That wasn't an easy realization. Like you, I just told myself I was having fun, making the most of my new bod. But I came to understand what I was doing. And I came to realize no matter how many times I hooked up, no matter how many loads I took, that didn't make me any more lovable." He snorted. "That fat guy, I came to find out, was just as lovable as the new thin one. And I think it took my realization of that truth for me to understand what I really wanted."

"Which was?"

"Don't you know, Bobby?" Wade stared at him through the darkness of the car's interior.

Bobby knew. "I think I do."

"What I really wanted, Mr. Nelson, was love. And I learned that I was good enough to wait for it, to not settle for less than hot sex and romance, all in one package." Wade laughed. "I'm not saying I'm some saint. We have bodies; we have needs. But I no longer hook up indiscriminately. I want to know the guy before we have sex. I want to know if there's even a small chance we might have a connection." He grabbed Bobby's hand and squeezed it. "I want to feel a spark."

Bobby took his hand away. "And you didn't feel a spark with me?"

Wade snatched Bobby's hand back, brought it to his lips, and kissed it. "Not yet. But I don't do blowjobs in cars anymore. At least not with a guy I just reconnected with and, really, hardly knew before tonight. It's not my style."

Bobby sank back into the upholstery, his mind a jumble of thoughts. "So where does this leave us? I get on a plane tomorrow, bound for Chicago."

"Maybe I'll come see you. That is, if I get an invite." Wade grinned.

"You'd do that?"

"Come see you? In a heartbeat! I've never been to Chicago."

"Well, maybe you could look into flights for next weekend?" Bobby asked hopefully.

Wade shook his head. "Let's give it a little time, Bobby. Everything I told you tonight, I told you because I suspect we have some of the same issues. You just haven't dealt with yours yet. When you do, then maybe we can get together. Maybe then, we can even feel a spark." Wade grinned.

Bobby said, "Maybe I should just move back here to Seattle." Bobby thought of what he had in Chicago—a sterile, high-tech apartment, a job that paid him very well yet gave him nothing in the way of personal satisfaction, a bunch of sex partners who never once had led to a "spark," and worst, a best friend who had turned his back on Bobby. The turning away was justifiable, he knew that, but it didn't lessen the pain. He missed Caden every day.

"Don't take this the wrong way, but the fact that you would say that tells me you're not ready," Wade said. "No, you go home. You see that therapist you mentioned in the park, you work on loving yourself first, then we can plan a weekend." Wade gnawed at his lower lip.

"You'd wait for me?" Bobby was all childish hope.

"I can't promise that. But right now, I'd like to see you again. Like to see where this might go. I'm not saying I won't wait. I'm not saying I will. But that's not the point. You need to work on yourself for Bobby, not for Wade."

Bobby stared down at the floor, knowing in some part deep inside that Wade was right. Finally, he raised his head to look at Wade. "One last kiss?"

Wade came across the seat and kissed Bobby tenderly, one hand stroking his cheek, but there was no tongue. When they pulled away, Wade stared into Bobby's eyes, and the look turned his insides to jelly. "Go. Find you. And then call me."

"I will."

Bobby got out of the car and headed up the walk. He turned to wave at Wade, but he was already gone.

Part Two

Chapter Six

Bobby sat at Sea-Tac Airport waiting for his flight to begin its call for boarding. Outside, Seattle's famous (infamous?) skies pressed in, the large airport window revealing a sky painted entirely in shades of gray and white. His view of that sky and the planes outside was obscured by drizzle that ran down the glass.

Bobby had gotten here two hours early; he was compulsive that way. Michelle had offered to ride with him to the airport, saying she could take a cab home. But Bobby had argued against the idea. For one, there was no need for his mom to go to the expense. But more importantly, after last night with Wade, he wanted time to be alone with his thoughts, with what Wade had revealed about himself.

Michelle had reluctantly agreed, sighing and saying, "My little man is all grown up. I guess he doesn't need me to find his way for him."

At the front door, when they were saying their goodbyes, was when Bobby had relented and took his mother up on her offer. Tears stood in the corners of her eyes, threatening to drip over, and her voice was husky. He knew it was because there was a big old ball in her throat. "You take care, son. And don't worry about your mom. I'll be okay. Maybe I'll even get a job. Imagine that!" She had laughed, but her face revealed only sadness and, Bobby thought, a kind of panic at being alone for the first time in her adult life.

"You know what?" Bobby had said. "Why don't we just call the rental company and have them pick up the car from here? It's a little trouble, but I'll pay for it. Would you still be willing to run me out there?" He smiled. "I'd like your company for a little while longer, anyway."

"You sure?" Her face had brightened so much, as though she was in shadow before and the sun had just moved out from behind a cloud.

"Of course I'm sure. Come on, let's go get the car."

Now, Bobby was glad (for once) about all the security measures implemented since 9/11, because it ensured the goodbyes between him and Michelle were quick. She dropped him off at the sidewalk outside departures, they hugged briefly as Bobby hoisted his bag out of the trunk, and both pretended that Michelle would not collapse into sobs the moment she pulled away.

Bobby waved from the curb as his mother merged with airport traffic. He wondered when he would see her again but knew he would not let ten years pass before the next time.

She needed him.

And maybe he needed her just as much.

Now, sitting here in the idle, suspended-time universe that was an airport, he tried to read a book on his iPad but found himself reading the same passages over and over again when he realized not one word had registered. He closed the cover on the device and looked around.

Across from him sat a young father and son. Both were adorable. The more licentious Bobby couldn't help but notice the dad was hot, in his baseball cap, chamois shirt, jeans, and hiking boots, with dark stubble covering his chiseled jawline. But Bobby couldn't think in sexual terms, for once in his life, because he was so enchanted by the careful way the father treated his little son, a towheaded boy of about six.

Their heads were close together, like conspirators, and the father was making the son laugh. Bobby couldn't quite hear what the man was saying, but he liked to imagine he was trying to allay the little boy's nerves about getting on the plane, maybe for his first flight.

The dad adjusted the little boy's navy blue jacket, pulling it down and smoothing it around him, then chucked him under the chin. The little boy looked up at his father with the most amazing blue eyes. Such clarity! Such color—like summer skies. And there was so much love and admiration in those eyes. Bobby could read, better than he could the book on his iPad, complete love and devotion. He could see, in that single glance upward, that the little boy felt safe with his dad, as if he knew no harm could come to him as long as that man was by his side.

Suddenly, Bobby found it hard to swallow. The tiny ball in his throat expanded, making it hard to breathe. Tears sprang forth, running down his cheeks. *Where the hell is this coming from?* he wondered.

The handsome guy looked over at him, a frown replacing the smile he had had for his son. "You okay?"

Bobby just nodded, unable to speak. He gathered up his carry-on items and walked hurriedly to the men's room.

Once inside the stall, he sobbed as though his heart was broken.

*

It was late afternoon when they touched down at O'Hare International Airport. Bobby had a window seat, so he could look down on the city he had called home for more than a decade as the plane began its descent. There were the familiar waters of Lake Michigan, shimmering and blue verging on aqua under sunny skies (so unlike Seattle). There was the familiar skyline—the John Hancock, the Sears Tower, the Standard Oil building, Lake Point Tower, the magnificent condo buildings of the Gold Coast.

And yet Bobby felt like a stranger landing in a city to which he had never been. *Shouldn't this feel like coming home? Shouldn't there be some eagerness to get back to my condo and my job? Resume my regular life?*

Bobby felt no passion for things that he suspected must be comforts for most people, returning to the place where they laid their heads at night. He wondered, as the plane touched down on the tarmac, jostling him and causing his ears to finally pop, if he was simply numb from being back home on the West Coast, from having to see his father one final time, dead.

He thought of the little boy and his dad again, looking around to see whether they were on this flight, but he didn't see them. He knew he would remember that simple scene for a long time to come, maybe forever. He would remember because it was an image of something he had longed for his entire life.

*

Back in the sleek, elegant, ultramodern box in the sky Bobby called home, he had put away the clothes he had packed (Mom had washed everything for him before he left), sorted through the mail (all bills and advertising), and stared out his floor-to-ceiling windows at Lake Michigan, which today was an almost Caribbean aqua under the spring sun.

He wasn't due in to work until tomorrow and wondered how he should fill his day and night. In the old days, before he had lost his best friend, Caden, he would have called him up, and the two of them would have headed out to Boystown or Andersonville for cocktails and cock. But Caden had Kevin now, and even if Caden and Bobby were not on the outs, he doubted very much Caden was interested in the kind of carousing evening the pair used to make their habit.

He dropped his iPhone into the charging unit with speakers, after setting it to his Pandora "New Age Ambient" station, and simply sat for a while, facing the windows, watching the late afternoon sunlight fade into dusk.

He supposed he could shower, shave, moisturize, and dress himself in denim and black Spandex and hit the bars himself. They were within walking distance of his condo, and maybe a drink would serve to lighten the bleak feeling of desperation that hung over him like a moist blanket. Maybe a drink and a little hottie (or a big one) to come home with would fix him up. That was a combo that had always worked in the past for him, for keeping his mind free of pesky self-reflection.

Yet Bobby remained rooted in his leather chair, feet up, seemingly without the energy to move.

The sky outside faded to lilac, then gray, and finally to the inky black of night.

Bobby had thought of getting himself something to eat, mixing a drink, getting online, and cruising for a manmeat delivery but he did none of those things.

He simply didn't have the energy.

Or the desire.

He thought of Wade, considered calling him, and the prospect made him smile, but a little voice inside told him to wait, that it was too soon.

Eventually, he dozed off in the chair and dreamed of his father. In the dream, he was screaming at the man, as he never had. A great rush of anger poured forth from him as he listed his father's parental shortcomings in a loud, rage-and-sorrow-choked voice, while the man stood there and listened, shocked. In the dream, Bobby screamed at his father until his throat was raw, until the heat of anger fairly overtook him.

He awakened as the sun was rising over Lake Michigan, its bright golden light lifting his eyelids. Bobby opened his eyes, the dream memories scattering, and felt his face, which was damp. He had trouble getting his breath.

What's wrong with me?

Chapter Seven

"I don't know what's wrong with me. Ever since I got home from my dad's funeral, I seem to have lost all my passion, all my interest. I get up, go through the usual motions—coffee, shower—and go to work, where I do my job, and then come home. I sit in front of the TV all night, watching whatever network I happen to land on, and I go to bed."

Bobby looked at his therapist, whose warm brown eyes met his with understanding and sympathy. Camille waited for him to continue.

"I didn't used to be this way."

"How did you used to be?"

Bobby laughed. "I used to be a horndog, an incorrigible slut. I had a different guy—sometimes more—every day. You know how many times I've had sex since I got home last week?"

Camille shook her head.

"Zero."

"And that's a bad thing?" Camille asked.

"Well, yeah."

"Do you want to have sex?"

"That's just it. I don't. And that's not me."

Camille nodded, leaning forward to place a hand on Bobby's knee. "Would it help if I told you your behavior is actually very normal for someone who's just lost a parent?"

"But I hated my dad!"

"It doesn't matter. He was still your dad. He still occupies a huge space in your personal history. Don't you think that maybe your lack of interest in sex, and in life in general, might be due to the fact that you're attempting to process this loss?"

"But it wasn't a loss," Bobby argued, perhaps a bit too vehemently.

Camille smiled, toying with her frizzy hair for a moment. "Bobby, do you really believe that?"

"Yes! He made my life hell. He was a self-centered perfectionist for whom nothing I ever did was good enough. We had zero bonding. I can't tell you how many times, growing up, I fantasized about him dying." Bobby thought for a moment and then sprang up from his chair. "For Christ's sake! When my mom asked me about a happy memory with my father, you know what I did?"

Camille shook her head.

"I made one up. I couldn't think of a single thing." Bobby sat again. "I don't see how you can call his passing a *loss*." Bobby spat out the last word.

Camille said nothing for a moment, then softly said, "Sometimes the biggest losses are for things we never had, for things we long for. Maybe your father's death represents a big loss to you because now you know you'll never connect with him, not how you wanted."

The words hit Bobby like little pellets, stinging. He didn't want to hear them. He had spent almost the whole session complaining about his dad, about his visit home, which really wasn't a home at all, where, if anything, he felt displaced, longing for a past that never really happened.

And now Camille was telling him his current funk was due to the fact that he was longing for a relationship with his father. His father! He didn't need a relationship with someone as vain and shallow and flat-out mean as that man. It didn't take a PhD in psychology to know that!

"Our time is almost up." Camille placed her notepad on the table beside her and leaned forward, so her face was close to Bobby's. "I'm going to say something that might surprise you."

Bobby slumped back in his chair, crossing his arms over his chest. "Shoot."

"Be receptive, Bobby. Listen." Camille shifted. "We haven't done much work together yet, but I've heard enough from you in two sessions to understand that there might be a link to the promiscuity you told me about when we first met and your relationship with your father."

"Oh, I've been through all this already. I talked it out with a friend in Seattle. He thought that my hooking up might have had something to do with unfulfilled longing for a father I never had."

"And what did you think about that?"

Bobby shifted. He felt weird, like his heart was suddenly beating too fast. He couldn't seem to make the brain, tongue connection to form words. Finally, he said, somewhat desperately, "Didn't you say our time was up?"

Camille sighed, glancing down at her watch. "We're a little past." She smiled. "I can see you want to be anyplace but here. But I'll tell you, escaping *here* isn't going to help you escape your demons. You can go now, but I want you to think about the connection I just described. And maybe we can talk about that next time."

Bobby said nothing, but thought, *if there is a next time*, as he hurried from Camille's office. He slammed the door behind him.

Just as suddenly as his sex drive had vanished, it reappeared—with a vengeance.

*

Bobby didn't want to think about anything as he took a cab north from Camille's office to Halsted Street. It was just past 4:00 p.m. on a Wednesday afternoon in late March, and the day was surprisingly, unusually temperate for this early in the spring. The sun was shining, the breeze blowing was actually warm, and people were out on the sidewalks in droves. As they headed north on Lake Shore Drive, Bobby could see that the trails along the lakefront were alive with walkers, runners, bladers, and bicyclists.

Nothing like a sunny spring day after a punishing Chicago winter to bring everyone outdoors.

The spirit of the day was completely at odds with Bobby's mood, which was dour. Every time he thought of his session with Camille, he shifted his mind away, concentrating instead on where the cab was taking him—Sidetrack, the busiest bar along the Halsted strip. The weather, Bobby reasoned, would be the catalyst for a busier-than-usual happy hour. And a crowded happy hour, filled with hot men, drinking, talking, laughing, and cruising may *not* be just what the doctor ordered, but it was what Bobby ordered.

He needed to get back to being Bobby. A few vodka and cranberries, some mind-blowing sex, and he just knew he'd be back to normal. He'd be Bobby again.

The cab left him at the corner of Belmont and Halsted. Even though they weren't quite far enough north yet for the entrance to the big video bar, Bobby tapped the driver's shoulder at the intersection's red light. "I'll get out here."

The warm air felt good, and so did the sun on his face. He found himself smiling as he took in the rainbow pylons that lined the street and the fact he was certain almost every man he passed was gay.

He was home.

This was who he was: Bobby Nelson, sexually active gay man. Young, single, handsome, and on the prowl.

He had only been depressed because he hadn't been doing what came naturally to him.

As he walked north, he caught the eyes of several good-looking gentlemen, several of whom did the classic head swivel of gay men on the street everywhere, so they could check out Bobby's retreating form and, perhaps, make lingering eye contact one more time. Bobby had gone home with men based on as little as this simple gesture.

Inside Sidetrack, as Bobby had predicted, the walls were lined with guys, all staring up at video screens. Right now, a scene from *The New Normal* was playing, and everyone laughed at the appropriate moments. The scene was followed by a couple of kids from *Glee* doing a rousing rendition of "Somebody That I Used To Know."

The song made him think of Caden, and he quickly scanned the crowd, hoping to see his old friend. But Caden was nowhere to be found, and Bobby reasoned maybe that was for the best, since a confrontation, even if it was a reconciliatory one, was not what he had come to Sidetrack for.

Bobby made his way through the crowd, searching fruitlessly for any previous tricks, and finally landed in front of the bar. The bartender, he noted, was gorgeous—a shaved-head, bearded man who looked to be all of about twenty-five. He wore a tight black tank and faded jeans. Both arms were alive with color. Sleeve tattoos trailed down both muscular arms, a riot of twisting vines, flowers, and bursting stars. Bobby grinned when—at last!—he felt a familiar tightening in his groin as he watched

Tattoo Guy hold up and agitate a silver cocktail shaker, then pour out a perfect martini.

Finally, the man, god, whatever, stood before Bobby. His irises were ice blue, emphasized even more by startling black lashes. The eyes met Bobby's, and his knees just about turned to water.

Yes! I am back!

The bartender asked, "What can I get you, sexy?"

"Vodka, cranberry," Bobby said, his gaze never wavering from the stud's blue eyes. He felt a connection—familiar, primal—pass between them. "And your phone number," Bobby boldly ventured, feeling confident and brazen, even. It was a feeling he had missed.

The bartender laughed and turned away to get Bobby's drink. He set a cocktail napkin down and placed the tall glass before Bobby, saying only what Bobby owed.

Bobby fished his wallet out and handed the guy a ten. "Keep the change."

The bartender flashed him a killer smile, with the kind of pearly white teeth that only came from professional whitening, and started to turn away.

"Hey!" Bobby called after him. When the bartender turned around once more, he looked quizzical, his heavy black eyebrows drawn together in a question. Bobby grinned. "Aren't you gonna give me that number? I was very serious. I'd like to know when you get off."

The bartender ambled back up to him, put his face almost close enough to Bobby's for a kiss, and said, "Hey, man, I'm flattered, but I have a husband at home. Not a good idea for you to call me. But if I didn't, I'd be on you so fast." He patted Bobby's cheek and walked away.

A man Bobby had not noticed before, even though he stood right next to him, spoke. "Justin is always like that with us older guys. Likes to flirt so he gets big tips. Can't say that I mind. He is hot."

Older guys? Bobby was outraged. He had just turned forty—was he now an "older" guy? He took in the man standing next to him holding a glass of beer in one beefy paw. *He* was definitely on the downside of forty, maybe forty-five, forty-six, but still hot in a daddy way. His plain white T-shirt and jeans revealed a fit body, broad shoulders, a thin waist, and pecs that had obviously seen much attention in a gym. His head, too, was shaved, but unlike the bartender's, his baldness was probably due to nature or the desire to conceal gray or a thinning hairline.

Bobby liked the way a patch of silver hair poked out from the top of the guy's T-shirt. He was drawn to the man's intense brown eyes, his full lips, and the salt-and-pepper grizzle that coated his cheeks. The facial hair thickened around his mouth and chin, forming a scruffy goatee.

There was no denying he was hot. Still, it disturbed Bobby that the man found *him* "older."

"Ah, I had to take my chances. I'd kick myself if I walked away from that and didn't at least try."

The man laughed, and Bobby liked it—it was deep and full. Bobby let his gaze roam south and saw that the man's faded denim revealed a nice package. Well, more than nice, huge actually, bulging, just about begging to be caressed.

Bobby stuck out his hand. "Bobby."

The man's grip was confident, firm. Bobby liked that. "Aaron. Aaron Shaw." He smiled. "I believe in exchanging full names. So few people do anymore." He winked.

"Bobby Nelson. So, Mr. Shaw, what brings you out to Sidetrack on a Wednesday afternoon?"

"The hankering for a Blue Moon with a big slice of orange. Love this stuff. Have to limit my intake, though. Used to be I could drink a lot more, but now it goes right to the gut." He patted a stomach that looked firm but had just the slightest beginnings of a paunch. Bobby was surprised he found it sexy. "And you? What brings you to Sidetrack? And please don't be a wiseass and say something like a car...or the El."

"The hankering for a man." Bobby pointedly looked the guy up and down, sending his eyebrows up for a second, flirting.

Instead of grinning, or winking, or licking his lips, Aaron actually frowned, which took Bobby by surprise. Even though he quickly turned that frown upside down, as the saying went, Bobby was taken aback. "You come on a little strong, don't you?"

"I don't know. I just don't believe in playing games. I see something I like, I admit it."

"Well, thank you. But really, I was just here for a beer and maybe some conversation. If you're okay with that, we'll get along."

"Boyfriend at home?"

Aaron cocked his head. "Why would you ask that?"

Bobby knew the answer. It was on the tip of his tongue to say, "Maybe that's why you're not jumping at the opportunity to hook up with me." But he had second thoughts, thank God, and decided uttering such words would be more than a little vain, even for him. Still, the afternoon, so far, had not gone at all as he had imagined it would.

"Just wondered."

Aaron laughed. "Want to be sure you aren't wasting your time?" It was Aaron's turn to raise his eyebrows. "Sorry. I shouldn't draw conclusions."

"I don't think talking to you would be wasting my time." Suddenly, Bobby felt defeated, dejected. Just as suddenly as his good mood had arrived, it deserted him. He met Aaron's gaze and said, "I'm gonna hit the restroom."

Aaron smiled, but he looked away. Bobby figured he knew he was being brushed off.

Bobby started away.

"Hey!"

He turned back to Aaron, who was holding out a business card. "Take this. It has my email and my cell on it. Maybe we could meet up some time. Talk. Grab coffee or a beer."

Bobby glanced down at the card before pocketing it. "Sure thing, man." He hurried away.

The high-tech men's room was like a sanctuary, and Bobby was relieved to be away from the crush of bodies in the large bar. He ambled up to the urinal, hoisted himself out, and let go.

There was a guy standing next to him. Bobby had taken in the basics when he entered the washroom. Stats came to him easily; he was so practiced at sizing men up with a single glance. This one had black hair, olive skin, was probably about five feet eight, with a compact build and a bubble butt. In profile, Bobby could see the guy sported a mustache, unusual these days, but oh God, adorable. His black hair was gelled into an alluring mess of spikes. Probably late twenties, early thirties. Hispanic.

And Bobby couldn't resist glancing down at the guy's cock. It was uncut, a kind of purplish brown, and thick. Right now, a stream of golden piss was issuing forth from it, splattering the bowl.

Bobby had to concentrate to keep his own dick from rising in admiration.

Bobby noticed the guy's stream slow to a trickle, then a few drops, and then nothing. But the Latino didn't put away his cock. No, he shook it a few times, which was normal, then began stroking himself, working the cock quickly into a firm column of flesh, at least seven and a half or eight inches long. Bobby could feel two things—his breath coming quicker and the guy's gaze on Bobby's dick, which was hardening as he stroked himself.

Bobby didn't say a word. He stroked himself to full hardness, spitting on his hand and working it up and down the shaft as his new friend did the same.

Bobby didn't want things to end here. He glanced over his shoulder and saw no one entering the washroom. He met the Latino's eyes, grinned, and then bent over, taking the guy's cock in his mouth with one fluid motion, swallowing it all the way down to the base, to where the guy's black pubes tickled his nose.

The guy moaned and rested his hand on the back of Bobby's head, thrusting even more deeply into his throat. Bobby took the cock like a champ, closing his eyes, relishing the slightly salty taste of the uncut dick in his mouth. He moved his head a bit away from the cock, pulling back the foreskin to lick out the drop of precome already poised at the guy's piss slit.

This quick, down and dirty heaven was brought to an abrupt halt by the guy stiffening (and not in a good way) and then three sharp taps on Bobby's back. Bobby straightened up and stared into the other guy's chocolate eyes, a question on his face.

The guy nodded over Bobby's shoulder while hurriedly stuffing his cock back into his jeans.

Bobby turned and looked.

Aaron stood there at the entrance, leaning against the wall, watching, a sardonic grin on his face. "Sorry to interrupt, fellas, just need to take a piss."

Bobby felt heat rise up to envelop his face and neck. He put himself away with difficulty—he was still half-hard—and started out of the washroom.

Aaron grabbed his arm as he went by. "You need to be careful," he said softly.

"Oh, fuck you. Mind your own business."

Instead of looking outraged, Aaron's face revealed only concern. "It's just that a couple guys were arrested last week in here for doing just that. The owner doesn't want that kind of thing going on here. He could lose his license. There are plenty of back room bars for that, or the baths up the street."

Bobby watched the Latino retreat quickly, brushing by them as he edged his way out of the men's room, eyes cast downward.

"Shit," Bobby whispered to Aaron. "That's ruined."

Aaron sidled up to the urinal and took himself out. Bobby heard the splatter of piss hitting the aluminum. He didn't dare look.

Aaron spoke over one shoulder. "Look, man, I didn't mean to come off as the morality police or anything. From where I was standing, that looked damn hot. But I just didn't want to see you get in trouble."

"Thanks."

Bobby turned to leave.

"Use my number. Give me a call," Aaron called out.

Bobby didn't answer, but hurried back out into the crowd, hoping to find that the Latino wasn't totally humiliated and that he remained in the bar.

Breathing a deep sigh of relief, Bobby spotted him standing on the upper level, alone, holding a bottle of Bud in one hand.

Bobby rushed up to him. The Latino met his gaze and, to Bobby's immense relief, grinned.

"Sorry we were so rudely interrupted—and just when things were getting interesting."

"Well, I guess, contrary to my fantasies, the whole world is *not* my sexual playground."

"More's the pity," Bobby said. "I'm Bobby."

The guy shifted his beer to his left hand so he could shake Bobby's with his right. "Carlos."

"I'm very pleased to meet you, Carlos." Bobby glanced down at his bottle and was able to determine it was three-quarters empty. "I was just gonna go grab another cocktail. Would you like another beer?"

Carlos winked and leaned close, whispering hotly in Bobby's ear, "What I'd really like is for you to suck my cock some more."

Bobby straightened up. "Well, I think that can be arranged. To use the age-old cliché, your place or mine? I think in public is kind of ruined for us, at least for now."

Carlos said, "I got a roommate at my place up in Edgewater. So that's not cool. You gotta place?"

"I certainly do. Follow me."

*

Twenty minutes and one cab ride later, Bobby found himself flat on his back in his bed, his calves on Carlos's shoulders, as the Latin guy thrust deeply into him. Bobby was enjoying this, and his groans and cries to "fuck me harder" confirmed it. He liked the way Carlos's thick cock stretched him open, sending electric waves of pleasure not just through the area being penetrated but also throughout his whole body. Bobby's own dick was rock hard, and he dared not touch it. Carlos's thrusting had him *this close*. He glanced down at his dick and watched the precome ooze out of it, pooling on his flat belly.

"Oh man, you feel so good. I could fuck you all night."

"Go for it," Bobby gasped. A little come leaked out of him as the head of Carlos's dick hit his prostate.

Maybe Carlos would have liked to fuck Bobby all night, but it was only seconds later as Bobby watched Carlos's face morph into something twisted as his orgasm approached. He clenched his eyes together and his mouth dropped open. "Fuck! I'm gonna come!"

"Shoot it in me, baby! I want every drop." Bobby ground his hips down on Carlos's pulsating cock, enveloping it completely in his hole. He loved this part, watching his fucker's face go from tense as he shot to more relaxed as the come and sexual tension ebbed out of him.

Bobby reached up to touch Carlos's gorgeous face while he worked his own cock up and down. "Keep it in me. Keep it in me," he muttered, as he drove himself to his own climax. In only a moment, he shot, the white come arcing up over his belly to land on his chin and chest.

They both laughed, Carlos collapsing on top of Bobby.

Carlos pulled himself carefully from Bobby, rolling onto his back next to him. Bobby watched as he unrolled the condom from his half-hard cock, eyeing the load inside with hunger. *Would it to be too slutty of me to snatch that out of his hand and suck the come from it?* Bobby decided it would. Besides, Carlos had already flung it into the wastebasket beside the bed.

"You mind if I have a smoke?" Carlos asked.

"Yeah. I kind of do. Is that okay?"

"Sure, I understand." Carlos sat up, and Bobby admired the muscles in his strong brown back. He traced his hand along the spine. "I need to get going anyway." Carlos stood and began to struggle into his jeans.

Bobby got up on one elbow. "What? I was hoping you'd stay. Maybe have round two? Breakfast in the morning?"

Carlos laughed. "Dude, I don't think my wife would like that."

"You have a wife? I thought you mentioned a roommate."

Carlos grinned and pulled on his T-shirt. "I suppose you could call her that too. But she's gonna be wondering where the hell I am." Carlos leaned over and gave Bobby a fast peck on the lips. It was funny, Bobby thought, how quickly all the passion died once a guy shot his load.

"You want my number?"

Carlos paused at the door to the bedroom. "I could take it, but I might not ever call. I don't do this kind of thing very often."

Sure you don't. "No worries. I'll see you around."

"Thanks, buddy. I can see myself out."

Bobby lay in bed, body tense, as he listened for the sound of the front door opening and closing. Within seconds, it did. Bobby leaned over and plucked the condom from the wastebasket. He held it in front of him, eyeing the thick load within its receptacle tip, imagining himself turning it upside down above his mouth and letting the come flow into him.

That would be hot. But it would also be unsafe.

Instead, he upended the rubber above his chest and let the come run onto himself, mixing with the drying remnants of his own load. He rubbed it into his skin, whispering, "Carlos."

He rolled onto his side, staring out at the night, which had crept in while he and Carlos were fucking and now pushed against the glass as if it wanted admittance.

"Carlos," Bobby whispered once again, wishing he had stayed. He closed his eyes against the darkness and imagined the two of them in bed together, Bobby's head on Carlos's chest, laughing and talking softly. He imagined falling asleep together, spooning.

He would have liked to have at least talked to him. Maybe shared a laugh. Discovered what they did and didn't have in common. Made plans to meet a second time.

Dream on.

Wearily, Bobby got up and headed for the shower, ass sore and, in spite of the orgasm he had just had, feeling completely unfulfilled.

Just as he was about to step into the shower, Bobby heard his phone ringing from the bedroom. He smiled when he saw the picture of the handsome redhead who came up on its screen.

Bobby pressed Accept. "Cody! I haven't heard from you in ages. What's up?" Cody, a bearded, beefy redhead, had once been one of Bobby's fuck buddies. Once, because it had been at least six months since he had heard from the man. But back then, they had gotten together for some very satisfying sex at least a dozen times—why, it was almost a relationship! But when Cody stopped calling and two, three months had passed, Bobby had assumed that the statute of limitations had run out on their friends-with-benefits status. He had moved on and had had, oh, literally hundreds of new "friends" since the advent of Cody. Bobby assumed the same was true for his long-lost "friend."

"Well, I was just thinking about you."

"Yes?" Bobby grinned in spite of himself. That mood that Carlos had left in his wake? The unfulfilled one? The one that was quickly catching up with Mr. Carlos as he headed out of the building? It was doing a U-turn and heading back to the elevators.

"Going through my contacts and I came across your stunning picture."

Bobby laughed. "Get out!"

"No, seriously, I *came* across it. Had to clean the screen off and everything."

They both laughed.

"I like that. So what's going on? I haven't heard from you in ages. To be honest, I was pretty sure I wouldn't ever again."

"Well, I've been busy."

"A man?"

"Oh, you know me so well!"

"Serious?"

"He just moved in last week. Bobby, I'm in love. Bliss!"

And Bobby's mood, which had gone from unfulfilled to optimistic, took another U-turn, grabbed the elevator doors to prevent them from shutting, and headed back down to the lobby. "Well, good for you," Bobby said, hoping he sounded convincing. *But why*, he wondered, *is Cody calling to tell me now? To rub it in?* Now he was just being self-pitying. For all Cody knew, Bobby was happily settled in his own little love nest with a man who was kind, smart, gorgeous, and who drove a Porsche.

Shallow much?

"So, what prompts the call? Not that I'm not glad to hear from you again, but this just comes so out of the blue."

"I know, I know. But, uh, Andy was looking at my contacts with me, and he was very impressed with your picture. *Very* impressed." Cody lowered his voice to a whisper. "I showed him some of the other pics too, the naked ones. He about shot when he saw those." Cody's voice returned to normal. "So we talked a little about you, saw it wasn't all that late, and, um, don't quite know how to put this, but—"

Bobby rolled his eyes. "Let me guess. Is this a booty call?"

Cody laughed. "I guess we've shared so many of those in the past, you recognize my siren song when you hear it."

"But I'm confused. I thought you just said you were blissfully in love with this new guy—setting up housekeeping and everything. What did you say his name was again? Andy?"

"Right. C'mon, Bobby, you know I could never be monogamous. We play together. I'm *emotionally* monogamous to Andy; he'll always come first in my heart."

Good luck with that.

"Anyway, we were doing a little partying, nothing serious, it *is* a weeknight after all, but we were in the mood for a third, and you came up—along with our dicks. So, what do you say? You still single? Available? I won't even ask if you're up for it because you're the one person in Chicago that I can always count on being up for it." Cody laughed.

Bobby didn't know what to say. The silence stretched out. Bobby glanced at the clock and saw that it was going on ten. He had to be at work in the morning.

"Bobby? Has your situation changed? It's cool if it has. It was still nice to talk to you."

"No! No, I was just trying to decide if I want to come out on a work night."

"Are you getting old or something? Two hot guys here—horny and hard! Just waiting for you. You gonna turn that down?"

Bobby grinned but felt sad. "I guess not. You still over in Lincoln Square?"

"Eastwood Avenue, second floor. How long?"

"Just gonna hop in the shower, and then I'll be right over. Less than an hour."

"Sounds good. You won't regret it. See you soon!" Cody disconnected.

Bobby hung up the phone, looked again at the darkness pressing in, wondering if that's what it looked like inside his heart.

He sighed and headed back into the shower. He had a date!

*

Bobby lay snuggled between the two men in their king-size bed. Cody must have moved in with the older Andy, because none of this furniture, all very sleek, very Room and Board, had belonged to Cody when he knew him. Cody was more the type to haunt thrift stores for midcentury modern stuff. He said it reminded him of his childhood in Des Plaines.

Bobby noted how quiet they all were, now that they had all come. Bobby had been what he referred to as "spit-roasted:" one guy up his ass (Andy) and the other down his throat. During the course of a prolonged and sweaty fuck, the couple had switched off, using Bobby's orifices three times each, finally ending up in the same positions as when they started. At least they hadn't suggested double penetrating him. Bobby wasn't sure even he could handle that, especially not with Andy, who sported at least nine inches.

Now, lying between the two sweaty and muscular bodies, Bobby remembered Andy's nine inches, his compact, almost muscle-bound frame, his black high and tight buzz that made him look like a marine or a police officer, the coarse black hair that covered the man from head to toe. He remembered him from not just this evening's ass pounding, which had left Bobby breathless and aching in an oh-so-good way, but from several other times over last summer, when Andy had visited Bobby at his Lake Shore Drive condo.

They had originally met at Steamworks, the bathhouse on Halsted. Andy had been one of a trio who had gangbanged Bobby one memorable hot summer night.

And now here Andy was with his former fuck buddy, Cody, in what passed for wedded bliss in Chicago's gay community. Small world.

"So," Bobby asked, "tell me the story. How did you guys meet? How long have you been together?"

Cody quickly got up on one elbow to look down on Bobby. His green eyes shone. Bobby wasn't sure if it was from the candlelight or happiness.

Cody smirked. "Wish we had some romantic story to tell, but the truth is we hooked up online. When I saw this one's pic on Adam4Adam, I was in love. Who wouldn't be, right? With that body and that dick? I didn't even think the man was in my league. But it worked out fast. You know how it goes, sometimes you can spend hours on those sites, cruising, chatting, sending messages back and forth, exchanging pics..."

Bobby knew.

"Anyway, it was like that with us. I got online, and five minutes later, Andy was headed over to my place. I like to think it was fate. And Andy agrees, don't you, honey?"

Andy growled from his side of the bed. Bobby assumed it was in agreement.

Cody continued, the happiness he felt obvious from the big smile on his face. "And it went really fast after that first time too. And that first time? Wow. Well, you know." Cody nudged Bobby, and Bobby politely laughed.

Cody got up and moved to the other side of the bed so he could cuddle up next to Andy. Bobby watched as he stroked the hair on Andy's chest and reached up to tenderly kiss his neck. Cody whispered, "I just love this guy. With all my heart. He's the 'one.' You know what I mean?"

Bobby nodded and wished he did.

Andy looked over at Bobby with his dark eyes, smiling. "Soul mates."

"That's great, guys."

The hot sex he had shared with the two of them no longer mattered. Bobby now felt like a little poor boy, standing outside a candy store, nose pressed to the glass, longing for things that would always be out of his reach. He looked at how contented Cody looked with his head on Andy's chest, the older man's arm wrapped protectively around him. In spite of what they had just done, they appeared to be such a sweet couple, so completely in love.

Bobby didn't think he could bear to lie here as the pair drifted off to blissful sleep in each other's arms.

It felt as though a lot more than a mere few inches separated him from them.

He sat up and reached for the jeans he had left in a crumpled heap on the stained-black hardwood floor. He slid into them, back turned to the boys on the bed, staring at the wall before him. To that wall, he said, "Gotta get up early for work in the morning. Thanks, guys. This was great."

He listened for one or the both of them to protest, to ask him to stay the night, or at least for another round, but it was only Cody who said, "Got it. It was good to see you again, Bobby."

"Yeah." Bobby looked over his shoulder at the couple. "This was fun."

"We'll do it again," Andy said, sitting up and pulling on the boxers he had worn when he answered the door. "I'll see Bobby out, hon."

"Okay." Cody pointed the remote at the plasma screen mounted on the wall opposite the bed. It had been playing porn, but Bobby could hear him switch the porn off and the TV on. *The Golden Girls* theme was playing.

Bobby couldn't wait to get out of there.

Andy closed the bedroom door and then followed Bobby down the hall to the front door. There, they paused.

"Thanks for not mentioning that we'd hooked up before." Andy smiled. He opened a small desk situated in the entryway and rooted around in it.

"No problem."

Andy scrawled something on a sheet of paper and straightened up. "I mean, Cody would be cool with it. We met on a cruising site, after all, but I think we were both wise to just keep things to ourselves."

"Very wise. Your secret is safe with me."

Andy pressed the piece of paper into Bobby's hand, then grabbed him and pulled him close so his rock-hard body touched every inch of Bobby's. Bobby was getting hard in spite of himself. He felt the same stirring from within Andy's boxers.

Andy licked his ear and whispered, "Man, that is one fine ass you got there. I'd like another taste with us just one-on-one, on the down low, because Cody and I are supposed to play only together, but I would love to drop by your house again sometime, fuck you senseless." Andy growled.

He did that a lot.

Bobby pushed away from him. He looked into the man's sexy dark eyes, remembering the scene of contentment he had just witnessed between the couple, and hurried, wordless, out the door.

Once he was in the street, he tore the paper on which Andy had written his number into tiny pieces and tossed it in the gutter. He felt the hot prick of tears in his eyes.

He began walking east, toward Damen Avenue. At this hour of the early morning, he knew a cab would be hard to find, especially here in Ravenswood. But the brown line L station was only a couple of blocks away, and he could catch that, take it to Belmont, and walk home from the station.

The train was nearly deserted.

Bobby gingerly took a seat, ass still sore from the poundings it had taken in the last twenty-four hours. *God! Have you really taken three dicks up there in one day? You slut!* Bobby thought the appropriate response to this thought would be a quiet chuckle to himself, but instead he simply felt sad.

He stared out the window at the backs of apartment buildings as the train sped south and east. Many of the windows were dark, but a few gave off a warm yellow glow, and Bobby thought that indicated home. Sometimes, he would see a person moving around in a kitchen, opening and closing the refrigerator door, or the flickering light of a TV in a living room. When they were stopped at the Irving Park station, he saw a couple, male, lying in bed together. They were not doing anything risqué, both of their faces aglow with the light from e-readers or iPads on their laps. Their bare shoulders touched, and in that brief moment, Bobby witnessed their companionable silence.

He felt just as isolated from this scene as he had from watching Cody and Andy in bed together, drifting off. He hoped *this* pair, glimpsed only briefly, had more going on than the couple he had just been with.

The train lurched back into motion. Bobby had been so absorbed in staring out the window, he hadn't noticed that someone else had boarded the train.

Someone was occupying the seat opposite him, his back against the windows, long legs stretched out before him so his Nikes dangled into the aisle. The guy stared at Bobby, an impish grin playing about his lips. *How do they always know?* Bobby wondered. *And what does this one want? A blowjob or to bash my face in? It's hard to tell, especially on a public conveyance like the L.*

This guy had a mop of black hair, part of which hung down to cover one of his dark eyes. He was olive-complexioned, tall, and wore faded jeans and a Northwestern hooded sweatshirt. Middle Eastern? Hispanic? Bobby couldn't tell for sure, but he imagined an uncut, plum-headed dick nestled between those spread thighs.

The guy smiled bigger at him. He was either making fun of Bobby or trying to start something.

Bobby threw caution to the wind and smiled back, raising one eyebrow quizzically.

Ever the suave, romantic gentleman, the man squeezed his crotch, never ceasing his eye contact with Bobby. To be sure Bobby got the message, he licked his lips.

Bobby nodded. *Oh, he's all subtle charm.*

The man stood and was suddenly on the seat next to Bobby. He reeked of alcohol and cigarettes. Bobby felt trapped, leaning back toward the cool glass of the window. Glancing behind him, the guy reached down and squeezed Bobby's dick, which—damn it—was getting hard, in spite of the stranger's not-so-alluring aroma and the brown teeth he revealed when he smiled.

You really aren't considering this, are you? For one, haven't you already had enough for one day?

Buddy, you're not even horny. And two, this guy is beneath you. You are so far out of his league it isn't funny.

Or maybe he's just what you deserve...

Still, Bobby's dick was hard. He felt, as he had many times in the past, that his dick stole all the blood from his brain.

He leaned over and whispered in Bobby's ear. "I get off at Belmont."

"Me too," Bobby said, questioning his motive for responding.

"You got a place?"

Bobby shook his head. "No." He thought maybe that would end things.

But this guy was undeterred. "I got a studio, right across the street from Dunkin' Donuts. We can be there and undressed, man, in like ten minutes. You up for it?" He gave Bobby's dickhead a squeeze as the train slowed when it pulled into the Belmont station.

Bobby wasn't sure what to think. A part of him didn't know how to say no. It would just be easier to follow him off the train, go to his apartment, and have sex. It would all be over in less than a half hour, and then he could go home and maybe, finally, sleep.

Bobby moved the hand gently from his crotch. There were people, after all, standing on the El platform, and they could see them.

He didn't want to do this and wondered why he felt compelled. Was it really easier to go through with it than it was to utter one simple two-letter word: no?

He looked over at the guy once more, at his eager grin, and Bobby's stomach gave a little nauseous lurch.

"Okay. I'll follow you."

The train stopped, and the door slid open, accompanied by the familiar gong. Bobby watched as the stranger stood, and still wondering what the hell he was doing, he eyed the man's ass.

He didn't feel in the least horny.

Bobby sighed and stood, then walked to the door. His potential fuck buddy was already out on the platform, facing away. The flash of flame from a lighter illuminated the area around his face, indicating he simply could not wait to light up a smoke.

Is this what you really want?

Bobby stepped off the train, a million invisible hands and inaudible voices telling him not to follow.

The guy looked over his shoulder, eyebrows raised.

And Bobby stepped back onto the train, just as the doors were closing. With a sigh, he plopped back down in his seat as the train lurched into motion.

He stared out the window at the man standing there, a cigarette dangling from between his lips, watching the train's passage, features twisted by confusion, or maybe the surprise of rejection.

Whatever. Bobby was simply glad to be going home, glad that, for once, he had not followed through.

He could catch a cab to his condo from the station at Fullerton.

Chapter Eight

"So, why didn't you go home with this guy? What did you say his name was?" Camille looked down at the notebook in her lap, flipped a couple of pages.

"I didn't. I don't know his name. I never did. Honey, we were just strangers on a train."

Camille cocked her head. "And you hooked up? Right there on the L?"

"Do you counsel many gay men? I am sure we are not the first gay men to board a train single and get off of it a couple, at least for the next hour or so."

"I wasn't judging. I just wondered. So, this guy, as you said, made eyes at you, then asked you back to his place..."

"And I was going to go." Bobby blew out a breath, unsure if he even wanted to reveal what followed, but what was he here for, in therapy, if not for getting at his own personal truth? "But something stopped me."

"Which was?"

Bobby didn't say anything for minutes. He glanced around the smartly appointed office that looked more like someone's living room, all done up in soothing shades of beige and sage green. He stared down at his hands as though he had never seen them before, clasped primly on his khaki-covered lap. "Um, maybe I didn't go because I wasn't really horny anymore. After all, I had been with three different guys that day." His grin, he knew, was sheepish.

"So you would have gone if you had been horny?"

"Maybe I would have." Bobby stopped. He knew horniness, or the lack of it, had nothing to do with why he had almost followed the guy off the train. He leaned forward so his face was closer to Camille's. He noticed, for the first time, that she was beautiful. Her hair was a brownish halo, and her body was lush—most people would call it fat, but it was curvy in all the right places, and it was the kind of body within which he imagined a man or a child could find comfort.

Bobby went on. "The truth is, I didn't get off the train because I knew, even when I was considering going home with him, that I didn't really want to. And *that's* what puzzles me."

"Tell me more about that."

"I don't understand why I'd even entertain having sex with someone I didn't find attractive, and I don't get why I would pursue sex when my balls had literally been completely drained."

Camille let out a little snort of laughter.

Bobby smiled. "It's not funny."

"I'm sorry. The 'balls drained' thing just hit me wrong." Camille crossed her legs, leaning forward so she could place one hand on Bobby's knee and look more closely into his eyes. "I want you to try to give voice to your motivations—tell me why you wanted to follow him and what stopped you from doing it."

Bobby leaned back in his chair. "I don't know. I just don't know."

"I think you do."

Bobby bowed his head. Again, as he had felt before in this very office, he felt a powerful urge to flee, to simply get up from this comfortable leather chair and bolt from the office. Be outside, where he could breathe once more.

"Could it be that..." Bobby's voice trailed off, and he knew he was giving Camille a very helpless look. "Could it be that my sex drive is ruling me, rather than the other way around?"

Camille nodded. "What do *you* think?"

"I think that's not news to anyone. I've been that way for years. But at least before, I had standards." Bobby stared down at the distressed tongue-and-groove wooden floor.

"Let me ask you this, Bobby. Has this happened to you before? In other words, have you gone through with something sexually even though you knew it was inappropriate?"

He again felt constricted, as if his only recourse was to run from the room, but he forced himself to answer. He thought of the many times he had slept with guys he had, for example, invited over from Craigslist. There were many who had shown up at his door, looking nothing like the photographs they had posted. They were older, or fatter, or the pics were not even of them. Yet he had slept with all of them because, well, why? Because they were there? Because it was easier to just go through with the sex act than to say he was sorry and close the door? Did that even make sense? Yet he had done it, time and time again. He had given his friend Caden the notion, on their innumerable pub crawls back in the day, that he went only with "fucking gorgeous" guys—his term—but that was not the truth.

Bobby realized he went with almost anyone who would have him. And that included half of Chicago.

He thought of a line from a book he had read somewhere, and it sprung forth now, as if highlighted. It was about accepting the love we think we deserve.

Did he think he deserved indiscriminate, unsatisfying sex?

"Yes," Bobby said, looking at Camille. "Lots of times." He sucked up what little courage he felt remaining with him and forced himself to say the words. "I'll sleep with just about anybody, whether I find them attractive or not. It's like I'm never satisfied, and I'm always thinking the next man will be better."

"The next man will love you?"

Now that really gave Bobby pause. He slammed back into his chair, as if Camille had stood, drawn back her hand, and slapped him across the face hard enough to make his head swivel.

Bobby said nothing. What could he say? To agree with a statement like that, well, it just made him feel pathetic. Worthless. Unlovable.

Camille spoke again. "I apologize, Bobby. I can see from your face that maybe it was too soon to ask a question like that. I just want you to think about it. I know it hurts."

She stood up from her chair and moved to the desk situated behind them. Bobby didn't look, but he could hear her rooting around in a drawer. It reminded him of Andy searching for a piece of paper so he could write down his number to facilitate cheating on the guy who was head over heels in love with him.

Camille returned, bearing a pamphlet in her hand. She sat back down across from Bobby and handed it over.

He glanced down at its simple cover and read the title: "Sex Addicts Anonymous. A Pathway to Recovery." There was an oval logo with a rising sun, bearing the legend, "From Shame to Grace."

Bobby held it back out to Camille. "I don't need this. You think I'm an addict?"

"What I think is that it doesn't matter what *I* believe." She took Bobby's hand holding the pamphlet and gently, firmly shoved it back to him. "All I ask is that you read this. I'm not saying you have to admit anything. I'm not saying you have to go to any meetings, make any choices. Just read the fucking pamphlet. Simple. It's only a few pages."

Bobby looked at her, tense, feeling as if she were shining a bright light in his face. He wanted to shrink from her gaze.

"It won't bite you. There's a quiz in there." She smiled. "Take it and see what you think."

"I'm not an addict," Bobby said.

"I never said you were. I simply asked you to read a pamphlet and take a quiz." She tossed her notebook onto the side table. "Our time is just about up. Your homework is to read the pamphlet and take the quiz. It should take you ten minutes. But I hope you'll think about it after, and that might take a lot longer. We'll talk about it next time."

Bobby shook his head. "This is pointless. It's not what I came here for." He tried to hand the pamphlet back to her, but she wouldn't take it.

"See you next time, Bobby."

*

Bobby was alone on the El, traveling north. Outside, the sky was dusky gray tinged with purple as evening fell. He had gone to see Camille after work that day, so the train was not as crowded as it would have been an hour or so ago, at the peak of rush hour. He actually had a seat alone at the back of the train car with only a wall behind him.

He wondered if he had subconsciously chosen that seat for himself so he could cautiously open the pamphlet. He did so now, looking around guiltily, certain he would see someone suddenly standing beside him, staring down and smirking at his reading material.

If anyone comes along, this goes into my messenger bag and out comes my Kindle.

He turned immediately to the "Questions for Self-Assessment." And he looked no further than the title. *What? Are you afraid to read the questions? Afraid of what they might reveal?* Even though the questions he asked himself were his own thoughts, he thought he could hear Camille's voice asking them.

He took a deep breath, shut his eyes for a moment, and looked at the first question. It asked him if he kept secrets about his sex life. If he led a double life. He snorted with laughter. Of course he didn't. Who was more out there than Bobby?

Then he reminded himself of what he had just thought of when he was with Camille, how he had always told Caden he only went with the most "fucking gorgeous" men, that his bar was set very high. That he had standards. And that was not true at all. Bobby had been with guys he wouldn't have been caught dead with in public, some who really could be referred to, by no stretch of the imagination, as ugly, yet he maintained to Caden and other "worthy" tricks that he only accepted the best.

So he supposed the answer to that first question was a "yes." Sort of.

The next question asked him if his sex drive had driven him to have sex in places or with people he wouldn't normally choose. Well, yeah, he had already answered that—about people—in the first question. And places? Public places? Good Lord, Bobby had been a regular at the long stretch of park that ran along the lakefront between Montrose and going all the way up to the gay beach at Ardmore. He had blown guys in the summer months at the Bird Sanctuary at Montrose, concealed by trees and bushes. He had gotten fucked once in the back of a white delivery van by a cigar-smoking daddy while a carload of teenagers partied, unaware, to hip-hop music in a car nearby. He had once had sex with a Northwestern student in an alleyway that ran beneath the El tracks, while commuters traveled above them. The answer to number two was an unqualified yes.

Maybe there was something to this. He went on to number three. It asked him, basically, if he needed *more* in terms of frequency and variety to achieve the same levels of relief. Three dicks on one day, he reminded himself, almost four. And that was not even his personal best. What about the night at the bathhouse in Seattle? What about his last visit to Steamworks, when he had lost count of the number of guys he had sucked off in the glory hole room?

Oh *yes*.

Number four asked him about pornography, and Bobby thought of the cache of DVDs that must have numbered in the hundreds in his bedroom closet, portraying everything from sweet, simple vanilla sex to raunchy bareback orgies that included felching, watersports, and fisting. And now, he simply streamed porn right to his computer, watching the latest offerings from sites like MachoMoe. He could spend hours stroking himself until he was raw and sore.

Oh *yes*.

Five wanted to know if his relationships became distorted because of his sexual preoccupation. If sex was destructive... And Bobby shut his eyes, no longer able to look down at the type on the page. What relationships? I am forty years old, and I can truthfully say I have never had one, not really. Even the ones that lasted longer than a couple of weeks or months were fuck buddies—never anything more than that.

How could sex be destructive to his relationships when, if he were being honest, he had never really had one?

He didn't know how to answer question five.

Six wanted to know if he wanted to get away from his partners after sex, if he felt shame or remorse. *Hmmm...* He certainly had made no habit of sticking around to cuddle with his tricks when he went home with them or hooked up with one at the baths. But did he feel shame? Remorse? That was pretty strong language. He had always thought of himself as this happy-go-lucky horndog, no regrets, lots of sex.

But if that was the case, why was he seeing Camille? Why was he so miserable? Why did he feel that something was missing from his life?

And don't you dare even think that that missing thing is love. Don't you dare.

Bobby guessed he would give a qualified yes to number six. He glanced down and saw he was halfway through the questions.

Number seven asked if his sex life had caused him legal problems. *Not officially. Not on record. The case was dismissed, and I had an attorney make sure the record was expunged.* But while the official record may not exist, Bobby's memory had not been expunged of that summer evening in the men's room along the gay beach, where he had briefly sucked the cock of a cute dark-haired guy about his age, one he had later seen in a Sondheim musical at the Athenaeum. He recalled how hinky that encounter had felt, how there were too many people standing around watching. With a grin, he had stood up from his work and said to the guy, "Sorry, but this is a little too public even for me."

He had hurried out of the restroom, thinking there was no harm done. He had been crossing the grassy field to get to the underpass that would take him to Bryn Mawr Avenue when he heard the alarming quick burst of sound, the *whoop* of a police siren as the cruiser crossed the grass and rolled up behind him. Bobby remembered how his heart had just about stopped, how he had a quick moment of desperate denial as the car stopped right behind him, and a voice cautioned him to stay where he was.

The handcuffs, the fingerprinting, the mug shots, and the three hours spent in a jail cell all were etched indelibly into his memory, regardless of whether or not there still existed a legal record of his transgression.

So, another yes.

Question eight asked him if his sex life interfered with his morals or his "spiritual journey." Bobby quickly thought he could answer "no" to that question. But then he thought of the term "spiritual journey" and wondered about that. Did the phone call telling him of his father's death start the clock ticking on his own spiritual journey? Was he on a journey right this very minute?

Bobby looked out the window and laughed. An older man with a bald pate and bifocals turned in his seat to look at him. Bobby wondered if he pegged Bobby immediately as a sex addict, or just your garden-variety loon who enjoyed taking a spin courtesy of the Chicago Transit Authority.

Question nine asked him about the threat of disease. Bobby chuckled again, more softly this time. *Threat? Let's see, I've had the clap half a dozen times; I am taking daily medication (Valtrex) to ward off the herpes I was diagnosed with when I was twenty-seven; I have gone through the series of injections to cure syphilis a couple of times, and I have had bacterial parasites back there more times than I can count. So yes, I guess my sex life has posed the "threat" of disease.* Somehow—Bobby didn't know how—he had made it through all of this without becoming HIV positive.

He sometimes wondered if he was immune to that particular scourge of the gay community. Wasn't that possible? Wasn't there some literature to that effect? If anyone should be HIV positive, it was Bobby. His condom compliance was dedicated, but far from 100 percent.

Question ten again made him want to fling the pamphlet to the floor and stomp on it. It asked him if his pursuit of sex had ever made him feel hopeless, alienated, or suicidal. *Do I really want to think about that? Do I really want to sit here on the L and wallow in self-pity about how lonely and isolated I sometimes feel? Does it ever cross my mind that if I did jump off a bridge or OD'd on Ambien, no one would care?*

Bobby didn't want to ponder those questions too long, for fear they would drag him into a black pool of depression from which he'd find it hard—if not impossible—to emerge.

So he simply answered *yes* to that one, too, and moved on.

The next-to-the-last question wondered if Bobby's fantasies ever caused him problems, even if he didn't act on them. He smiled to himself. There had hardly been a fantasy that had crossed the seedy, pornographic theater of his mind that he hadn't, at some point, brought to vivid Technicolor life. *So, Mr. Smartass Sex Addicts Anonymous, the answer to that question is no.*

Finally, the questionnaire concluded with asking Bobby about avoiding sexual activity compulsively. If he had a fear of intimacy…

Well, hell no.

Bobby looked for how to score himself but was disappointed to find there were no guidelines, like "If you answered six or more questions with a yes, you are a sex addict. If you answered at least four with a yes, you are a horndog. Three or fewer, then you are a nun."

No, the booklet just "scored" responses by encouraging the reader to seek more help, through the Sex Addicts Anonymous's website, reading materials, or group meetings, if any of the answers to the questions made the quiz taker "uncomfortable."

Bobby was beyond uncomfortable.

In fact now, as he looked up from the brochure, he found he had been so absorbed in the questionnaire he had completely lost all sense of time and place.

He was at Howard Street, at least a dozen stops past where he should have gotten off at Belmont.

The canned announcement informed him he had reached the end of the line.

Yeah, tell me about it.

Bobby got off the train, thinking how he needed to cross to the other side to catch a southbound train, and if he should never see Camille again, or if he should call her tomorrow and schedule another appointment just as soon as she could squeeze him in.

He stopped on the bridge above the train tracks, pulled out his phone, and located Camille among his contacts. He pressed the button that would connect him to her.

He got her answering machine.

"Hello, Camille? It's Bobby Nelson. Is there any way you can fit me in tomorrow? Let me know."

He hung up and made his way down the stairs. A southbound train was just rumbling into the station.

It would take him away from the end of the line.

Chapter Nine

Bobby stood outside the Unitarian Church in Evanston. The beginning of April had brought with it chilly temperatures, a fine, misty drizzle, and completely negated the promise of spring. Bobby shivered in his leather jacket, looking up at the gray fieldstone edifice of the church.

Do you really want to be here? There's still time to turn away, walk the few blocks to the Main Street L stop, and head south and home. No one is forcing you to do this.

Except someone was, Bobby realized. Himself. After taking that quiz and a tear-filled session with Camille two days ago, he knew he needed to seek help. Knew that his preoccupation with sex was more than just horniness, knew it was controlling him instead of the other way around.

He knew too that all of this "acting out," as the literature described it, was most likely a substitute, a smoke screen for something missing in his life.

He couldn't hide from his feelings forever. Couldn't run from the thing he wanted most—whatever that thing was.

The meeting was supposed to start at seven, and Bobby had arrived at a quarter after. Typical. And now, he delayed going in even more by standing outside in the cold, hemming and hawing.

Just go in. Find the basement recreation room.

He watched a couple of people hurry by, their heads bowed, shoulders hunched against the drizzle and the cold. Bobby sighed and, finally, forced himself to put one foot in front of the other, feeling like he was taking steps toward a gallows or gas chamber.

He chuckled grimly—would he come out of this alive?

He heard voices as he approached the room. Low male voices. Camille had helped him find a couple of groups that were specifically for gay men, one in the Boystown area where Bobby lived (too close to home, too likely to run into someone he knew) and this one, in the North Shore suburb of Evanston.

Bobby opened the door to the room, wincing when it squeaked. The voices stopped, and about a dozen male heads turned to look at him, making Bobby think of how it felt when he entered a bar. The room, though, was nothing like a bar. It looked more, oddly enough, like a room for a church social or a Bible-study group. Bobby supposed the space was used for just such purposes, but it seemed an odd backdrop for a bunch of perverts, excuse me, sex addicts. There was an urn of coffee set up on a long table and a couple of paper plates filled with store-bought cookies. The men sat around another long folding table, and Bobby noted many of them had the

SAA handbook, what Camille called the twelve-step bible.

The men stared. Fresh meat.

One of them, a short, mousy-haired fellow who put Bobby in mind of the actor Steve Buscemi, stood up. "Welcome. Come on in and find a seat."

Bobby took a seat adjacent to the table they were gathered around, but not at it. Several of the men smiled at him.

"First time?" the Buscemi look-alike asked.

"Oh, honey," Bobby said, "you don't know how many years it's been since I've been asked *that* question."

This made all of the men at the table laugh and relaxed Bobby enough to at least not feel like he was in immediate danger of throwing up.

"Okay. Most of the guys who come here for the first time want to just observe. Would that be your plan too?"

Bobby nodded, feeling his face go hot for reasons he couldn't quite put his finger on. "Yeah. Sorry I'm late. The L…"

The men went back to their discussion. Bobby wanted to listen, but it was hard, what with the blood roaring in his ears, his breath coming more quickly, and his overwhelming urge to simply flee.

He stared down at the floor in an attempt to calm himself, but also because he didn't want to make eye contact with anyone. He listened as one of the men spoke, his deep voice almost hypnotic.

"I acted out again last week."

There were murmurs, Bobby supposed meant to be comforting, around the table.

"I told myself I would stay offline. I even canceled my membership to all the cruising sites. But I was just on my computer, you know, checking email, when I got an instant message from this guy I knew from, of all places, Facebook.

"We had hooked up a couple of times in the distant past. He was a good bottom, you know?" The guy laughed.

"He asked if he could come over, and it was all over for me. That was all it took. What am I supposed to do? Chuck my computer out the window?"

What did this mean, Bobby wondered. Were these guys feeling guilty simply because they were having sex? That didn't seem right to him. Sex was normal, wasn't it? A simple biological human urge.

Another man asked the first if there were other times after the Facebook friend had come over.

Silence. Then the first man sheepishly admitted there had been more times. In fact, there had been a dozen other times, over the space of two days. And in that time, he had used too. "My good friend Tina came by, and she made me throw all my good intentions right out the door."

Bobby looked up to see "Buscemi" nodding. "That bitch has a way of doing that. Crystal meth works on our brains, as many of you know, and it just rips away who we are, just making us these big, empty holes needing to be filled—at any cost."

The men around the table nodded, and Bobby wanted to point out that the guy who was doing the main talking was a top, but then thought his humor wouldn't be appreciated.

Bobby had never used crystal, or Tina, but many of his fuck buddies had. It made them sweaty and insatiable, fun for an hour or so, but these guys, when they were "spun" as they called it, wanted to go on for hours and hours, sometimes days. As much as Bobby liked sex, he couldn't keep up that kind of pace, and so he now avoided the meth heads and the coke whores. They actually had too much stamina for him. And he didn't want to join them because he feared what he would do if he lost what little control over his body and libido he currently had.

Bobby sat back in the chair, accepting that nothing more would be expected of him this time than to listen. And he did—to stories from a chronic masturbator, whose penis was now scarred from so much self-abuse, the skin having been rubbed off more times than he could count; from the married man who was scared to be there, whose wife had encouraged him to come, not because of his sexual compulsivity, but because she thought the group would be a cure for his homosexuality; from a guy who frequented Steamworks, the baths on Halsted, so frequently that the entire staff knew him by name and who was so in debt to credit cards upon which he had charged rooms that he was facing bankruptcy. Really.

Bobby wondered if he was actually like these men. Maybe he did pass the quiz with flying colors, but was he really that out of control?

It was then he noticed a familiar face around the table. He hadn't noticed him at first because his back was to Bobby, but when he turned to speak to the guy sitting next to him, it all came back.

That's the guy from Sidetrack. The one who rebuffed me. What was his name? Alan? No. Adam? No. Aaron, that was it, Aaron. Bobby took in the shaved head, the salt-and-pepper stubble, the intensity of his dark eyes even from Bobby's vantage point. *So is that why he didn't want to hook up with me that afternoon, because he's trying to stay "clean?" Where's the fun in that?*

Bobby studied Aaron, thinking it was such a waste. Here was this hot man (Bobby had not forgotten the surprisingly large basket, the lean, tight body), and he was frittering away his time at a group meant to thwart sexual behavior. It wasn't right. The two of them should have been hooking up, enjoying the pleasures of each other's flesh, rather than sitting around a folding table in some church basement.

Maybe Camille had been wrong in suggesting this. Maybe he had been wrong in thinking it was for him.

Politely, Bobby sat and listened to the rest of the meeting, to the heartaches, the failures, and the triumphs, but was so focused on getting away from these men, this place, that he heard little detail of what was said. At the conclusion of the meeting, he did close his eyes as the men recited what Bobby had come to learn was called the Serenity Prayer.

"God grant me the serenity to accept the things I cannot change, the courage to change the things I can, and the wisdom to know the difference."

Bobby wondered if he could ever change himself, or if his personality, his traits, obsessive or otherwise, were simply too ingrained to entertain transformation. If he couldn't change, what the hell was he doing here?

He had stood, as all the other men had, when they recited the prayer, but had not joined their circle of clasped hands.

Then the leader said something Bobby hadn't heard of in his research about the group.

"We don't always do this," he said, "but I think it's good to reiterate 'The Promises' every so often, to remind us what's in store for us. To give us hope. Aaron, why don't you recite them?"

Bobby watched as Aaron thumbed through his book.

"Page eighty-three," the Steve Buscemi look-alike urged.

"Right." Aaron found the page, cleared his throat, and began reading from the handbook.

"If we are painstaking about this phase of our development, we will be amazed before we are halfway through.

1. We are going to know a new freedom and a new happiness.

2. We will not regret the past, nor wish to shut the door on it.

3. We will comprehend the word serenity.

4. And we will know peace.

5. No matter how far down the scale we have gone, we will see how our experience can benefit others.

6. That feeling of uselessness and self-pity will disappear.

7. We will lose interest in selfish things and gain interest in our fellows.

8. Self-seeking will slip away.

9. Our whole attitude and outlook upon life will change.

10. Fear of people and of economic insecurity will leave us.

11. We will intuitively know how to handle situations which used to baffle us.

12. We will suddenly realize that God is doing for us what we could not do for ourselves.

Are these extravagant promises? We think not. They are being fulfilled among us—sometimes quickly, sometimes slowly. They will always materialize if we work for them."

The men were silent, and Bobby, for some peculiar reason or perhaps some reason he fought to *not* consider, felt the heat of tears rise to his eyes and a lump to his throat as he heard Aaron voice these promises.

He realized they were all things he wanted—and didn't have. He wondered if he ever could.

No.

He had been here long enough, tormented himself enough, and he was not about to let this little group of oh-so-caring souls see him cry. He didn't think he could bear their sympathy and concern.

He didn't make a fuss. He didn't say anything. He didn't dash from the room as if someone had yelled "Fire!" No. He simply moved slowly, quietly, eyes on the prize of the exit door, and left.

Outside, the cold air, which had chilled him before the meeting, now felt good, bracing. Bobby gulped in lungfuls of it, as though he had been forced deep down under water.

He looked around. While he was out here, darkness had drawn its silent curtain across the world. Rain pattered down. For some reason, maybe because he was in Evanston and the Rogers Park neighborhood where Caden and Kevin lived was only a couple of miles away, he thought of his old friend, wondered what he would say if he could see what Bobby had gotten himself into tonight.

Caden. How he wished he could talk to him. His old best friend would surely understand and have some words of wisdom and encouragement for him. But he had burned that bridge, plowed that trail asunder. Betrayal did not make for good friendships. Bobby shook his head.

But when he found out Dad died, he did call me. He called me. Hope?

Bobby's thoughts were interrupted as he heard the door opening behind him, deep voices, the smell of cigarettes being lit. He looked over his shoulder to see the group had emerged. They laughed and chatted with one another, making Bobby feel even more isolated.

They all looked so normal. If they were coming out of a Catholic church, Bobby mused, they probably would have been mistaken for the Knights of Columbus. Now, Bobby wondered if anyone passing by would even begin to guess at what kind of meeting the men were leaving.

Bobby started off in the direction of the L station at Main Street. The rain was coming down harder, and he didn't want someone trying to catch up with him, to talk to him in soothing and sympathetic tones.

Didn't want it? Or couldn't bear it?

Bobby wasn't sure as he picked up his pace, head down against the rain.

"Hey! Wait up."

For a second Bobby considered breaking into a run, but somehow was unable to transfer the notion from his brain to his legs. He stopped, feeling like maybe he should put his hands in the air, in a kind of surrender.

He felt a hand on his shoulder and turned to see Aaron standing there, the water dripping down his face. He spat against it and then smiled at Bobby. "We've met before."

"At Sidetrack." Bobby nodded.

They stared at one another. Bobby gave an involuntary shiver.

"There's a Starbucks a block west of here. Wanna go get a cup of coffee? My treat," Aaron said.

Bobby started running through his catalog of excuses, built up over the years to get away from men, but nothing suitable would emerge. Besides, a part of him was pulling him toward this encounter with Aaron. Whether he was unavailable or not, the man was hot, even in this icy rain. So he simply said, "Sure. Why not?"

*

They spent a long time *not* talking about where they had just been. They had exchanged occupations. Aaron was an English teacher at a private school in the Kenilworth suburb. "I teach rich kids how to write their college entrance essays," he quipped.

Bobby wondered why he was meeting all these men who taught English all of a sudden.

They told each other what their favorite TV shows were. Both agreed on *Mad Men*, but Bobby said he found *Project Runway* a guilty pleasure, and Aaron confessed a passion for *Breaking Bad*.

"Although, just to put it out there, I never do that stuff."

He referred to the drug the show revolved around—crystal meth.

They talked about where they lived. Aaron had a small house in the Rogers Park neighborhood, just south of them, west of Clark. "It's a typical Chicago bungalow, and I've lived there for more than fifteen years. I love it."

They discussed political leanings. Both, predictably, were liberal, left-leaning Democrats. They even discussed religion. Aaron confessed he had been raised Catholic but no longer felt welcome in that church. "Not with the church's official stance against our kind," he said. In spite of his falling away from the church in which he had been brought up, Aaron told Bobby that he considered himself a "deeply spiritual person."

Bobby said, "I'm not religious at all. Maybe it's because if I was a believer, I'd be worried about burning in hell for all eternity. I'd get that on fornication alone."

It wasn't until after two cups of coffee each and a shared slice of lemon pound cake that Aaron finally brought up the meeting.

"So—not to pry or anything, but what brought you to the meeting tonight?"

Bobby thought a lot about the question—about the countless hookups, the almost all-consuming need for sex, engaging in it even as he was telling himself he didn't want it, about the sexual connections with men he never even felt attracted to. He considered telling him that his medical record would reveal numerous sexually transmitted infections. He could have told him about how fulfilling his fantasy of being the bottom in a gang bang with a dozen men had not been everything he had dreamed of. In fact, after the fourth guy, he was sore and bored and, at the end of it all, he took home an anal parasite and a case of syphilis. He wondered how Aaron would take it if he told him how he had destroyed his relationship with his best friend, his only friend, by trying to steal his boyfriend.

"My therapist suggested it." Bobby took a sip of coffee and regarded Aaron over the rim of the cup. He noticed that the man had dark eyes, like his, but Aaron's were flecked with gold, which made his stare intense and, Bobby couldn't deny it, sexy.

Aaron smiled, took a drink of his coffee, and waited.

Bobby laughed. "You're wondering *why* my therapist suggested it."

Aaron put up his hands. "Well, yeah, but as I said, I don't want to pry. We can talk about something else if you want."

"No. She just thought the group might be good for some of my issues. You know, everyone is there for the same thing: sexual compulsion, right?"

"Yeah." Aaron, for once, did not meet Bobby's gaze.

"So can I ask about you?"

"Come to the group often enough, and you'll get my story. In lurid detail."

Bobby nodded. "Okay."

Aaron slid back his chair and crossed his legs. "I started going three years ago." Aaron sighed. "I used to do a lot of coke. My favorite thing to do was get an eight-ball, drag out a big stack of bareback porn DVDs, and alternate watching them with doing lines and cruising online sites for hookups. I would have guys come over all night long, and by the end of the night, I have to tell you, I wasn't too particular." He smiled, but the warmth was absent from his eyes. "As long as they had a hard dick, they were *pretty enough*." Aaron stood suddenly. "I'm gonna grab a refill. You want anything?"

"God, no. I'll never sleep." Bobby watched him at the counter, laughing easily with the female barista, a buxom redhead, in spite of what he had just confessed. Bobby had to admit he admired the confident way Aaron walked and stood, the way his ass rode high, filling out his jeans nicely.

When Aaron sat back down, he resumed his tale, still not really looking at Bobby throughout much of it. "I might have continued going on like this until I got too old for it, or the coke stopped my heart, but one night, I met this guy online, invited him over, and he turned out to be a real nut. Remember I told you I live in my own house? So I am pretty much alone.

"Well, this guy wasn't gay. His modus operandi was to cruise the sites to see if he could figure out who might have a little money; then he would assault and rob them."

"God. I'm sorry. He did that to you?"

Aaron nodded. "I should have known something was up when he got there. But I was too coked-up to see the red flags. All I could see was this hot Latino thug type, and that just fueled my fantasies. But I didn't get it when he didn't want me to touch him. I still didn't get it when he wouldn't take off any clothes. And I should have sent him packing when he pulled out his cell and said he had a couple buddies who might be interested in coming over. Would I like to get tag teamed?

"But I didn't catch on to the numerous red flags the universe threw my way. All I could think about was sex.

"He invited his buddies over all right. Three of them." Aaron's eyes went a little blurry as he remembered, and Bobby wondered if he was going to have to comfort a crying man, right here in Starbucks.

"They, under the pretense of hot sex, tied me up on my bed. Have you ever heard the phrase 'too stupid to live'?"

Bobby nodded.

"That was me. All I could think about was getting fucked, when it should have been obvious these guys were not at all interested in sex.

"Long story short—they didn't just rob me, they tortured me for over three hours. They burned me with cigarettes, one of them pissed on me, they took turns punching me and kicking me. One of them twisted my balls so hard, I screamed." Aaron's gaze went somewhere else, and Bobby wondered what he was seeing. Aaron continued.

"But no one heard.

"They finally rifled through the whole house, took anything portable enough to sell, including my laptop, and any cash I had laying around, and left."

Bobby sighed and shook his head. "Wow. I am so sorry, man. I guess an experience like that would put anyone off sex."

Aaron grinned. "No, you don't get it. I wasn't so much put off. What happened to me wasn't sex, or even anything close to it. I got that. But the experience made me step back and consider my attitude about sex, about what mattered, what was important.

"It made me see the endless hookups weren't giving me any pleasure, not really. Not beyond the momentary zap of an empty orgasm. It made me see I wanted more.

"But habits like that die hard. It took a couple more empty encounters and a lot of sleepless nights for me to finally get to a point where I realized I had a problem. And then another month before I had the nerve to go to SAA."

"And then what? It was like magic? A switch was flipped?" *Oh, please say yes.*

Aaron laughed. "Nah, man. It doesn't work that way. You know what the first step is? Of the Twelve Steps? I can't quote directly, but it's something about admitting we're powerless and that our lives are—what's the word?—unmanageable. Man, that rang so true for me. By the time I stepped into the room for that first meeting, I knew I had a problem, but that first step laid it out so clearly for me. You know?"

Bobby did know. Camille had quoted that first step to him, and while he hadn't agreed out loud with her, he had recognized himself immediately.

Aaron went on. "But I slipped up, messed up, half a dozen times before I got somewhat on the right path." He sighed. "I recognize we're not perfect beings. We're all human, but that is no excuse not to strive to be something better, to try to make our lives more fulfilling and whole." His dark eyes met Bobby's. "Sorry. I didn't mean to preach at you. I guess my point was to answer your question, and the answer is no, it was not like a switch being flipped. It wasn't that easy. It took me a long time to examine my life, to really take stock, before I could even begin making any real progress. I'd take two steps forward one back, over and over again." He shrugged. "Old habits die hard. And old tricks don't just go away. And the temptation to find new tricks is way too easy, as I'm sure you know." He winked at Bobby, and Bobby could feel his face heat up as he recalled what Aaron had witnessed in the men's room at Sidetrack.

Aaron put a hand on Bobby's knee. Bobby looked down at the hand, then back up at Aaron, who was smiling. He noticed then that Aaron's smile was kind of lopsided, yet utterly charming. He had a little gap in his front teeth that made him even sexier, rather than detracting from his manly good looks. "Bobby, you're at the start of a journey. It's normal to be afraid, to maybe even think you're better off *not* hitting that trail but staying right where you are. Inertia can have a powerful hold on us. But we both know you showed up at that meeting for a reason, and you didn't make the decision to come lightly."

Bobby felt an almost irresistible urge to kiss the man, right here in this clean, well-lighted place. He could even imagine it, how his lips would feel against his own, the moment when his mouth would yield and open to admit Bobby's tongue. He could taste the coffee in Aaron's mouth, the smoky warmth, the essence of *him.*

Weakly, he forced himself to speak, but his words came out soft, uncertain. "So where are you? Do you just never have sex again? I mean, if I were going to AA, wouldn't that be the goal? Just not to have another drink—ever? Because, man, I don't know if I can sentence myself to a life of no sex." He laughed, tried to imagine it, could not.

Aaron pulled his hand away, sat back. Bobby wanted to snatch the hand back; wanted, really, to ask Aaron to come home with him. He longed to see what was under that T-shirt and more: what was under those jeans.

But he knew that to make such a proposition would be wrong.

Wouldn't it?

Aaron said, "No! No. I couldn't do without sex either. Right now, though, my only sex parties are with Mr. Thumb and his four buddies, but that's okay. Because I want to find sex and love in one package, and I think that's worth waiting for. And even if it's not, I might be able to settle for affection, companionship, and"—he wiggled his eyebrows—"hot fuckin'."

Bobby felt a jump in his crotch simply from hearing Aaron utter the word fuck.

"It's about turning away from what we know is bad for us. I don't believe sex in and of itself is bad—God no—I think God put it in place for us to enjoy, to take pleasure from, to find joy in. Sex is a good thing! We're not saying it's not, not at all. But we are saying that maybe sometimes we get off on the wrong course when it comes to sex, that maybe we abuse it, rather than simply using it as a part of a natural life."

"I get it. I think."

"No, you don't. And it will be a while before you do."

"In the meantime"—Bobby leaned forward to whisper—"you wanna come home and fool around?"

Aaron shook his head, smiling. "Case in point. You haven't heard a word I've said, have you?"

"Well, I feel affection for you—already. Didn't you say you'd settle for that?"

"And I for you, Mr. Nelson. And a few years ago, I would have been on you like nobody's business, but now I think you'd be worth waiting for. How's that?"

"Disappointing."

"Yeah, well." Aaron finished his coffee, got up, and threw the paper cup in a recycling bin. When he returned to the table, he said, "Have you thought about a mentor?"

"No. What's that?" he asked, although he knew.

"Someone to help you along on the journey. Not really a navigator, but someone to help you find your own way."

Bobby thought he knew where this was leading. "So would you be mine?"

"Your what? Valentine?"

"Yeah...my Valentine. But remember, I expect my Valentines to put out."

"You don't give up, do you, Blanche?"

Bobby caught the reference and chuckled. "My mentor. If you think I need one, would you be mine?"

Aaron rubbed the fur on his chin, moved back so he was balanced on the chair on two legs, then slammed back down. "No."

Bobby let out a surprised laugh. "Why not?"

"I'll let you think about that." Aaron turned his hairy arm so he could grab a quick look at his watch. "It's getting late, and I, at least, have work in the morning. Wanna grab the purple line south together?"

"No. I think I'll stay here a little longer."

"Okay. See you at the next meeting?"

"Yeah, sure."

Bobby sat, feeling wistful, sad, hopeful. He knew he wanted to stay back simply so he could watch Aaron walk away.

Why didn't he want to be Bobby's mentor?

Chapter Ten

Bobby got home to his condo feeling confused, lost. He no longer knew where his place in the world was. Once upon a time, after an evening out, it would be an automatic given that he would get online or bring up Grindr or Scruff on his phone and find someone with whom he could find a few minutes' oblivion. Now it seemed there were forces beyond his libido pulling at him, questioning him. The effort to go online just seemed like too much.

He turned the TV on and scrolled dispiritedly through the channels. He thought about watching *RuPaul's Drag Race* or that Douglas Sirk chestnut, *Imitation of Life*, on Turner Classic Movies, but he knew his mind couldn't settle enough to concentrate even on mindless fare like RuPaul or a well-worn tearjerker like *Imitation of Life*.

He went to the kitchen, pulled out ice, cranberry juice cocktail, and vodka and mixed himself a drink in one of his jumbo tumblers. Hey, it would help him sleep.

He took the drink to the living room, sat on his leather couch, and kicked off his shoes. He pulled his phone from his pocket and switched off the button that silenced it. He always did that when he was out with someone. He liked giving a man his full attention when he was with him. He alternately felt sorry for or held in contempt other couples he saw out these days (straight and gay both), who were busy on their smartphones, rather than busy with the person right there before them, across the dinner table.

Didn't they realize what they had?

He saw, though, when he glanced down at the screen, that his phone being silenced had caused him to miss two calls. One was from his mother, and the other was also from a Seattle number. He didn't recognize the number, but there weren't many people it could be tied to, because his mother and his sister were pretty much the only numbers he had in his contacts list.

Wade? Could Wade have called him? *I thought the deal was to wait until I found myself for me to call him.*

To verify that the call was indeed from Wade, Bobby pulled out his wallet and extracted Wade's card.

The number matched.

Second thoughts? Maybe he realizes what he missed. Bobby grinned.

Bobby's first impulse was, naturally, to call the handsome man. But a part of him quickly put the kibosh on that idea, knowing he had a mother in need.

He pressed the button that would return her call, checking his watch and then reminding himself it was two hours earlier in Seattle.

"Bobby?"

"Yeah, Ma, it's me. How are you?"

His mother blew out a sigh. "Ah, well, you know, this is taking some getting used to. Whoever coined the term, 'merry widow' was full of it. It just seems so weird rattling around the place by myself. I get up in the morning and expect to find him next to me, or listen to see if he's in the bathroom." She snorted out a brief burst of laughter. "You know what I did yesterday morning?"

"What?"

"I got up and made poached eggs...for two." She laughed again. "Your mother is going off her rocker."

"Mom, that's perfectly understandable. It'll take time. Is Dawn helping you out? Does she come by? Bring the kids over?"

"Almost every day." His mother lowered her voice to a whisper, even though Bobby was pretty sure she was alone. "And it's driving me nuts! Where did that girl get her ideas? Certainly not from me! I am sick to death of hearing about family values!"

They chuckled together.

"What did you do with the eggs?"

"I ate them!" She burst into laughter again, but Bobby could hear the near hysteria that was on the edge of the guffaw. "With your father gone, I have been consoling myself with food far too much. I may have lost a husband, but two new guys are staying at my place way too much these days."

Bobby was taken aback. "What? Who?"

"Oh, don't be that way. As if... I'm joking. I'm talking about Ben and Jerry. That duo has caused me to gain five pounds. I'm thinking of joining a gym. There's one that's right along the water, over in Fremont. It's close enough that I could walk on nice days."

Although Bobby couldn't imagine his mother in a gym, or even gym clothes, he said, "That might not be a bad idea. Get you out of the house. You might meet some new people too. Maybe take a spin class?"

"Yeah, yeah, I'll think about it."

They fell silent, and Bobby was about to ask if there was anything he could do for his mom when she cut in, saying abruptly, "I'm so damn alone."

"I know. I know, sweetheart." Bobby wished he could reach through the phone and stroke his mother's face and tuck her hair behind her ears. "You want me to come back? I could be on a plane this weekend."

"No, dear. You have a life out there in Chicago. A job. Responsibilities. I can't expect you to hop on a plane just to be by your mother's self-pitying side."

"Oh, Mom, it's not like that." *Besides, I am being a little selfish—I could see Wade again.*

"No, Robert. I need to learn a little independence, even if it's just to get away from that insufferable sister of yours. I was thinking about maybe getting a job."

"A job? You?" Bobby failed to keep the surprise—and alarm—out of his voice. His mother had never worked, although she had once come close, shortly after graduating, to teaching a class of third graders. But her impending marriage to his father made her decide against it.

"Yes, me. I'm not that old. I do have a college degree, and maybe I could take a few classes, get my teaching certificate renewed. I could sub at first, see if I liked it."

"You have been giving this some thought, haven't you?"

"Bobby, no one takes an interest in our lives as much as ourselves. I have to get my butt out of the house if I'm lonely here. No one's going to do it for me."

"I love you, Mom."

She didn't say anything for a moment or two, and Bobby wondered if what he had said was not what she had been expecting. The Nelsons, after all, were not a particularly demonstrative family. "Well, I love you, too, Bobby."

They talked some more—about teaching, about the chill and rain in Seattle, about Bobby's job, but he had heard little more beyond the words, "I love you."

He at least had a mother who loved him. And that was no small thing.

When they hung up, Bobby reiterated his offer to come back out west.

"As much as I would love to have you here, I'm going to say let's not have all the fun so close together. No, why don't you wait until August or September when it's beautiful out here?"

They both agreed that sounded like a plan and hung up.

Bobby glanced down at his phone, wondering if it was too late to return Wade's call. *Don't be stupid. It's only eight o'clock out there.* Wade hadn't left a message. Maybe he didn't want him to call back.

Again, don't be stupid. He called you. So he must want to talk to you.

Bobby entered Wade into his contacts. And called him back.

The phone on the other end rang three times, and Bobby expected it to go to voice mail. He was taken by surprise when he heard Wade's deep voice answer the phone, pleased that he had used Bobby's name. That must mean he had entered Bobby's number into his contacts.

"Bobby? How are you? I just got in. I teach an evening class tonight."

It made Bobby feel warm inside to hear Wade's voice. He could picture his handsome, chiseled face on the other end, his dark eyes. "I'm good, just trying to ease back into life here." He debated about whether he should tell Wade what had really been going on with him, the therapy and the initial visit to Sex Addicts Anonymous. In the end, he decided it would be way too much information. "How are things with you? I was kind of surprised to see you called."

"Things are good, but something came up that made me think of you, and I wanted to run an idea by you."

"Oh?"

"Yeah, my best friend, a woman who teaches French here in Seattle, originally came from Chicago. All her family is back there. Anyway, long story short, she told me she's planning on going back in July and asked if I wanted to come along."

Bobby could feel his face heating up with anticipation and maybe something a little akin to joy.

"And you said?"

"Well, I've never been to Chicago, but I always wanted to go. I'm a bit of an architecture buff, and Chicago, probably more than any other American city, has all this amazing architecture, much of which, really, was built all at once."

"After the big fire," Bobby said.

"Right. So, I know the Architecture Foundation does this amazing riverboat cruise."

"Yeah, it *is* great. The company I work for took a bunch of us on it last summer for a department outing. A lot of history here."

"Plus, there's so much to see—Millennium Park, the Art Institute, the Field Museum, Navy Pier." Wade took a breath, and Bobby was beginning to wonder why he was being consulted at all about this obvious tourist trek. He was not, after all, the triple A. "And you."

Bobby was so sure Wade would never get to that last point that he almost didn't hear it. But he did. And he smiled.

"Oh yeah, me. There is that." Bobby laughed.

"Well, of course I'd like to see you, which is why I'm calling."

God, please say you need a place to stay. Please say it. Bobby stared out the window at the night, his mind already filling up with fantasies about having Wade right here under his roof, doing things like showering in his bathroom. Bobby imagined the steamy room and how he could slip in naked and—

"I just wanted to be sure you're going to be in town the first week in July. Sabine, that's my friend, wants to come for the Fourth. I'd hate to come all the way out there and miss out on seeing you."

"Do you need a place to stay?" Bobby, single-minded, blurted.

"What? No, no I don't think so. Sabine's parents have a big house up in—what was the suburb? Something ritzy—I can't remember."

"Lake Forest? Kenilworth? Winnetka?"

"Winnetka sounds right, but not quite."

"Wilmette?"

"That's it! Anyway, they have a big old house near Lake Michigan, and she said there's plenty of room. They also have a home up at a place called Lake Geneva in Wisconsin, and she said we could go up there for a few days too."

"Sounds like you're all set, then." Bobby's spirits took a nosedive. Why was he getting all excited, anyway? He hardly knew the guy. Yes, they had gone to high school together, and yes, they had connected (even shared a kiss) on his recent trip back home, but really, the amount of time the two of them had spent together had been short, very short. Dispiritedly, he asked, "So what were you thinking? Maybe we could get together for dinner while you're here?"

"Well, yeah. Sure. But maybe spend a little more time together than *that*. I was thinking that when Sabine went up to Lake Geneva with her family, I could bow out and maybe hang with you. If you're up for it, you could show me around. Take me to that Boystown that I've read about."

Bobby grinned. "Oh, I could be a world-class guide for that part of town, that's for sure." Bobby did not want to stick his foot in his mouth by offering his place up again, so he stayed quiet on that score. "I can show you lots of places off the beaten path here in town, not all of them gay. But Chicago is a great food city, and I could take you to some real hidden gems."

"That sounds great. So you think you'll be there? I mean, I don't expect you to be there if something comes up, of course, but just wondering—as it stands now."

Bobby thought about the summer stretching out before him and how, really, he didn't have a single thing planned.

"Yeah. I think there's a very good chance I'll be here." He wanted to pinch himself, bite his lip, pull his hair, to prevent himself from saying the words, but they tumbled out anyway: "And you know you can stay here. I live right on Lake Shore Drive." *Shit. Why couldn't you keep your mouth shut?* Bobby slammed his hand into the bed, cursing his lack of self-control, even in this small way.

"Well, thanks, Bobby. I'll think about that. We don't have to make any decisions right now."

"No, you're right. July is still a few months away." Bobby moved to the window, looked down at the drive, alive with headlights moving north and south. He felt isolated, wondering what he should say next.

Wade made it easy for him. "Well, bud, I need to get moving here. I have a shitload of compositions to read and grade before I go to bed tonight. I just wanted to touch base with you and make sure you're going to be in town when I get there. How lucky am I? I'm really glad you'll be in town, Bobby. And I'm really happy I got to hear your voice tonight."

Bobby felt like his emotions, with this short and simple phone call, were on a roller coaster. Right now, he was riding high.

"The feeling is mutual, Wade. I'll look forward to seeing you, spending more time together." Before hanging up, Bobby gave Wade his email and Wade returned the favor.

Bobby hung up the phone, feeling he had something to look forward to.

*

His mother handed him a picnic basket. "There's my world-famous ham salad in there, on marble rye. Potato salad, dill pickles, a nice bottle of chilled Riesling, and apple turnovers for dessert."

"You didn't have to do this."

"Of course, I did!" His mom laughed. "How often does a mother get to see her son go off on his first date?" She pushed him gently. "You better get going. You don't want to keep him waiting."

Bobby started away from her and cast a glance back at his mother over his shoulder.

"There's cutlery, napkins, plates, and glasses— everything you need—in the picnic basket. I even remembered a corkscrew! Now shoo!"

And just like that, his mom was gone, and Bobby found himself standing alongside the Chicago River. The picnic basket was on a park bench beside him, and if he looked west, he could see the docking station for the riverboat tours and, above that, traffic bustling by on Michigan Avenue. He admired the gothic presence of the Chicago Tribune tower rising up and the white elegance of the Wrigley Building, across Michigan Avenue. The newer skyscrapers, with their chrome and glass, had nothing on those two old grande dames.

The sun was up high. Noon? Its rays beat down on Bobby—summer hot, but they felt good as the cooler wind, rushing across the water, made for a very pleasant contrast.

It was quiet. Bobby had never seen the riverfront so empty, especially on a perfect summer day like this one. His gaze moved to the east, where he spied Navy Pier and its iconic Ferris wheel jutting out into the sparkling blue waters.

Maybe everyone is at the pier today.

"Maybe they are." Bobby jumped a little and turned to see Wade standing beside him. The man looked gorgeous, wearing a simple white tank that showed off the muscles in his shoulders, arms, and chest to good advantage, and a pair of navy blue cargo shorts. On his feet, of course, were the requisite flip-flops. Bobby noticed his feet, the well-manicured toenails and the little tufts of dark hair that crowned each toe.

"What?" Bobby asked, grinning. "Now you can read my mind? How did you know I was thinking everybody must be over at the Pier?"

"I can read your mind, sweetheart. I always could. Even back in high school, I knew what you were thinking. And, oh! The filth that went on in that teenage mind. Gave me fantasies for years." Wade chuckled. "Come on, give us a hug!"

And Bobby fell into his arms, reveling in the delicious sensation of being completely enveloped in Wade's strong arms. Off Wade's firm body came the scent of sandalwood and a slight undercurrent of sweat that Bobby found undeniably sexy. His cock stirred in his cargo shorts—camouflage for him. Wade stroked his back and slid his hand up under

Bobby's black T-shirt to rub his shoulder blades and trail his finger down Bobby's spine.

In spite of the heat, Bobby shivered. "God," he whispered in Wade's ear. "You're gonna make me come in my shorts."

Wade pulled away, dark eyes twinkling with mischief. "Not yet." He took Bobby's hand and led him silently along the path that ran parallel to the river, passing through the cool darkness of the tunnel beneath Lake Shore Drive, where he stopped, turned Bobby toward him, and kissed him deeply, their tongues dueling. When he moved away, Bobby was breathless, casting his gaze around to see if anyone had witnessed their passionate kiss.

But the area all around them remained sun-dappled and empty. Strange.

Wade took his hand again, and now they were finding a place in the grass that bordered the running/blading/walking/bike trail that ran along Lake Michigan. Bobby looked out at the boats moored along the waterfront, how they bobbed in the glimmering waters.

He saw not even one person aboard any of the boats.

There were no runners or bikers along the trail either. The grassy area all around them was deserted.

Bobby sat down with Wade in the grass, opening the picnic basket and pulling out first the bottle of wine. He handed it to Wade, along with the corkscrew. "It's strange, you know?"

"What?" Wade expertly pulled the wrapper from the top of the wine bottle and inserted the corkscrew and began removing the cork.

"There's no one around. Usually, on a day like this, that trail is a traffic jam of bikers, runners, and bladers. Yet, I don't see anyone."

Wade motioned for Bobby to hand him the wineglasses, and he poured each of them a glass. "That's because today is our day. No one else's." He smiled and held up his glass. "A toast. To our very first date."

They clinked glasses.

The wine tasted crisp, icy, as it coursed down Bobby's throat.

The next thing he knew, he was lying in Wade's arms, his head on his chest. It seemed as though the two of them had talked for hours. Indeed, the sky above them had grown gray, edging on dark, the water lit up brilliantly as the sun set behind them, below the skyscrapers to the west.

A gust of wind rose up from the water, bringing with it the smell of the lake, and Wade repositioned himself so he could kiss Bobby once more. Bobby watched as Wade's face came closer, blotting out the sky.

*

And Bobby awakened. Morning light was coming in through the blinds at his windows, and he sat up and stretched, feeling contented and happier than he thought a dream should have any right to make him.

He wandered over to his windows to open the blinds and gaze down on the day, which was much like the one in his dream, the water shimmering under a brilliant ball of orange. Across bustling Lake Shore Drive, the early morning runners and bikers were already out, crowding the trail.

Bobby stretched again, yawning. He felt he had not had such a satisfying slumber in years. Already, the images from his dream were fading, but not enough to prevent him from searching for Wade down below, somewhere along the water.

Chapter Eleven

"So it's going well for you?" Camille straightened her pencil skirt and crossed her legs, giving Bobby the full attention of her gaze.

"Two months sober now." Bobby smiled. "If you had told me, when I first walked in here, that I would go two months without sex, I would have said you were the one desperately in need of therapy." He laughed. "But the time has been good, and I have to honestly say: one, going without is beginning to get on my nerves, and two, the time away has been a revelation."

Camille cocked her head.

"Yeah. It's really made me stop and think about what's important to me and showed me how destructive my past behavior has been."

"So are you ready for more sex?"

"What? Right here? With you? On the floor? Sorry, hon, I don't swing that way. I thought you knew that."

Camille giggled. "I was hoping maybe you were bi. A fine specimen such as yourself really should not be denied to roughly half the population."

"You know what I think about bisexuality. Just one stop on the road to Gaytown."

"Well, I don't know about that. But getting back to my question, however ineptly put, do you think you're ready to try to be sexual again?" Camille hastily added, "With a man."

Bobby shook his head. "My mentor says I should have more time under my belt before I get under someone else's belt. Maybe even a year." Bobby yanked at his close-cropped hair and gave a little scream. "I don't know if I can stand it."

"There's always masturbation. You still do that, don't you?"

"I'm not dead. All that jizz has to go somewhere."

Camille rolled her eyes.

"Too much information?"

"There's no such thing as TMI in this office." Camille examined her long, French-manicured nails for a moment, then looked back at Bobby. "So remind me what step you're on now."

"Well, I've gone through, in a major way, three of the steps. I made that admission that I'm powerless. The next two are, as you know, all turning over what happens to your higher power." Bobby bowed his head for a moment, thinking of the meetings he had attended, his emotional breakthroughs, and his arguments with the group assembled that he didn't really hold much stock in God and organized religion. It was his mentor who made him see the light.

His mentor was a little guy, about five feet five, named Hank. He was about Bobby's age, maybe a few years older, with a rim of mouse-brown hair around a bald pate. He wore round wire-rimmed glasses and had a potbelly. Not someone the old Bobby would have looked at twice, but what he said on that particular day, when Bobby was struggling with the concept of a higher power, made him stand out. He said, "It's not about God, necessarily. And it's not about organized religion, though that works for some of us. It's just about finding that centered place which exists in all of us and all around us. Your higher power can be the universe and its mystery. It can be nature. It can be *you*, your instincts—what comes naturally to you. It's just about surrendering yourself to something greater—and letting go. Fighting with yourself is not the answer."

The words had resonated with Bobby, and, at the time, he had thanked Hank and said he understood, because he did. Something shifted within him during that meeting. It was as though he had laid down his shield and sword and thrown up a white flag. Instead of making things harder, that giving up, that laying his trouble in the hands of a higher power (whatever that might be to Bobby) made it easier.

"Hank, that's my mentor, really helped me that day. It's *why* he's my mentor. So, to answer your question, I guess I'm on my fourth step, which is all about making a moral inventory, and I've been working on that. With my history, it's gonna take some time."

Camille nodded.

"But Hank says it's okay to not complete the steps in order. He says that we have to do what works for us, and if another step is calling to us, we should listen."

"And is another step calling to you?"

"God, yes. Almost since the start, the eighth step."

"Which is?"

"You don't have these memorized? What kind of therapist are you?"

"A good one. And, no, I don't have them memorized, smartass. Shall I look it up or are you going to tell me?"

"The eighth step is about making a list of people we harmed—and making amends."

"You're talking about Caden?"

"You've been listening. I know I can be shallow, self-centered, vain to a fault—see I have been working on that moral inventory—but nothing has ever crushed my heart as much as losing my best friend. As we've talked about—many times—in here, I am totally to blame for what happened between us, but that doesn't lessen the pain of not having him in my life anymore." Bobby sighed, looked thoughtful for a moment, and continued. "I thought maybe, after a couple of meetings, I would make some new friends in the group, and I have—"

"Aaron?"

Bobby felt the heat of a blush rise to his cheeks. "Yeah, him and some others. But my point is, even with having some people I can really call friends, where sex doesn't come into the equation, I still miss Caden." He stared hard at Camille. "It's like a piece of *me* is missing."

"And you've never apologized to him?"

"Oh God, no. I have. Many times. Emails, texts, voice mails. He's pretty unwilling to talk to me." Bobby lowered his head, the shame, like a wave of nausea, filling him. "But I need to see him, to look him in the eye, to make him understand that I know what I did and how wrong that was. I need him to know that I am willing to do whatever it takes to make amends."

"Define 'whatever it takes'."

Bobby didn't hesitate. "Up to and including saying I will go away for good if that's what it takes for him to understand. I would leave him and Kevin alone, never see them again, even though it would totally break my heart."

Camille nodded. "I think you're sincere, Bobby. And I believe you really do want to make amends for the right person—who, as you know, is not you, necessarily, but him."

"Any advice for me on how I can make this happen? In all this time, he has been unwilling to see me."

"What does he like to do?"

Bobby didn't have to think. "Run. He runs like he's being pursued. Every day. Lakefront. Usually in the mornings before work."

"Well, you could try to bump into him on the trail. Kind of a last resort. I might try first another email, a sincere one about how you know you done him wrong and that you want to make it up to him."

But Bobby was hardly listening. He knew Caden was more likely to see his name in his email box and to simply delete it, maybe without even having read it.

No, he would be out tomorrow morning, rain or shine, with a latte for himself and a bottle of water for Caden. He would position himself on a bench overlooking the gay beach at the end of Ardmore. He knew Caden often passed this way on his runs south, because the two of them had made cracks about the cruisy men's room there and how there were often guys out on that particular beach in the summer as early as 8:00 a.m.

Of course, Caden might not opt to run that day, or he might choose to take the trail north, up to Evanston.

But Bobby had to try, and he had an inkling, maybe even a premonition, that he would be right.

When he looked up, Camille was telling him their time was up.

Bobby stood and said, "Hopefully, I'll have something special to report next time."

"Good luck, Bobby."

*

The next morning, Bobby rose extra early so he could take the train north to the stop at Bryn Mawr and have time to walk to the beach—and to do all the rest before he had to be at his office downtown. He looked out his windows at June perfection. The lake was shimmering and aquamarine, looking almost tropical, the sun, a dazzling orange ball, soared above a few fluffy white clouds that put Bobby in mind of heaven. He recalled reading somewhere a poem describing light on water as sequins and now understood the image.

He checked the weather app on his phone and saw that the looks of the day did not lie. Already, at 7:00 a.m., it was a very pleasant seventy-two degrees.

If Caden didn't run today, it would be a miracle.

Bobby showered and dressed in a pair of madras shorts and a linen shirt. He put on, then took off, a straw hat, thinking the look was too affected. If sincerity was what he wanted his friend to come away with from this impromptu meeting, then he should make the attempt to at least look like—for once in his life—he wasn't totally focused on his appearance.

He headed out.

*

Bobby thought he should do this morning beach ritual a bit more often, especially on days like this one. The breeze off the water was cool in contrast to the sun, and simply sitting here on a bench under a tree and looking out at the broad expanse of endless water, sipping his latte, was perfection, centering.

Bobby began to think this was a very good idea. At the worst, he would have had a calm hour or so to simply relax and be (what some of the guys in SAA might refer to as a kind of meditation) before he had to head into his job downtown. And at the best, he could hope he would not only see Caden, but would strike a kind of accord with him, opening the door to reestablishing their friendship.

Many runners were out that morning, and Bobby's heart lifted a little, his nerves energized, when he would see a male form coming toward him. He thought of how, in the past, he might have been tempted to lock eyes with one of the coltish young men jogging by and try to lead them into some sort of sleazy, furtive encounter in one of the stalls in the men's room behind him.

Ah well, as the song goes, the girl can't help it.

And, truth be told, he did have thoughts like these, some that even bordered on fantasy, when a particularly hot guy dashed by, but he knew that would not help him on his journey to self-awareness. Ah shit, who was he trying to kid? The real reason was that if he did score and went off to give a blowjob in a bathroom to some stranger, he might be otherwise occupied when Caden ran by, thus defeating his whole purpose.

So he let his mind do the coupling, and he stayed there, being buffeted by the breeze, watching and waiting.

"What are you doing here?"

Bobby jumped at the voice. He turned and saw Caden standing behind him. He wore a T-shirt and a pair of pale blue nylon running shorts. He was breathing hard, and his shirt was soaked with sweat.

He looked like an angel dropped down from heaven. Bobby felt a mixture of emotions overcome him, chiefly the desire to simply get up and run away, wondering what he was thinking, or to stand and throw his arms around his friend, or to simply cower there, and hope he'd remember how to engage his brain and tongue at the same time to produce speech.

Finally, he uttered the truth, the simple truth. "I was waiting for you." He did not add that he was surprised to see him and his careful surveillance was structured all around spying Caden running toward him as he came from the north. It had never figured into the equation that Caden would run behind him, although it should have, since that was where the freaking lakefront trail was located.

"You were? Why?"

Bobby's peace, brought on by the calming waves and lovely morning, shattered. Caden did not, by any stretch of the imagination, look happy to see him. A kind of fire danced in his eyes, and Bobby wondered if it was controlled rage. He looked down to see Caden clenching and unclenching his fists, his knuckles whitening with the pressure.

Go ahead and slug me. It's what I deserve, anyway. So, if you're thinking of hitting me, I won't stop you. I won't even try to defend myself. In fact, I would welcome it. Bobby didn't utter any of his thoughts. He simply set his paper coffee cup down on the pavement and finally stood to face Caden.

They faced one another for several moments, simply staring, each breathing hard, but for different reasons. "Why did you stop?" Bobby asked.

"Because it's not like you to be out here just sitting on a weekday morning. Shouldn't you be downtown playing the corporate cog or maybe back there in that bathroom, getting nailed by some 'fucking gorgeous' guy you met out here?" Caden sneered.

Bobby wondered if he had done the right thing. He still didn't understand why Caden had bothered to not only stop, but to make contact. Maybe, Bobby could hope, in some delusional way, that the gesture was a good thing, the opening of a door?

Well, we can dream....

"I guess I deserved that. Would you sit down here for a minute? I just want to talk to you, and I thought this might be the best place to catch you."

"No. I won't sit down." Caden looked away, brushing the sweat off his forehead and flinging it to the ground off his fingertips. "And I don't know why I stopped. I guess seeing you just kind of took me by surprise, like you were some kind of mirage. I had to get closer to see, and then, I don't know, I blurted something out. I probably shouldn't have." He turned, looking as if he was about to run off.

"Caden, please don't."

Caden stopped, staring. His breathing had just about returned to normal.

Bobby grinned. "As Joan Rivers always said, 'Can we talk?'"

Caden shook his head. "I don't know what there is to say, Bobby."

"Maybe *you* don't have much to say—"

Caden let out a short, bitter snort of laughter. "Oh, I have *a lot* to say. And I doubt very much you want to hear it."

"Would it surprise you if I said that even though I could guess I won't like what you'd say, I'd still love to hear it? Maybe even need to hear it?"

"Nothing coming from you would surprise me." Caden looked away from Bobby's gaze and stared out at the water. "I gotta get back. Kevin has the morning off, and we had plans to go to the Heartland for breakfast."

"That sounds nice."

"Well, don't hold your breath for an invitation."

"Caden...please. Don't be so mean."

Caden laughed at that. "That's rich coming from you." Caden sighed and sat on the opposite end of the bench from Bobby. "What the fuck do you want?" He continued to stare, resolute, out at the water.

Bobby so wanted to reach out and touch his friend lightly on the arm, simply to reassure him that his intentions this morning were honorable, that he appreciated Caden's willingness (albeit strained) to stay. But he knew even the slightest touch could send

Caden dashing off, like a spooked animal, so he kept his hands folded in his lap.

Now was his moment. What could he say? What were the right words? Bobby closed his eyes for just a minute, feeling the lake breeze and the sun's warmth on his skin. He knew what he had to say. It wasn't complicated. It was simple, actually. The trick would be getting Caden to accept his words, to take them into his heart and mind and digest them.

Bobby prayed things weren't too far gone between the two of them for that to happen.

"I have been a shit to you. A complete and utter shit. It's not a pretty word, but there's no other way to put it. I could make excuses, like I thought you were through with Kevin when I went after him, but there are no excuses. There are reasons, of course, and I myself am just beginning to understand them, but there aren't excuses. My behavior with you regarding Kevin was inexcusable."

Caden chuffed out a breath, outraged. The little snort told Bobby he agreed.

Bobby went on. "And I wanted to say that I am so sorry. I hurt you. I violated the trust you put in our friendship. I have no one to blame for what happened but myself. I get that. And I don't blame you for hating me." Bobby reached out to Caden with his gaze, aching for just a look, a simple glance that might show he was, even a tiny bit, getting through to the man.

But Caden stared out at the water, stared hard, as if watching for a boat to come in, or a plane to suddenly land upon the water.

"I wanted to say that I will do whatever it takes to make amends to you and Kevin. Anything."

There was a long silence in which Bobby desperately hoped Caden would say something, but Caden kept his own counsel, not revealing anything. The silence, acting almost as if Bobby wasn't there, was the worst thing Caden could do, worse than even screaming at him or hitting him.

It made Bobby's heart feel as though it was shriveling up inside.

Finally, Bobby licked his lips, which were very dry, and made a good-faith effort to slow the thundering pace of his heart. He didn't want to utter the words that would come next, but he had to say them, to demonstrate to both himself and especially to Caden, that he was sincere.

"I will do anything it takes to make things up to you guys," he repeated. "And that means if I need to leave you alone and never see you again, then that's what I will do." Bobby slumped back against the park bench, feeling as though he had just thrown up. It wasn't an elegant comparison, but it was real.

Again, the silence intruded, long enough for Bobby to notice the roar of the traffic behind them on Lake Shore Drive as it curved onto Hollywood, the *slap-slap-slap* of running shoes hitting the pavement as two runners—one male and one female—dashed by, huffing. Behind them, a man called out, presumably to a child, to "Just keep pedaling. Have faith!"

At last, Caden turned to him and met what Bobby knew was a hungry gaze. And God bless Caden, he was smiling. Perhaps, Bobby thought, his words had gotten through, made a chink on the armor of his defenses.

Bobby, tentative, lifted his own lips to smile in return, his heart leaping just a little in his chest. He leaned forward.

Caden said, still smiling, "That sounds like a great start."

Before Bobby even had a chance to process the words, to wince and recoil from their sting, Caden was on his feet again and running north, away from Bobby. He did not look back.

Bobby was so crestfallen, so hurt, that he had to repeat the words to himself and tell himself that what Caden was saying was that he never wanted to see him again. It was what he had expected, what he knew in his heart would happen, but that didn't lessen the pain. It was as though a bank of black and foreboding clouds had suddenly usurped the sunny day.

He watched Caden running away, his figure growing smaller as he retreated. Then he turned at Ardmore and disappeared between the high-rises lining Sheridan Road.

Gone.

Forever.

Bobby got to his feet, suddenly weary to his very bones, and kicked the half-empty cup of coffee at his feet angrily into the grass, then went and fetched it and put it into a trash can.

He wanted to run after Caden, to catch up with him, grasp his shoulders, and talk, talk, talk to him until he made it right.

But Bobby knew there was no way to make it right. He understood to do what he wanted to do, to pursue his old friend, would only make matters worse. Doing that would be selfish. *Really, you'd be doing it more for yourself than for him. Leave him alone.*

Bobby knew the truth of his thoughts and slumped back down on the bench. He glanced at his watch and saw that, if he hurried to the El train, he could catch it and still be in his office only a little after nine.

But the prospect of going to work now just seemed, well, sickening. He pulled out his phone, called his office, and left a message on his boss's voice mail that he wasn't feeling well, which was the truth, which was—honestly—the understatement of the year.

Bobby got up from his perch on the bench and started walking. Gone was the beauty and serenity of the early summer morning, even though the sun continued to shine, the waves to roar, and the breeze to blow. The day now reflected the slight nausea in Bobby's gut and the darkness in his head.

He felt numb as he walked along Hollywood, the traffic roaring alongside him, seeing only the detritus of urban blight before him instead of the beauty of the day—the trash in the gutter, the graffiti on the buildings lining the boulevard upon which he walked. Even the cars going by him seemed to all have damaged mufflers, their fading paint pocked with rust, spiderweb cracks in their windshields.

He didn't want to think about anything, simply letting his feet propel him forward. Eventually, Hollywood turned into Ridge, and, finally, Bobby veered north to head up Clark Street.

Later, he might say that he didn't know where he was headed, but he walked there as if on a mission, even though he never made a conscious decision to go there.

In the Andersonville neighborhood, Bobby paused in front of the nondescript façade of Mangroves, one of the oldest and sleaziest bathhouses in the city. It had been, once upon a time, too low-rent for even Bobby to consider, except maybe on a lark, or if he had too much to drink at one of the bars nearby and was too horny to go home without getting his itch scratched. But normally, Bobby would have opted for Steamworks, down in Boystown, with its relatively plush appointments and its decidedly younger, buffer clientele.

Now, he stood outside Mangroves, simply staring at the faded white brick, the blackened windows, the discreet neon sign on the door that bore nothing more than the legend, *Enter*.

Bobby laughed bitterly. He'd never thought of the sign as a double entendre, but now he did.

Do you really want to go inside? His mind roused him from the near stupor he had walked to this destination in. *You'll ruin all your hard work. Your six weeks of sobriety. Think of how disappointed Camille will be. Think of what the guys in the group will say. Think of how you'll feel afterward.*

None of it mattered. Bobby pushed through the door and entered the small lobby, which seemed even darker after the brightness of the sun outside. The lobby reeked of disinfectant, a bleachy smell that burned in Bobby's nostrils. Behind the glassed-in front desk stood a burly man with a red beard in a green T-shirt that stretched mightily over his broad chest and potbelly. Bobby thought how he was just Caden's type, and then quashed the thought.

I don't want to think about him.

He stepped up to the desk, noticing the lubricants for sale behind the burly guy, the rolled towels stacked neatly on the counter, the pegboard with its keys.

He spoke through a hole in the glass. "I need a membership and a room."

"ID?"

Bobby pulled out his wallet and slid his driver's license under the glass. *You can still turn back now, no harm done.*

Bobby batted the voice in his head away like a pesky fly. He had come too far to turn back now; he knew that in every fiber of his being. Nothing could pull him away from the course he had set himself on, nothing.

The clerk went through the motions of entering Bobby into the database on Mangroves's computer, then writing out a temporary membership card. He took Bobby's license and put it in a lockbox, then turned to give the key, along with a towel, to Bobby. "Twenty bucks. And you're in Room 58. Need anything else?"

Bobby met the man's eyes, noticing how the pupils practically ate up his irises, and wondered what drug he was on, wondered if he could get some. But he was too shy to ask, so he simply pulled two twenties out of his wallet and asked for a bottle of ID Millennium Platinum lube. The clerk handed it to him and told him what time he would need to check out.

"Thanks." Bobby took his towel and key, waiting for the clerk to buzz him through the entrance door.

The place was run-down, even more than Bobby remembered. The carpet, even in the dark, showed itself as threadbare and stained. *Do not wander around barefoot, whatever you do!* Paint chipped from the walls, spotted cancerously with mildew. The posters—one sheets of newspaper ads of gay strip shows the place did on the weekends—hung crookedly on the wall in their dime-store frames.

Cheesy synthesized music served as a soundtrack as Bobby made his way through the dimness.

Bobby stopped off at the men's room adjacent to the lockers to take a piss. As he was washing his hands, he looked up in the mirror to see a lanky guy bustle in next to him. The man was thin, bordering on emaciated, his ribs showing and his body decorated with an art gallery of tattoos. He had a scraggly beard and stringy hair. He spat what looked like come into the sink next to Bobby. Bobby stared at the goo and gaped. "What was that?"

"My latest love affair." He regarded Bobby in the mirror and winked, then stooped to rinse his mouth with tap water. Then he rushed away as quickly as he had entered.

Bobby shook his head, wondering if he had imagined the guy, if he was some come-eating specter doomed to repeat the same scene over and over again.

In the locker room, Bobby spied several guys changing from street clothes into towels around their waists.

He turned away to find where he would be spending the next few hours of his life. His room was down a flight of stairs, on the basement level, where the steam room and hot tub were. Bobby wondered if he would need to visit either, and if he did, would he bring something unwelcome home with him.

Shut up, he told the voice in his head. And he made his mind go blank.

He passed a tall African American man on his way to his room. The guy was huge, sporting a shaved head. His towel, instead of around his waist, was slung over his shoulder. Bobby couldn't blame him. Even soft, the guy's dick looked to be about six inches long.

Bobby met his dark eyes, holding his gaze for a second. He wasn't ready for more of a connection than that, but wanted the man to know that, maybe later, you'll get your chance.

Bobby continued on to his room, the door of which was open. He ducked quickly inside and closed the door on the black man, who had followed him. He turned the rheostat so the room was fully lit.

Sad. Along one wall was a single cot, with a many-times-bleached sheet covering the thin mattress. Opposite it ran a long mirror on the wall. Next to the cot was a box where one could put one's belongings and also use it as a sort of side table.

Bobby dimmed the lights again and began to undress, hanging his cheery summer clothes on a hook on the back of the door. He put his wallet and watch inside the box, closed it, then set the bottle of lube on its top, along with a handful of freebie condoms he had grabbed from a tray on the wall.

Finally, he opened the door and sat, naked, on the bed. The rolled towel lay beside him, and Bobby thought he should wrap it around his waist, but at the moment, simply didn't have the energy. Instead, he took the cap off the bottle of lube, removed the safety seal, and then replaced the cap.

He left the bottle sitting open on the box next to the bed.

Then he lay on his stomach in the dimness and waited.

It wasn't long before he sensed eyes on him. He lifted his head and saw the black man staring in at him, eyes intent, a small grin playing about his features. Bobby placed his face back down on the thin mattress. *Why not start with the best?*

He listened to the man's tentative footfalls as he entered the room. Bobby shut his eyes as the man touched him, running a warm hand slowly down his spine, pausing to linger at his lower back, then moving down to massage and caress his ass.

The guy's breathing came heavier, but he didn't speak. Bobby felt him weigh down one side of the bed as he sat. He continued to massage Bobby's ass, but leaned over and placed a delicate kiss on the back of his neck, then another between his shoulder blades, another at the base of his spine, which made Bobby shiver. The man parted his legs roughly, then knelt between them. He leaned over Bobby, and Bobby gasped as he felt the wet of his tongue painting a line of saliva between his ass cheeks. Pulling his cheeks apart, he began what passed for foreplay in this neck of the woods, alternating tongue-fucking with finger insertion, working more and more fingers into Bobby's hole as he made it wetter and wetter with his tongue.

Finally, Bobby felt the man rise up, felt the heat of his cock at his hole. He started to push inside. Bobby reached back, not to guide him, because he was certain this guy knew what he was doing, but to check to see if he had wrapped that monster in a condom.

He hadn't. Bobby let out a rush of air, debating for only a moment or two whether he should just let the guy go ahead, to plow into him and fuck him bare. The idea made his heretofore soft dick harden, especially the thought of the cock shooting its load deep inside him, one of Bobby's favorite fantasies.

But reason, even in his numb sadness, won out. He mouthed the first and last word the pair of lovebirds would exchange. "Condom."

Relieved and disappointed at the same time, he waited as the man reached over, tore the foil packet open, and took a moment to roll the rubber onto his cock. Bobby lifted his head to make sure. In places like this, he wouldn't put it past someone to pretend to put on a condom, then plunge in raw anyway.

Safe as he could be, Bobby shut his eyes and lowered his head back to the mattress.

From the feel of it, the guy was enormous. Bobby winced, one hand instinctively flying back to press against the man's stomach as he pushed in, to stop him from further entry. He needed a moment just to get used to the pressure, the stretch, and to allow the white needles of pain to dissipate.

They did. Bobby looked back, nodded, and then the man pressed in more. More. At last, Bobby wiggled back against him, swallowing the last couple of inches with his ass, squeezing down on the cock.

God. I have missed this.

The man began to fuck, forcing himself all the way in to where his rough pubes met the baby soft skin of Bobby's ass, then withdrawing almost all the way out, ramming it back in again to the hilt. With each thrust, his tempo increased a bit more, until they were moving in rhythm, Bobby bucking against him to swallow him in deeper and the man almost savagely—at last—pounding him. This went on for a long time, leaving no doubt as to his fucker's stamina and endurance, until they were both drenched in sweat. At one point, the guy flipped him over on his back, and Bobby stared up into the man's face, his clenched-shut eyes, his mouth open, panting and groaning.

Their eyes, though, never met.

The man's tempo got faster, impossibly so, and his breathing quickened to match it. Bobby knew he was going to come soon, and he watched as the orgasm drifted across the guy's features, as he bucked, plowing deeply into Bobby, and then was still.

Bobby could swear he could feel the rhythmic spasms of the guy's cock as it emptied into the condom.

The man looked down between Bobby's spread legs as he withdrew, thoughtfully holding onto the base of the condom so there would be no spills. He tied off the rubber, its receptacle tip chock full, and flung it into the trashcan in the corner.

Two points.

He patted Bobby's chest in thanks, got up, and left.

It was then Bobby realized the door had been left open the entire time, and a crowd had gathered.

He caught the eye of a young man, little more than a boy, really, watching with the kind of dumb wonder that indicated to Bobby that this was the first time he had ever witnessed such a scene, at least in real life and not via the magic of porno.

He was cute, perhaps a Northwestern undergrad, slumming for the day. His body was tight and lean, covered in brown fur. A lock of dark hair fell over one eye. He had a Celtic tattoo band running around one of his biceps.

Bobby smiled at the boy. "You want to be next?" The boy did, and Bobby raised his legs in acceptance, in welcome.

The boy was much quicker, predictably, than the black man.

And Bobby still hadn't come.

There were many more after the college boy. Two in the steam room, one a blowjob to completion and another, a hairy silver-haired daddy, yet another fuck, as Bobby stood, legs apart and arms braced on the sweating tile walls while he pile-drove into him, grunting and reaching around to painfully twist Bobby's nipples, tug his balls.

He went back to the room and lost count of the number of guys who came in for a moment to be sucked, with Bobby on his knees on the gritty floor, then bolting away to see what else the bathhouse had on offer before coming. Others stayed to fuck him.

None stayed to talk.

By the time Bobby left Mangroves, it was late afternoon and he had had some form of sexual congress with eleven different men.

He stepped out into the bright sunshine, which hurt his eyes after the dark of the baths, and made him feel like he was stepping into another world. A stranger in a strange land? A bus roared by.

When you slip, you do it in grand style.

And Bobby leaned against the building, feeling all at once sick, and as though he was about to cry. He shook his head, reminding himself that self-pity was not a pretty thing.

He scanned Clark for a bus or a cab, but all he saw was a passing parade of cars and, here and there, a bicycle.

The cloak of numbness, which had enveloped him when he walked up here from the beach, surrounded him once more, although Bobby had to concede that the two were for completely different reasons. The first allowed him to do something he knew he shouldn't, the second was an avoidance response to a crushing wall of remorse and shame he knew awaited him. But right now, Bobby felt nothing—not lusty nostalgia for the men and loads he had taken, not guilt, not shame. Only a simple emptiness washed over him, making him wish for some kind of emotion, making him wonder why he felt nothing other than a dull, throbbing ache in his ass.

He spied a bus heading south down the street and thought if he wanted to catch it, he should hurry to cross to the other side.

But something held him back. He stood and watched as the bus pulled over, disgorged a few passengers, and took on a few more in their stead. It roared away.

This afternoon, Bobby decided, he would walk home. It wasn't a terrible distance, after all, three, maybe four, miles. In that distance, he could perhaps reconnect with himself and try to feel something, try to understand why he had just done what he did.

He turned and started walking south on Clark, past St. Boniface cemetery and its hush, its ancient stones right in the middle of the bustling metropolis. How soon would he join the ranks of those resting there? And was there sex in heaven? Hell?

The logical route, the scenic option, would be to turn at Foster or some other east-west street and head down to the lakefront, stroll along its sun-kissed trail to get home. It was not only the most expedient way, it was also the most beautiful.

But Bobby was not in the mood for beauty or tranquility. He wanted grime, noise, exhaust fumes in the air.

He wanted *not* to be reminded of his encounter with Caden.

Would he really never see him again?

As he headed south, crossing busy thoroughfares and taking little note of the apartment buildings and retail outlets he passed, whimpering interrupted his purposeful stride and dogged concentration on keeping his mind free of thought.

Bobby paused, listening, trying to hear beneath the din of traffic and the calls of street vendors selling Mexican treats.

There. It's almost like crying.

He turned and looked around him, but other than discarded cans, papers, weeds, and endless concrete, he saw nothing that could be making the noise, which had, anyway, stopped.

The crying began again simultaneously with Bobby thinking his imagination was playing tricks on him and beginning to walk onward once more.

He really listened this time and was able to discern the direction from which the sound issued. Just before him was a little side alley, a passage for deliveries for the bar/restaurant next to it. He peered into the gloom of the sun-starved, brick-paved alley and saw only a lone dumpster, its bright blue paint pocked with rust.

He stepped into the alley, and the crying grew louder.

At the back of the dumpster, hidden from the street, he saw the source of the sound: a shivering (in spite of the warmth of the day) little brown Chihuahua, its ribs showing and the remains of fast-food wrappers before it.

Huge brown eyes, looking even huger, Bobby thought, on account of the dog's emaciated condition, stared up at him. The dog went quiet, yawned, and rapidly licked its lips a couple of times. It gazed up at Bobby almost defiantly, in spite of the poor shape the animal appeared to be in.

Bobby was transfixed, and their eyes meeting seemed to erase the sounds of the day around them, isolating the pair, one two-legged, one four.

Bobby stood a couple of feet away from the dog and didn't want to spook it. He squatted down on his haunches, murmuring softly, "It's okay. What happened to you, little fella? Or are you a little girl?" It was hard to tell, with the way the dog sat. "Did someone leave you back here? Are you some street-smart survivor?"

Bobby slowly reached out, just letting his hand float, steadily, in the space between them. The dog eyed the hand with what Bobby thought were alternating shades of suspicion and hunger. He wondered if other hands had ever held out a treat to the little dog, or if perhaps human hands appeared to it as weapons, as something that would strike its tiny and terrified body.

Bobby dropped his hand. "I won't hurt you. I promise. You and me, we're both alone today." Bobby inched a little closer, and the dog yapped at him in warning. He moved a couple more inches, and the dog bared its teeth, a low growl issuing from deep in its belly.

"I would never hurt you. But I'll let you come to me." And even though it would ruin his expensive shorts and leave him smelling like the dumpster, Bobby sat down on the bricks of the alley and leaned back against the dumpster, legs splayed out before him.

"I have all the time in the world."

But all the time in the world is not what it took for the dog to begin a slow, cautious, one-step-forward-two-back progression toward him. Bobby didn't make eye contact, simply stared ahead, wondering what the hell he was doing. *You really should just get up and go. This little critter is not your problem. What's the game plan here, anyway?* In spite of the thoughts ricocheting through his brain, Bobby didn't move, casting a glance every so often out of the corner of his eye to see that the dog had drawn a little closer, a little closer.

Finally, the little creature was at his hip, sniffing. Bobby did nothing but stare straight ahead.

Finally, Bobby dared to move to put a gentle hand on its tiny head. The dog darted back, yelping as if Bobby had struck it.

They regarded one another. "We're never going to get anywhere without trust," Bobby said softly. He thought he saw a glimmer of that emotion in the dog's eyes. Or maybe he saw what he wanted to see. Regardless, the dog moved forward once more and allowed Bobby to hold his hand out close enough for it to sniff.

He petted him. In their little dance, the dog revealed to Bobby that he was, indeed, a male. And, for a Chihuahua, quite a well-endowed one. "You little stud," Bobby whispered, laughing.

The dog settled under Bobby's sure strokes, moving closer until he had placed one paw on Bobby's thigh, as though he wanted Bobby to lean in so he could tell him a secret. When Bobby stopped petting him to look down and regard him, the dog nudged Bobby's hand with his head, as if to say, "More. More."

"Can't get enough, huh?" Bobby asked, resuming the petting and scratching behind the ears. He chuckled. "You and I have that in common."

At last, the dog crawled onto his lap and curled up in the warmth of his crotch. He fell asleep. "Well, would you look at that," Bobby wondered. Bobby stared down at the dog, not sure what to do next. "You're gonna give me fleas—to add to the crabs I probably just got up yonder." Bobby's laughter, bordering on tears, startled the dog awake, and he stared up at Bobby, head cocked.

"What am I gonna do with you?" Bobby whispered. He wished there was a collar with a tag on the dog. That way, he could at least do the logical thing and try to find his owner.

He couldn't just leave him here. Not now. They had forged some sort of bond in a few quick minutes. Bobby sighed. "That's the way it goes with me and well-endowed males. Can't help it." He laughed, and again, the dog met his eyes, as if he too wanted in on the joke.

Bobby thought he could take him to the pound. He looked down at the poor little creature—his bordering-on-starvation body, the slight underbite that made his lower teeth stick out. This was not a pretty boy.

"You're just a streetwise thug, aren't you?" Bobby scratched the dog behind the ears. "Rough trade."

Bobby wondered what would happen if he took him to the pound. No, he didn't really wonder. Who would want this little guy? Especially if there were puppies to compete with, as he was sure there would be, or if there were purebreds and cuter dogs, as Bobby knew there would be.

The most likely scenario, Bobby knew, was that the dog would be gassed after its however-many-days were up.

And already, as he looked down at the brown-eyed face, so ugly it was cute, he knew he could never sentence this animal to a certain death.

"You son of a bitch," Bobby said to the dog, noticing how he wagged his tail at the epithet, which made Bobby chuckle. "I guess that would be true of any male dog, wouldn't it? But seriously, what am I gonna do with you?"

Bobby sighed; he already knew the answer. To leave the dog sitting there would break his heart, especially if he, as he did in Bobby's imagination, followed him.

So he stood up, wiping the back of his shorts with his hands, feeling both grit and grease in a single swipe. The dog stared up at him, tail wagging, as if it knew not what was in Bobby's mind, but what was in his heart.

Part of him—the part that worked downtown, the part that ogled the Barney's and Room and Board catalogs, the part that wondered how soon he could trade in his BMW for the latest model, the part that guzzled designer cocktails, the part that worked them off at a chic gym—did tell him he should just walk away. After all, the dog could belong to someone, a child, maybe, and he had just darted out of an open door. Distraught owners were combing the north side for him right now.

Right. A dog in this neglected condition most likely belongs to no one, and, if he does, that owner doesn't deserve him.

So he squatted down next to the brown dog, holding out his hands in a little cradle. The dog hopped right into them. "Oh, so you're easy. You and me, we're two of a kind. You've probably waited your whole life behind that dumpster, anticipating the moment I would walk by and hear your pitiful cries. Don't worry. I know all the tricks to snare a man. You don't fool me. The real trick is keeping one."

Bobby stood, cradling the dog close to his chest. He looked out at life pulsing by on the street beyond the alley's mouth and wondered how he had gotten here. The sun, he could tell from the quality of light, was beginning to set—the shadows were long and the air was cooler.

Bobby held the dog, and the pair of them emerged from the alley as if they had been made for each other, both clinging to the other for dear life. Never had the cliché, Bobby thought, been more apropos.

Just before Bobby turned the corner to begin the long trek south again, he asked the dog, "Now, what are we gonna call you?"

Bobby paused, thinking, and the name came to him all at once, brought on, not surprisingly, by the Chihuahua's surprisingly large member. "Let's call you Johnny, Johnny Wadd," he said, christening the pooch after porndom's biggest—literally—star, John Holmes.

As he headed south on Clark, holding onto Johnny, who really weighed so little he barely registered, Bobby had a bracing thought.

He'd felt more connection, more joy, more happiness from the few moments with this dog than in all the eleven times he had been fucked earlier in the day.

"What does that say about me?" he wondered to Johnny.

And Johnny's large brown eyes regarded him, but he kept his own counsel.

Chapter Twelve

Bobby awakened to the smell of urine on the pillow next to his head and the stink of regret inside his head. He reached over, feeling the little handful of warmth and fur that was Johnny Wadd, and tugged him close. "You're supposed to go outside," he mumbled sleepily, shoving the soiled pillow to the floor.

Unshaken, Johnny curled up next to Bobby's chest and began to snore.

What the hell are you doing? Bobby wondered, staring up through the darkness at the ceiling. *I know you haven't been all that selective in the past, but taking this little guy to bed with you has to be one of your dumbest moves ever. I mean, he's probably completely ridden with fleas, and now you and your home are too.* Bobby thought this in spite of the fact that his first order of business, once he'd gotten Johnny home, was to give him a long, luxurious bath using Kiehl's shampoo. He then left a shivering Johnny in a file drawer lined with towels and a throw pillow while he ran out to Walgreens for dog shampoo with flea-killing properties.

He absently petted the dog, hoping against hope that maybe the dog wasn't afflicted with fleas, just as he hoped he had not been afflicted with crabs at the bathhouse earlier that day.

Hey, sometimes we get lucky. Sometimes misfortune passes us by.

The smell of urine was not what had awakened him. Nor was the feel of a strange male he had just met in bed next to him sleep-interrupting. (After all, there was nothing new about the latter.)

No, what had awakened him was remorse, guilt, shame.

He knew, when (if?) he went to a meeting tomorrow, they would inquire if anyone had recently slipped. Would he be man enough to raise his hand? Confess what he had done?

Or would he, like a weasel, keep his transgressions to himself, thus negating any chance for redemption?

Now, these were the kind of thoughts that keep a man awake at night.

He lifted his head from the pillow to glance over at the nightstand clock. It was only a few minutes after midnight.

Is it too late to call him? Will he be mad? Is it rude?

Bobby didn't know if he was being selfish or smart when he got up on one elbow, snatching his iPhone from the table next to him. Without giving himself a chance to second-guess, he located Aaron's number among his contacts and pressed the button to call him.

Aaron didn't sound as if he was asleep when he answered.

Bobby asked anyway. "You weren't sleeping, were you? If you were, go back to bed. We'll talk tomorrow."

"I'm fine. I was actually lying here on the couch, watching *To Kill a Mockingbird*. I must have seen it a couple dozen times, but it never gets old. And sometimes, drifting off to sleep with Atticus Finch's Alabama-accented voice in my ear is pretty perfect." Aaron paused for a moment. "So what's up, my friend?"

Bobby stared at Johnny, whose furry, spotted gut was rising and falling with his easy breathing. "I've got a male sleeping in bed next to me. I'm watching him right now, but he doesn't know it."

"So we had a slip?"

Bobby chuckled. "I didn't say a male of what species. This is a canine male."

Aaron let out a relieved breath. "I didn't know you had a dog."

"I didn't, until I found this little fella shivering behind a dumpster off Clark this afternoon." Bobby got up from the bed to stare out at the darkness, the traffic moving like an illuminated river along Lake Shore Drive below him. "I never could resist a stray. I did what I always do—brought him home. Now I am wondering if I am out of my mind. Look at him. Hang on." Bobby took a moment to bring up the camera on his phone to snap a picture of the sleeping Johnny Wadd and to send it to Aaron.

"I can see what you saw in him. How could you resist? Are you keeping him?" Aaron asked.

"I don't know that I have any choice. The real question is—is he keeping me?"

"Sounds like you're already past the point of no return."

"Way past." Bobby wondered if Aaron would remind him of something they had discussed in meetings—about not making big life decisions until you had a significant period of sobriety. Given the fact that Bobby's sobriety—when he found Johnny— numbered in only minutes, he thought Aaron would have every right to tell him he needed to get rid of the dog.

But he didn't.

They were silent for several moments, with Bobby debating coming clean to Aaron about the bathhouse. Finally, Aaron broke the silence by asking, "Did you just call to tell me about your new dog?"

"No. But you knew that, didn't you?"

"Given the hour and the slightest hint of evasiveness in your voice, I would say that, yes, I knew that." Aaron drew in a breath. "So what's going on?"

Bobby sat on a horsehair-covered chair he had positioned in front of his floor-to-ceiling bedroom windows, returning his gaze to the stillness of the dark night outside and noticing how the horizon to his south had an almost sickly orange glow, from the combined force of all the streetlights lining Chicago city streets. Could he tell Aaron what he had done this afternoon? Could he risk that the man would turn from him in disappointment and maybe even revulsion? Bobby felt his heart suddenly hammering in his chest, wanting, with every fiber of his being, to make some excuse and quickly hang up the phone.

"I was right earlier, wasn't I?" Aaron asked.

"What do you mean?" Bobby asked, although he knew.

"When I asked if you had slipped. You did, didn't you?"

Bobby let out a long sigh. "I'm just me," he said, apropos of nothing—and everything.

"Okay."

"I went to the baths. I did, like, a dozen guys." Bobby waited with bated breath for the recrimination, the hot force of the scolding and disappointment to come through the phone. He imagined the sting of it feeling like a slap to his face.

But no recriminations came. Aaron said, "Well, okay. So you slipped. You had sex, and a lot of it, from the sounds of it. That's now in the past. And you can't live in the past. You can only live in the present. So what do you want to do about it *now*?"

"Can I come over?" Bobby felt like his voice sounded like that of a little boy.

Aaron replied, "Why don't I just meet you somewhere? There's a little café on Clark and Irving Park Road called The Bored Room. It would be about halfway for both of us, and I know it's open really late."

"What will I do with Johnny?"

"Who?"

"My dog." Bobby felt a frisson of pleasure go through him—sudden—at uttering those two words.

"Bring him with? I don't know. I suppose you're going to have to answer that question a lot from here on out. That is, if you plan on keeping him."

Bobby glanced over at Johnny, now on his back, all four legs in the air, reminding Bobby of himself. He chuckled, but a warm rush of love coursed through him for this animal who had just barged into his life. "Oh, I plan on keeping him. The universe has given me no choice."

Johnny opened one eye and looked at Bobby.

"You up for going out?"

"I just said I was," Aaron replied.

"No, I was talking to Johnny." The dog stood on all four legs and shook itself, hopped down from the bed. It started sniffing the rug, moving in rapid circles.

"I will see you there within the hour," Bobby said in a rush, hanging up the phone with one hand and, with the other, swooping up Johnny. He held the dog close to him while he struggled into a pair of sweat pants and a T-shirt. "We are going outside, which is where good boys do their business."

He slid on a pair of flip-flops, grabbed his keys, and headed for the bank of elevators at the end of his hallway. This going down twenty-some stories to take the dog out to relieve himself was going to get old very fast. Bobby thought that, tomorrow, he would need to go to PetSmart and invest in some puppy pads.

*

The Bored Room was pretty empty this time of night. There was a woman hunched over her laptop, her pale face made paler by the screen before her. She was typing furiously. One barista lounged behind the counter; he perked up to look disapprovingly at Bobby when he walked in with Johnny, whose head poked out of a leather messenger bag.

"No dogs."

"He's a service dog."

"Oh yeah? What's your disability?"

"I'm mentally ill," Bobby replied, nearing the counter. "It's almost one o'clock in the morning. There's no one here, and the dog stays in the bag. You gonna be a hardass or let me slide?" Bobby was too tired and too disappointed in himself to deal in any other way with this urban hipster kid, with his shaved head, nose ring, unnecessary scarf, skinny jeans, and "ironic" Partridge Family T-shirt.

The kid eyed the dog once more, baring his teeth at him.

Johnny growled, then let out a fierce yap. He burrowed back down into the messenger bag. Bobby thought he was going to like this dog—Johnny had good instincts.

The kid asked, "What are you havin'?"

Deciding that sleep was most likely impossible, Bobby ordered a large drip with room for cream. While the kid, whose nametag told Bobby his name was Felix, drew coffee from an urn, Bobby scanned the empty café for Aaron.

I wouldn't blame him if he didn't show up.

Bobby took his coffee, asked the kid for one of the biscotti in a jar on the counter, and found a seat far from the raven-haired woman composing her memoirs. As Bobby expected, Johnny poked his head out of the bag, his nose twitching.

"I anticipated your interest." Bobby broke a piece off the biscotti and fed it to Johnny by hand. While he was doing this, he looked up to see Aaron enter.

Bobby savored the moment when he could simply watch Aaron before he realized where Bobby was. In spite of all the sex he had recently had, in spite of his resolve to try and somehow, some way, make his out-of-control attractions and sex life more manageable, he couldn't help but be struck once more by how handsome the man was. He had such an easy masculinity about him and confidence in the way he carried himself: shoulders back, dark eyes looking relentlessly forward. Tonight, he wore a pair of thin sweats that were made of feltlike material and closed with a drawstring. Bobby couldn't help but stare and couldn't slow his quickening pulse as he observed Aaron's thick cock swinging lazily beneath the fabric. *You son of a bitch. I know you didn't wear those on purpose, just to tempt me. You are not a cruel person.* Bobby forced his gaze to move upward and saw that Aaron wore a faded long-sleeved red T-shirt that bore the legend about some long-ago AIDS ride that went from Minneapolis to Chicago. *Yes, I can see how that shirt clings to your pecs, but I will not dwell on it.*

Bobby smiled when Aaron spied him. Aaron held up a finger, asking Bobby to hold on, and went over to the counter to order. In moments, he was seated before Bobby with a steaming beverage in front of him.

"What are you drinking?" Bobby asked.

"Herbal tea. Caffeine this late at night would keep me going until dawn's early light." He grinned. "And I don't need that. I have to teach in the morning." Aaron took a tentative first sip. "So, it's late and I'm not the kind of guy that's much good at small talk, so you want to tell me what prompted you to call in the middle of the night? Your slip?"

"Yeah. I don't understand why I did it."

"First off, you don't have to understand why—that might reveal itself somewhere down the road, but it may not. For your sake, I hope it does, because understanding our motivations when we act out are key to reining them in. To us being in control, rather than them."

"God. You sound like a counselor."

"I could be! I've slipped enough times to know the drill." Aaron's easy laugh put Bobby a little more at ease as he absently stroked the top of Johnny's head inside the messenger bag. "But, as I was saying, you don't really have to understand why you did what you did. At least not right now. You just need to look back at it and try to figure out what made you go there in the first place."

"That's easy. I tried to make amends to my best friend, Caden, and he pretty much told me to get lost." Bobby felt the beginnings of a tangerine sprout and grow in his throat and tried mightily to pull himself together. "That guy, really, was my only friend. I love him, but not in *that* way."

Aaron nodded. "That's bad news indeed. But life is all about disappointments and things not working out the way we hoped or planned. There's always gonna be shit. Are you gonna rush to the baths every time something doesn't go your way?"

Bobby snickered. "It does seem to put some balm on the wound."

Aaron frowned. "It does? Then what the fuck are you doing here with me?"

Bobby shook his head. "I know." Bobby reached into the bag and gently pulled out Johnny. "I'd like you to meet Johnny. Johnny, Aaron. Aaron, Johnny."

Aaron took the dog's paw in his hand and shook it. "He's a brute."

"Just my type." Bobby winked, arranging Johnny into his lap. The dog was asleep there within a minute or so, his head resting on Bobby's forearm. Bobby gently stroked Johnny's head, drawing comfort from the warmth of the small form. "When I found this little guy and spent some time with him, I realized I had more of a connection with him than with any of those guys I was sexual with."

"So much for the balm. Bobby, I think, from just what you've said tonight and from the little bit you shared in group, that I can draw a conclusion about your acting out. I say acting out because it's different from having sex, which can be a beautiful thing, but I don't think you even know that."

I bet it would be pretty damn beautiful with you. Bobby took in the full measure of the man sitting across from him. He simply could *not* turn off his libido, and deep inside he knew he didn't want to. Still, something wasn't quite right. In fact, something was very wrong. "You said you could draw a conclusion about me."

"Are you sure you wanna hear it?"

"Of course I do."

"Then open your ears and just listen; don't try to be defensive. Just listen."

"Yes, Dr. Phil."

Aaron rolled his eyes and took a sip of tea. "I think, for you, a lot of your sexual acting out at this point in your life is because you're using it to avoid pain. What happened to you at the baths earlier—or what you made happen—is a perfect example. You got hurt. Big time. The loss of a good friend can be devastating, just as much as losing a family member, maybe more so because this is a tie forged from something more conscious than blood. Let me ask you—how did you feel after your friend told you he didn't want to see you anymore?"

At first, Bobby thought it was a stupid and naïve question. Of course he felt devastated, horrible, crushed. But then something came to him, like the clichéd light going on over his head.

You felt none of those things. Remember?

Bobby cast his gaze down at the shiny dark wood surface of the table at which he sat. He looked up at Aaron. "I felt nothing."

Aaron nodded. "Do you understand what I meant, then?"

Bobby realized the numbness he felt, as he marched, on a mission he didn't even allow himself to be aware of, to the baths. There was a big wall, a blockage to ensure he didn't experience the pain of Caden's parting words—his telling Bobby that his offer to never see him again would be a "good place to start."

Caden had broken his heart. If Bobby was even the tiniest bit self-aware, he would have known that, would have maybe experienced the pain, cried, or kicked a can. But instead, he did what he always did—shut down his feelings, hiding them in some dark recess in a dusty back corner of his mind—and went out and, once more, attempted to use his body to give him succor for the emotional pain he tried to ignore. He bowed his head.

He jerked up again when he felt Aaron's hand on his shoulder. "This isn't easy. It's a process. A journey. You said you're seeing a therapist?"

Bobby nodded.

"That's good. You're what? Forty?"

Bobby considered telling Aaron he was thirty-three, as he claimed in several online profiles, but again, he simply nodded.

"For close to four decades then, you've probably been practicing denial, practicing using means outside yourself to bury your hurt. Maybe you grew up in a family where you weren't allowed to express your pain, your anger."

Bobby put up a hand. In his mind flashed a memory—a family frozen around a maple kitchen table, silent. A little boy sat cowering in his chair as a man, impossibly large, rose and towered above him. The man's hand was raised, ready to slap the boy. His features were contorted with rage far beyond whatever transgression the little boy had committed. A girl, a little older than the boy, sat across the table, staring, her glass of milk midway to her mouth. A woman to his left looked down into her salad, moving the lettuce around with endless fascination. Bobby snuffed out the scene. "Yeah, my family wasn't big on demonstrating emotion, so that makes an awful lot of sense."

"So you, like I once did, too, have a deeply ingrained pattern of avoidance. Instead of experiencing pain, letting it hurt, but then letting it go, we try to cover it up, pretend it isn't there, while all the while it festers within us, toxic."

"Wow," Bobby said, awed by his friend's insight. Everything Aaron said, Bobby knew was true. But knowing that didn't reveal any easy paths for change.

Then Aaron said something that surprised him. "Do you pray?"

Bobby quipped, "Well, I get down on my knees a bit."

Aaron chuckled. "Be serious!" he said gently. "I am—serious. Answer my question."

"You mean like to God?"

"To whatever you see as God...."

"No. I haven't gone in for that church stuff since I was a kid."

"You might want to, first of all, understand that praying doesn't have to be 'church stuff.' It can just be a quiet moment where you get in touch with yourself."

Bobby wanted to joke that he already spent too much time getting in touch with himself, but it was clear, even to his frightened mind and wounded heart, that such levity was not only inappropriate, it was hurting him. So he said nothing.

Aaron said, "You know the Serenity Prayer?"

"I should. We recite it every meeting."

Aaron shrugged. "Maybe you could start with that one. Just take a minute, before you go to work, before you go to bed and say it:

"God grant me the serenity to accept the things I cannot change,

"The courage to change the things I can,

"And the wisdom to know the difference.

"And when you do say it, take a moment to really think about what you're saying. Think about how it applies to you personally. These aren't just words. They mean something, simple as they are." Aaron leaned in close. "Take them into your heart."

"Okay. I'll try it."

"Just set aside a few minutes every day. Be thankful. Think of what you have over what you don't. In those few minutes, maybe just be still—and wait."

"Wait? For what?" Bobby asked.

"Silence." The word hung in the air for several moments.

Aaron looked down at his watch. "It's really late, buddy. And I have to get a few hours' sleep or I will be completely worthless tomorrow at school." He stood up. "You come on the L?"

"Yeah."

"You wanna walk to the stop together?"

Why did Bobby feel himself hesitate? More time alone with this kind and generous-of-spirit man should be welcome, a no-brainer, yes, but something held him back, almost as if he was afraid the tiny bit of magic Aaron had invoked in the coffee shop would fall to pieces if they stepped outside into the bigger world together.

Crazy.

"It's okay. I'll see you at the next meeting." Aaron reached down and squeezed Bobby's shoulder. That touch had more significance than anything sexual. Bobby couldn't understand why, but it brought tears to his eyes. He sucked in a big breath and said, "See you. And, Aaron? Thanks so much. You've helped. I owe you one."

"You owe me nothing. All I ask is that you do the same for someone someday." And with that, Aaron hurried out the door.

Bobby watched him, for once not concentrating on a man's ass as he walked away. He stared after Aaron until the night swallowed him up. Bobby was a cynic, and if you had told him, even as little as a few weeks ago, that people could come into his life for a reason, he might have laughed, responding that the universe was nothing more than a colossal set of coincidences.

But now he felt like he knew—Aaron had come into his life just when he was supposed to.

Johnny, in his lap, stirred, looking up at him with need in his eyes. "You want to go outside?"

Before Johnny could respond, Felix yelled sourly across the counter. "Dude, do you and your 'companion' there need anything else? Because if you don't, I'd kind of like to close up for the night."

Bobby looked down at his watch and saw that it was past 2:00 a.m. He resisted the urge to respond sourly. Instead, he smiled at Felix and said, "Thanks. We are out of your hair. I appreciate that you let us have the time."

"Yeah, whatever."

"Good night." Bobby groped in his bag for the leash he had brought, hooked Johnny up, and headed outside.

*

After he got home, and made sure Johnny slumbered on a fresh pillow beside Bobby's own, Bobby slid from his bed and knelt beside it. It crossed his mind he had never done this before, unless he was between the naked and spread thighs of a man lounging back on the mattress.

It felt weird. Stupid. Bobby remembered the Serenity Prayer and recited it quickly, giving a nervous little hiccup of a laugh at the end. He was ready to jump back into bed, already deciding that prayer wasn't for him, when Aaron's words, reminding him to really think about what the Serenity Prayer was saying came back to him. He stayed put.

He thought of the first line: *God grant me the serenity to accept the things I cannot change. What can't I change? My height? My eye color? The size of my dick? The fact that my wisdom teeth have never come in?* Bobby shook his head. He knew that's not what the prayer meant, and he wondered why he tried to avoid it. Was it because he was afraid he couldn't change this fucked-up essence of himself that, while allowing for plenty of casual sex, had thwarted any attempts he had made throughout his life to forge real love with another man?

What if I can't change that? What if I'm just a dyed-in-the-wool man whore? Should I accept that?

And Bobby felt something, a tightening of his skin, prickly. It was almost as though there was someone in the room with him. Nervous, he had a horror-movie moment where he glanced over his shoulder, expecting to see a dark shape barely discernible from the shadows.

It was as if another voice answered him. *What you can't change, maybe, is your physical aspect. What you might not be able to change is who you are, but who you are might be someone more than you think. Because mixed in with the slutty Bobby, the betrayer, stab-best-friends-in-the-back Bobby, there's another Bobby. There's a Bobby who is a good son, who loves his mother with all his heart. A good Bobby who is heartbroken that, even though it was his own damn fault, he has lost his best friend and who longs to make that wrong right. A good Bobby who can stop for a pitiful little creature cowering beside a dumpster and has the heart and the courage to take him home, despite whatever obstacles that might entail.*

There's a loving Bobby there. And that Bobby is afraid if he shows too much love, he might get hurt. Might be made too vulnerable.

So maybe the core Bobby—the one who may still be a stranger to you—is what cannot be changed.

Bobby looked around the room again. *Ah, this is just my subconscious talking.*

But even if it was only his superego, or whatever psychological term one might apply to the voice in his head—note to self: ask Camille—or even if it was God, that didn't change the fact that maybe, just maybe, the words were true.

But if the words were true—what did that mean?

The next line was all about having the courage to change the things he could. Did he have the courage to change himself? Or were his habits too ingrained, the path worn too deeply?

He didn't know, and the voice that told him there might actually be a good person lurking beneath the shallow, horny veneer also told him that the first step toward any change was recognition. And here he was. Look in the mirror.

Bobby got up, went into the bathroom adjoining his bedroom, and flicked on the light. In the big mirror above the double sinks, his own face looked back at him, showing him a tired man of forty.

Maybe it doesn't matter whether you know you can change or not. *Maybe right now it's enough to want to. That's the first step on the journey. Perhaps it's enough for now that you've set your foot on the path.*

He heard a clicking sound. Nails on marble. Johnny had come into the bathroom and sat on his haunches, looking up at him, as if to say, "Are you *ever* coming to bed?"

Bobby swooped the dog up and carried him back to the sheets, where, after planting a kiss on Johnny's snout, he fell deeply asleep.

Chapter Thirteen

"He's coming tomorrow."

"And how do you feel about that?"

"Excited. Nervous."

Bobby reclined in the leather chair in front of Camille. The fact that his old high school classmate and new friend, Wade, would be arriving at Chicago's O'Hare International Airport tomorrow afternoon actually filled him with all kinds of emotions, many of them warring with each other. He was eager to see Wade, to drink in his handsome face and form. He dreaded seeing Wade and drinking in his handsome face and form because he was terrified it would send him spiraling into all sorts of temptation.

Since his encounter with Caden at the lakefront about a month ago, Bobby had really knuckled down and worked on himself. He had attended SAA meetings almost daily, missing only when he was too tired from work. On those nights, he would simply go home, heat a Lean Cuisine up in the microwave, and fall asleep in front of the TV. Sometimes the only thing that kept him from remaining there all night was Johnny's insistent kissing, his signal that he needed to go outside for a final walk.

This was supposed to be the better life for which he was striving?

But Bobby was feeling different. Aaron had reluctantly agreed to become his mentor, replacing Hank, who had actually—and conveniently—moved to San Francisco. Bobby was able to play upon Aaron's sympathies when Bobby found himself suddenly left without a mentor. Aaron had more insight into Bobby, since he had wrestled with the exact same demons as Bobby: too much time online at sites like Manhunt, too many hours logged in at the baths, too many encounters, in desperation, with unsavory people with whom he might not have otherwise associated if it hadn't been for his addiction.

Hank's addiction, for heaven's sake, was too much masturbation. Now, the little guy took it to whole new levels, compulsively whacking off, "edging" he called it, for hours at a time. He had told Bobby more than once he had edged for almost eight hours. His penis was raw and now bore scars from his inability to stop himself from stroking.

But Bobby digressed—in his thoughts. He was thinking about how he had changed in the last few weeks. How, through the grace of Aaron, SAA, and yes, prayer, he had become a more centered person, someone he actually liked better when he looked in the mirror.

And then he thought of Wade's visit. Wade, he of the cleft chin, dark eyes and hair, and movie star good looks that harkened back to the days of no less than the likes of Mr. Rock Hudson.

There was temptation. In the flesh… And it could send his goals, his strides flying out the window to splatter on the pavement below as though they had never existed.

"Tell me why you're nervous." Camille leaned forward. Today, she wore a tight leather miniskirt, a loose silk blouse, and heels of the height that qualified for the term, CFM pumps (with CFM standing for, naturally, come fuck me). Bobby suddenly wondered if Camille dealt with some of the same issues he did when she wasn't on duty.

"I've been good, you know? I am really coming along in understanding who I am and why I behaved the way I did."

"Remind me about that."

"You know, it probably stems back to my dad and my relationship—or lack thereof—with him. I think I've been hungry for his denied love all my life. Maybe even more so because I was a little gay boy who grew into a big gay slut."

"Which is why you have the relationship with sex that you do?" Camille pushed her glasses, wire ovals, back up on the bridge of her freckled nose.

"Which is why I've had an *unhealthy* relationship with sex all my life." Bobby grinned. "I look forward to a time when sex and I can have a healthy relationship."

Camille nodded. "So when this Wade gets here from Seattle, what makes you think he'll want you? Why do you fear that?"

"Oh, that's cold. Look at me." Bobby laughed, sitting up straighter in his chair. Today, he wore a pair of linen pants and a formfitting raw silk T-shirt that showed off his broad shoulders and defined pecs. "I don't mean to brag, but I have been fortunate."

"Yes, you have." Camille eyed him up and down, and Bobby swore he could see something predatory in her stare.

"Anyway," Bobby went on, "you're right. Wade might not have the least bit of interest in me. It's possible. But what if he did? Could I resist a man like that?" Bobby had earlier sung the praises of Wade's pulchritude to Camille. "Could I say no if he offered, or if he made a pass?" The thought of it was both arousing and repellant.

"Why would you want to?" Camille asked.

"Because the group and Aaron tell me I'm not ready yet. They say that I haven't yet come to terms with how to express my sexuality, and I need time to understand where my abuse of it came from. I need to work on that before I can jump into bed with anyone."

"That's what *they* say. What do *you* say?"

"I say I don't know. I mean, I can think of lots of good reasons not to sleep with Wade, if the situation came about, which it very well might not, but when push comes to shove, or kiss to kiss, or grope to grope, or whatever, I'm not sure I'm strong enough to resist that temptation. Through all this, you know, my libido hasn't just shriveled up and died. It's standing there, proud and tall, waiting in the wings, just waiting for me to give it a cue to bound onto the stage. I'm jonesing a bit here. Add to the fact that this guy is gorgeous, it's summer in Chicago, and I really like the man, and you might have a recipe for a major slip."

"What have you been doing to avoid that? I mean, without Wade here?"

And Bobby knew. Prayer. Meetings. Aaron. That holy trinity had kept him clean, had allowed him, for once in his life, to get in touch with himself, not just on a superficial level, but more deeply, shining a light on the Bobby he had hidden from and hidden away for all of his adult life.

And the surprising truth that had come to him was this: *that* Bobby was not as reprehensible and out of control as he thought. *That* Bobby had the capacity for good.

"You still will have those tools—the whole time Wade's here, I assume." Camille cocked her head. "Is he staying with you?"

"Lord, no. He has a friend whose family is in Wilmette. He'll be staying with her most of the time."

"I don't usually offer such concrete advice, but I think it would be a good idea if he doesn't stay at your place, if it somehow comes up."

Bobby thought of how Wade's friend Sabine would be headed up to Lake Geneva for a couple of days. He would be lying if he didn't admit he had thought about Wade staying at his place while she was gone.

Bobby nodded at Camille. "You're right."

"I'm always right. That's why you pay me so much money." She laughed. "Did I ever tell you I was raised Catholic?"

Bobby shook his head.

"Well, I always tell people I'm a lapsed Catholic in need of a good spanking." She chuckled, raising her eyebrows. "And it's true. But one thing I learned from those years was about avoiding what the various nuns and priests in my upbringing referred to as 'the occasion of sin.'"

Bobby nodded. He knew all about the concept. He just wasn't sure he knew how to avoid it. But he didn't tell Camille that. "I'll keep that in mind, Camille. There is something else that's been bothering me, and it's an ongoing thing."

Camille cocked her head. "Go ahead."

"I've talked about this before, but it's still there. I suspect it always will be unless I can arrive at some sort of resolution."

"Caden?"

"Caden. I know you've said, and my group has said, that I need to just let go of that relationship, but I can't. I still think of him all the time, and even when I'm not, something will remind me of him and I'm right back where I started—yearning for him, missing that easy friendship we used to have."

"Bobby, this isn't about Caden. It's about you. Do you hear yourself? You talk about not having a resolution, about what *you* want. People don't always do what we want them to and, as much as I think you do need Caden's friendship and support in your life, you do have to accept that he's gone. If he doesn't want you back in his life—and all the evidence appears that he feels that way—then you can't force it. You do need to let go. You need to move on. You have other friends now, and I'm sure he does too."

Camille caught his gaze and held it. Her eyes were warm with sympathy. "This may sound cold, but maybe it would be easier if you thought of Caden as dead."

Bobby felt a jolt go through him, and suddenly an image of his friend laid out in a casket popped into his mind. "I can't do that!"

"Bad idea, maybe."

"Why won't he just forgive me?"

"I don't know. I'd advise him to, if he ever came to see me again. Forgiveness can be one of the most powerful and freeing gifts we can bestow on ourselves. I'd tell him that his carrying around this resentment toward you is harming him just as much as it is you, even if he doesn't want a relationship with you."

"Isn't there anything I can do?" Bobby knew Camille held no magic answers.

"You've tried everything, right? I mean, you've made a point to see him in person, you've called, you've emailed." Camille laughed. "You've texted."

Bobby nodded, morose. He supposed someday he would let go of his friend, but he felt incapable of it at the moment.

Camille asked, "You *have* written to him, haven't you? I don't mean like an email, I mean a real letter, sent through the post office, delivered to his home mailbox."

Bobby shook his head. "No. Who writes letters anymore?"

"Exactly! And maybe doing something like writing a heartfelt letter, in your own hand, and mailing it to him may be out of the ordinary enough that he'll pay attention to it. It may not change anything, but do you think it would be worth a try?"

"At this point, I have nothing to lose save a stamp and some time and everything to gain."

"Then do it."

*

That night, Bobby sat at the desk that, for the last several years of his life, he'd used as a portal for bringing men into his life. Whether it was just for the visual stimulation of sites like cam4 or Xvideos, or for bringing about the potential of a more physical, and no less pornographic, connection in the real world, didn't matter.

The condo was quiet. Johnny slumbered on his pillow on the bed. There were no sounds from outside, the traffic below on Lake Shore Drive a distant drone, barely heard.

Bobby had shoved aside his wireless keyboard and mouse to make room for the yellow legal pad he had before him, upon which he would compose his missive to Caden. It had been years, Bobby thought, since he had even owned stationery.

On the floor at his feet were several balled-up wads of paper, representing his previous attempts to transform the contents of his heart into inked scribbles on paper. Nothing seemed right.

He sighed. *Don't think about it too much. Just say what's in your heart. Let go.* There was a phrase he had read once upon a time, in a Mary Carr memoir, and it came back to him now with the force of divine advice.

The heart knows what the head don't.

And that other phrase, so oft repeated at the meetings that had become central to his life—*Let go and let God*—now gave him the kick in the butt he needed to begin.

The words are there; just wrangle them onto the paper.

And so he began.

Dear Caden,

I ask only one thing of you. Read this little letter to its end. After that, you can do what you want, but if you could just have the grace and kindness in your heart to do me the one simple favor of just reading this letter through to the finish, you will have my undying gratitude.

I'm sure you know why I'm writing—what happened last fall/winter between us, the moves I made that wrecked our friendship. I've said it many times before, but it bears repeating—I am deeply sorry. With all my heart, I regret what I did and accept full responsibility.

But you know that, right? You may not be able to get over it, but you do know that I'm deeply and terribly sorry. The last thing in the world I would ever want to do is cause you, my best friend, pain. The fact that my selfishness hurt you is an ache that is with me always. If I could go back and do things differently, I would.

But again, you've heard all this before, and I can see the impatience on your face and hear the thoughts in your head, about just balling up this note and throwing it in the trash or touching a match's flame to it.

But wait, there's more! As they say on the infomercials...

See, the one thing I don't think you do know is that my apology, my desire to make amends, to build a bridge back to you, is different tonight as I sit here writing this. Why? Because the Bobby you know is a different Bobby from the one writing this letter.

The Bobby you knew was vain and selfish. He was hedonistic and heedless in his pursuit of pleasure.

Frankly, Caden, I don't know what you ever saw in him.

But that aside, you must have seen something, back in the day, when a weekend wouldn't go by where we wouldn't see each other.

And I like to think the Bobby you saw is the one I've more fully come to be.

Here's my secret: Camille has helped me to understand that I have a sexual addiction. I have finally come to accept that. And if you think I'm going to pull out this condition, disease, whatever you want to call it, to excuse myself from past wrongdoings, especially to you, you'd be wrong.

No, I tell you this now so hopefully you'll understand the change within me, the change I've worked so hard for these past several months, with Camille, with Sex Addicts Anonymous, with caring people who have suddenly appeared in my life. They showed me that all the sex I was having was just an avoidance measure—a way to not deal with what was really preventing me from making a connection that actually mattered with another human being.

Like the one I had with you. Like the one I pray that one day we can have again.

I have come to see that I need to work on myself, to understand why I used sex as I did, before I can even have it again.

It may stun you to know that it's been weeks and weeks since I've had sex, beyond making love alone, as Bernadette Peters once sang...

Listen, this letter isn't about me. It's about you. I hope you are well. Healthy. Happy. I hope yours and Kevin's relationship has continued to grow and flourish. I hope you have found real love. No one deserves that more than you.

Until very recently, I thought—and didn't even realize it—that I didn't deserve what I now hope you've found. If you had told me I felt that way even a few months ago, I would have said you were crazy, but I know now it's true.

But I do deserve love. And by the grace of God, I will find it.

If you can see it in your heart to imagine a different Bobby, a better Bobby, I hope you'll be in touch.

If you can see it in your heart to consider, for only a moment and not for me but for you, forgiveness, I hope you'll be in touch. Or not. I urge you to let go of the pain I caused, for your sake if not for mine. I want your happiness to be unsullied, whether I figure into your future or not.

I really mean that.

I love you, Caden. That's all.

Bobby signed the letter with usual *x's* and *o's*, folded it three times, and slid it into the already-addressed envelope he had laid out on his desk. He placed a stamp on it, then turned to Johnny and gave one quick whistle.

Johnny raised his head and yawned, focusing his gaze on his master.

"Wanna take a walk? I need to mail this, and I don't want to trust it to the outgoing mail tray at the front desk."

Johnny seemed to understand. He hopped from the bed and, nails clicking on hardwood, walked to the front door, in front of which he sat, waiting for Bobby to put on his harness and leash.

Bobby set out with Johnny leading the way, hope in his heart.

Chapter Fourteen

Bobby awakened that first morning in July with two thoughts. The first had to do with the well-endowed stud snoring next to him and how deeply in love he had fallen with him in such a short time. He certainly had done little to earn Bobby's adoration, besides being so damn cute in a rugged sort of way. But he was completely unpredictable, which sometimes Bobby loved, but mostly hated. This unpredictably, however, ensured that things never got boring between the two of them. Bobby prized the excitement that came from that, from the knowledge that every day with this character would be different.

The other thing Bobby was so smitten with was the fact that this one really listened to him. His large brown eyes drank Bobby in with utter devotion, and when Bobby spoke to him, he gave Bobby his complete and undivided attention, as though he was processing deeply every word Bobby spoke.

Yes, his little Chihuahua mix, Johnny Wadd, had proved himself to be such a lucky find nearly two months ago that Bobby often wondered if their encounter in the grimy alley adjacent to a run-down bar and grill was fate.

Bobby had never imagined he'd be a dog owner, or a dog lover whose devotion very quickly knew no bounds.

Now, Bobby looked down on the little dog and watched his rising and falling chest with all the adoration a mother showers on her slumbering infant. Johnny had been all Bobby had hoped. He had quickly taken to housebreaking, using puppy pads when going outside proved inconvenient and saving the rest for the pair's frequent walks along the shores of Lake Michigan. Johnny adapted effortlessly to being a passenger in a bright orange canvas messenger bag purchased just for him because of its fabulous faux sheepskin lining. And, best of all, he was perfectly content to sleep through the night, a comfort on the pillow beside Bobby's head. The dog never asked for breakfast or to be taken out until Bobby was ready.

Bobby respected that. Now, why couldn't he find a two-legged male with such sterling qualities?

He rolled over, observing the bright blue sky, dotted here and there with puffy cumulus clouds that looked like nothing more than cotton balls. The day was fresh and open to all sorts of possibilities, which brought Bobby to the second thing on his mind upon awakening.

He knew Wade had arrived in Chicago two days ago. He had received an email from him that included his airline itinerary a couple of weeks ago.

Bobby was a little disappointed because, although he kept his phone on his person during nearly every minute of the previous forty-eight hours, even taking it with him to the bathroom, Wade had not called.

An optimistic Bobby had imagined Wade texting him, excited, the moment his plane touched down on the runway at O'Hare. *I'm here!* He would text. *Can't wait to see you!* Two days ago, every time he heard his ringtone or the peculiar little tweet he had selected to alert him to a text, he expected to look down and see one or the other would be from Wade. His mood grew fouler as the hours, and finally the days, progressed with no word from the man he had been looking forward, longing really, to see for the last couple of months.

Now Bobby tried to shut out the depressing, pessimistic voice in his head that said Wade wouldn't call, or if he did, it would be toward the end of his stay and would be to perhaps make arrangements for a quick lunch or coffee somewhere.

He knew he could call Wade. Of course he could, but he remembered how Wade had specifically said in his last email to Bobby that he'd be in touch when he got into town.

Bobby rose from the bed, yawned, and stretched. Johnny aped his master's movements, then hopped from the bed, tail wagging, an expectant gaze focused on Bobby. Bobby was grateful for the distraction.

"You ready to go outside? And then come back in, have a nice breakfast? How about I scramble up an egg for you?"

Johnny wagged his tail harder, mouth falling open and tongue lolling out. Bobby sometimes swore this creature could understand every word he said.

Bobby dressed quickly in a pair of cargo shorts and a black T-shirt from his favorite bar, Big Chicks, farther north on Sheridan Road. He slid into his flip-flops and grabbed Johnny's studded black leather harness, purchased because it was so similar to Bobby's own fetish wear.

"Let's go."

Johnny knew the drill by now and actually led Bobby down the long corridor to the elevator, head up and alert for any neighbors. The dog had quickly become a favorite in Bobby's condo building, with his woeful face, underbite, and feisty and outgoing spirit. Bobby swore in the short time Johnny had lived with him, more neighbors knew the dog's name than knew Bobby's.

Once outside, Bobby's spirits were lifted by the temperature, which he would have estimated to be somewhere in the midseventies, with hardly any humidity. A cooling breeze, in contrast to the sun, moved across Lake Michigan's waters, which today looked almost tropical, decked out in aquamarine. One of the things Bobby loved about living on Lake Shore Drive was the shifting moods and color palettes of the lake.

Bobby stopped as Johnny lifted his leg to pee on a shrub near the circular drive in front of the building. They moved on, with Johnny barking quick, gruff hellos to two other dogs, a black-and-brown shepherd mix and a Boston terrier, out with their owners, both gay men like his daddy. Bobby and Johnny had seen them both many times before, although Bobby was surprised he had never hooked up with either of the owners.

Or if he had, he didn't recall it.

Johnny began to circle atop a patch of grass once they emerged from the tunnel that ran under the drive into the lakefront proper. Bobby knew what this meant and drew out a plastic bag from the hydrant-shaped receptacle attached to Johnny's leash. He watched as the dog did his business, then stooped to clean it up.

"Make sure you dispose of that properly," a voice said from behind him.

Why, of all the nerve! Of course, he would dispose of the bag properly. Why wouldn't he? He always did. He didn't need to be reminded! He whirled, ready to give the person a piece of his mind. He was in no mood to be corrected that morning.

He turned around—and there was Wade. Wade...his eyes crinkled from the sun and his smile, which was huge. Wade, looking absolutely delicious in a pair of madras shorts, espadrilles, and a pale yellow linen shirt, open to reveal his hairy chest. His dark eyes, Bobby swore, sparkled with mischief in the sun. Wade seemed somehow larger than life, bigger than Bobby recalled, with broader shoulders, more imposing biceps, and calves that looked like they'd managed to swallow grapefruits. All of this musculature was highlighted by a thick dusting of coarse black hair that made Bobby a little short of breath.

Bobby had a quick flash of the young Christopher Reeve, when he had starred in his very first *Superman* movie. Fact of the matter was, Wade put Mr. Reeve to shame, even in his glory days.

Oh my God, what am I going to do? Bobby's fears about being tempted came crashing into his head, causing his already quickly beating heart to accelerate a little more. *How can I resist that? They say "Let go and let God," but hell, all I'm thinking right now is "Let go and let Wade." Let Wade—do anything he damn well wants.*

Bobby tried not to let the sudden storm that had blown up in his mind reflect on his face. He grinned. "I was wondering if you were going to be in touch."

Wade shrugged. "I wanted to surprise you." He moved closer and gave Bobby a brief hug. Johnny, jealous, yipped. "I hope that's okay."

"I don't know." Bobby looked down at the Chihuahua. "Is that okay with you, Mr. Wadd?"

"You named your dog Mr. Wadd?"

"Johnny Wadd." Bobby chuckled.

Wade stooped down for a glance under the canine carriage. "Oh, I see. Well, the name certainly fits." Wade laughed and stood back up, but Johnny was not about to let him get away, standing on his hind legs, propped up by Wade's own calves, and staring up at Wade with mournful eyes. Wade petted him, scratched him behind the ears.

After Johnny had apparently had enough attention, he wandered off to sniff a patch of grass that had probably been marked earlier by one of his peers.

Wade caught Bobby's eye. "I do hope I didn't overstep my bounds by coming down here. If you have other plans for the day, that's completely cool. We can maybe get something on the calendar for later in my stay."

"No, no, not at all. I'm glad you're here." Bobby grinned. "And I can't imagine a nicer surprise. How did you plan this, anyway? I don't remember giving you my address, and it had to be a crap shoot knowing I would be outside this morning."

"Well, you're one of those weird, dwindling few with a landline and listing in the phone book, although you are certainly not the only Robert Nelson or R Nelson in Chicago! I played the odds that this address would be yours—and I won. Sabine helped me out. She told me that the Robert Nelson just east of Boystown would most likely be you.

"And you told me you had gotten a dog in one of your emails. As a dog owner myself, I knew that it was pretty likely one of the first things you'd do in the morning is take your little critter outside." Wade cocked his head. "And if you didn't, or I missed you, I would have just called your cell."

They fell silent for a moment.

Wade asked, "So...are you free today?"

"Yeah! Yeah, I had kind of planned on spending time with you this weekend anyway, so the day—gorgeous as it is—is ours to enjoy, obstruction free."

"That's good."

"You wanna come upstairs?"

"Said the spider to the fly?"

Oh, buster, if you only knew... Instead, Bobby said, "You and me have a lot to talk about. Come on up, and I'll put some coffee on. You and Johnny can get better acquainted while I shower and make myself pretty."

"That should take about thirty seconds."

"Flatterer! But I'll take it. Come on." And Bobby, feeling suddenly as though he were walking on air, led Wade inside his building. What would he do—he couldn't help but wonder—if Wade tried to get into the shower with him? Wade didn't know it, but Bobby felt the responsibility for whether he reverted to old habits or not rested entirely in Wade's hands, which was not a good thought to have. *But they do say, in the group, we are powerless over our addiction. And yes, sir, I do feel pretty powerless right now.*

*

An hour later, Bobby found himself sitting across the table from Wade at Tweet, the restaurant next to Big Chicks and headed up by the same owner. When Bobby asked if Wade had anything special in mind for the day, Wade had responded, "I want to see the Chicago you don't necessarily get in the tourist guides. I mean, Sabine and I have been to Millennium Park, and we went up in the John Hancock. We rode the Ferris wheel at Navy Pier. We did the Architecture Foundation boat cruise. We had lunch at Pizzeria Due. We did the Art Institute. All cool, but I figured you've been here long enough to show me some things that are off the beaten path."

Bobby felt more than a little pressure, since the things Wade had named would have been some of the first things he would have suggested if he had not been challenged otherwise.

So Bobby was thinking, thinking, thinking. He would play the day by ear, but he would do his best to impress Wade. He wanted to impress Wade. His mind, already, was filled with thoughts of...Wade.

Bobby was grateful he had a car because living right in the heart of the city, he had many times considered just ditching it. But today, it would be easier to chauffeur Wade to the places he wanted to take him.

They finished their Bloody Marys and eggs Benedict and set out. "Where are we headed?" Wade asked, as Bobby used the remote to unlock the doors of his car.

"You'll see. But it's quiet, and although there are hundreds of people there, you'll be amazed at how little any of them has to say."

Fifteen minutes later, they pulled up in front of a Gothic sandstone arch that looked ready-made for a castle.

Bobby parked the car across the street. Wade looked over at him, and Bobby could see the uncertainty playing about his features.

Wade asked, "You brought me to a cemetery?"

"You said you wanted different. And Rosehill isn't just any cemetery. Aside from being a beautiful oasis right in the middle of the urban jungle, it's historic." He rattled off the names of some of the cemetery's better-known mausoleum and plot residents—"Charles Schwab, the Florsheim shoe guy, Oscar Mayer, the founder of Sears, the Schwinn bicycle guy, a whole bunch of former mayors and politicians, even a gangster who died in the St. Valentine's Day massacre."

"Sounds interesting."

"Oh, it is...and it's beautiful. And some of the monuments are amazing."

They began walking through the cemetery. A warm breeze buffeted them, and the quiet serenity of the grounds stilled them, until they came to one monument.

"You weren't kidding when you said some of the monuments are amazing," Wade said.

They had paused in front of the marker for Frances Pearce. Atop the large headstone rested a sculpture encased in glass. The sculpture was a lovingly rendered and detailed portrait of a young mother reclining with her child. "They say she died in childbirth, and her husband commissioned this statue. That's his grave over there." Bobby pointed to a much less remarkable memorial for Horatio O. Stone, nearby.

"It's beautiful." Wade seemed awed, and Bobby was glad he had brought him here. In spite of the beauty of the day, they had the cemetery almost entirely to themselves. He eyed the mother and child, reclining in each other's arms for eternity. There was a tranquility about the statue that left Bobby yearning for something he couldn't quite define.

"Local legend has it that on the anniversary of her death, the glass fills inside with a white mist."

"Really?"

"Now, I can't vouch for that personally, but there are people who swear it's true."

They walked on, pausing at the many mausoleums dotting the manicured grass, the obelisk honoring Senator Charles Farwell, tributes to fallen soldiers, going all the way back to the Civil War. Finally, Wade tugged at Bobby's hand.

"Let's sit down for a minute. That Bloody Mary and hollandaise sauce have clouded my head and thickened my blood. I need a break."

Careful not to sit in goose crap, which was plentiful here by this serene pond dotted with geese and even a couple of swans, Bobby sat next to Wade. For a while, they gazed out at the water, quiet, companionable.

Finally, Wade asked, "How have you been, Bobby? I know losing a parent is hard."

Bobby's mind flashed on his father. Just a quick image of the man smiling. There was a contentment surrounding this image, an unexpected sense of calm, and it made Bobby catch his breath. He wasn't used to thinking of his dad this way. If he could have predicted this moment, when Wade conveyed his sympathy and concern for Bobby's loss, he would have thought he simply wouldn't care.

"Yeah. Life becomes different when a parent goes." He stared off at the greenish water, bedazzled with what looked like sequins, courtesy of the sun. Another image came to him—Dad sitting at their kitchen table on Queen Anne, reading the newspaper, magnifying lenses perched on the bridge of his nose. He didn't know if this was fifteen, twenty years ago or more, but it was something he remembered about his father. Every night, after dinner, he would bring out the day's *Seattle Times* and page through it, concluding with the crossword puzzle. Bobby didn't know why this particular image chose to present itself now, save for the feeling it gave him, one that he realized he'd had as he helped his mom clear the dishes from the table—a feeling of security, of sameness, of, dare he think it, family.

He didn't want to become maudlin on this gorgeous summer day, so he turned to Wade and smiled. "I have a lot to tell you."

"Oh?"

"Yeah, remember that little scene you witnessed at the baths in Seattle? And what we talked about afterwards?"

"Of course I do," Wade said softly.

"Well, when I got back here, I dug deep and thought really hard about who I am, why I am, what I'm doing." Bobby recounted his slips, those uncertain steps toward sobriety, toward understanding that sex could be an instrument of joy and connection and how his abuse of it had actually removed the pleasure from it, making it instead something to bury his head in. Or the head of his dick, he quipped, but he didn't smile. He told Wade about Sex Addicts Anonymous and the community of friends he had found there, people who shared his concerns and walked with him on a journey that was baffling and filled with pitfalls but was made easier by the company, by the simple knowledge that there was a small community of people who cared if you succeeded or failed. He told Wade about Camille, his sexy therapist, who appeared to have just a tiny bit too much appreciation for Bobby in the way she leered at him when Bobby suspected she thought he wasn't looking, but ultimately, how she led him toward making profound conclusions about his life. And, of course, he mentioned Johnny. "That dog was like my dumpster-found savior." Bobby laughed, shaking his head. "I never thought I'd fall in love with a dog. But I did. And a well-hung one at that! Leave it to me. I never denied being a size queen!" Bobby laughed and then grew serious. "Caring for Johnny has shown me a side of myself I didn't know existed."

"What side is that?"

Bobby didn't want to say, although he knew the answer was "unselfish." The response would simultaneously put him in a bad light and a good one. "I don't know. Isn't there some saying about not really knowing how to get love until you give it?"

Wade shrugged. "Probably. Hallmark, maybe?"

"Whatever. Johnny made a difference, made the path I'm walking on right now easier."

Wade stared at him, and Bobby felt the force of his gaze penetrate him, almost like the sunlight streaming down. He felt *seen*.

Wade said, "There's something different about you. I can see it. Feel it. You seem calmer, somehow, than when I saw you last in Seattle. I know you were fresh off your father's death, but that wasn't all of it. There was something so deeply unhappy in you, it almost radiated off you." Wade touched his face, and Bobby let out a little gasp, feeling tears rise to his eyes. "It's different now."

Bobby stared into Wade's dark eyes for a long moment, and it seemed the pastoral setting around them dissolved, fading away, so that it was just the two of them, alone, suspended, linked in a kind of void.

He didn't know if it was wrong or not, a slip or not, but Bobby had never felt a moment more right to do what he was about to do. He leaned forward only a little, because they were sitting so close, and kissed Wade.

Wade's mouth, warm, sweet, and spicy from their breakfast, opened to accept his tongue, to accept *him*. They pressed their faces together, tongues dueling, lips locked in a passion so sudden and fierce it nearly knocked the breath right out of Bobby.

Who knows how long the kiss would have gone on had it not been interrupted by the long blast of a car horn, which prompted the geese sitting nearby to take flight. Bobby and Wade broke apart, panting, and looked to see an ancient powder-blue Valiant glide by, not twenty feet away. Two old women were in the car, wearing twin gray upsweeps of hair and twin faces of disapproval.

Wade laughed. "Didn't you see the sign?"

Bobby got up, brushing the grass from his ass. "What sign?"

Wade stood too. "The one at the front that said 'No Public Displays of Affection.'"

Bobby pushed him. "There was no such sign."

"No, but maybe there ought to have been—for us." Mischief danced in his eyes.

Wade took Bobby's hand, interlacing his fingers with Bobby's. "Come on. Let's see what else you've got up your sleeve."

Bobby didn't know if he meant regarding what he wanted to show Wade about Chicago, or if he meant in the physical contact department. Either way, Bobby felt he had stepped into a dangerous, bottomless well of temptation, and he didn't know how he could ever emerge. He glanced at Wade, at the way his dark, wavy hair absorbed the sunlight, and wondered if he even wanted to.

*

"Are you sure this is okay?" Bobby had taken Wade to the Heartland Café in Rogers Park for dinner. The place was iconic, a leftover from hippie days when tofu was king and macrobiotic was a word people tossed around with seriousness. Bobby remembered Wade liked to eat naturally and for that reason, plus the relaxed atmosphere of the laid-back-to-a-fault eatery, had brought him here.

They had wanted to sit outside, since the day was holding steady in its promise of glory and sunshine. It seemed that dusk was hours away, when in fact it was only an hour and a half distant, heading fast over the western edge of the city. But a large crowd thwarted their wish, all of whom wanted to sit outside, and their request for the first available table got them near the covered patio, but not on it. Still, with the windows open, they could enjoy the warm breezes that wafted inside.

"This is great. How long has this place been here?"

Bobby shook his head and grabbed a piece of pita bread from the bowl they had ordered to share as an appetizer and loaded it up with hummus, avocado, and tomato. "As long as I've lived here and I think well beyond that." He peered around him at the rustic interior, listening as a jazz trio began tuning up on a little stage set up in the window of the main dining room. "From the looks of the place, and the stuff they have on sale in the gift shop, I'd guess they opened in the late 1960s."

"Before we were born."

"Yeah."

Bobby stared into Wade's dark eyes and thought how he could drown in them. He also thought he should be taking a quick break to duck outside and call Aaron, to let him know he was in such a state of temptation, but something always prevented him. He could say it was the arrival of their waitress, a cute blonde with a nose ring, dreads, and a butterfly tattoo, who introduced herself as Betty, or he could attribute it to their appetizer being set in front of them and his hunger after a day spent exploring what seemed to be the whole north side of the city—and beyond. They had gone to the top of the lighthouse in Evanston, on up to see the architectural wonder of the Baha'i Temple in Wilmette, then headed west to hop on I-94, and then back south toward the city and to the Wicker Park neighborhood, where they had spent hours among the stacks, comparing notes on the more unusual offerings at Quimby's Queer

Bookstore, which, despite its name, was not a GLBT establishment.

Yes, he could attribute his not calling Aaron, or any other member of SAA whose numbers he had carefully programmed into his iPhone so he would have them at the ready in times of need, of which this was a perfect example, to any number of reasons outside the most basic one. The one, which, if he were being completely honest with himself, he would know was the true reason.

He simply didn't want to.

For to call Aaron or some other member of the group might cause an interruption in this day, might indeed, as Bobby well knew, put an end to it.

And he couldn't do that. The day had been magical, and continued to be so. There had been no more kisses, but the same intimacy that had gripped them by the pond at Rosehill remained with them throughout the day, exemplified by stolen glances that lingered for a fraction of a second longer than what might be considered normal, or a hushed whisper that placed the two of them into a bubble of exclusivity, or even the provocative brush of a hip against a hip or a quick touch of one hand to another.

And, throughout the course of the day, they had shared their stories with one another, catching up on what had gone on with each of them in the intervening years between high school graduation and the present. Bobby wasn't shy, and this was the amazing thing. He freely shared his decade of sexual adventuring with Wade, recounting what was really a tale much more of quantity than of quality. But the wonderful thing, the thing that made him feel closer to this man from the city in which Bobby had grown up, was that Wade listened and never judged him.

It was as if at last someone, outside the more rigid confines of a therapist's office or a twelve-step group, saw him for who he was and accepted him. Understood him.

Bobby knew in the past he had wanted men and that want sometimes went beyond the physical, but it was always an unspecified yearning, a desire to possess, to have what he perceived the rest of the world having while he alone was denied.

But with Wade, he felt a meeting of the minds, a connection that was as powerful emotionally as it was physically. Wade knew him, knew where he was from in a geographical sense, but also on a much broader scope, understanding the roads Bobby had traveled, the wrong turns he had taken, and his desire, at age forty, to avoid those wrong turns for the time he had remaining.

All of this flashed through his mind as he gazed into Wade's eyes, as they chatted over nothing, sharing their food, their beers. Underneath the table, Wade's foot, freed of its shoe, rested on Bobby's bare instep, and the pedestrian touch was more exciting to Bobby than a blowjob, sending a rich, pulsating current of electricity that pulsed and radiated up his legs, went directly to his groin, and radiated outward to envelop his heart.

Betty showed up with their dinners—buffalo chili for Bobby and a seitan stir fry for Wade—and smiled down at them as though she too was in on what was going through the couple's minds, or at least Bobby's at any rate.

"Can I get you two anything else?"

"No, thanks," Bobby said, but he wanted to add, *Yeah. Why don't you go ahead and bring us the check? I want to get this boy home.* But, of course, he had no idea Wade would even come back to his place after dinner, and if he did, what would happen there. In spite of the closeness they had shared throughout the day, Bobby wasn't at all sure Wade was on board for more than hand holding and soulful gazes. And Bobby didn't know if he was either, which, in and of itself, was something of a small miracle.

The old Bobby probably would have blown Wade at least once in the car by now and coerced him into fucking him in the bathroom stall of the men's room in the basement of the Baha'i Temple. He snorted with laughter at that last thought.

"What?" Wade looked up from his plate of vegetables, his eyebrows coming together. Betty walked away.

"Just a funny thought, that's all. Nothin'." Bobby dug into his chili. "You know, I've had an amazing time with you today. Better than I could have ever imagined."

Wade covered Bobby's hand with his own. "Me too. I hope we can spend some more time together while I'm here."

"Oh, I'll be either heartbroken or furious if we don't. Probably both. Besides, I haven't shown you Graceland yet."

"Graceland? Elvis?"

"No, it's another old cemetery on the north side. Some of the biggies in Chicago history are buried there—Marshall Field, Mies van der Rohe, George Pullman, Louis Sullivan—and it's reported to be really, really haunted. When we get back to my place, I can show you some pictures that ghost hunters have taken in the cemetery that are supposed to be real. You don't want to miss out on that."

"You and cemeteries. Who knew? And who knew they could be so much fun? I'm down for Graceland." Wade pulled his hand away. "But what's this about coming back to your place after dinner? I hadn't been issued any such invitation. I assumed after this, you'd drop me back at Sabine's family's house in Wilmette. That's why I thought you came all the way back up north."

Bobby felt his spirits take a plunge. He supposed the trial he was anticipating wouldn't be a trial at all, not when the object of his temptation had just pretty much ruled out any "occasion of sin" as the lapsed-Catholic Camille might have termed it.

Wade reached over and startled Bobby by touching his cheek. "Hey, I never said I wouldn't come back, just that I hadn't been asked. Don't look so crestfallen. You'd make a lousy poker player."

All at once, Bobby realized that maybe *not* having Wade back really wasn't such a bad idea. He didn't know if they would end up being intimate or not, but maybe there was a certain pleasure, one which he would have to confess to himself he had never experienced in his self-indulgent life, in *waiting*. Anticipating. Letting the excitement build, and build.

Delayed gratification was a concept Bobby had no familiarity with, until now.

"So you would like to come back?"

"Maybe. Just for a nightcap." Wade grinned, and Bobby felt his common-sense resolve melting.

He said the next words in a rush because he knew if he didn't get them out quickly, he would never say them. "It would be fun, Wade. But you know all we've talked about, all those things I told you about how hard I've been working since I last saw you?" He started to go on, but again, Wade squeezed his hand, halting him.

Wade smiled. "I know. It's okay."

They fell silent, and Bobby cast his gaze around the busy restaurant. He hadn't noticed because his focus had been so intent on his dinner companion, but tones of navy, lilac, and gray had replaced the summer's blue skies that had been in place when the pair had sat down.

He also hadn't noticed the other couple, two young men like themselves, sitting at a corner table outside on the patio. Bobby felt his heart ascend and lodge in his throat.

One of the men, dark-haired, intense, wire-thin, and wearing a white tank and faded, ripped jeans and flip-flops, was totally immersed in his companion across the table. It was almost like Bobby could draw a straight line between the pair's eyes. That's how connected they were. The other guy, blond and bearded, was broad-shouldered, with muscular biceps and shoulders straining the thin fabric of the black T-shirt he wore.

They were a beautiful couple, and Bobby thought anyone could see that, gay or straight. Such good looks transcended gender.

Another thing: anyone with a pair of eyes in his or her head could see was that the two were hopelessly in love. The way they gazed soulfully into each other eyes, how they laughed together, as though they were conspiring, their whispered words across the table put them in a small world all their own in spite of all the people surrounding them, laughing, eating, drinking, and even walking by on the sidewalk. All of these things told a great and potent love story.

It almost brought tears to Bobby's eyes.

Wade flicked Bobby's hand with a finger, making Bobby realize he had fallen silent for perhaps too long. "What are you staring at?"

"Those two." Bobby nodded at the couple on the patio.

Wade turned discreetly to look. "Man, what a pair of hotties." He turned back to Bobby, grinning.

Bobby shook his head. "Oh, it's more than that, my friend. Can't you see it? Can't you just practically feel how into each other they are?" Bobby said, his voice barely above a whisper. "I envy them." He wasn't even sure he had spoken loud enough for Wade to hear.

Wade looked again. "Yeah, now that you mention it. It's pretty obvious they're smitten."

Bobby stared at them again, shutting out the other diners and even Wade. He knew them. They were Caden and Kevin, his former best friend and the boyfriend who Bobby, once upon a time, had attempted to steal from him, thus sealing the end of their friendship. It made his heart hurt to look at them. For one, he missed Caden so terribly, and he knew what a good man Kevin was—honest, simple, compassionate, not to mention sexy and smart—and felt a deep sense of regret that neither of them was in his life. For another, the fact that their love for each other was so obvious caused a sharp twinge of longing, painful, to course through him.

He felt like the easy love they had, unselfconscious, real, and impossible to ignore, was something which had been denied to him. Bobby wondered if he even had the capacity to feel the way they did, if he had the depth of emotion within him to experience that kind of love.

He looked over again at Wade, who had stopped eating and was staring at Bobby expectantly. "What? Is there something you're not saying? It's like those two have you transfixed. Do you know them?"

Bobby had shared a lot with Wade throughout the course of their day, but the one thing he did *not* share was what had happened with Caden. He could easily let Wade know what a slut he had been—after all, the man had seen him in action at the baths in Seattle—but he just couldn't bring himself to let Wade in on what a shit he had been as well. He just never saw a reason to reveal himself in such an unflattering light. Now he wondered if he had made the right decision, holding this piece of his history back. If anything were ever to grow between him and Wade, as Bobby hoped it would, he knew that making a clean breast of things would be the best course to take.

"Yeah," Bobby said softly, taking a sip of his beer. "I know them both."

"And?"

And Bobby told him the whole story of how Caden had once been his best friend and how Bobby had betrayed their closeness to chase after the man now sitting across the table from Caden. Bobby swallowed hard, summoning up all the courage and resolve he possessed, and forced himself to let Wade in on the duplicity he had instigated, how he had almost prevented the scene they now saw before them, not twenty feet away. When he finished, he fully expected Wade to shake his head and say something along the lines of "Wow. I didn't know you could be so rotten."

But he didn't, because Wade was kind. Wade had a good, nonjudgmental heart. "I can see how much this means to you," Wade said. "And I can hear the regret in your voice. You really miss him, don't you?"

"Oh God, yes." Without thinking, he blurted out, "Caden was my only friend."

"Really? I thought I was your friend. And those guys in your group?"

"Of course you are, Wade. Of course you are. And the group has delivered to me some really good friends. But Caden was my best friend. He stuck with me when I was at my most hateful, my most promiscuous. And when he and I were together, he really was the only man I could truly call friend. The others were just encounters or, at best, fuck buddies. No one who gave a damn about me." Bobby sucked in a big breath. "But I don't want to sit here feeling sorry for myself. I take responsibility for what I did. And I know that the price I'm paying now—although it's really high—is, in the end, fair."

"Have you apologized to him?"

"Dozens of times. I emailed, called, texted, everything. I even lay in wait for him at the lakefront just to tell him I wanted to make amends."

"And none of that got through?" Wade shook his head. "I mean, what you did was pretty terrible. I'm sorry, but it was. But if you've apologized in good faith, and it obviously looks like everything came out okay in the end for *him*, then I don't understand why your old friend Caden is being such a dick."

Bobby felt a surge of warmth for Wade, inspired by his obviously coming to his defense. He also felt protective toward Caden. "He's not a dick," Bobby said quietly. "He's a good guy who never deserved what I put him through." Bobby shoved his chili away from him, covering it with the paper napkin that had been in his lap, no longer hungry.

"Well, maybe he just needs a little more time," Wade said. "He might still come around."

"I can hope." Bobby shrugged. He caught Betty's eye and motioned her over. "Could we get our check?"

"Sure thing, hon. Need anything else?"

Bobby shook his head, and Wade said, "The check will be fine."

Bobby said, "I'm sorry. I should have asked if you wanted anything else. That was selfish of me."

"It's okay," Wade said softly. "You probably want to get out of here, don't you?"

"Yeah. I don't really want to run into them."

"Why don't you slip out now, and I'll meet you at the car."

If Bobby didn't love this man before, he did now. Wade's kindness was rare, and Bobby thought no one had ever looked out for him quite like this before. He took out his wallet, but Wade waved him away. "My treat."

"But—"

"Don't argue. Next time, it's on you. And I want upscale." Wade chuckled.

Bobby hurried out of the restaurant, keeping his gaze focused on Caden and Kevin. He was sure they had never spotted him.

They were too focused on each other.

*

Outside the restaurant, darkness had fallen completely. Bobby hurried west, even though he had parked east of the Heartland, just so he could avoid an encounter with Caden and Kevin. They would surely see him, since they were seated just off the sidewalk. It was easier to go around the block than to experience the pain of coming face-to-face with the couple. He was sure there would be dirty looks, downcast eyes, and silence that grated worse than if they had stood up and yelled at him.

Wade hurried after him. "Hey, wait up! Didn't we park in the other direction?"

Bobby stopped and turned, explaining the method to his madness.

"I'm so sorry you have to feel this way, Bobby."

They walked to the car in silence, the chirping of crickets and the rush of traffic on Sheridan Road their only accompaniment. Once in the car, Bobby started to push the button that would start the ignition, and then pulled his finger away, laying his head on the steering wheel. He was breathing hard and felt tears were close behind.

Wade ran his hand over Bobby's back in slow circles, saying nothing. And the truth was, the simple touch meant more to Bobby than any words ever could. He didn't know what Wade could say, anyway, that would make him feel better. But the feel of the man's hand on his back was soothing, and it was enough to stave off his tears.

After a moment, Bobby sat up straighter, dislodging Wade's touch. He blew out a shaky breath. "I'm okay." He started the car and pulled out onto Glenwood Avenue.

The drive back to his condo on Lake Shore Drive was quiet. The only words spoken were from Wade, who commented on the lighted towers lining the drive on the west side and the huge expanse of dark on the east. They had the windows down, and Bobby finally tuned his Sirius radio to a classical station and set it to low. He wasn't in the mood to play tour guide anymore.

He didn't know why seeing the two of them hit him so hard. Well, no, that wasn't really true. Perhaps it was more accurate to say that there were many reasons seeing them had such a profound impact. The difficulty lay in deciding—if that was even necessary—on which one was the most significant.

For one, he had yet to see the pair together. Even when all the drama took place last winter, he had never really seen Caden with Kevin. The couple's happiness, the obvious joy they found in one another's company, was a sharp pain to his heart, making him wonder if what he saw on their faces, the way their hands casually linked across the table, would be something he would ever experience. But then he thought of how selfish such thoughts were. He realized that he could be happy for them (and he was), but sad for himself.

For another, seeing them drove home the point (hard) that Caden wanted nothing to do with him. He had never answered Bobby's heartfelt letter, let alone ever responded to the countless apologies Bobby had sent his way. The fact that he obviously was indifferent to Bobby and had moved on with his life hurt more than the knowledge that he hated Bobby. At least with hatred, Bobby thought, there was still some feeling left.

The last reason Bobby felt so desolate was the fact that seeing the pair had such a power over him. That simple sighting in the restaurant had pretty much ruined the wonderful day he had been sharing with Wade.

Wade broke the silence as they exited at Belmont. He chuckled and said, "So I *am* coming back to your place?"

"What?" Bobby stopped at a red light. He had been so lost in thought that he almost forgot Wade was on the seat beside him. *That's a first. A hot man in the car with you and you not even aware of his existence. Bobby, oh, Bobby, what's happening to you?*

"I thought you'd take me back to Wilmette. To Sabine's."

Bobby laughed, feeling heat rise to his face, remembering how he had made a point of nixing the idea of Wade coming home with him after dinner. In his upset, he had just driven on automatic pilot, and since his default setting for being out anywhere was to go home afterward, he had simply headed south.

"I'm sorry. I was preoccupied and just did what comes naturally. I didn't mean to presume, and I certainly wasn't up to..." Bobby's voice trailed off. Up to what? His old tricks? Being duplicitous? Making like a spider to a fly? "I can turn around easily enough."

"Why don't you just go home? You have a guest room, right?"

Bobby felt a shiver inside. In spite of all that had gone on, he didn't know how having Wade in the condo overnight might go. It was too much temptation, especially if Wade was even in the smallest way willing.

"Um, yeah."

"It's got clean sheets and everything, right?"

Bobby laughed. "I honestly don't think it's ever been used." When Bobby bought the condo, he had thought some of his family might venture out from Seattle to visit him, but none ever had. "But yeah, it should be fine."

What are you doing, Bobby?

He pulled into his space in the parking garage and looked over at Wade. Even in the fluorescent lighting, Wade managed to look stunningly handsome. *I guess that's one way to define true beauty: you look good no matter what the lighting is.* Bobby got out of the car, having no idea how the rest of the night would play out. Would he succumb to the temptations that had been part and parcel of him all of his adult life? Or would his mood save him because, for the first time he could remember, he was just too down to contemplate going down on a hot man?

Inside the condo, Bobby switched on some lights and turned to Wade. "Would you like something to drink? The nickel tour?"

"Later. I think, right now, the best thing is to get you into bed."

Bobby stood near his floor-to-ceiling windows, paralyzed. Here it was. The temptation—Wade couldn't have laid it out more clearly. What else could getting him into bed mean? He supposed he could go through with it...

Wade must have seen what was going on with Bobby, writ large on his face, because Wade laughed. "By get you into bed, I meant only that I would tuck you in and get you a drink of water, read you a bedtime story if you require it. I'm too tired to have the energy to do much else."

Bobby was touched. The offer meant more to him than if Wade had pounced on him once the door was closed, tearing off his clothes, as had just about every other man—save for Caden—Bobby had ever had up here.

"Go on," Wade said. "I'm sure I can find the guest room."

"Are you sure? Maybe I should check and see if there are sheets on the bed?"

Wade turned him around. "I'll be fine. If there are no sheets, I'll find some. I'm quite capable of making up a bed myself."

"Okay. Thanks for this." Bobby was suddenly so tired. It was like every bit of life had been drained out of him. He walked, like a zombie, toward his bedroom. At the threshold, Johnny waited for him, staring up beseechingly at his master.

"Oh shit," Bobby whispered to himself. "I forgot all about you. Come on." He patted his leg, indicating that the dog should follow him to the front door, where his leash and harness hung on a hook by the door.

Johnny panted as he trailed Bobby. At the door, though, Bobby was surprised to see Wade already waiting, crouched down on the floor with the leash and harness ready in his hands. He grinned up at Bobby.

"Are you for real?" Bobby asked.

"Of course."

"Why does someone like you have to live all the way across the country?"

"I could ask you the same thing," Wade answered. "Can you give me the keys? Johnny and I here will take a little stroll, and we don't want to wake you when we get back."

Bobby grabbed his keys out of his pocket and handed them to Wade. "Enjoy. And thanks again."

Wade got Johnny "saddled up," stood and kissed Bobby lightly on the lips, which sent a shiver through Bobby, making him long for more, making him wish Wade would hurry up and go. "Sleep. You'll feel much better in the morning. You'll see."

Bobby watched until the pair exited through the front door, Johnny casting a puzzled stare back at Bobby, as if to say, "What? You're not coming along? What is this shit?"

After they were gone, Bobby felt there was no better refuge for him than his own bed. He didn't even bother to turn on any bedroom lights as he stripped down, dropped his clothes on the floor, and collapsed on the bed.

It wasn't until much later that he awoke. The condo was silent, and even the constant whoosh outside of traffic rushing north and south on the drive, was silent. He stood, feeling awake and not groggy in the least, and went to his windows, where he stared out at the night. The drive below him was indeed empty, and Bobby wondered what wee hour this could be, when not a single car was present on Lake Shore Drive.

Did that ever happen?

He wondered how Wade was sleeping. He hoped it was deeply.

He rummaged around in his dresser and pulled out a pair of boxer shorts and a T-shirt and slid them on. He walked out to his living room, enjoying the stillness.

Where was Johnny? The little dog was like his shadow when he was at home, and now he was nowhere in evidence.

But there, by the window, he could see someone sitting in one of the leather chairs he had positioned there for staring out at the water and its changing moods. He neared the chair, thinking it was Wade, but when he got closer, he stopped and gasped in shock.

It was not Wade, but his father.

Robert Nelson, Senior sat, taking in the tranquil night. He didn't look at Bobby, but he must have sensed him there, because he spoke to his son. "I don't know why we never came to visit. You have the most amazing view. Is that a Ferris wheel?" He leaned forward to look south, at Navy Pier and its principal landmark, a wheel that honored the Ferris wheel built for the World's Fair in 1893. It turned slowly, its lights a beacon in the night.

"Yes, Dad. That's exactly what it is." Bobby drew in a breath and sat in the matching chair opposite his dad. "What are you doing here?"

"I came to see you. I had the sense there were some things left unsaid between us."

Bobby chuckled, but there was little mirth in it. "That's an understatement, Dad." He felt he could be free with what he said. None of the fear and anxiety his father usually inspired in him was present, probably because Bobby didn't believe his father was really there. This had to be a dream, a sleepwalking dream, perhaps.

"Like what?" Bobby asked.

"Like that you never knew how I felt about you?"

"How could I, Dad? You never told me."

"I didn't know I had to."

"You did. I never knew."

"I guess I just thought being there for your mom, your sister, and you said it all. I worked all my life at a job I hated just so I could take care of all of you. Where I come from, a man who provides for his family shows his love that way."

"And I thank you for that."

"Do you?"

"Of course I do. Without your money, I could have never had all I have in this life," Bobby conceded. "You were a good provider."

"But you wanted something more."

Bobby felt something catch inside him, and he drew in a frantic, quivering breath, telling himself to be calm. He could only nod and hope his father saw.

"What did you want?"

Bobby felt the tears, hot, spring to his eyes. "You. I just wanted you. I wanted you to be there for me. I hungered for it." Bobby cast his mind back, way back, to ninth grade, when he had been on the track team, running the mile relay. Bobby had never been good at sports, but at least he could run. And deep down, he hoped that this effort would please his sports-obsessed father, who was always parked in front of the TV on weekends, no matter what kind of sport was being broadcast, watching avidly.

Maybe, for once, he would notice his son, take an interest.

And it had been good, when the first meet came about and his father insisted on driving him down to the field on that drizzly Saturday morning. Bobby looked out the car window when he got there and saw all his teammates arriving, many with their own fathers in tow. His excitement rose as he imagined his father cheering him on as he rounded the track, as he chatted with the other boys' fathers.

But his father just pulled up in the car, put it in park, and turned to his son. "Just give me a call when you're done."

Speechless, Bobby had gotten out of the car. He turned to watch his father drive away, hoping that he would realize nothing could be more important than this track meet on this morning in May. He watched, mouth open, until the Audi disappeared completely from view.

At the meet, his relay team placed first, and Bobby ran his quarter mile fast enough to break the school record.

What did it matter?

"It did matter," his father said, startling him, jolting him out of memory.

"Why would it matter to you? You couldn't even be bothered to give up the two hours of your day to stay and watch me."

"Oh, but I did. You just didn't know it. I parked the car and came back, and I watched you from beneath the bleachers. I was so proud."

"Bullshit."

"You ran that quarter mile like you had a tiger on your tail." His father laughed.

Bobby wished it had been true. This was some kind of crazy, fucked-up dream, some wish fulfillment.

"I was there, Bobby. I saw you break that record."

"Then why did you never say anything?"

His father bowed his head. When he spoke, his words came out halting and soft, unlike the confident manner he usually used when he spoke. "I couldn't."

"You couldn't? Why the hell not?" The tears rolled down his cheeks. "It was all I ever wanted."

"It wasn't in me. Sad, isn't it? But we sometimes learn by example, and my father—"

Bobby held up a hand. "I know. He beat you. He hit your mother. You were a prince compared to him."

"Yes."

The two men fell silent. They said nothing for the longest time, and then his father rose. "I have to go back."

Bobby didn't look at him.

"I know this is supposed to end with me telling you how much I love you and how proud I am of you, but that wouldn't be me, now would it?"

Bobby looked up at the man. He was already growing shadowy and insubstantial, as if his form were fashioned from smoke.

"No" was all Bobby could say. He knew to say more would have his voice coming out broken and choked, and he couldn't bear to display his weakness to his father.

"I can say this, though, son. You'll never have any kind of relationship with anyone until you realize you must accept them for who they are. You may get a little; you may get a lot. But only when you start from the point of what's possible, rather than what you hope for, will you ever find love."

Bobby had barely registered the words before he realized he was sitting alone in the living room. He felt something cold and wet on his toes and looked down to see Johnny, licking.

Bobby stood. "You telling me you need to go outside? It's the middle of the night." He shook his head. "Come on, then."

When Bobby returned, he unleashed Johnny, who made quick sticks to their shared bedroom, and imagined him hopping up on the king-size bed and curling up in a tight little ball on one of the pillows.

Bobby didn't follow him, not immediately. Instead, he went and stood outside Wade's door, his head inclined, listening. He thought maybe he'd hear him snoring, or at least breathing, but nothing was audible through the thick door.

Wade was inside. Bobby was out here. All it would take to broach that separation would be for Bobby to reach down, turn the doorknob, and walk into the guest room. He could glide silently through the darkness and sit beside Wade on the bed. He could reach out a gentle hand and play with his dark curls, run it over his chest, let it wander farther south...

He could imagine it all, standing there in the stillness that comes only in the middle of the night, and he felt himself growing aroused as he thought of Wade awakening and not being startled but, instead, reaching up with one hand to grasp the nape of Bobby's neck and pull him toward him to kiss. Wade's mouth would be warm, wet, like a Seattle spring night. Bobby could practically feel the burn of Wade's stubble on his face, the hunger in Wade's mouth as the kiss grew more passionate, as Wade threw back the sheet with one hand and pulled him down on top of him.

He could imagine so much but wondered if acting on this fantasy, even if all was reciprocated as he imagined, would be the course toward something healthy. Or would it, in the morning, look like nothing more than a trick, another mistake in a long line of them?

Was Wade worth waiting for?

Bobby turned and went to his room. As he knew he would be, Johnny was curled up on the pillow that would be next to Bobby's head. The dog looked up for a moment, yawned, then tucked his head back between his forepaws and returned to his slumber.

Ah, to have a dog's life...

Bobby sat on the floor at the foot of the bed, his back resting against it, legs sprawled out lazily before him. He knew the possibility of sleep was over for this night, and he wondered, then, if Aaron would be awake.

He glanced at his clock on the nightstand and saw it was now nearing 5:00 a.m. There was a possibility the guy could be up, sure, but Bobby would wait until morning to call.

Instead, he sat, looking out the window, and watched until the sun rose slowly over the lake's still waters, throwing shades of orange, pink, and pewter across the horizon.

He thought of his dad, and he wished the wish all children have for parents who have died, whether there was a good relationship or a bad one—for more time.

Because with time, any wrong can be righted. Death wiped out that chance.

But he remembered, then, his father's parting words to him, about how we had to accept, sometimes, the things we are given, if there is ever to be a chance at, well, *anything*. It was what the Serenity Prayer told him, and he finally got it.

Accept the things we cannot change.

In order to ever love his father, he had to love his memory as he was, not as Bobby wished he had been. When he could begin from that point, maybe there would be room to see things he had never seen.

Chapter Fifteen

Bobby was up before Wade, grinding Sumatra coffee beans and brewing a pot for the two of them. He figured, since they had breakfast out the previous morning, he would actually try to prepare something for them himself. He opened his big Subzero stainless steel refrigerator to find it nearly empty. The top shelf held an empty Brita water pitcher, and the remaining shelves were populated with a couple of take-out containers, a box from a restaurant dinner Bobby had all but forgotten, a loaf of stale bread, and a bottle of hazelnut no-fat coffee creamer that was probably good for another decade. The contents, really, should all be flung into the garbage.

"Feel like a little walk?" he said to Johnny. There was a small gourmet food market on the ground floor of his building. The prices were insane, but it was convenient.

And they didn't mind Johnny, as long as Bobby kept him in one of his reusable shopping bags, his head out to take in the sights.

When he returned, loaded down with a dozen eggs, turkey sausage, orange juice, cream cheese, and half a dozen bagels, Wade was up and in the kitchen.

"Good morning," Wade said, turning and reaching out to grab the shopping bag from Bobby. He set it on the counter and handed Bobby a cup of coffee. "I didn't know how you take it."

"Black's fine. Thanks." Bobby sipped the coffee and said, "Look at you."

"What?" Wade grinned.

"I don't know whether to ask you politely to put some clothes on or to take off what little you're wearing." He waved a hand. "Ah, I know what I wanna ask, so go put some clothes on, please, before you find yourself ravished."

Wade laughed and headed off to his bedroom.

The man had worn only a pair of pale blue boxers with a seashell design. The simple pair of shorts just made everything else that was exposed (and even the couple of things that weren't) that much more alluring. Bobby couldn't help but grow breathless at the sight of the muscular calves and thighs, crowned with coarse, dark hair, the perfect chest, broad and well-defined, with a treasure trail that disappeared into Wade's shorts. And the thin cotton material couldn't hide the fact that Wade was, well, blessed.

Bobby was tempted to follow him into the room, accuse the man of being a tease, and attempt to take what he thought was rightfully his.

Instead, he busied himself with making breakfast. By the time Wade returned, barefoot and clad in his shorts and shirt from the day before, Bobby was already whisking together the eggs and heating up a bit of olive oil in a skillet.

"Better?"

"I guess. No, actually, that shirt is wrinkled, and I can't stand seeing you in yesterday's clothes. Go into my room and find yourself some comfy shorts and a T-shirt. I think we're close to the same size."

Wade disappeared, which allowed Bobby to finish the breakfast he was attempting to make. When Wade returned, Bobby thought he couldn't imagine a sexier outfit on a man than what Wade had pulled from his closet and drawers. Funny how the simplest things, when draped over the most luscious body, could take on proportions that were something like haute couture.

Wade smiled. "Dude, you're staring."

"My, my, you are a sight for sore eyes."

"In these old things?" Wade wore a pair of faded Levis with the knees in shreds and a well-worn Egyptian cotton button-down white shirt with the sleeves rolled up. He was barefoot. He was stunning, and Bobby just about forgot the eggs he was scrambling.

Half hard and nearly panting, he forced himself to turn back to the stove. The eggs were beginning to brown on the bottom, but Bobby thought that was okay. Apparently, though, Wade begged to differ.

He came up behind him, wrapped his arms around Bobby, and peered over his shoulder into the pan. "Those will *not* do, sir. Why don't you let me take over?"

Bobby would have gladly let Wade take over—the breakfast, his body, his world. He just murmured something unintelligible that sounded like assent and moved to sit at the granite countertop that doubled as a breakfast bar.

His dick was rock hard. He wondered if Wade knew. He had an urge to free it from the confines of the shorts he had on, letting its head out to sniff the air, to take the surface temperature of the lust that hung in the air, like the aroma of Sumatra coffee that had just brewed.

But that would be perverted, wouldn't it?

He tried, somewhat desperately, to concentrate on Wade in the simple act of scrambled egg preparation. "The key to perfect scrambled eggs," Wade said, "is low heat. I mean, really low, like where you can barely see just a tiny rim of blue flame." Wade whisked five eggs in a bowl, adding some salt and pepper and a dollop of half and half. "Whisk hard, baby, to incorporate some air—makes them fluffy." He poured the eggs into the pan. "Now, it may seem like nothing's happening, but slowly, you'll see, the eggs will begin to set. That's when you use your wooden spoon to just gently nudge the eggs, so they begin to form soft curds." Wade paused to pour Bobby more coffee and remove the sausages Bobby had placed in the oven earlier to roast. As he was transferring them to a paper-towel-lined plate, one dropped to the floor. Johnny was on it, as though he had been born waiting for the moment when a sausage would drop from heaven, just for him to devour.

And Bobby was wondering if a sausage (not turkey) had dropped from heaven for him as well. Wade finished up the eggs and buttered the toast.

As they were eating, the words just fell out of Bobby's mouth, perhaps inspired by the simple brush of their thighs touching beneath the breakfast counter. "You know, I could get used to this. Waking up with you in the morning."

Wade turned and looked at him, and Bobby could see the emotion on his face, happiness, he thought, tempered by wariness.

"I'm sorry. Was that too forward? Too fast?"

"No, no. I'm touched." Wade put down his fork and leaned over to give Bobby a light peck on the lips. When he pulled away, he wiped a speck of scrambled egg off the corner of Bobby's mouth. "I'd be lying if I said the same thought hadn't crossed my mind."

This time, it was Bobby's heart that welled up—if not with love, then at least with the possibility of it.

Suddenly awkward with one another, they finished their breakfasts hurriedly, saying little.

As Bobby loaded the dishwasher, he asked, "So what do you want to do today?"

"Well, I need to call Sabine. I'm pretty sure she leaves for Lake Geneva today with her family." He paused for a moment, staring at Bobby with a question in his eyes. "I need to arrange to get some keys from her so I can stay in the house while they're up there." He gnawed on his lower lip. "Unless—"

Bobby closed the dishwasher and let out a big breath. There were limits to what he could endure, and the words tumbled out before even the smallest part of his brain could censor or even question them. "You can stay here."

"Are you sure?"

"Oh, man, not at all. But you can stay here."

Wade came up and threw his arms around Bobby. They stood that way for several moments, their bodies connected in a line of silken electricity from head to toe. For the first time since he was about fourteen, Bobby feared he might come in his pants.

It was Wade who pulled away first, and Bobby was, in fact, having those early tremors that foretold imminent orgasm. *Good Lord! This is crazy!* He tried to will down his erection and the erotic pleasure coursing through him like the most powerful of drugs. "Listen, why don't you go ahead and take a shower. I'm going to walk Johnny. I'll be back in a bit."

Before Wade could speak, Bobby grabbed the leash and harness, called for the dog with the phrase he was always certain to respond to, "Puppy, come!" and got him fitted in record time. They were out the door within seconds.

If Bobby hadn't removed himself so quickly, he didn't know what he would have done. Yes, he did, and he didn't know if he was ready.

*

Outside, once his hard-on had wilted enough to return some thinking power to Bobby's brain, he stopped at a bench along the lakefront, pulled out his phone, and called Aaron.

"Good morning, starshine," Aaron greeted him.

"The earth says hello," Bobby responded, and the men chuckled together, in a conspiracy of being old enough to recognize the song lyrics pulled from the musical, *Hair* and not *Hairspray.*

"All hilarity and *Name That Tune* aside," Bobby said. "I need to talk."

"Okay. I was just sitting out on my deck, enjoying the morning with a nice cup of Earl Grey. I have all the time in the world, Bobby. What's up?"

Bobby had a moment, with the sun shining down on his face, the roar of the surf hurling itself against the beach, his dog lying contentedly in the grass at his feet, and a good friend listening on the phone, when he felt simply—blessed. There was no other word for it.

"I find myself sorely tempted," Bobby began.

"Have you done anything yet? Where are you?" There was a note of urgency in Aaron's voice, and Bobby wondered if Aaron thought the call was coming too late to prevent Bobby from making a mistake.

Bobby quickly outlined the scenario, filling Aaron in on Wade, how he had known him from as far back as high school, when, really, Wade was a completely different person. "Yeah, I'm lusting for him. The man is completely hot. But this is different."

"How?"

"Ah, in the past, I always thought with my little head, you know? The one between my legs."

"It's been the curse of men since time immemorial," Aaron said. "No need to beat yourself up about *that*."

"Well, there's more to it than that. I really care about this guy. I mean, sure his touch can be so sexy, but it can also, in a weird way, and hopefully this doesn't sound too romance novel, but he also touches my heart. I want more than to get him in bed. I'm having thoughts of a much broader nature.

"I want to get him into my life."

Aaron didn't say anything for a long time. So long, in fact, that Bobby asked, "Are you still there?"

"Sure," Aaron said hurriedly. "Sure, I'm still here. Just processing what you just said. So you think this guy, this Wayne, you believe he might become someone special?"

"Not become. Is. I know. And his name is Wade."

Aaron laughed. "Sorry about that. Wade, Wayne—it's an honest mistake. So, have you, um, acted out with him?"

"We've come close, but no, I've always managed to pull away, and right now I just don't know if I'm doing the right thing. You know? You, the guys in the group, even Wade all talk about waiting to be physical with someone until there's some sort of emotional connection instead of just a sexual one, especially for guys who are struggling, like us. But

Wade isn't going to be here much longer, and I'm afraid I'll be kicking myself once he's gone."

"Then go ahead and do it. Fuck him."

Bobby almost gasped. The baldness of Aaron's reply shocked him. And it shocked him that he was shocked. "I don't know if that's a good idea. I mean, I knew Wade in high school—well, not really—we were just passing ships. I am just getting to know him now."

"And you feel like you're falling for him?"

"Well, yes."

Again, Aaron didn't say anything for several moments. "I think you know what to do, Bobby. I think the answer is in your head and in your heart. You have to listen to those two and not your dick. Your dick will lie to you every time. If there's one thing I've learned, it's that."

Bobby laughed, then grew more serious as he thought of the many, many times his dick had lied to him, leading him into situations for which he now felt regret and remorse. His dick took the message of "to thine own self be true" to heart.

Bobby watched as a pair of rollerbladers went by. Two guys with tight-fitting denim cutoffs showing off spectacularly muscled and tanned thighs and calves. The top halves matched the bottoms as well. His dick told him to make eye contact with them.

He didn't listen—for once.

"I get it."

"Then, you know what, Bobby? I'm going to trust you to do what's right." Aaron barely took a breath and then said, "Listen, I'm kind of busy here. I've gotta go. I'll check in with you later."

Bobby was puzzled. At the start of their call, hadn't Aaron mentioned something about having all the time in the world? He thought, though, it would be rude to point this out. So he simply said, "Okay." With the usual goodbyes, Bobby disconnected.

He looked up at the brilliant blue sky and then down to see Johnny, patiently waiting, parked at his feet.

Could he trust himself? Really? He had a lifetime of spectacularly poor impulse control to tell him the answer was a resounding no. But, unless he was prepared to just take Johnny and hole up somewhere else, hidden, until Wade left town, he would have to see if this time would be different.

"C'mon, kiddo, let's see how we can entertain our friend today." And at the thought of entertaining Wade, an image popped into Bobby's head—himself on his bed, on his back, legs in the air, with one finger invitingly inside his hole, his gaze focused lustily on Wade. *Stop it!* he said to himself and to his dick, who had raised its head at the imagery.

Bobby and Johnny headed into the tunnel that ran beneath Lake Shore Drive. He clarified, as much for himself as for the dog, "Let's see what *touristy* things we can entertain our friend with today."

*

In the end, Bobby decided on taking Wade to the beach. Sure, there was the fact that they would be almost naked, tanned, muscular skin glistening in the sun with a vague whiff of coconut to make it even more alluring, but they would also be in public. Too, there was the fact that the blue waters of Lake Michigan lay just a few feet away. That water, as inviting as it looked, was ball-shrinkingly cold. A dip of a toe in its frigidity could put an end to libidinous thoughts in a flash. Plus, Bobby avoided the gay beach at Hollywood and took Wade farther north, to the beach at the end of Fargo Avenue, where he and Caden used to come, once upon a time.

Here, it was quiet, with only a scattering of sunbathers and one lone lifeguard, a heavyset young girl with hair bleached almost white by the sun, walking up and down the shoreline.

They had come at Wade's request, who had asked to do something a little more sedate today, since, yesterday, they had been all over the north side.

"It's like the ocean here," Wade said, sitting cross-legged on the old pinstriped sheet Bobby had brought for them to sprawl out on. "It might as well be, since you can't see to the other side." He lay back on the sheet, his shoulders almost touching Bobby's. The heat and closeness of Wade had a million different thoughts, mostly antithetical, coursing through Bobby's mind. Part of him wanted to scoot over just enough so their shoulders would touch, but he would be adding kindling and gasoline to a flame, so he stayed put.

He listened to the steady pound of the waves on the shore and closed his eyes against the sun. The air was a pleasant contrast, a layer of cool, from where it rushed across the water, and hot higher up from the sun beating down.

It didn't take long for him to fall asleep. In his dream, he was back in Seattle with Wade. The two of them walked the trail that encircled Green Lake, on the city's north side. They were hand in hand and, although the day was sunny and clear, the water and the trail were free of other people. Their only company was a few ducks, some of which paddled lazily in the water while others gathered, restless, on the pebble shore of the east side beach.

The feel of Wade's hand in his gave him a sense of security. Although no words were spoken, Bobby had the sense that the two of them were a couple, and a couple who had been together for more than just a short time.

As if to confirm this, Wade turned to him, smiling, and asked, "What do you want for dinner tonight, honey?"

Bobby felt something catch in his throat, a quickening of his heart. The simple question spoke to a kind of familiar domesticity that Bobby had thought he would never experience.

Since there was no one around, Bobby pulled Wade to him and kissed him, his tongue tasting the sweetness of Wade's, his skin absorbing the roughness of Wade's beard, scratchy, like sandpaper, and entirely arousing.

"You." Bobby said when he pulled away from the kiss. "I want you. Inside me. And then, after a little nap, I'll get up and make us something light, maybe a frittata with green onions and Beecher's cheese, a little salad."

He looked into Wade's dark eyes, feeling as though he were sinking into the depths of the water just beyond them.

The next thing he knew, he was on his back, on pale blue sheets, while a bamboo-bladed ceiling fan spun lazily above them. Cool, dry air blew in through an open window, rustling the sheer curtains.

And Wade was there. Bobby's legs were on his shoulders, and he stared up at Wade's handsome face as he thrust into him. Wade's eyes were closed, squinched together, and the rapid pace of his breathing matched the tempo of his thrusts.

Bobby loved watching Wade's face, and one word came to mind to describe it, a word that made Bobby ecstatic, and that word was *rapturous*.

His expression was giving Bobby so much pleasure that that alone was enough. Bobby could feel the stretched skin of his dick, its rigid fullness, yet felt no need to touch it. As Wade thrust harder into him, his hips going faster and faster, Bobby cried out as he felt the first jets of his own come land, molten, on his chin, his chest, his belly.

Bobby awakened, and the beach around him seemed surreal. He looked over at Wade, who lay on his side, asleep. Bobby smiled, liking to think they shared the same dream.

He reached down and surreptitiously felt himself beneath his board shorts, and his hand came away, shockingly, sticky.

Good God, I think the last time I had a wet dream I was a Boy Scout! Bobby got up, glad that the shorts were a riot of dark colors and that his come stain would not be too noticeable, and traipsed past a couple of adolescent boys who tossed a Frisbee back and forth.

He gasped as the cold lake water hit his feet, but summoned up his resolve and forced himself to wade quickly into the water. A wave rushed to shore, growing larger, and its cold slapped Bobby's belly. Walking in was a bad idea. He quickly raised his arms and dove into the next wave, holding his breath and going deep, until he could feel the pebbles and sand on the submerged sandbar beneath him. He swam out farther to where the water was darker and deeper.

When he emerged, blowing out a wet puff of air, the shore seemed a long way off, and it took him a minute to find Wade on it. *I love you,* he thought simply. *I don't think it's just lust or infatuation; I think it's love. Sure, it's lust, but it's love too.* Bobby dipped back beneath the water, going down, down, until he thought his lungs would burst, then shot back up to the surface.

The water around him was dappled with silver, and he saw Wade walking across the beach, then braving the waves to swim out toward him.

Bobby would wait for him to come to him.

*

The rest of the day was a revelation. Bobby supposed it was the kind of day that two old lovers might look back upon and see as the beginning of something special. It wasn't so much what they did, but the togetherness with which they did it.

They had spent a couple more hours at the beach. Since both of them were blessed with olive skin and had been smart enough to use at least a number six sunblock, neither was burned. Instead, each sported a deepening golden color, making their flesh that much more desirable and touchable. They had walked along the beach together, admiring the buildings south of them in the distance and the outcropping of buildings north of them—the campus of Northwestern University.

After the beach, Bobby took Wade to a small café on Sheridan Road, known for its poetry slams and open mic nights. The place was in an old ballroom of what was once a lakefront hotel, now a condo, and one side of the café was a wall of windows that faced the glorious lake waters, which today were frisky, with large waves breaking on the boulders beneath the windows.

Bobby knew this place because he and Caden used to come here on the weekends for brunch. It may have been small, and the menu limited, but everything was always fresh and organic, and the coffee was stellar.

Today, with the sun and the water outside and the faded elegance inside, Reve, as the café was called, was a magical place.

After they had found a table near a window and ordered iced teas, Bobby excused himself to go to the bathroom. When he returned, he paused a few feet away from the table. Wade was on his phone, chattering away and laughing.

Bobby had a flash of totally unreasonable jealousy. He was probably only talking to the friend he had come with, the woman called Sabine. But unreasonable was jealousy's stock-in-trade, wasn't it?

As he approached the table, Wade looked up, spotted him, and quickly ended his call.

Bobby didn't like himself for asking, but couldn't resist. "Who was that?"

Wade smiled, maybe too big, and responded, "Nobody. Just a friend from home." He hurriedly picked up a menu and began scanning it. "Oh wow, everything on here looks so good. It's going to be tough to decide."

Although a part of him wanted to press Wade for details about the call, Bobby recognized just how ugly doing something like that would be. "The avocado with red onions, cherry tomatoes, and pita is outstanding. So simple but so good. Probably because they get the best ingredients."

They passed the rest of their lunch talking about nothing, and Bobby wondered if there was something a little bit falsely bright about their conversation, which revolved mostly around the movies they were hoping to see that summer.

He told himself he was imagining things.

*

"Is this the right way?" Wade asked, as they headed west on Fargo.

"I just wanted to show you where my old friend, Caden, is living now." Bobby knew it was stupid, and perhaps even stalkerish, to drive by the apartment building where Caden now resided with Kevin. He didn't know why he did it, other than an absurd hope that he might see one or the other of them, perhaps sitting on the concrete ledge of their balcony that overlooked the street.

If he could no longer talk to his old friend, he could at least see him. Or so he hoped...

They cruised by the building, an old redbrick six flat, built, Bobby supposed, around the turn of the century.

It looked so much homier than his box in the sky. Tenants had put hanging plants, flowers, and herbs outside on their balcony. A woman with dark hair, who looked vaguely familiar, walked a chocolate-brown pit bull along the sidewalk.

Bobby slowed...and there he was. Caden.

"That's him," Bobby whispered, almost reverent. Caden was reaching up to water a hanging spider plant on the second floor balcony of the apartment where Bobby knew the two of them would be living. (Mutual acquaintances had told Bobby of this arrangement. He had certainly gotten no change-of-address notice from Caden himself.) He still looked long and lean, his dark hair glinting in the sun. He also looked very much at home, wearing only a pair of plaid boxers and a ribbed, sleeveless T-shirt that Bobby had always called a "wifebeater."

He sped away. He didn't want to linger to see Kevin come out to join Caden on the porch.

Once they had made the trip down Jarvis, headed east, and were back on Sheridan Road, heading home to change for happy hour and dinner, Wade asked, "Why did you do that?"

"What do you mean?" Bobby responded, never taking his eyes from the road.

"Why torment yourself? You're like a lover who can't let go."

The description was apt. He shrugged. "I don't know. I just can't let it go, as you say. I just never got any kind of closure with him that meant anything to me."

Wade squeezed his shoulder. "Bobby, you're a good man. We are all flawed. You know that, don't you? You're not the only one, and there are plenty of people in this world who want you, even if that bozo doesn't."

"He's not a bozo," Bobby said softly, but he smiled.

*

They ended up staying in for dinner. Wade offered to cook, and so the pair had headed out to Whole Foods to get what he would need for their simple supper—a bottle of Riesling, a salmon fillet, which he planned on grilling after marinating it with brown sugar, soy sauce, and lots of chopped garlic, and the ingredients for a quick kabob: cherry tomatoes, mushrooms, red onion, and orange peppers.

They had talked far into the night, watching together as Navy Pier, south of them, became illuminated.

Wade slid his arm around Bobby and lowered his head to Bobby's shoulder as they watched the slow turn of the Ferris wheel at the very end of the pier.

"I'm tired," Wade announced. "Can we clean up the dishes in the morning?"

"Of course." Bobby kissed the top of Wade's head. He took his hand and led him back to the threshold of Bobby's own bedroom. They paused just outside, and Bobby leaned in for a kiss that was slow, passionate. Wade ran his arm lazily up and down Bobby's back, and Bobby decided, in that moment, it would be okay to sleep with Wade.

After all, they had had a perfect day together, really getting to know each other. They had a common history. Throughout the day, their exchanged glances, quick touches, just the nearness of being together had all been forms of flirtation.

It would be all right. What he wanted now to happen with Wade bore no kinship, no resemblance, really, at all, to a bathhouse encounter or even a one-night stand with someone Bobby had perhaps brought home from the bars.

This was two men who cared about one another.

He pulled away from the kiss, tugging Wade toward the interior of his bedroom.

Wade halted. "Wait. What are you doing?"

Bobby grinned. "Just taking the next natural step, I thought. I mean, hasn't the day been leading up to you *not* spending the night in my guest room?"

"I thought you wanted us to take our time, Bobby. I thought that, from all you told me, you were giving yourself a break from sex—to see who you were, to find out what you really wanted."

"And I want you," Bobby said softly, his ardor and erection simultaneously beginning to flag.

Wade put a hand on Bobby's chest, but it was not a caress. It was a gesture that said "stop" more than anything else. Maybe, "don't come closer."

"Look, sweetheart, I've had a wonderful day with you. I really like you, and maybe I shouldn't try to speak for you. I can't say what you're ready for. But I can say what I am. And I'm not at a place where I can follow you into that bedroom, much as I'd like to, much as my dick is telling me to not be a fool and get in there and get yourself some of that." He laughed, but Bobby didn't join him.

Wade went on. "I'm not at a place where I can trust you just yet, Bobby. You seem like a wonderful guy, one who's really committed to growing, and I can't tell you how much I respect that, but even if you don't need more time, I do. I need to see you're right for me.

"I need to see you're not the guy I saw taking on half a dozen guys at the baths."

This last statement felt like something sharp plunged into Bobby's gut. He actually gasped.

Bobby could tell from the sudden regret on Wade's face that he knew his remark cut to the quick, wounding. "Oh, shit, I shouldn't have said that."

They said nothing, standing there in the darkened hallway for what seemed like an hour, but was really only a minute or two. "No, no," Bobby said, "I guess I deserved that. You need to trust."

"That's part of it."

They looked at one another, their eyes connecting in the gloom.

Bobby said, "I'm going to go to bed now. Maybe tomorrow we can check out the Museum of Science and Industry."

"Sure."

They parted. Wade started away but returned to give Bobby a chaste peck on the lips. "Good night. And thank you so much for a wonderful day."

Bobby watched him retreat the few feet it took for Wade to go into the guest room and close the door.

Bobby waited a while, stinging, but realizing, somewhere, that perhaps Wade had done him a favor, saving him from doing something he might have come to regret, especially with Wade being so far away.

And Wade hadn't really closed the door, had he? He had given Bobby hope. He just needed more time.

That was all.

Bobby was about to turn and go into his room, when he heard Wade's voice, through the guest room door.

Bobby moved closer, hating himself for listening, but rationalizing the eavesdropping by telling himself that Wade's words were indistinct. But he could hear laughter and the rise and fall of excitement in Wade's voice, and Bobby wondered to whom he was talking.

While he had been listening, Johnny had crept up silently, to sit patiently at his feet. Bobby looked down to meet the dog's dark and expectant eyes. He motioned with his head for Johnny to follow him.

In the entryway, he applied leash and harness and said, "I guess I couldn't expect you to go to bed without your evening constitutional." Bobby opened the door but glanced longingly down the hallway, still hearing the murmuring of Wade's voice. He stepped into the hallway with Johnny and told him, "He's probably just talking to that woman, Sabine, firming up plans for the rest of the trip." They continued on to the elevator.

Once descending, Bobby said, "I'm sure that's it. Aren't you?"

But Johnny was keeping his own counsel.

Chapter Sixteen

The morning brought with it disappointment. Bobby had endured a restless night, feeling rejected, even though his logical mind told him otherwise and that Wade's saying no to his advances the prior night had everything to do with respect and consideration for Bobby's own feelings, for the very commonsense move of waiting until they were both ready for a more intimate connection.

Yet his heart told him otherwise. And it was his heart that grieved as he ground coffee beans, filled his coffeemaker with water and the coffee, and set it to brew.

The sky outside reflected his mood. During the night, dark gray clouds that reminded him of Seattle had amassed along the horizon, their nearly black lower edges promising rain by afternoon.

While the coffee brewed, Bobby took Johnny for a quick walk down to the lakefront, where Johnny found one of his favorite companions, a little Boston terrier named Lily. The pair of them playfully made their "downward dog" motions to the other, barking, and getting their owners, Bobby and another middle-aged man, slightly older than Bobby, tangled in the dogs' leashes.

It was curious to Bobby that he knew Lily's name but not her owner's, even though he had seen the pair out walking many times.

When he returned to the condo, Wade was in the kitchen, sitting at the breakfast bar, fully dressed in a pair of jeans, a plaid button-down shirt, and a pair of red suede shoes that looked like Chuck Taylors but were actually Prada. Bobby knew, because the shoes, as was the rest of the ensemble, were his.

Wade had not made the trip back to Wilmette to fetch any of his own clothes. Perhaps they would do that today?

"Good morning!" Bobby called out, more cheerily than he felt, as he stooped to free Johnny from his confines.

"Hey there."

Bobby poured himself a cup of coffee. "I hope you slept okay?"

"Oh yeah, fine." Wade sipped his coffee, staring out at the lackluster day, so different from its predecessor.

"Good thing we did the outdoorsy stuff yesterday," Bobby said. "Looks like it's going to be a perfect day to be indoors. You're gonna love the Museum of Science and Industry. Did I mention it's one of the only buildings left from the big World's Fair?"

Wade didn't say anything for a moment. Then he said something that made Bobby's heart sink. He knew what was coming. "About that."

"Yes?" Bobby sat down on the stool next to Wade.

"I talked to Sabine last night—"

"Oh, so that's who I heard you talking to?" The question just slipped out, and Bobby wanted to kick himself for asking it.

Wade ignored it. "And she and her family are coming back from Lake Geneva a little early. She wondered if I wouldn't come back up and join her and her family for dinner at their country club."

Bobby snorted. "Sounds fancy."

Wade ignored this too. "I thought I might like to go." He looked quickly at Bobby. "I mean, if that's okay with you."

Bobby felt as though he might cry and then judged that reaction to be over the top, stifling it. "Of course, anything you want to do." Bobby had envisioned an entirely different morning for the two of them. He also hoped Wade might ask him to join Sabine and her family at dinner, but no offer was forthcoming. "Anyway, dinner's later. We still have the day."

Wade grinned and looked at him sheepishly. "I thought maybe I'd get back up there this morning. If you can't drive me, I can take the train. There's a station at North and Clybourn, right?"

"How did you know that?"

"Everything's online."

"It certainly is." Bobby thought of the many men he had delivered right to this very condo, simply by going online for a few minutes. He was wondering if he would have one delivered today, to put a little balm on the sting of this latest disappointment. "I can drive you. Don't be silly." Just because he hoped to make Wade feel a little bit bad, he added, "I have the whole day free."

If Wade felt any sting from Bobby's last remark, he didn't show it. Instead, he stood and said, "Thanks. This way I can give you your clothes back, although I'm tempted to keep the shoes." He started toward the hallway. "Don't worry about breakfast. I'm going to grab a shower."

Bobby stood. He couldn't help it. "Wade. Wait."

Wade turned.

"Is everything okay? We were getting along so well yesterday, and this morning, you're like a different person."

Wade stood frozen for several moments, as though he might be pondering how to answer Bobby. Bobby wanted him to say anything other than a denial. He didn't think he could bear it if Wade simply pretended all was well, when they both knew it wasn't.

Wade made a turn from the hallway and went to sit on Bobby's couch. "Come here." He patted the empty space next to him, and Bobby hurried to take it, sitting close enough so their bodies touched.

Wade stared out at the gray day as he spoke. "Listen, Bobby, yesterday I got a little confused. Things were fun and close and flirty, and I loved that, but I wasn't expecting it. I really thought we were just starting out on a friendship."

Bobby swallowed hard, wanting to wince.

Wade looked at him. "But I discovered I liked you, really liked you—and that caused all kinds of mixed emotions in me. See, I don't know whether I need that right now, not with everything else going on in my life."

"What else?"

Wade didn't say anything for a minute or two, his face lost in thought. "Oh, lots. The point is, we talked about taking it slow, which is the real reason I wanted to go back to Wilmette today."

"So Sabine and her family aren't even back yet, are they?"

"What? Of course they are—or will be, by this afternoon." Wade thought for a moment. "I think we both need time. I need time to know you better, to know I can trust you, and trust your feelings, which I suspect are very new. And I need time to know myself better."

Bobby waited for more of an explanation, but none came.

Wade stood. "Are you sure you don't mind running me back up north?"

"Not a problem," Bobby said, his voice gone toneless, dull.

As Wade started away, Bobby asked, "Will I see you again?" Once more, he hated himself for the note of desperation he knew was in his voice, but he couldn't help it.

Wade smiled. "Sure."

An idea popped into Bobby's head, and he latched on to it, like a drowning man grabs a life preserver. "I was thinking of coming to Seattle in a few weeks, while the weather out there is still nice and sunny." He laughed. "It's so rare. And I thought my mom would appreciate the visit. She's been a little lost since my dad passed away."

Wade nodded, sympathy obvious in his dark eyes. Bobby wondered if his mentioning this trip to Seattle was a manipulative move on his part, especially the part about his mom.

"That would be wonderful, Bobby." He turned and went back to his room. Bobby listened to the click of the bedroom door closing.

Bobby looked over at Johnny, who had curled himself into the leather chair opposite. "Did you hear him? He said it would be wonderful."

*

Later that day, after Wade was nothing but a bittersweet memory and a violent but quick thunderstorm had cleared the clouds from the sky, Bobby's phone rang.

It was Aaron.

Bobby was quick to answer. "Thank God you called," he blurted out. "I mean, it's good to hear from you."

Aaron was leery. "Everything okay? Is he still there?"

"I assume you mean Wade?" Bobby chuckled. "No, he went back to Wilmette this morning. He heads back to Seattle tomorrow, so I probably won't see him again this visit."

Aaron let out a sigh. *Of relief?* Bobby wondered.

"Well, that's good to hear. I was just rambling around my house today with no plans, and I was hoping you might be around. Maybe we could do something?"

What was that saying? When God closes a door, he opens a window? "That would be great. What did you have in mind?"

"Why don't you come over around five and find out?"

"Okay…"

"See you then." Aaron hung up, leaving Bobby confused, yet grateful.

*

When Aaron opened the front door to Bobby, Bobby raised his nose to sniff the air spilling out of Aaron's bungalow. It was like a wall of olfactory heaven—tomatoes, red wine, oregano, garlic, basil, all rode out to him on a cloud.

Aaron grinned. "That look! That's what I was going for." He gestured Bobby inside the house, where the smell of tomato sauce simmering was augmented by the comforting jazz of Oscar Peterson's piano. "Come on in. Make yourself comfortable."

Grinning, Bobby took a seat on the overstuffed distressed-leather couch. It was as though Aaron had somehow read his mind and was offering him just the kind of comfort he needed on this day.

"I just need to give the sauce a stir and make sure it's at a good simmer, and I'll be right back." Aaron headed toward the kitchen. "It's my mom's recipe. She was Sicilian. Passed away three years ago. Making this sauce brings her alive for me all over again. Isn't it funny how food can do that?" Aaron didn't wait for Bobby's reply, but continued on into the kitchen. In this house, unlike the great room concepts of so many condos and homes of the twenty-first century, the kitchen was separated from the living room by the dining room. Bobby could see that the table was already laid with what looked like good china and crystal, and the warmth of the room—all the rooms, really—made him feel immediately at home. All the dark wood molding and baseboards, original to the house he was sure, along with the stained glass above the fireplace with its built-in bookshelves, harkened back to a time when people related on a level that was different from how they did today, what with the instant global connections of "places" like Facebook.

Aaron returned, holding a glass of red aloft for Bobby. He handed it to him, looking around on the floor. "You didn't bring him?"

At first, Bobby thought he meant Wade, and then dismissed the idea. "You mean Johnny? I didn't want to be presumptuous."

"Get out of here. I invited you over to see him, not you, you dolt."

There was a moment of silence, and then Aaron laughed. "Joke. But Johnny is always welcome here. I've been thinking about getting a rescue myself."

They sipped their wine in companionable silence, and Bobby relaxed, the hurt of Wade's sudden departure being slowly erased by the warm surroundings and the wine. "This is good."

"A nice Chianti," Aaron said, echoing Hannibal Lecter.

"I'm glad you had me over."

"I'm glad you could come."

They sat in silence for a while, sipping their wine. Bobby took in the wall of bookshelves opposite him, noticing how they were a hodgepodge of art books, hardcovers, and mass-market paperbacks. None of the books was pristine. All looked well-read, with worn spines and faded covers.

"You're quite the reader."

"I'm voracious. I like everything from mysteries to biographies to thrillers." He chuckled. "Even some love stories. I've been getting into some gay romance lately. There's way more out there than you'd imagine, some of it awfully good." He grinned. "And some of it awfully bad. But you read, you learn how to separate the wheat from the chaff."

"I'll have to check some out."

Bobby looked at Aaron and, once again, appreciated how perfectly this man was put together.

It didn't matter that today he was clad only in a pair of old gunmetal-gray sweats and a Big Chicks black T-shirt; he still looked amazing. It didn't matter that he was almost bald and what hair he had was close-cropped and salt and pepper. The lines around his eyes, deeply etched, told a tale of someone who laughed and smiled a lot. And his body? Well, Bobby didn't think it would be appropriate to get started on that. But Aaron was lean in all the right places with just a hint of a pot belly, which, rather than detracting, only made him sexier.

If only you weren't my SAA sponsor… But wait, where is your mind going, young man? I thought you were all about Wade. I am, I am. But that doesn't mean I can't appreciate what's in front of me.

"Penny for your thoughts." Aaron nudged Bobby's shoulder. Hard. He almost spilled his wine.

Bobby reacted quickly, not wanting to confess what he'd really been thinking. "Those romances you were talking about. Who are some of the more popular guys?"

"You mean authors? That's the funny thing. Most of them are women, and straight women, from what I hear." Aaron got up and brought back a paperback. "Try this one. I guarantee you'll be hooked."

Bobby looked down. The book was called *Mongrel* by an author who had the gender-neutral name of K.Z. Snow. Bobby looked up from the book's cover.

"It's steampunk. I can't explain it, so don't ask. But just read a little of it, and you'll get lost in this woman's world, the writer's, I mean. It's a whole new universe, fascinating and touching all at once. Pure escapism."

Bobby said, "Just what I need."

"And I need to put the water on to boil. Hungry?"

"Always. Ravenous." And to Bobby's surprise, he was.

*

Over dinner, Bobby decided to open up and tell Aaron the truth about Wade, about his feelings. He told him the whole story, starting with when Wade had seen him at the bathhouse in Seattle. He felt comfortable revealing this sordid episode to Aaron, who seemed unfazed by it. After he had described the events in the gloom and grit of the bathhouse, he looked up at the man over the rim of his wineglass, searching for judgment or condemnation in his eyes, and found none. Aaron merely waited for him to go on. Bobby told him the rest, wrapping things up by describing his disappointment of earlier that morning. "I really thought things were going well," Bobby said.

"And who says they weren't?"

"What?"

"Why are you casting everything in a negative light? So the guy needed some space. So what? That doesn't mean he was rejecting you. It doesn't mean he never wants to see you again."

"I guess you're right."

Aaron waved a hand at him. "Ah, you're just agreeing with me to get me to shut up. As Judge Judy's always saying—and yes, she's a guilty pleasure—put on your listening ears."

"Okay, okay." Bobby realized he was right. He wasn't really listening. He was just going along, clinging to his own gloom and doom. He didn't understand why.

"I think you believe, and I know this because I thought that way myself once upon a time, that if things don't end up immediately in bed with a guy for whom you have feelings, then there must be something wrong. But, Bobby, listen—there are lots and lots of people out there, some of whom have been couples for years, straight, gay, what have you, who took their courtship a little slower, who got to know each other before hopping into bed together.

"And I'm here to tell you, that doesn't have to be a bad thing. Sometimes, anticipation can make everything that much hotter."

Bobby laughed. "I wouldn't know. I've hardly ever anticipated. I was always shoot first and ask questions later. Like, what's *your* name?" He was laughing, but at the same time, wondering what was wrong with him.

"Just because this guy, this Wayne, wants a little time might mean just the opposite of what's got you so down. Maybe he sees you as someone special and, for *that reason*, doesn't want to rush into things. Did that ever cross your mind?"

"Not really. I guess I'm just a hippie love child at heart. You know: if it feels good, do it." Bobby didn't bother to correct Aaron again on mispronouncing Wade's name.

"And where has that gotten you?"

Aaron's question hung above the dinner table, waiting for a response Bobby wasn't willing to give, at least not yet. Aaron saved him from the uncomfortable silence by saying, "Just think about things, man. Give him time. Give yourself time."

"Time. I guess I never felt I had enough of it." Bobby cocked his head. "I'm forty. I don't know how forty got here this quick." He shrugged. "Maybe I'm worried I'll be sixty just as quick, and still no one will love me and no one ever will."

Aaron made a "tsk" sound. "Christ, Bobby, that prophecy will come true if you keep feeling sorry for yourself like that."

Bobby stared down at the table, ashamed. He knew what he admired in Wade, in Aaron, in other men—confidence. Strength. He thought of the men he had been attracted to, and the ones that were most attractive were often *not* the best-looking ones, but the ones who seemed the most comfortable in their own skins. The ones who seemed to be saying, with their body language, with the way they handled themselves, the way they just had of being, *take me or leave me.*

Bobby wondered if he had ever exuded that kind of confidence, or if he had simply relied on his looks for far too long. Forty these days was not that old, but it was no longer young. He couldn't trade on those looks forever, not when there was a whole new crop of twentysomethings and thirtysomethings edging him out of the race.

"You're right," Bobby said softly. "I'll have to work on that."

Aaron sighed. "I didn't mean to chew you out. I just want you to take a look at the man in the mirror, as my buddy Michael Jackson once sang. And I don't want you to look at how pretty that guy is, how sexy, how well put together, although you're all those things, and damn it, in spades. But look at what's beneath that gorgeous surface. You might be surprised." Aaron was staring across the table at him, and Bobby could swear—and this was not conceit—there was a kind of hunger in his eyes, a tenderness, too, and Bobby wondered if Aaron saw beneath the surface and what he saw there.

"Thanks," Bobby said softly. He then looked up at Aaron, wanting to break this serious spell, this moment of self-examination that felt like being exposed to too bright a light. "What's for dessert?"

Aaron chuckled. "Knowing you, I'm surprised you didn't ask that question first."

Bobby got it. He grinned and wagged a warning finger at Aaron.

"Can't you tell? Sniff."

Bobby had noticed a smell in the air, almost pungent, beneath the smells of the garlic, herbs, and tomatoes in the spaghetti sauce—the smell of licorice.

"It's anise. I made pizzelles."

Bobby shook his head.

"They're thin little Italian waffle cookies, and they're delicious with a nice little cup of espresso, which I'm going to make for you right now."

Bobby watched Aaron disappear into the kitchen. He couldn't keep his eyes from focusing, for a moment, on the easy rise and fall of his ass, which was firm and high, but he also noticed how comfortable he felt, how at home.

He leaned back in his chair and again thought of that saying, how when God closes a door, he opens a window.

*

Bobby didn't see Aaron again until Wednesday night's meeting, and the pair didn't have much of a chance to talk then because Aaron had to hurry home after the meeting.

"No coffee? I was hoping we could talk," Bobby had said to him outside the church where they had met.

"Can't tonight, Bobby. I've got someone waiting at home for me."

Bobby had been surprised at how much Aaron's simple admission stung. Why? He had no claims— other than friendship—on the man. He was interested in Wade, or Wayne, as Aaron liked to call him, anyway. Right?

"Oh, I see," Bobby had mumbled.

Aaron burst out laughing. "I don't think you do. See, I missed you bringing Johnny over so much on Sunday that on Monday I went down to the animal shelter and got myself a dog. I've been meaning to do it for a long time. She's a sweet little mutt, just under a year old, coarse black fur, pointy ears, and these almost amber-colored eyes that are *so* expressive. Kind of looks like Toto from *The Wizard of Oz*. You'll have to meet her. *Johnny* will have to meet her—he's gonna fall in love. I called her Frieda. I don't know why. The name just seemed to fit." Aaron moved toward the L stop at Davis. "We can take the L south together if you want."

"I want."

"And on the ride there, we can make plans for Johnny and Frieda's first date this Saturday. I mean, if he's available. I was thinking forest preserve."

"I'll check with him when I get home and let you know."

And so now, Bobby found himself doing something he never thought he'd do, even as recently as six months ago: walking along a trail in a forest preserve in one of the city's western suburbs with a handsome man and two very playful dogs.

Upon meeting Frieda, Johnny immediately tried to mount her.

Aaron barked out his own laugh. "Just like his old man!"

Bobby yanked at the leash. "Johnny! Manners!" But he needn't have, because Frieda proved herself a strong, independent woman, and she turned and snapped at him. "What you deserve," Bobby said to Johnny.

It took only a moment or two for the dogs to begin playing together like old friends, Johnny's initial play of sexual dominance quickly forgotten. *If only human relationships could be so easy.*

The day was magical, in spite of the heat, the mosquitoes, and the persistent drone of traffic whizzing by on the expressway a mile over from the preserve. Bobby felt alone with Aaron and the dogs and contrasted what he might have been doing on a summer Saturday a year ago at this time. He might have been at the gay beach, wearing either a thong, if he was feeling really daring and slutty, or a pair of board shorts that showed off his abs to good advantage, on the lookout for the tannest, most muscular guy on the beach, whom he would always somehow charm into coming back to his place with him. They would have sex, fireworks maybe, or more likely a lot of buildup to a few minutes of frantic coupling.

And then he would never hear from the guy again.

Or, if it was raining, Bobby would be online, on Manhunt or Adam4Adam, fielding offers to party, offers to fist, offers for vanilla sex, but never anything deeper than that. This scenario would often end up much as the beach one, with the same result of feeling like he had eaten a meal, yet still was hungry.

Now he understood why.

He watched Aaron as he bent down to pet Frieda's sweet little face and thought what a good man he was, what a good friend. After the debacle with Caden, he thought he'd never have anyone in his life he could again call friend. And yet, here he was, delivered like a gift.

Aaron came up to him, surprising him, Bobby was so lost in thought. "This city boy needs to get back to buildings and concrete. What do you say we take the dogs to the beach?"

*

They next found themselves at the beach at the end of Touhy Avenue, in Aaron's Rogers Park neighborhood. Because the day was so warm, the beach was crowded with sunbathers and swimmers and the grass bordering it thick with people having picnics, people who had pitched tents and set up portable grills, the smoke of charcoal in the air. Music blared from portable players, and the cries in the humid summer air were raucous. Vendors with aluminum carts sold Mexican corn on the cob and frozen treats.

Even though dogs were technically not allowed on the beach, Aaron and Bobby had managed to creep by the lifeguards' eyes to take Frieda and Johnny out on the breakwater that jutted into Lake

Michigan's silver-blue waters. The breakwater, a concrete pier of sorts, was peopled with fishermen and others, just strolling out for a glimpse of the skyline south of the beach.

Bobby had gotten into some heavy wrestling with Johnny and was laughing heartily as the dog playfully nipped at his hand, wriggling away, and then coming back for more tickling.

He was so absorbed in his play with the dog, he almost didn't notice the shadow that fell across them. And when he *did* notice, he just assumed it was Aaron.

But it wasn't.

It was Caden.

He looked up, squinting into the sun, and Caden, to him, appeared like some sort of mirage, as though Bobby's eyes were deceiving him. Even though Caden's face was in shadow, Bobby could tell he was smiling.

A smile from Caden? Bobby's heart gave a little leap, and he blurted, "Caden?"

"You remembered." He squatted down next to the pair of them and scratched Johnny behind a pointed ear. Johnny eagerly sniffed him. "Who's this little guy?"

"This is Johnny. Johnny, meet Caden, an old friend."

Caden sat down on the concrete next to them. Without any more preamble than what had just occurred, he said, "I've been thinking about giving you a call. Sort of on the fence about it."

"Oh?" Bobby looked over at him, knowing his expression probably revealed both fear and hope. Aaron hovered nearby, but soon called to Frieda and walked to the other end of the pier.

"Yeah. After I got your letter. I have to admit, it did touch me, and it crossed my mind that I might be holding onto a grudge a little too long."

Bobby smiled, but before he could say anything, Caden continued.

"But I still wasn't sure. Eternal damnation, as far as I was concerned, was too good for the likes of you."

Bobby sighed. Is that what this was about? Another chance to berate him? He was tired of it. But he felt he deserved it, and if it made Caden feel better, well then, he should have at it.

"Kevin read your letter too. You know what he told me? Him. The one you really almost hurt the most, Bobby. He said it was time to forgive you."

Bobby gazed out at the water, suddenly feeling chilled in spite of the heat.

"I didn't know. I just didn't know."

They were silent for a long time. Finally, it was Caden who spoke again, because Bobby had no words.

"I didn't know until just a few minutes ago, when I saw you out here with that dog. I thought if any guy can love a creature that hopeless-looking—and I'm sorry, Bobby, but that little guy is a poster boy for so ugly he's cute—I thought if that man can love a dog like that and be as into it as you obviously are, well, that guy can't be all bad.

"Seeing you with Johnny here pushed me over the edge. It made me remember that somewhere inside that buff, exfoliated, and tanned exterior a heart was buried. It made me see why, once upon a time, you and I were friends. Good friends.

"I remembered what you wrote to me, the sincerity and hope in that letter, and I knew how hard it must have been for someone like you to write those words, and I thought, actually just now, that you must have changed.

"Because even if you do have a heart, which I acknowledge, you still had a lot of growing to do. I saw evidence of growth today."

Bobby felt a mixture of emotions, mostly relief, colored by joy. Was this a new beginning? Or was Caden merely preparing him for the news that he was forgiven, only to follow it up by saying something like "But you do understand—we can never be friends again."

But that's not what Caden said. "So, I thought I'd come over and just tell you, friend, that I forgive you. You pulled some real bonehead shit that's mostly unforgivable, but I saw before me today a guy who may have learned something. I think I knew that when I read your letter, but I just needed to see your heart in action—and today, the universe provided me that opportunity."

Bobby looked away, out at the water once more, eyes bright with tears. He sniffed quickly and forced the waterworks away. When he turned back to

Caden, he was all smiles. "Thank you. You don't have any idea how much this means to me."

Caden stood up. "Hug?"

"Of course." Bobby stood, too, and felt the warmth of Caden's arms encircle him. He squeezed Caden to him, not caring who saw, and oblivious to Johnny's frantic yelps and jumps on his leg, desperate to get in on the action.

Bobby closed his eyes, reveling in the warmth of Caden's embrace, the feel of their bodies pressed together, marveling that he did not feel this was a sexual moment, but a moment born of the heart and maybe even the soul.

He had loved Caden so much, loved him still, and the fact that he had lost him had been a kind of hell for Bobby. This moment was akin to being lifted out of the pits.

Caden whispered in his ear, after the hug had gone on perhaps just a shade too long. "Hey. Your boyfriend's gonna get jealous."

At first Bobby thought he was referring to Johnny, but then he realized the truth—he meant Aaron. He pulled away and looked down the pier to see Aaron and Frieda, whom Aaron had rolled over on her back and was scratching away, much to the dog's delight.

Surprisingly, Aaron was chatting with another man, a beefy blond with a beard. Kevin. This was all a dream, right?

"Oh, he's just a friend," Bobby explained. He didn't say anymore, but hoped there would be time, sometime soon, to tell Caden all about how Aaron had come into his life.

Caden laughed and started back toward them. "Well, I gotta admit, Bobby, you two sure looked like a couple. Anyone could see that. The way that man looks at you..." He winked. "And a very hot couple."

Bobby felt heat rise to his cheeks. "Thanks. But, as I said, just buddies."

Caden nudged him. "Really? Nothing more? You and a hot guy like that? Come on!"

And Bobby grinned because he knew the truth. And knew he had changed.

Caden said, "Let's go join them. I'm sure you want to say hi to Kevin."

Bobby felt a cold fear grip him in the gut, almost like a cramp. "Are you sure? Doesn't he hate me?"

Caden shook his head. "He forgave you a long time ago. He's a better man than I am. I've learned a lot from living with him." Caden peered at Bobby. "It will be fine. It will all be fine."

And as the two of them walked toward the other two men, both of them stood, smiling. It would be fine.

It really would.

Chapter Seventeen

Bobby touched down at Sea Tac on what was, for Seattle, a blisteringly hot summer day. It was an afternoon early in August, and the captain announced over the speaker that it was "It's sunny and clear, with temperatures hovering around eighty-five. Humidity: zilch. A gorgeous day to hike Mt. Rainier, if you're so inclined, or take in the sights the lazy person's way: from the top of the Space Needle." A few people chuckled, but most were intent on bringing their phones to life.

Bobby wore cargo shorts and a black T-shirt. He put down the book he was reading, on loan from Aaron, a tale of suspense and romance called *The Heart of the Jungle*, by Jeremy Pack, and couldn't believe he was back in his hometown again so soon. After all, the time between his last visit and the one before that had been nearly ten years.

But his mother needed him, he was sure. When he would talk to her on the phone, she would put on a falsely bright front, chattering on about the part-time clerical work she was doing for the Episcopalian church she belonged to across Lake Union, and her grandchildren. Bobby knew for a fact his sister,

Dawn, and her husband were so wrapped up in their suburban lives and those of their children, they scarcely gave Michelle a second thought. Besides, Bobby was attuned to the emptiness in his mother's voice, that film of sadness that clung to her cheerful words like a skin.

He wasn't buying it.

This visit would be a surprise. He hadn't told her he was coming.

As people in front of him began reaching into the overhead bins for their belongings, Bobby considered the other reason he had come—to see Wade.

He had spoken to him several times on the phone, but he had always had the misfortune of catching Wade at a bad time—just when he was heading out the door, or when he was driving, or out to dinner with friends—so their conversations had been brief. But they had texted here and there, and Bobby had posted a countdown to his visit on Wade's Facebook page.

He couldn't wait to see him again, to hug him, and maybe get into one of those lip-locks the two of them couldn't resist, no matter their best intentions. As he retrieved his bag and snatched up the paperback, he smiled as he thought of Wade's dark eyes and how he could just about sink into them.

They didn't have to make any drastic moves this visit, but he hoped they would move forward just a bit. Even though it was sooner than he said he would again have sex, Bobby had decided if the situation arose, as it were, he would take advantage. Wasn't the whole point to combine sex with caring and love? He knew what he felt for Wade, and how much stronger those feelings would only grow once they consummated their union physically.

After all, Wade was a man with whom he was falling in love, serious enough that he was thinking of moving back to Seattle. Yes, he knew even thinking such a thing, making such a monumental life change, was rash, but if it meant Wade became a more serious fixture in his life, it would be worth it.

Bobby got in line to get off the plane and moved slowly behind his fellow passengers. He felt like he was inching toward his future, and that optimism filled him with hope and lightened his heart.

*

Once he had rented his Toyota Prius, Bobby headed north on I-5. He had regrets about not springing for a convertible, because the day was in glorious bloom. In the distance, the Space Needle and the downtown skyline rose up like sparkling towers, a testimony to how perfect the weather could actually be in Seattle, contrary to popular belief. The mountains he had just flown over, blue-gray and tipped with white, stood almost ethereal in the distance, out to show themselves off against the backdrop of the clear blue sky.

In no time at all he was taking the exit at Mercer and heading north on Dexter to his mother's condo.

As he made his way up the front walk, he imagined Michelle's look of delight when she opened the door to him. He rang the buzzer for her unit. *What if she's not home? No worries. You will go over to Fremont and have a latte, or you would head north to Green Lake and take a stroll around its borders. On a day like this one, there is sure to be much eye candy, running shirtless around its waters.* Bobby was grinning as his mother's voice, metallic, came through the intercom.

"Yes?"

Bobby wasn't sure, for a moment, if it was his mother speaking. She sounded so old, and tired for this early in the afternoon. What was it? Two o'clock?

He disguised his voice. "UPS. Delivery for Michelle Nelson."

His mother responded wordlessly, and in a second, Bobby heard the click of the glass front door's security mechanism releasing. He grabbed his bag from the pebbled concrete and hurried to open the door.

Because she lived directly back from the front door, Bobby could hear Michelle unlocking and opening the door.

They stood for a moment, simply facing one another. And Bobby could not say for certain who was more shocked.

Bobby, his eyes still adjusting to the somewhat dimmer light of the lobby, was shocked at his mom's appearance. His mother had always been as meticulous about her looks as he had. In fact, Bobby always thought he got his vanity from her. She was always perfectly coiffed and attired in the latest fashions, bought from frequent shopping expeditions to places like Seattle's own Nordstrom or the even more upscale Barneys.

Today, she was still in her bathrobe, a quilted affair in faded dusty rose that Bobby had never seen, probably because it was something she wouldn't have been caught dead in a few years ago. He glanced down at his watch. Yup, it was a little after two, and Michelle was not dressed.

Unheard of.

Her blonde hair, usually looking silky and freshly cut, today was weathered and dry, streaked through with gray and in need of a trim. It framed a tired face, one Bobby marveled at because, in the short time they had been apart, it seemed to have doubled the number of wrinkles.

"Honey?" Michelle asked questioningly. She laughed. "I thought you were the UPS man."

Bobby dropped his bag, hurried to Michelle, and gathered her in his arms. She felt smaller and less substantial. He hugged her close, in spite of the fact that, well, she was a little ripe. Bobby wondered when she had last showered.

"I'm so glad you're here. But you should have called," Michelle whispered into his neck. "The place is a wreck. *I'm* a wreck." She looked up at him, and Bobby saw the tears standing in his mother's eyes. If for no other reason than this moment, Bobby was glad he had made the trip.

Michelle took his hand and led him into the condo. As usual, the view from the floor-to-ceiling windows was magnificent, revealing a shimmering Lake Union, dotted with sailboats and lined with houseboats and yachts. The rise on the opposite shore revealed the buildings and streets of the Eastlake neighborhood and, beyond that, stands of pine, as if there simply to frame the majesty of the Cascade Mountains, today standing clear and tall in all their glory. A seaplane neared the water, getting ready to land.

It was breathtaking.

Bobby couldn't say the same for the condo. He had never, in his entire life, seen the home where his mother lived so dirty. The coffee table was a riot of open and shut magazines, newspapers, and remotes. Half-full glasses and cups littered the end table next to the couch. A pair of jeans lay across the seat of a chair, and a green blouse, wrinkled, lay over the top. A film of dust covered everything. There were stains and crumbs on the carpet.

Bobby shook his head. "Mom, what did you do? Fire the cleaning lady?"

"Actually, yes." Michelle began hurriedly gathering up the reading materials from the coffee table. "What do I need a cleaning lady for, now that your father's gone? Keeping up this little place isn't that much work, and it gives me a way to fill my time."

Except you haven't been filling it. At least not with cleaning. Bobby didn't dare utter his thoughts. He didn't want to hurt his mom's feelings.

She hurried into the kitchen, and he heard her stuffing the newspapers into the garbage. When he heard water running, he joined her.

The kitchen was also a mess. Dishes, caked with half-eaten food, filled the sink and lined the counter space adjacent to it. The dishwasher stood open, full of dirty dishes. To his shock, a cockroach skittered across the granite.

Michelle was trying to stuff some of the dishes into the already-overcrowded dishwasher. Bobby stopped her. He took the plate from her hand, set it down, and took her in his arms again. She clung to him, and before he could say a word, she was sobbing.

He let her cry for a while, stroking her hair and whispering, "It's okay. Shhh." Finally, he said, "Mom. Mom, what's going on? This isn't like you."

She sniffed and pulled back so she could look up at her son. "It's nothing, Bobby." Her smile was falsely bright and her breath was horrendous, but Bobby didn't recoil. "If you had called first, I would have had this place shipshape." Her grin slipped to sheepish.

"I wanted to surprise you," Bobby said.

"Well, you certainly succeeded." Michelle laughed, turning away from him. "Let me go hop in the shower, and I'll get this place cleaned up. The guest room, though, is as you left it, I swear." She started away from him.

Bobby gently grabbed her arm. "What's going on, Mom?"

She stopped, considering him. "Don't you know?"

"Of course I have an idea, but why don't you tell me."

Michelle grasped Bobby's hand firmly and led him into the living room, where they both sat on the couch. She looked out at the day, but it seemed as though she wasn't really seeing it.

"I just don't care," she said softly. "Not anymore."

Bobby gnawed at his lower lip, feeling a lump form in his throat. He didn't want to hear this, but he had to. And he knew the wrong move would be to leap in at this moment to tell her she was wrong, to tell her about all the people who loved her, himself most of all, who were there for her. There would be time for that later. But right now, instinct told Bobby to simply let his mother speak.

"There's not much reason to clean up, Robert. Myself or this place. Who's gonna see it? Your dad used to take such pride in my looks." She chuckled. "I made sure he never even thought about a trophy wife. Not when I was around. But now? Who? George next door? He sees me when I go out to get the mail or the paper, and he says 'Hi,' but he couldn't care less. I doubt if he's even noticed."

Bobby was sure that wasn't true. The change in his mother in the recent past had been dramatic. She looked twenty years older than when he had last seen her.

"Doesn't Dawn bring the kids around? You're always talking about them when I call. I assumed you were spending lots of time with her and her family."

Michelle looked at him steadily. She said softly, "The last time I saw Dawn and the kids was when you were last here, my dear."

"What? They haven't been by in all this time?"

Michelle shook her head. "Oh, there was one Friday, she was going to take me to lunch downtown, said we'd do a little shopping. A real girl's day. I got myself all ready and waited. She called about ten minutes after she was supposed to be here and said one of the kids had come down with the flu. Now, I ask you, why couldn't she have told me that, if it was true, in the morning?

"After that, I just didn't think it was worth getting myself dressed, or cleaning, or any of that shit that needs doing. You know what? Not doing any of that has made not one bit of a difference. No one cares." Her voice had gotten shrill and strident.

She stood, pressing a hand to her face. "Really, Bobby, now that you're here, and, oh, you look so nice, you make me ashamed. Let me go clean up."

Bobby did. He watched as she walked slowly from the room, hoping a shower would revive her.

Quickly, he threw his bag into the guest room that was, as promised, pristine. He hurried back into the kitchen and turned the water to hot. He wanted to have a good dent made in these dishes before his mother emerged from her shower. He hoped the rushing of the water and the clinking of flatware and dishes would cover the sound of his sobs.

*

"Would you like to come out to Chicago for a visit, Mom? You know, I could spring for that, no problem. And we could make it a regular thing. I've got a view that rivals yours, and there's so much to do in the city. Theater, restaurants, boat cruises in the summer, concerts..."

They had moved on to Karen's, an unpretentious little diner in the Ballard neighborhood, near the shipyards. Out the plate glass windows, huge hulks of fishing boats, moored for now, provided their backdrop.

Michelle had undergone quite a transformation, and Bobby hoped his presence had helped spur it. When she had emerged from her bedroom after showering (and nearly an hour later), Bobby had to give his mother a wolf whistle. The playful note was not simply to cheer her up (although there was a measure of that in it), but because it was true.

It was amazing what hot water, soap, shampoo, lots of makeup, and the right clothes could do.

His mother gave a little turn before him, and Bobby flung the dishtowel he was using over his shoulder to give her his undivided admiration.

Michelle had erased years with carefully and tastefully applied makeup, a straightening hot comb to her blonde hair, giving it back some of its sheen, and donning a simple burgundy sundress with small white flower appliqués. Her white toeless heeled sandals added some height—but then, so did her posture, which sprucing herself up had also improved.

Bobby knew both he and his mother had always ascribed to the tenet: it is better to look good than to feel good.

And now, as they sat with their salads in Ballard, Bobby still hoped his mother's change in appearance heralded a corresponding upswing in mood. He didn't think he could bear seeing her again as he had this morning.

It had about broken his heart.

"Oh, I'd like that," Michelle said, responding to his idea about coming to Chicago. "I'd love to see your place. I've never been."

Bobby set down his fork. "Why is that, Mom? You know, this isn't to make you feel bad or anything, but the whole decade I've been out there, I always imagined you coming out to see me. I'd buy a new chair for the living room and wonder what you'd think of it. Or I'd have the guest room painted, and I'd wonder if you'd approve of the color. I used to imagine you coming out, especially in my early years out there, and all the things I would show you, the places I would take you."

Bobby stared out the window, realizing all at once how much it had hurt that no one in his family had ever come to see him.

Hey, don't feel sorry for yourself, buddy. You never went to see them either.

Bobby knew it had been a kind of standoff. If his family wouldn't come to him, he wouldn't go to them. But where had such an attitude gotten them? Ten years apart, time that could never be reclaimed.

Bobby wasn't about to dwell on the negative, though. So he picked up his fork and dug into his salad again. "Why don't we plan something for early October, then, while the weather's still nice. You can stay for a week. Johnny will love you."

"Johnny?" Michelle smiled. "New man in your life?"

"Little man, I suppose." Bobby pulled out his phone and summoned up a picture of Johnny, caught in the act of lounging on Bobby's bed, the pillows arranged nest fashion, eyes up at the camera.

"Oh, he's adorable! When did you get him?"

And Bobby told her most of the story of the day he had found Johnny (leaving out the part about his bathhouse visit—he didn't want to fry her hair), and in the telling, he realized something—he, like his mom, was not only concerned about his appearance, he was a nurturer.

*

When they got back to the condo, Bobby felt like his mother had truly undergone a transformation. It made his heart swell to think and hope that he had had a little something to do with that. His showing up at her door, he liked to think, had demonstrated that someone did care. And he believed it was that, more than anything else, which helped her begin to climb out of her depression.

Bobby was glad he had come, because he knew it would take a lot more than just cleaning up and his presence to get his mother back on the road to life. Oddly enough, he thought his own journey might just give him some insights that he could share with Michelle, about the happiness that comes with understanding and loving yourself.

He knew his mother had been cast adrift by his father's death. But Bobby understood, now, that one man could not be totally responsible for the happiness of someone. No one person could be the be-all and end-all for anyone. Happiness came from within, not without.

Really, Bobby? You know that? Bobby grinned at his inner voice. *I'm trying.*

His mother surprised him in his thoughts when she returned to the living room bearing a Cole Haan shoe box.

Bobby cocked his head. "Shoes? Just what I need! More shoes."

"A girl can't have too many," his mother quipped, grinning. She composed her features into a more serious mien and sat next to Bobby, settling the shoe box in his lap.

"I meant to give you this when you were here for his funeral. But my mind was so scattered then, and everything went so fast, you were already back in Chicago by the time I thought about it."

Bobby lightly ran his hand across the box's weathered cardboard top. "What is it?" He had an absurd vision of himself opening the box and finding inside a miniature version of his dad, just waiting for Bobby to come along and release him.

"This was in the back of your dad's closet. I never knew he kept it, not until after he passed and I went through his things. I thought you'd like to have it." She patted his hand. "You know what? I'm stuffed after lunch and all the excitement of you being here. Would you mind if I went to my room and had a little lie down?"

Bobby shook his head. "No. But what's—"

His mother put a finger to her lips, shushing him. She got up and started out of the room, but paused by the hallway leading back to her bedroom. "Just look through it," she said.

She disappeared around the corner.

Bobby looked down at the box, not opening it for several moments. He knew his mother didn't really need a nap. Since when had Michelle ever taken a nap, anyway? She was leaving him alone with this box she had found in his father's closet for a reason, but what was it?

He pulled the top off the box and gasped at the first thing he saw.

It was a Lucite disc on a chain, meant to be used as a key ring. A photo of a seven-year-old Bobby, hair slicked down and wearing a seersucker sport coat, looking smart in spite of the freckles across his button nose and the missing front tooth, grinned up at him from inside the clear plastic. On the sheet of paper inserted beneath it, written in clumsy green Magic Marker, was the message:

Dear Dad,

Even though you're never home, I still love you. Happy Father's Day.

Love,

Bobby Nelson

Bobby felt something inside him clench and unclench. He remembered making this at Sunday school for his father, remembered giving it to him, so proud of his creation. His father had put it aside, he recalled, and thanked him, but had moved on quickly to the next gift in his stack.

Bobby had never seen him actually use the keychain.

Bobby had thought his gift hadn't made an impression.

Yet, here it was, after all these years. Why had his dad saved it?

You dolt, isn't it obvious?

Bobby set the keychain aside and began pawing through the box. It contained, in bits and pieces, his whole life. Here was a report card from third grade, when Bobby had made all As. There was a cheap purple ribbon he had gotten when he was twelve, for participating on his junior high school's track team. There were all sorts of things Bobby would have imagined no longer existed, piled up on the unquenchable fire of memory.

But his father had saved them.

A tiny pair of socks, black-and-orange striped, from when Bobby must have been a toddler.

A papier-mâché puppet Bobby had long forgotten that he had made as a child. It was supposed to be Morticia Addams.

A picture of Bobby and some pretty girl—what was her name? Maryalice, that was it—at his senior prom.

A clipping from the *Seattle Times* that had a picture of Bobby, taken at Pike Place Market. He had only been standing in the background, near a new restaurant that had opened. He hadn't even been named.

His acceptance letter to college.

A note from the university to Bobby's parents when Bobby had made the dean's list.

A picture of him and his dad and mom outside the house he had rented with four other guys senior year of college, Bobby standing tall above both of them in his cap and gown.

A postcard from Chicago, showing fireworks over Navy Pier. Bobby flipped it over and read, "Just moved in! I have this view from my place. Can't wait for you to come and see it!"

And finally, at the very bottom, was a note. To him. From his dad. Words and sentences were scratched out, and Bobby could see from the date at its top that his father wrote it about five years ago. His father had written him a letter? Even though the man had never sent it, the fact that he had taken the time to sit down and compose a handwritten letter to him touched Bobby's heart and made it hard to swallow.

He looked out at the clear summer day, watching as yet another seaplane landed on the waters of Lake Union, unsure if he should read what his father had written.

But there was no resisting. Who could look away from what had become essentially a missive from the dead.

Dear Son, the letter began. When had his dad ever called him "son"? When, in fact, had he ever even referred to him by name? It was odd, really. Seeing himself referred to as "dear" and "son" by his father sent a jolt through him, not unpleasant, but shocking all the same.

I have been meaning to write this letter for some time, ever since your mother told me, a couple of months ago, that you were gay.

Bobby put the letter down, his hand trembling. He figured a lecture was in store. Perhaps the letter was to disown him or tell him that no son of his would be a pervert.

He read on, though, expecting and bracing for bad news, harsh words.

She said that when you told her you were gay, she remarked, "Never tell your father; it'll kill him."

Bobby remembered that. He could hear his mom's voice over the phone. This was way back. He had come out to his mother when he was a sophomore in college.

But your mother felt, finally, that I should know. Know you. Know my son, as he really was. She wanted me to have a clear picture of you, come Hell or high water. She knew she had pretty much ruined any chances of you being straight with me (ha ha), so she felt the time had come for me to know, so I could see you for who you really are.

As you can tell, since I'm writing this, the news didn't kill me.

Hell, it didn't even surprise me. For Christ's sake, you and your cousin Cathy used to play with Barbies when you were kids. You did a paper in school on "the disco era." You had no interest in sports. I think I knew all along.

I just never really put it on a front burner until your mother told me.

I just wanted to let you know that I'm no less proud of you, Bobby. You're still a great guy, smart, accomplished, and handsome. Just like your old man (ha ha).

Your mom asked me, after she told me, if I felt any different about you. I asked her why. You're still my son. I love my son, you, gay, straight, purple, green, whatever the hell you are.

From the moment I first held you in the hospital, I loved you. Who you love doesn't matter to me, as long as you're happy. That's all I ever wished for my kids.

I hope this note can open some doors for us...

And there the letter ended, as if someone had surprised his father in the writing of it. Bobby brushed away the tears that had rolled down his cheeks as he read. "Why didn't you ever send this?" he wondered aloud to the empty room. "It would have made such a difference. We lost so much."

He set the letter down beside him, drawing his knees up to his chest and encircling them with his arms. He laid his face on his knees and wept.

When he was done, he was reminded of what he now knew—that you could only love someone for who they were, and not who you hoped they were.

His father had done that.

And now, he needed to do the same.

He had always thought there was no love lost between father and son because there was none there to begin with.

He had been wrong. And even though Dad was gone, Bobby could still love him for the man he was, a man who, after all, wasn't nearly as bad as Bobby once thought. A man who had loved his son…

What more could Bobby want?

Michelle crept into the room at last, a tentative smile on her face. She stopped about three feet away from him, hands at her sides, waiting.

"He loved me, Mom. He loved me." Again, with the tears! Bobby brushed them away and went to allow Michelle to gather him up in her arms.

Chapter Eighteen

"Where would you say would be the most romantic place in town to take someone you wanted to impress?" Bobby and Michelle sat outside, on the condo balcony the next morning, cups of coffee before them. "It's been years since I've lived here, and I really don't know anymore."

Michelle took a sip of her coffee, thoughtful, as she stared out at the water and the mountain range opposite them. "Once upon a time, I would have said Canlis. It's just a short walk from here, and it's kind of an institution. But institutions aren't all that romantic, huh?" She laughed. "No. It's funny, when you asked that, one place popped into my head, right away, so that must mean something."

"So?"

"There's a little, kind of rustic place in Pike Place Market called Maximilien. It's French, excellent food. But the place just has this ambiance that's unforgettable. It helps that it has views to die for. Time your reservation so that you'll be there for the sunset. The views are amazing—Puget Sound, the Olympic Mountains. And they have it set up, even if you don't get a window table, there are mirrors all over the place so you can still have the view." She put her hand over Bobby's. "But make sure they give you a window seat."

"Have you been there, Mom?"

Michelle's eyes immediately teared up. "Your dad took me there. On our last anniversary. I had never been, and it was a surprise." She looked far away, and Bobby assumed she was remembering the evening. In spite of how far he had come, Bobby still was surprised his mother loved his father as much as she obviously did and, for that matter, that his father was enough of a romantic to plan a night out like this for Michelle.

Now, now. That's not the way you want to think. Remember the box. Bobby wondered if "remember the box" would become kind of a mantra for him now, any time he recalled his father.

"Yes, Maximilien. It's the most romantic. Who are you thinking of taking?" she asked, playful.

And Bobby told her all about Wade.

Later, he called the man himself.

He got voice mail, as he had the last couple of times he called. He assumed Wade was busy getting ready for the new school term. There was a sinking feeling of dread inside him too. He wasn't stupid, after all. But he couldn't imagine why Wade would be avoiding him. So, as he had learned to do on this journey of late, he decided he would be optimistic.

"Hey, Wade, it's Bobby. Hope you're well. Listen, my time in town is running short, and I do want to see you before I leave. I'd love to take you to dinner, if you can spare the time. I'm thinking Friday. Let me know."

Bobby disconnected and was surprised when his phone rang, not five minutes later. It was Wade.

"Hey! Good to finally hear from you!"

"Sorry. I was just coming in the door when you called. Listen, about dinner—"

"Don't you dare say no. I just talked to my mom, and she steered me toward what she said is the best French in town, with, as a bonus, the best views. I really want to just have some quiet time with you, Wade. It seems our times together have always been so hurried and even a little bit strained." Bobby's voice became softer, and he hated the desperation he heard in his next sentence. "I need to see you."

Wade was quiet for a moment or two, and then he finally said, "No worries. I'm free on Friday. Where did you want to go?"

And just like that, all of Bobby's worries disappeared. Friday night would be a memorable one, a night, Bobby just knew, that would go down in his romantic history as a landmark. He already pictured their eyes meeting across a candlelit table. "Let me surprise you. What do you say we meet under the big clock at Pike Place Market at, oh, around seven?"

"Sure. Sounds good. Dress?"

"Don't you dare wear a dress. You know I like 'em butch."

Wade laughed. Finally, he had gotten a chuckle out of the guy.

"You always look good, no matter what you wear. But I would guess no shorts, something a little nice, but no need for a tie."

"Got it. See you Friday."

Bobby was thinking of asking if they could get together for lunch, a drink, coffee, or something before Friday, but Wade had already hung up.

*

Friday arrived with Bobby in the guest room with every article of clothing he had brought along strewn across the bed. Michelle peeked into the room. "Whatever you wear, you'll look sensational. Sweetie, you could wear a bathrobe and look delicious." She came up to him and pinched his cheek. "You got the best of both of us, that's for sure. My handsome son."

Bobby could actually feel heat rising to his cheeks at his mother's flattery.

"This is important, Mom. I want to look good for him."

"That's sweet. I didn't think young people cared as much about clothes these days. I thought it was all about comfort...and tattoos." She moved to the bed, sorting through what Bobby had laid out. She lifted a moss-green linen short-sleeve shirt and paired it with black jeans. "Wear these. Simple. Masculine. Comfortable." She winked. "And quick and easy to get out of."

"Mom!"

"Oh please, now is not the time to pretend to be Mary Poppins. It's a little late for that, sweetie."

They both had a laugh over that. Bobby looked down at the clothes and saw his mother was right. Simple would be best. He had a pair of black leather sandals that would look great with the ensemble.

His mother paused in the doorway, turning to say, "And underwear—if you *do* wear it—make sure it's clean. One never knows."

Bobby played dumb. "Knows what?" He had the sudden feeling he and Michelle were on the road to becoming not just mother and son, but very good friends.

"When you might be struck by a bus, of course. What did you think I meant?" She didn't wait for his response, but left him to get ready.

*

Bobby arrived in front of the big clock in front of Pike Place Market, which had now become iconic as a Seattle landmark, fifteen minutes before seven. He was eager, anxious, and wanted to be sure he was positioned so he could watch Wade walk toward him.

All around him, tourists swirled, chattering, stopping to take pictures. One walked up to him and asked where she could find the original Starbucks. Behind him, the fish market had, as usual, attracted a crowd, as the workers there made lots of noise and created a big show out of tossing huge whole fish back and forth. Bobby didn't quite understand the appeal, but the tourists lived for it. It must be on everyone's must-see list when they came to town.

He saw Wade coming down Pike Street, and for a moment, time stopped, and all the people around him blurred as if by magic, making him stand out. Wade too had dressed simply, in a white cotton button-down shirt and jeans. A gust of wind off Elliot Bay lifted his hair off his forehead. Bobby liked watching him like this, catching him for a moment unawares. Bobby admired his confident stride and how the sun had darkened his skin even more since he had last seen him.

He was stunning. He practically glowed. And, apparently, Bobby was not the only one who thought so. As Wade progressed through the crowd, he saw at least three heads swivel to watch the man's progress, one of them male.

At last, Wade stood before him, a big smile on his face. They said nothing, but Bobby was delighted that Wade's first move was to pull Bobby toward him and give him a peck on the lips. Bobby wished for a more lingering kiss, but they were deep in public throngs, and any further display of affection, even in a city as liberal and tolerant as Seattle, might turn heads for the wrong reason.

"It's so good to see you," Bobby said. "So very good." He touched Wade's arm lightly, the connection of their skin electric, to lead him into the marketplace and to Maximilien.

*

The view—and the sunset—delivered on its promise of spectacular. Bobby had booked a table at one of the windows, and he and Wade watched, wordless, as the sun set over the Olympic Mountains, etching the sky with hues of slate blue, lavender, and tangerine. Those same colors reflected on the waters of Puget Sound and off the windows of a ferry, gliding soundlessly across the bay.

The room was actually hushed for a few moments as the sun made its descent behind the jagged and majestic peaks.

It was amazing that something that really happened every day could still stun with its beauty, leaving the viewer in a state of awe and wonderment, almost childlike.

As they watched, Bobby placed a gentle hand atop Wade's, rubbing the coarse dark hair. Wade drew his gaze away from the setting sun to meet Bobby's eyes, and the two men stared at one another for long, delicious seconds.

Talk over a duo of foie gras and sea bass for Bobby and cassoulet for Wade, had revolved around Wade's upcoming school year, how Bobby was tiring of his work in corporate marketing and his desire to make a change, to do something more meaningful with his life.

They had danced around talking about each other and where their future was headed.

Bobby felt like now was the time. The beauty of the sunset, the light pressure of his foot against Wade's, and several glasses of wine loosened his tongue, giving him courage.

"I've really missed you. After you left Chicago, it was like you took a piece of me away. And tonight, tonight, I feel like that piece is back."

"I complete you?" Wade teased, chuckling.

"Stop! I'm trying to be serious here."

Their waiter came along and cleared away their plates. "Would you gentlemen care to see a dessert menu?"

They had shared a bottle of pinot gris with dinner. Bobby said, "I'm not interested in dessert, are you?" He raised his eyebrows. "At least not here." He felt his face flush as Wade didn't respond to the latter comment. Perhaps he hadn't heard, even though he had shaken his head no to the idea of dessert. Bobby looked up at the waiter and said, "Do you have Veuve Clicquot?"

"Of course."

"Bring us a bottle, please."

"Right away."

As the waiter left them to fetch the champagne, Bobby turned back to Wade. "It's my favorite bubbly. Hope you don't mind. Now, where were we?"

Wade looked neutral, his handsome features betraying nothing. He glanced out the window, where the sky, near the top, was darkening to navy. The mountains were silhouetted now in pale gray light.

Bobby said softly, "I was telling you how much I missed you." He picked up Wade's hand again. "And how good it feels to be back together."

Wade smiled. "That's sweet."

Bobby waited for him to go on, but after a few moments passed, he continued. "I've been thinking a lot, you know, about life in general and things. And I have come to the conclusion that I'm not getting any younger and I should go for the things that matter.

"I was actually considering coming back here to Seattle. My mom would love it, but more importantly, I'd like to be close to you, to see where things might go." He smiled and squeezed Wade's hand. In a voice barely above a whisper, he said, "You're a special man. Special to me. And I think there's tremendous potential here." He stopped short of telling Wade he loved him. Even Bobby knew it was too soon for such declarations, but looking at the man across the table, Bobby knew he was falling for him.

Falling hard.

Bobby wished Wade would say something. But he was silent, not saying a word as the waiter came back with the champagne and poured a flute for each of them.

Bobby raised his glass. "To coming home."

They clinked and sipped. "So, you haven't said much about my idea of maybe moving back."

"I think you should do what you want to do."

Bobby stared down at the table, and the denial he'd been cultivating all evening collapsed in front of him like a house of cards. It was clear that Wade didn't reciprocate his feelings—or at the very least, not at the same level as Bobby. He felt pathetic as the desperate words tumbled from his lips. "Wouldn't you like to see me come back? We could get to know each other better, date, you know, a real *courtship*." He laughed at the old-fashioned word, but inside, his heart raced. A line of sweat trickled from his neck down to the small of his back. He gulped the entire flute of champagne and poured himself another glass.

Wade hadn't touched his, a fact that had not escaped Bobby's notice. And now, Bobby could see discomfort stamped on Wade's features. Wade shifted in his chair, his gaze wandering out the windows, at the other diners, at a waiter passing by with a plate of steak tartare.

Finally, Wade looked at him, his gaze level, his expression elevated from discomfort to resolute. He drew in a breath and said the words that had struck terror into the hearts of lovers since time immemorial. "Bobby, we need to talk."

No. I don't want to hear this. I don't want to talk. I want to hug, kiss, fuck, walk along the waterfront hand in hand in the moonlight. I want to chart a course for a future together. I want you to make my dreams come true. I want to lay the foundation for a life together. Oh, Wade, I want you. Bobby took another long swallow of champagne. Now, it tasted bitter, like carbonated vinegar on his tongue. "What?"

Wade said, "Bobby, you're a great guy—handsome, funny. You're everything I hoped for in a man."

Maybe he isn't going to say what I thought. Maybe it's just me, being a pessimist again, hating myself so much that I couldn't imagine someone loving me. Bobby sat up straighter, listening.

"And I think we would have really had a shot. But sometimes life has a funny way of throwing in a curve ball when we least expect it." Wade traced a pattern in the table's surface for a moment, staring down. When he looked back up, he was smiling, and Bobby could see that Wade found it hard to contain his joy. "I met somebody, Bobby. We had a couple dates right before I came to Chicago, and it was cool, but things hadn't really gelled. I didn't know where things would go.

"But when I came back, it was like everything fell into place. And I fell for *him*. Hard." Wade shook his head. "He's perfect, Bobby. I think he's 'the one,' if it doesn't sound too hokey to say that."

Wade took Bobby's hand again, squeezed it, and let go. "I know you had hopes for us, and I did too. But David just took me by surprise, took me by storm. Hell, we're talking about living together."

"David?" Bobby said dully.

"Yeah! I was hoping maybe you'd want to meet him. We could grab a drink on the Hill after we finish up here."

Bobby felt the rich food he had eaten roil in his stomach and tasted a splash of bile at the back of his throat.

This was not happening.

This was a nightmare.

Bobby shook his head. "I don't think so." He knew his voice came out toneless, dead.

"That's okay. Maybe another day before you leave."

Bobby stared at Wade, as if in just a few minutes and with only a few words, he had changed into someone else entirely. Someone Bobby hated. "Are you really so stupid?"

Wade looked stunned, hurt. "Excuse me?"

Bobby, with a shaking hand, pulled out his wallet, glad he had gone to the ATM prior to this dinner. He took out three hundred-dollar bills and slapped them down on the table. "That should cover dinner. There should be enough left over to buy David a drink when you meet him later. Tell him I said hi."

"Bobby, don't."

Bobby realized if he didn't get out of the restaurant *right now* he would be sick. He stood, crossed to Wade, and squatted. He grabbed Wade's chin and kissed him, passionately, deeply, his tongue halfway down the man's throat.

Wade jerked back and away. "What's wrong with you?"

"I wish I knew."

Bobby turned and hurried from the restaurant.

*

He didn't know if the Stallion had been his destination when he made his way from the very romantic restaurant, away from the hordes of tourists converged on the public market, who all suddenly seemed too happy for their own good, away from *Wade*, but now he found himself on a seedier part of Summit Avenue, in front of the bland façade of the bathhouse he had visited last time he was in town.

At least tonight, he thought, *Wade probably won't be inside to witness whatever I get myself up to.*

And what he wanted to get up to—his weeks of therapy, sessions with SAA, long talks with Aaron, all be damned—was to take as much cock as he could before dawn sashayed back into town, lightening the sky for decent people. People unlike him.

Bobby thought a good gang bang, one cock after another, a cock up his ass and one down his throat, multiple times, multiple loads would be just the thing he was longing for, just the thing to deliver sweet oblivion. He grew excited as he paced outside, the summer breeze warm and dry, imagining come dripping from the corners of his mouth and from his ass.

Why had he been denying himself? For what?

This is what I'm good for, what I really want—and what's wrong with that, anyway? Leave that love shit for those who know what to do with it.

Bobby was about to head inside, no second thoughts, when a guy crossed the street, coming toward him.

For a moment, his heart leapt because, through the darkness, he thought it was Wade. But then, as a streetlight revealed the man, Bobby saw that this guy couldn't have been more different from Wade.

He was probably about six two, and looked like he weighed about one hundred sixty pounds. He wore a beaten-up, dirty tank top and baggy jeans that were just barely succeeding in hugging his hipbones, dragged down farther by the big chain that held his wallet in his back pocket.

One arm had a sleeve of tattoos, but it was too dark to make out what they were. Bobby could make out, though, the ring of tattoo stars that moved, like a constellation, around his throat. His hair was a riot of reddish-brown spikes. When he got closer, he smiled with brown teeth. "Dude. You goin' inside?"

In spite of the brown teeth and in spite of the current of acrid aroma—a mix of body odor and something unidentifiable, something chemical—that rode across the couple of feet separating them, and even in spite of the aura of sickliness that the man exuded, Bobby, in his current state, found the guy hot, a temptation, a very bad boy gone to ruin, and he didn't give a fuck. The guy pulled out a pack of Marlboros and lit one up. "Well?"

"Yeah. I was just headin' in."

The guy surveyed him, looking him up and down. "They're gonna eat you alive in there, man."

"What I was hoping."

"Chip."

"Bobby."

"The Stallion usually doesn't get specimens like yourself. You are definitely a cut above."

"Thank you. You're not so bad yourself."

Chip snickered. "Fuck."

They stood silently for a couple of minutes. Bobby watched as Chip smoked. Finally, Chip patted his front right pocket. "You party?" He leaned in close to Bobby.

Bobby had never been big on drugs. He had been with many guys high on T, on G, on E, the whole fucking alphabet, but had never indulged in anything more than a bit of pot and alcohol himself. Sex alone had always been enough.

But maybe tonight should be different. After all, how often does one get dumped unceremoniously by the man one hoped to love?

"Fuck yeah," Bobby said. "You got favors?" he asked, using the lingo he had heard bandied about online.

Chip dragged deeply on his smoke, blew a cloud toward Bobby. "I'm the candy man, dude. You want a slice? A gram's eighty dollars."

Here he was, perched on a precipice. Everything inside him was telling him to just say "Aw, fuck it," and leap. Just descend into oblivion. Into hot sex. Into his body amped up on meth, sweating, insatiable. It all sounded good.

Until it didn't. Until an image of a Cole Haan shoe box came to him and, inside it, years of love, hidden away.

It sounded good until he looked at the sores on Chip's arms, the way his hand trembled as he took the cigarette from his mouth, the look of desperation in his yellow-cast eyes, at the sweat that coated his skin like glue, stinking. He was high, of course. He sought oblivion too.

Just like Bobby.

All at once, Bobby realized something—he was *not* like Chip. Not anymore. But he could be. So easily. All he had to do was give in to self-loathing, give in to lack of respect for himself, lose the possibility that someone could love him, just say "fuck it." He could live for the moment. Go inside with Chip, buy a Baggie full of crystalline rocks, crush them up and snort them, then go on the prowl for dick.

He would forget everything, save the hunger for dick.

But something stopped him. It wasn't just the rotating images of faces in his mind—Mom, Dad, Aaron, Caden—but the thought, for maybe the very first time, that he was past this. Sure, he could get high, play the power bottom all night long to a shitload of strangers, but when morning rolled around, he'd still have to deal with his disappointment over Wade.

He'd still have to wonder what the next step in his life should be.

Only that next morning, when his ass was raw and sore, eyes bleary, he knew he would not feel elation or satisfaction, or even nostalgia.

All he would feel was remorse—and the fear that maybe he had picked up more than some nasty memories on his debauched night.

His same hopes, his same problems, would still be there waiting.

Doing this, this bathhouse adventure, this drug, wouldn't change anything. He never used to know that, but he knew it now.

And that knowledge couldn't be ignored.

In spite of Wade's proclamation earlier, Bobby knew that someone would love him. People already did. That special man he longed for, though, would *not* be waiting inside the Stallion. That much he knew for certain.

He would wait out there.

Somewhere.

All these thought processes coursed through Bobby in a blink, some only felt and not articulated. He put a hand on Chip's bony and damp shoulder and squeezed it, looking into the dealer's rheumy eyes. He felt compassion for the man, a kind of sweet sorrow, and the hope that Chip might someday find the path to something better, something more real than the false promises a bathhouse and a gram of crystal meth offered—before it was too late.

"You know what, bud? I'm gonna pass."

He didn't wait for a response, but simply turned and walked away, heading for his car, heading for home.

Chapter Nineteen

Bobby awakened the next morning in a different place. Yes, the memory of Wade's rejection still stung, still hurt, hot and tender to the touch. Dashed dreams had a way of doing that. But we all had to live with dashed dreams, and to learn to give up on them and pursue what was attainable. Sometimes, Bobby thought, attainable was good enough. After all, what else did we really have?

Gain the power to change what we could, accept what we could not.

Wade was a beautiful man, inside and out. The possibility of not being with him left an empty void in Bobby, an ache. But at least now he knew the truth. Now he could move on with his life. And there was something to be said for finding out what Wade had revealed so soon, rather than, maybe, oh, six months after he had uprooted himself from his life in Chicago and moved here.

Perhaps Wade's rejection was a blessing.

Bobby snorted, rolling over on his side so he could look out the window at yet another sunny morning. *I wouldn't go that far. A blessing? Not yet.*

Last night had been a test. He had been hurt, laid lower than low (and not in a good way!), and he could have gone to default behavior and done what he always did, using sex as a balm on the hurt, to make him forget. The only problem with that was sex for that purpose was really, in the end, snake oil.

It couldn't work. Maybe for a few seconds or a few minutes it could, but it was a false promise.

And Bobby was through with those, or at least as much as he could hope to be.

He turned again, onto his back, tracing the course of a crack in the ceiling along its route from a corner to the light fixture. He thought, with more than a little shame, of how he had treated Wade. He had behaved like a spoiled child who didn't get his way.

A self-aware man, a grown man, a confident man would have dealt with his hurt later and shown his friend a smile, told him he was happy for him. Finding love in this world was a rare and blissful thing, Bobby imagined, especially at the start, and he should have conveyed that message to Wade instead of acting like a petulant brat.

Cut yourself some slack, man. Wade doesn't come out all lily-white in this scenario, you know. He could have—and should have—mentioned this new guy to you sooner. It was low of him to lead you on as he did. Bobby shook his head. He understood where Wade was coming from, even if his actions were less than honorable. *We're all looking for love, and it's not always easy to make the right choices, especially when those choices might jeopardize the love we're after.*

Make amends. Bobby knew it was the right thing to do. *Be the better man.*

He groped for his phone on the nightstand, pressed the Home button, saw that he had slept until ten, and decided it was not too early to call Wade. As he scrolled through his contacts and pressed the name on the screen that would connect them, Bobby hoped he would get the real man and not his voice mail.

"Hey." Wade's voice was soft when he answered, and Bobby wondered if he was expecting his call. That would be nice. It might show that Wade gave him a little credit.

"Hey. Listen, I wanted to apologize for last night. I shouldn't have rushed away like that. I acted like an idiot."

"It's okay. I know you came out here thinking we were maybe going to get something started, and you had every reason to think that. There were sparks between us when we were in Chicago. But I should say I'm sorry too. I should have told you about David way before you took me to dinner. I don't know why I didn't." Wade blew out a sigh, and Bobby could hear regret. "I guess part of me thought you'd just be here for a short time, and I could deal with it later. But when you started talking about moving here—"

Bobby laughed. "Gave you a scare, didn't it?"

Wade chuckled. "Yeah, kind of. But seriously, I knew I needed to, you should pardon the expression, be straight with you."

"I'm not gonna say I thank you for that."

They were silent for a moment or two.

Bobby continued, "But what I *am* gonna say is that I'm happy for you. I'd be lying if I said I didn't wish I was in David's shoes. But I'm glad you've met someone who's so special to you that you would call him the 'one.' That's a remarkable thing, wonderful, and I wish you and David a lifetime of joy. I mean that." Bobby paused and then added, "And, if things continue this way, you guys have the option to get married here in Washington." Bobby surprised himself at his sincerity and how good he felt about conveying his happiness to Wade.

Bobby heard the delight in Wade's laughter at that, the hope, the promise that was Wade's to anticipate.

"Thank you, Bobby. Are you sure you don't have time to meet David?"

"You know what? No hard feelings, but I think these last couple days I'm reserving for Mom. She's been really down, as you might expect, about my dad passing away, and I want to show her a really good time before I leave."

"You're a good guy."

At those words, Bobby felt something clench inside his chest. Was he? Really?

"You take care, Wade. And if you and David ever get back to Chicago, you be sure to call me. We'll do dinner."

They hung up, and Bobby settled back into the pillows. He thought he might drift back to sleep, but Michelle pounded on his door.

She called from outside. "Are you going to sleep the day away? Only two days left, sweetie. I'm putting coffee on."

Bobby sat up. "I'll be out in ten minutes, Mom." He stood and slipped into a pair of flannel sleep pants and a T-shirt. He called through the door, "I love you!"

"Love you more!" his mother called, her voice getting softer as she made her way into the kitchen.

Before Bobby headed out to join her, he stopped in front of his window to look across the water and recognize something else he felt—relief. He could have been lying here this morning, both physically and emotionally sick from bad behavior the night before, and he had respected himself enough to say no.

"Well, bully for you!" Bobby muttered to himself. "Don't get too big of a head. You have a lifetime of decisions laid out before you, and I would hazard a guess that not every choice you make will be the perfect one. It's a constant struggle."

"Who are you talking to in there?" Michelle must have returned to his door.

"Just myself, Mom. Crazy as a shithouse loon, as Gram used to say."

Michelle laughed at that. "Coffee's ready."

*

The next couple of days, as he had told Wade and promised himself, Bobby focused on his mother. The sun, more of a friend with benefits to Seattle than an enduring romance, stayed copious and glorious, and they drove up to Mount Rainier and rode the gondolas, timing it so they could have a sunset dinner at the restaurant on the summit. They rode the Seattle Ducks, something neither had done, even though Michelle saw the land/water vehicles from her windows almost every day. They had shopped downtown, strolled Green Lake, had dinner at the Dahlia Lounge and indulged in their magnificent crab cakes and sinful house-made doughnuts. They had even gone up to see his sister, Dawn, and her family in Snohomish for a cookout.

That day, Bobby had cornered his sister in the kitchen and risen to his mother's defense. "Mom tells me you haven't been around much at all since Dad died."

She had opened her mouth to start defending herself, but Bobby raised a hand to stop her.

"I don't want your excuses. I just want your promise that you will make time for her." He told Dawn the condition he found his mother in when he arrived.

When she heard, Dawn said nothing for several moments. "I had no idea," she finally whispered.

"Yeah. No idea. That's my point. I'm not saying this to make *you* feel bad, but for *her*. Go see her. Have her up for dinner, for one of the kid's soccer games, for a weekend here and there. She's our mother, and as we just found out, our parents won't be around forever."

He had looked pointedly at his sister, sorry for the tears standing in her eyes but glad he was making an impression. "And we might not always have the chance to say the things or do the things we wish we had done."

He thought again of the box, but he didn't tell Dawn about that. That was his. Alone. Both a treasure and a hurt to cherish and keep...

When at last the morning arrived for Bobby to head back to Chicago, Michelle sat on his bed, refolding his shirts in perfect retail-store symmetry as he packed. "I'm going to miss you," she said.

Bobby walked over to her, stooped to give her a little hug. "Me too. But you're gonna come out to Chicago for a visit, right? October?"

She nodded, staring out at the day, which had finally reverted to Seattle default. The skies were gray, and a light mist danced in the air.

"I'll book a ticket for you when I get home. You're gonna love it."

At last, he was ready. He stood with Michelle at the front door. She said, "You know I could still drive you." She grinned. "Be a pain in the ass to the rental car company again and have them pick it up from here."

"Mom, it's no trouble. Really, it's better this way." He gathered his mother up in his arms, holding her close. She felt so small and frail, as if a gust of wind could snatch her away. Bobby found himself not wanting to let go, to be strong for this woman who had always been strong for him, raising him up not to be a perfect man, but a man all the same, and one who was smart enough, finally, to understand how to make good choices.

"Thank you, Mom," he whispered in her ear.

She obviously didn't want to let go either, clutching him tighter. She whispered back, "You don't have to thank me. This is your home. You are welcome here anytime."

"I know. I didn't mean just that."

"What then?"

"Everything." Bobby squeezed her again and, at last, pulled away, searching his mother's eyes. "You're gonna be all right?"

She nodded. "Yeah."

Bobby opened the door.

"Call me when you get home, just so I know you made it okay."

"I will, Mom."

He could see the tears welling up and knew the best thing now was to cut things short. "I love you. Take care."

"I love you too, Bobby," she murmured, her voice weak. "I'll see you soon."

"Count on it."

And he was out the door.

*

A few hours later, he touched down at O'Hare, looking out at a brilliant Indian summer day. The leaves he could see were just beginning to turn, yet heat shimmered in barely visible waves from the tarmac. He had a weird thought, one that sprang from out of nowhere: he was home. Sure, he had grown up in Seattle and his immediate family was still there, but this city, with its crime, its traffic, its endless parking nightmares, snow, and frigid temperatures, had become his in the decade he had lived here. He knew its good points—the vibrant theater community, its Cubs fans with their bottomless well of optimism, the beauty of Lake Michigan in its ever-changing moods, the skyline viewed at night from Lake Shore Drive near Navy Pier, the kind of people who lived and loved here: hardworking, no-nonsense, but with a big capacity for affection, and much more—and they superseded all the bad, at least for him.

He had grown up here, in a way. And what he had gone through, in only the past few months, he realized, had been a sudden growth spurt. He chuckled internally at the notion that perhaps, at age forty, he had at last released himself from the troubled bonds of adolescence, a late adolescence, but an adolescence all the same, with its attendant aches, confusion, and growing pains.

Weird.

The flight attendant, a cute, butch blond with a buzz cut and eyes the color of ice, had flirted the entire flight, even bringing him a warm cookie from first class. He helped Bobby get his carry-on down from the overhead compartment.

"You live here?" he asked.

"I do." Bobby took the bag from him.

"So do I. And it just so happens this flight is the end of my day and the start of a week off."

"Good for you." Bobby moved into line to get off the plane.

"I don't know your situation or anything, but I'd love to get together for a drink, maybe? If you're available, if you're free…"

The old Bobby would have jumped at this chance. Hell, the old Bobby probably would have already done the guy in the lavatory. But that Bobby was gone, or at least far enough away that already Bobby was feeling a certain nostalgia for him, even if it was tinged with regret and remorse.

"I'm kind of seeing someone," he said to the blond, surprising himself. He didn't know if it was a convenient lie that had sprung to his lips, or perhaps the truth.

The blond nodded, grinning. "Of course you are. A man like you wouldn't be single." He sighed. "Some smart guy snatched you up ages ago. Am I right?"

"Oh, if you only knew." Bobby moved on.

*

It always amazed Bobby how exhausting simply sitting on a plane for several hours could be. He knew he could catch the Blue Line train right here in the airport, switch to the Red Line downtown, and be almost to his house within an hour, but he just didn't feel like the hassle, not with the fatigue and the bags he would have to schlep along.

So, after claiming his checked bag, he opted to splurge on a cab once more.

He stepped out into the bright, shimmering day. Even though it felt about eighty and the humidity was thick, there was something in the air nonetheless, undeniable, that felt like fall. He was scanning the bustling lanes of traffic for an available cab when he heard a deep voice behind him.

"You looking for a ride into the city?"

The voice sounded familiar, and Bobby turned.

It was Aaron, and Bobby was suddenly at a loss for words. Not only did Aaron hold a bouquet of bright purple irises in his hand, he held back a very elated Johnny, who strained to get at Bobby, to be reunited with his master and savior.

Bobby was *home*.

He squatted and patted his thighs for Johnny to come to him, and Aaron let up some on the leash so the dog could leap on Bobby, licking his face and trying to French kiss him. He laughed, petting the dog, scratching him behind the ears. The woeful face, with its bright button eyes and underbite, tugged at Bobby's heart. "Oh, I've missed you, stinker."

Finally, he stood and turned to Aaron, who held out the flowers. "I got these for you."

Bobby laughed, taking the flowers from him and reveling in their vibrant purple hue. They were his favorite, always had been. "Why? You didn't need to do this. I thought we agreed I'd come by and get Johnny once I got home."

"I thought it would be a nice surprise." Aaron's eyes twinkled, and his smile felt as much like a homecoming as a hug, although he wanted that too.

Bobby glanced around for Frieda. "You didn't bring your girl?"

"Johnny told me that he wanted you all to himself and that if I thought he was going to wait around at my house for you to show up, I had another thing coming." Aaron stepped in close, and Bobby got the hug he had wanted, wanted for far longer than maybe even he realized. The feel of Aaron's body pressed close to his own was magic—the solidity of it, the firmness of chest against chest, the sandpaper of Aaron's beard against Bobby's neck—all of this erased their surroundings for several moments, until Johnny, jealous, began pouncing on his calf and nipping. Before pulling away, Aaron whispered in Bobby's ear, "Don't flatter yourself. I planned this as much for me as I did for you."

Bobby stepped back, unable to contain his smile, his joy. "How did you know where to find me?"

Aaron nudged him. "You silly queen. You, traveling without a checked bag? Get serious! I knew you'd come out of baggage claim, and I just kept my eyes peeled for the best-looking guy to come out of those doors."

Bobby didn't say any more. He couldn't. Words eluded him, but he knew that this feeling of happiness and homecoming was something that felt, all at once, strange, unique, and wonderful. All he could do was stare at the man and the dog and think three words: *I am blessed.*

"Come on." Aaron finally broke the spell. "I have a dandelion salad, corn on the cob, and sliced tomatoes from my garden all waiting at home—a nice detox dinner, because I'm sure you overdid it out there. Car's this way." Aaron handed Bobby the leash and looked for an opening in the traffic so they could cross.

*

Later, as the light outside faded to dusk, and a breeze, cooler than the day, blew in to ruffle the sheer curtains at Aaron's bedroom window, Bobby lay with his head upon Aaron's fur-matted chest, glorying in the steel of it, the easy rise and fall of his breathing. He ran his fingertips through the hair and stopped for a moment to tweak one of Aaron's nipples.

"Cut it out." Aaron's voice was husky, sounding as though it was minutes away from sleep. "You'll get me started all over again."

"And that would be a bad thing?" Bobby wondered.

Aaron chuckled, and Bobby relaxed more into his arms as darkness claimed the room. He could hear Johnny, curled in a ball at the foot of the bed, softly snoring.

"You think this was okay?" Bobby finally pushed the words out, into the dimness.

"It was fuckin' fantastic. Are you kidding?"

Bobby grinned, flattered. The post-dinner sex had been intense, starting at the dining room table with a simple kiss to say thanks for a splendid meal. But that kiss was like dropping a match on gasoline-soaked tinder. In moments, Bobby was aflame and glad Aaron was too.

There was now a trail of clothes from the dining room to Aaron's bedroom upstairs. They tore them off as they went, tripping, popping buttons, laughing as T-shirts got caught in elbows as they struggled to get them off faster, faster, never fast enough. They had deep-kissed at the table, fondled one another in the living room, and Bobby had gone down on Aaron on the stairs. In the bedroom, their connection was fast, electric, almost brutal, Aaron barely taking time to lube up and roll a condom over his sizable cock before plunging hungrily into Bobby with abandon.

Bobby was so ready for him at that point, all he could do was thrust against the man, grabbing Aaron's ass cheeks to propel him deeper inside. There was no pain, only scorching heat and exquisite pleasure.

It had been over in minutes, yet neither complained.

Now, the quiet was a brilliant contrast to their fucking, their lovemaking, which Bobby had no idea was coming when he stepped out of baggage claim only a few hours ago. He said, "That's not what I meant. I think you know that. And thank you very much. But really, everyone at group says we should wait, like a year, before being intimate."

"It's a good guideline," Aaron said.

"It is? You could have fooled me."

"It's a guideline. I believe in following my heart, not my head, and certainly not arbitrary guidelines. It was right today, wasn't it?"

Bobby hugged him closer, so hard it was as though he wanted their bodies to merge into one. "Yes" was all he could manage to say.

"I know what you're saying, Bobby. But ask yourself this. Is what we just did anything like what you used to do? Online, at the baths, when I first found you going down on that guy in the men's room?" He chuckled. "No, of course it wasn't. This was real. There's gonna be—I just know it—not only a second time, and, baby, that's coming soon, but a third and a fourth."

Aaron got up on one elbow to gaze down at Bobby. "And there will be more than sex for us. I know it. Here." He touched his chest, above his heart.

He lay back down, talking to the ceiling, to the dark, but most of all, to Bobby. "When you went back to Seattle, I was sick. I knew you weren't just going for your mom, although I know that was part of it, but for that guy."

"Wade." Bobby pictured him in his mind and, already, felt something different for the man:

affection, respect, and happiness for him to have found love.

"Yeah, I know. I used to say 'Wayne' just because I was pissed off and frustrated that you were so into him, but I couldn't dare let it out, so I mangled his name. Stupid, I know.

"Anyway, when you went out there, I knew it was to be with him, and I realized that you could very well come home and tell me your good news, that maybe you guys were in love, maybe you were moving out there or he here, whatever. And I knew that news like that would break my heart. I would have lost you forever.

"I was kicking myself that I hadn't been more up front with you about my feelings, feelings which, I might add, have nothing to do with sexual addiction. This, what we just did, has nothing to do with it. I don't believe that and I never will.

"I love you, Bobby. There, I said it. Too soon. Impulsive. Rash. But I mean it. And I intend not to give you another chance to slip through my fingers. Ever."

Bobby traced his fingers over Aaron's lips. "Glad to hear it. I don't think I knew I loved you until I saw you standing outside baggage claim with those flowers and my dog." Bobby buried his head in the fragrant warmth of Aaron's neck and whispered. "It was a family portrait, and now I know that's all I ever wanted."

"All?" Aaron pushed Bobby over on his back and moved in to kiss him. "All?"

"Not all." And Bobby wrapped a hand around the back of Aaron's neck to draw him near.

Epilogue

CHRISTMAS

"I can never remember. Forks on the left or the right?" Bobby paused, a handful of flatware clutched in his hand. All around him, the place was decorated for Christmas, with the centerpiece being a seven-foot Douglas fir, decked out in tiny white lights and Radko ornaments.

"Sweetie, didn't your mother teach you any of the common civilities?" Wade called from the kitchen, where he had just closed the oven after taking a quick peak at the brussels sprouts he was roasting.

"Don't you badmouth my mom. Just answer the damn question."

"The left." Wade came into the room, trailed by the aromas of a roasting duck, the sprouts, garlic, lemon, and fresh herbs. He took the flatware from Bobby and gave him a quick peck on the cheek. "Why don't you let me finish up here? You still need to get dressed. Kevin and Caden are going to be here in what? Less than an hour? And you need to get dressed, mister."

"Oh, whose idea was it to have an early holiday dinner, anyway?" Bobby looked down at himself, still in his slippers, sleep pants, and a long-sleeved T-shirt. "I guess I should take a shower and put on some fresh clothes."

"Go make yourself pretty. I'll take care of things here."

Bobby pulled Wade into his arms, giving him the kind of hug reserved especially for bears, of whatever variety one might have in mind. He whispered, "Did I ever tell you how glad I am you and I worked things out?"

"Over and over. You've become the original heart-on-his-sleeve man." He squeezed back and then released Bobby. "I'm glad too, sweetheart."

"You're sure you're okay down here? I mean, I feel like you're doing all the work."

"Uh...no I'm not. If you think that, you're sadly mistaken, buddy. I just like to cook."

"You're not the only one."

Wade gave Bobby a swat on the ass as he headed out of the living room on his way to the bedroom. Bobby turned to wag a warning finger at him.

"Go on, go on!" Wade said, laughing.

Upstairs, Bobby opened the bedroom door softly, wincing when it squealed out its familiar squeak. He didn't want to wake Aaron. After they had opened presents that morning, Aaron had gone back to bed.

Bobby was relieved to see his man lying across the bed, mouth open in a snore. He couldn't help but think how, even though Aaron had spoiled him with presents that morning, Bobby would have been happy with no other gift than the one before him.

A man. *His* man. He'd had so many, many men, a deluge, but he had never had one that was his alone, until just a few months ago. He had thought, for a while, that having a man of his very own was something he could only dream about, that he was destined to enjoy the embraces of a multitude of men, but never to find just the right one, like some kind of hell only Dante could dream up.

But Aaron had been there. He'd always been there, and had not turned away from Bobby even when he saw him at his worst, even when Bobby had revealed to him things he had done in what he had once believed was the pursuit of hot sex, but in the end proved to be nothing more than a futile and soul-sucking search for love.

And love was the one thing he thought he'd never find. Yet Camille and Sex Addicts Anonymous made him realize that, if he never did find love, it was okay—not ideal, far from it—but okay. He was comfortable enough now, in his own jaded and heavily fingerprinted skin, to know that real joy comes from within.

Finding Aaron had been a bonus, a gift, a treasure, something he hoped he'd never take for granted.

Bobby sat on the bed, brushing his fingers lightly across the stubble covering Aaron's cheeks. That gesture awakened him. Their eyes met, and Aaron smiled. Bobby leaned down to kiss him. Aaron roughly pulled him close, so that Bobby's body covered Aaron's like the blanket Aaron had thrown off in his sleep and that now lay in a heap on the side of the bed.

Aaron said nothing, just growled, raising his hips up against Bobby. Bobby felt his hardness, as if a billy club had sprouted between them.

"Oh my!"

"Dreaming of you." He thrust his hips up again. "Do we have time for a quickie? Please, please, say yes."

Bobby laughed and whispered, "What about our houseguests?"

"Wade and David? They have each other. They can do the same if they overhear and get excited. And if they don't like it, fuck 'em. They can stay at the Holiday Inn."

Bobby looked deep into Aaron's eyes, which twinkled with lust, mischief, and, Bobby thought, best of all, love. Aaron cocked one eyebrow in question.

Bobby rolled his eyes. He reached into the nightstand drawer, found a condom and their pump bottle of lube and got the two of them ready, although there wasn't much to do. Never losing eye contact, he slid down on Aaron, taking him deep inside.

"Merry Christmas, baby," Aaron half gasped, half said.

But Bobby didn't say anything. He rode Aaron like a racehorse and didn't stop until he watched the beautiful contortions he now knew well on his lover's face, didn't stop until he spurted his own seed on Aaron's chest and belly.

The whole thing took only a few minutes, and Bobby slid down, so they disengaged, and he could lie next to Aaron, panting, his come a kind of glue between them.

Aaron, finally able to speak, said, "This idea of you moving in has really worked out." He patted Bobby's ass. "Makes things very convenient. What was it Dorothy said at the end of *The Wizard of Oz*? Something about not looking any further than your own backyard for your heart's desire." Aaron kissed him. "You're my heart's desire—in every way there is."

Bobby thought about saying "There's no place like home" but rejected the idea as too hokey. In the end, he said the words he had longed to say to someone all his life, even if, for a time, he hadn't known it.

"I love you."

About the Author

Real Men. True Love.

Rick R. Reed draws inspiration from the lives of gay men to craft stories that quicken the heartbeat, engage emotions, and keep the pages turning. Although he dabbles in horror, dark suspense, and comedy, his attention always returns to the power of love. He's the award-winning and bestselling author of more than fifty works of published fiction and is forever at work on yet another book. Lambda Literary has called him: "A writer that doesn't disappoint…" You can find him at www.rickrreedreality.blogspot.com. Rick lives in Palm Springs, CA, with his beloved husband, Bruce, and their fierce Chihuahua/Shiba Inu mix, Kodi.

Email: rickrreedbooks@gmail.com

Facebook: www.facebook.com/rickrreedbooks

Twitter: @rickrreed

Website: www.rickrreedreality.blogspot.com

Other books by this author

Unraveling

Sky Full of Mysteries

The Perils of Intimacy

IM

Chaser

Coming Soon from Rick R. Reed

Blue Umbrella Sky

Milt Grabaur stared out the window of his trailer, wondering how much worse it could get.

The deluge poured down, gray, almost obscuring his neighbors' homes and the barren desert landscape beyond. The rain hammered on his metal roof, sounding like automatic gunfire. Milt shivered a little, thinking of that old song, "It Never Rains in Southern California."

He leaned closer to the picture window, pressing his hand against the glass and whispering to himself, "But it pours."

That window had given him his daily view for the last six months, ever since he'd packed up a life's worth of belongings and made his way south and west to Palm Springs and the Summer Winds Mobile Home Community. This same picture window, almost every single day, had shown him only endless blue skies and sunshine. An errant cloud or a jet contrail would occasionally break up the field of electric blue, but other than that, it was azure perfection. Milt reveled in it. He'd begun to think these expanses of blue, lit up by golden illumination, would never cease.

Until today.

At about three o'clock, that blue sky, for the first time, was overcome with gray, a foreboding mass of bruised clouds. Milt wondered, because of his experience in the desert so far, if the clouds would be only that—foreboding. The magical gods of the Coachella Valley would, of course, sweep away those frowning and depressing masses of imminent precipitation with a wave of their enchanted hands.

Surely.

But the sky continued to darken, seemingly unaware of Milt's fanciful imagining and yearnings. At last the once-blue dome above him became almost like night in midafternoon and the first heavy drops—fat beads of water—began to fall, first a slow sprinkle, where Milt could count the seconds between drops, then faster and faster, until the raindrops combined into one single and, Milt had to admit, *terrifying* roar.

And then an unfamiliar sound—the drumroll and cymbal crash of thunder. The sky, moments after, lit up with brilliant white light.

The rain fell in earnest. Torrents of the stuff.

The other trailers, his neighbors, nearly vanished in the relentless gray downpour. The wind howled, sending the rain capriciously sideways every few seconds. The palm trees in his front yard swayed and bent with the ruthless gusts, testimony to their strength, despite their appearance of being stalklike and weak. The wind tore dry husks of bark from them.

At first Milt was unconcerned, thinking the rain could only do good. It would bless the parched succulents, cacti, and palms that dotted the rocky, sandy landscape of the park, maybe even bring them to colorful life, forcing a brilliant desert flower, here and there, to bloom. His decade-old Honda Civic, parked next to the trailer, would get a wash, the thick layer of sand and dust chased away, almost pressure-cleaned.

For the half a year he'd been here, Milt had been amazed at how clean everything could look when, in actuality, anything outdoors was quickly covered in a veneer of fine sand, almost like gritty dust. Milt was forever wiping off his patio furniture, cleaning the glass surfaces of his car. But this minor inconvenience was more than outweighed by the stunning and almost surreal appearance of the Coachella Valley and the desert, a wild beauty which far surpassed anything even an optimistic Milt had dreamed of when he had made up his mind, somewhat suddenly, to shed his old life in Ohio and move out to Southern California.

He stared out at the gusts of wind, the flashes of lightning, and the almost-blinding downpour and realized he had no idea it could be like this. The trailer park was smack up against the San Jacinto mountain range, and Milt realized with horror that not only would the little park suffer from the copious water falling from the sky, but it would also be the beneficiary, like it or not, of runoff as it came hurtling down the mountain face.

As if to confirm his notion, Milt gasped as he noticed the street in front of his trailer.

It was no longer a street.

Not really.

No, now it was a creek. A creek notable for its rushing rapids. Water was speeding by at an unprecedented pace. Milt sucked in some air as he saw a lawn chair go by, buoyed up by the current. Then a plastic end table. An inflatable pool toy—a swan—that Milt supposed was in the right place at the right time. But the damp throw pillows whizzing by, like soggy oyster crackers in soup, were not.

Milt turned to look behind him at the sound of a whimper.

"Oh, what's the matter, sweetheart?" He held out a beseeching hand to the gray-and-white pit bull mix he'd picked up from the Palm Springs Animal Shelter over on Mesquite the first week he'd gotten here. "It's okay."

She looked ferocious but was a big softie, easily frightened, shy, and with a disposition that made Mother Teresa look like a terrorist. Ruby, he'd called her on a whim, in honor of the kind lady that lived two doors down from him when he was a little boy back in Summitville, Ohio. *That* Ruby, like this one, had always been kind but retiring, shying from the slightest spotlight.

This Ruby, right now, was terrified, her tail between her legs, backing toward the shadowy corners of the room, eyes wide with fear. Milt reached out, trying to grab the frightened dog, but she scurried away and dashed out of sight down the narrow hallway leading to his bedroom, nails clattering, slipping and sliding on the tile floor. Milt sighed, knowing exactly what she was doing even though he couldn't see her—scurrying under his bed to cower among the dust bunnies and cast-off shoes.

It would take hours—and treats—to coax her out. Milt knew from experience...

He returned his attention to the storm raging outside, which showed no signs of abating.

Plus—and this made Milt groan—there was a new wrinkle to the carnage. Not only were the streets around his trailer now rapidly flowing rivers; Milt also realized with horror he was about to get flooded.

He gazed down on standing water several inches deep spread out across his patio. It covered the outdoor rugs he'd bought, with their whimsical cactus design, soaking them like washcloths. It rose up the sides of his patio furniture. Milt swore he could see it getting higher and higher.

Worst of all, Milt watched the water hover just outside the sliding glass doors, waiting, perhaps, for an invitation to come inside.

Ah, the hell with it, the water seemed to say, *why wait for an invitation? This party needs crashing!*

And it began to seep in... A little at first, and then faster and faster, until his entire floor was covered.

Milt involuntarily cried out, voice high-pitched and terrified, nothing like the butch forty-two-year-old he thought himself. "Help! Flood! Somebody, please!" The cry was pure panic. Logically, he knew no one would hear.

What that helper would do, Milt had no idea, but he simply wanted someone to be with him in his predicament. The thought flitted across his consciousness that he'd been here six months, and it wasn't until today and the advent of a rainstorm of biblical proportions that he realized he didn't want to be alone. He swore as warm water covered his bare feet at the exact moment his power went out, plunging his little sanctuary into murky dark.

And at this very unnerving moment, Milt realized—gratefully—someone just might have heard his pleas for help. There was a pounding at the back door, rattling the glass jalousie panes. He turned, confused for a moment—he'd cast himself as a sole survivor, a man against nature, alone.

The pounding continued. A voice. "Hey! You okay in there?"

Milt crossed the living room and the small galley kitchen to get to the back door. But when he opened it, there was no one there. The wind pushed at him, mocking, and the rain sent a drenching spray against him. Despite getting soaked, Milt leaned out, gripping the door's frame with both hands for balance, and looked around.

Even though the covering of storm clouds had made it seem as though a dusky twilight had fallen, he could see that there was no one there.

He wondered if he'd imagined the knocking and the voice. He really didn't know his neighbors, having kept to himself since he'd moved out here because he just wasn't ready to connect with others again. He'd given so much to his Corky during those final tortured months… Sometimes Milt felt he had nothing left to give anyone again *ever*.

And a dog, cowering and bashful as she might be, had been company enough.

His little reverie was shattered by a second round of knocking, this time at the sliding glass doors in his living room. "Okay, so I'm not hearing things." Milt turned away from the back door and headed to the sliders.

Outside, a young man stood, drenched from head to toe, in a pair of neon-pink board shorts and, well, nothing else. *Maybe there's flip-flops.* Milt couldn't see the guy's feet. His jaw dropped as he hurried to open the door. In spite of all that was going on—the storm, the flood, the risk of his home being destroyed—he couldn't help his thoughts, notions he'd decided long ago died within him.

I am looking at an angel; that's all there is to it. He's going to sweep me away in those muscular arms, lifting me right up to heaven and setting me down gently next to my Corky.

Milt shook his head. A short burst of laughter escaped him, almost as if someone else were chuckling in his living room with him.

The guy *was* handsome, a tanned and buff dreamboat. Corky would have loved him, saying, once upon a time, that looks like this boy's should be illegal, or at least sinful. Milt smiled.

Even though his hair was plastered to his head, Milt could tell it was thick and luxurious—right now the color of dark wheat, but Milt was certain that in dryer moments, it was as gold as the pure, unfiltered sunshine Milt had grown accustomed to being greeted by every morning. He had a body that made Milt, if only for a moment, forget the storm *and* the fact that he was a widower, still grieving nearly a year after losing his man. Muscles, smooth bronze skin, and a six-pack had the power of oblivion, of taking precedence over everything else.

Stop, he mentally chastised himself. He flung open the slider, noticing the rain had—at last—slowed to a patter and the winds had died down almost completely. Milt, though, couldn't seem to put lips and tongue together to form a greeting or ask a question or to even say anything at all. His eyebrows came together like two caterpillars possessed of their own will.

"Hey there, man. I heard you calling out for help." He jerked a thumb over his shoulder. "I live in the unit behind you." He smiled, revealing electric-white teeth that made Milt's thoughts go even more blank or even more lascivious, he wasn't sure which. He shivered.

The guy gave Milt a more tentative smile, the type you'd give to the kindly neighbor down the street who'd just emerged from home wearing nothing but a pair of saddle shoes and a big smile. Milt wondered if the guy thought he was encountering a person who couldn't speak, or maybe someone whose mind had completely deserted him. Lord knew Milt was familiar enough with people like that, having only very recently seen to every need of a person just like that.

"Are you okay, buddy?"

Milt managed a smile, despite the fact that his feet squished on the soaked carpeting. *Oh Lord, is everything ruined? How much is this going to cost? Is it going to wipe me out?* "Yeah," Milt sputtered. He glanced behind him. "It looks as though I'm getting flooded." There appeared to be at least a couple of inches of water covering the floor of his trailer. He groaned.

The young man leaned in to survey the damage and gave a low whistle. "Yikes!" He leaned back out so he could face Milt. "Bet you didn't think you needed to worry about flooding in the desert?"

Milt shook his head. "Well, it wasn't foremost." He glanced behind him again, feeling like his sanctuary had been violated—as it indeed had. And what fresh hell would spring forth from the damage? "What am I gonna do?"

"Well, my opinion is you need to get yourself the hell out of there. As I said, I'm right behind you, *up* the mountain a tad, so I'm still dry. You wanna grab some of your stuff just in case and come on over?"

"Stuff?"

"Yeah, man, like, I don't know, a laptop, maybe? Family pictures? Important papers? You know, just in case. The stuff you'd run out of here with if the place caught on fire."

"Oh, right." Milt sighed. "This is awfully kind of you."

"Hey, we're neighbors. At Summer Winds, we look out for each other. I've been wanting to meet you, anyway. Sucks that it has to be under these circumstances. But come on, I've got a dry house, air-conditioning, and enough candy to send you into a diabetic coma." He laughed.

Milt stood, his mind beating a hasty retreat. He shouldn't feel indecisive, but he did.

"Or if you have other plans..." the man finally said. "Indoor pool party?"

"No. No! I'd love to come over." Milt looked around his place once more. Most of his stuff was up high enough that it wouldn't get wet, unless the trailer toppled over or something, but there was one thing he couldn't just leave behind. "I need to get Ruby."

"Ruby?"

"My girl, my dog!" Milt snapped, as if his visitor should know. He immediately regretted his tone, but his neighbor simply seemed to be taking his dire straits way too lightly.

"Ruby. Cute name. I've seen you walking her. She's sweet. Go grab her. She's welcome too. Animals of all varieties are welcome in my crib." He winked. "I used to have a dog myself, a Yorkie, Bergamot, that thought he was a Doberman." He frowned. "But he passed away last winter. Coyote got him."

Milt jerked a little in horror. "I'm sorry."

Milt couldn't imagine losing his dog—he'd already fallen hopelessly in love with Ruby. He felt a deep-seated twinge of empathy. "The storm shook her up. Let me just see if I can coax her out from under the bed." Milt didn't think the task would be too tough, since it was now wet under the bed and Ruby hated water. He turned and started away, sloshing through the hateful water. Midstream, so to speak, he changed his mind and turned back.

He held out a hand. "I'm sorry. Milt. Milt Grabaur. I'd invite you in, but my place, as you can see, isn't exactly presentable." He laughed and then felt like bursting into tears.

"If you knew I was coming, you'd have baked a cake? A sponge cake?" He snorted and shook Milt's hand with a big calloused paw. "Billy Blue."

Milt smiled. "Seriously?"

Billy shrugged. "Yeah, my mom and dad had a great sense of humor. Or thought I was destined for the stage, instead of cashier at Trader Joe's. The advantage of a name like mine, silly as it is, is that people tend not to forget it."

"I think it's a lovely name." Milt met Billy Blue's gaze—and thought how fortuitous it was that his irises matched the color of his last name. *And you're a lovely man. Handsome, built like a brick shithouse—and sweet as pie.*

"I'll be right back with Ruby." He turned and this time did manage to slosh to the very rear of the trailer, where his wood-paneled master bedroom awaited. Before he even stooped down in the grimy water to coax, he began talking to Ruby. "Good girl. Nothin' to be ascared of, honey," Milt said in his most soothing voice, cadence and words dredged up from his boyhood memories of living near the river in the foothills of the Appalachians, in the northern panhandle of West Virginia. He squatted down, wincing a little as his knees came into contact with the spongy shag carpeting he'd hoped to replace one day, and lifted the bottom of the comforter, which was stained dark from the water.

Underneath the bed there was only a couple of inches of water, a pair of Keen sandals, and a metal storage box that contained Milt's "toys"—and we're not talking Fisher-Price here.

There was no Ruby. Nor any other living creature.

Milt got to his feet, groaning, and took stock of the entire bedroom, thinking perhaps Ruby had retreated to a corner or hidden behind the chest of drawers. But she was nowhere to be found, not even in the adjacent bathroom, which looked now as though Milt had taken a long, long shower and had simply not bothered to turn the water off.

Knowing she wouldn't be there, but checking anyway, Milt opened the frosted glass shower door to find it empty.

He made a tour of the trailer, getting more and more anxious with each step, with each empty nook and cranny. "Ruby?" he called out several times, each time his voice growing louder, as though sheer volume would make her appear.

But she didn't.

And the thoughtlessly left-open back door gave testimony to what had most likely happened. The poor terrified girl had probably tried to escape that way, running headlong into a fate worse than she was trying to escape. Milt hurried to the open door, peering out onto his little patio, hoping against hope she'd be out there, stub of a tail sending up splashes as she looked mournfully at him.

But Ruby was gone.

Milt felt as though his heart would break.

He closed the door behind him, sighing and wondering if he should leave it open, just in case she tried to return. Return to what? A trailer flooded with filthy—and probably bacteria-ridden—water?

He moved back to the sliders, looking over Billy's broad shoulders, hoping Ruby would appear on the doused desert landscape.

Billy smiled at Milt's return. "Dog?" he wondered.

Milt's breath caught. The day, or not really the day but only, really, the past few minutes, had been a disaster. *Disasters happen fast and savage in Palm Springs.* He wasn't sure he could speak without bursting into tears, without chastising himself for his own carelessness.

If only I hadn't left that damn door open.

"She's nowhere to be found." Milt shrugged.

Billy frowned, and his gaze seemed to reach out to Milt in sympathy, which made Milt want to cry even more. "She'll turn up." Billy changed his expression to a reassuring smile. "She's got it good— a man all to herself, and I assume a limitless supply of treats." He winked. "I wish I could say the same."

Ah, so he's one of us. I thought so, but one doesn't want to assume. "I'm sure you're right," Milt said, although he wasn't sure at all.

"You still want to come over? I got carnitas cooking in the Crock-Pot. Homemade tortillas. I may be blond, but I cook like the locals."

Milt managed a smile. The thought of food made his stomach turn, thinking of Ruby running around out there somewhere—with threats like coyotes, black widow spiders, and rattlesnakes all around, just to name a few. She might look fierce, but Milt feared she wouldn't last long up against the desert's more formidable predators.

At least it's not raining anymore.

"You wanna gather some stuff up?"

Milt shook his head. "It'll be okay." Barefoot, morose, he stepped through the sliders and outside.

"Atta boy. We'll get settled over at my place, and then we can do a little search-and-rescue mission. I'm sure she's not far away."

"I hope not." Milt followed Billy Blue into the unseasonably damp day. Steam was already beginning to rise off surfaces not under water.

The sun was beginning to come out again, revealing blue skies.

Milt couldn't see it, though.

Also Available from NineStar Press

Connect with NineStar Press

www.ninestarpress.com

www.facebook.com/ninestarpress

www.facebook.com/groups/NineStarNiche

www.twitter.com/ninestarpress

www.tumblr.com/blog/ninestarpress

www.ingramcontent.com/pod-product-compliance
Lightning Source LLC
Chambersburg PA
CBHW032156180726
48284CB00001B/69